For Marc...
En...

Ma Bremer's Boys

Dale Kueter

Dale Kueter

BookLocker
Saint Petersburg, Florida

Print ISBN: 978-1-64719-332-4
Epub ISBN: 978-1-64719-333-1
Mobi ISBN: 978-1-64719-334-8

Published by BookLocker.com, Inc., St. Petersburg, Florida.

Printed on acid-free paper.

The characters and events in this book are fictitious. Any similarity to real persons, living or dead, is coincidental and not intended by the author.

BookLocker.com, Inc.
2021

First Edition

A Mother's Love

A mother's love is something that no one can explain,
It is made of deep devotion and of sacrifice and pain,
It is endless and unselfish and enduring come what may
For nothing can destroy it or take that love away...

Helen Steiner Rice

Other books by Dale Kueter

- *Vietnam Sons*
- *The Smell of the Soil*
- *Motel Sepia*

"Ma Bremer's Boys"
main characters

fiction

Molly and Jack Bremer, parents of Peter, Bobby, and Hattie

Aliza and Orval Price, Molly Bremer's parents

Glenda (Goodman) Bremer, Peter's wife

Rosemary (Hitchins) Bremer, Bobby's wife

Hogg Mulder, Kansas Prison inmate

Tom Wendling, Cedar Rapids newspaper reporter

Rusty Ragno, enforcer for Chicago mob

Henry Bexler, west Kansas rancher

David Etting, Peter Bremer's lawyer

Jim Ryan, FBI agent in charge, Cedar Rapids

Norm Effron, Overland Park, Kansas, Chief of Police

Preface

Newspaper reporters retire with galleys of stories and characters collected over the years.

There are accounts of success and failure, tragedy and triumph, crime and goodness. The divergent individuals of life, I believe, are what attract many to journalism. That and the notion that we record the first draft of history.

One of my favorite stories was a calamity of small potatoes. An eighty-three-year-old grandmother from an upscale neighborhood is arrested by cops for shoplifting three capsules of Legg's pantyhose at a grocery store. The matter is recorded on the police blotter and viewed by a reporter.

The nosy writer checks it out. Grandma says she has no idea why she would steal nylons, "but please don't let my ailing husband know." Three pairs of nylons are piddling, but for her they might as well have been the Hope Diamond. She is aghast and cannot explain her actions. When her daughter and granddaughter visited the next weekend, "all I could see are two police officers approaching outside the grocery store."

This internal turmoil, this self-flogging over a minor matter, was not the kind of introspection suffered by the likes of Al Capone. In the end, we didn't use Grandma's name in the story. I accompanied her to court. Her sentencing was deferred and her record expunged in a few months. Case closed. Newsroom colleagues laughed, teasing that she "probably had a rap sheet a mile long."

"Ma Bremer's Boys" is not so unassuming. It centers on two sons who follow wayward paths in life and a single mother who suffers through it. While elements of the story are drawn from a lifetime of covering police and courts, it is a work of fiction. Different characters from different eras are blended into an account that is the author's creation. All dialogue is fictional.

The timeline, character development, and episodes are of the author's imagination. Any resemblance to actual events or persons, living or dead, is coincidental.

Place and time notations at the beginning of many chapters are intended to guide readers along the unsavory paths of the Bremers.

I want to thank several people, firstly my parents, for encouraging a farm boy to get an education and pursue the writing bug. Teachers, too. And the dozens of colleagues in the newsroom, the best workplace in the world. Over the years, I have received counsel from many – news tips from mayors, law enforcement officers, and janitors – and I thank them.

Guidance for this account was given by Kansas state officials, local and regional police, FBI sources, and historical libraries—all providers of information that keep fiction following the right roads. Writing suggestions came from personnel at Reedsy, the Alliance of Independent Authors, Patricia Buser, Jackie Brock and editor Francis Kelly. Also, thanks to Angela Hoy and the BookLocker team.

Mostly, thanks to my wife, Helen, who suffers my ideas and, because of her vigorous reading, is the best and kindest critic.

— Dale Kueter

*...for all mothers, especially Mary Helen, my wife,
and Luella, my mother.*

Ma Bremer's Boys

Chapter 1
Summer 1975, Iowa

The black Cadillac rumbled down the gravel road, its driver more like the occupant of a hearse than a man on a business trip.

The warnings had been explicit. Reckoning loomed like shadows in a dim alley. Peter Bremer gripped the steering wheel.

"Damn it!" he muttered. "Damn everything!"

The hot August sun, unrestricted by clouds, shot heat waves through Iowa's verdant landscape.

On the western horizon, he spotted dust boiling skyward, portraying the image of a tiny tornado plowing through emerald fields of corn. To most people, the ascending residue would be an insignificant blot on the serene countryside, but for Bremer it was foreboding.

His eyes fixed on the swirling billow; his mind was consumed by rising panic. It was as if some Mother Nature illusion was taking shape on a Grant Wood canvas. But this was no mirage, and his fears inhaled its full dimensions. For him, the danger was concealed in the unknown. Sweat beaded on his forehead.

Bremer seldom swore, but then seldom had he been in such dire straits. He stared, bound by bad decisions and unthinkable consequences. For a man cushioned in leather seats, he was about as uncomfortable as a person in an electric chair.

Unconsciously, he slowed his car as his gaze zeroed on the approaching speck. It alone ignited the powdery trail that punctured the azure sky. The vast dome over the Midwest was void of any tempest. The only impending storm was that which permeated Bremer's problematic life. He felt alone. Even success, his long-sought idol, was of no comfort.

Loose gravel ticked off the underbelly of the big sedan; it was the only sound other than the voice of baseball announcer Jack Buck:

"There's the windup. And the pitch from the Cubs' fine young right-handed pitcher, Steve Stone. Sizemore digs in, waiting for the pitch. Swing and a miss, and the side is retired."

St. Louis station KMOX came streaming into Eastern Iowa like a Bob Gibson fastball. But Bremer was oblivious to the broadcast. He turned the radio off.

Tall corn flanked the spiraling beige cloud that rose leisurely like prairie talcum. The dust plume hung almost suspended at times, taking its direction from the vehicle's propulsion and a nudge of the placid breeze. The only farmstead in sight assumed a peculiar poise, two round silos poking out of the horizon like sunburned fingers.

There was no one to yell to for help. Surely, he thought, there must be a farmer or mailman or county worker somewhere in the area. Maybe a Watkins salesman?

Anyone other than the portent of danger.

Solitude swelled Bremer's panic. He felt like he was without a place to hide from fear's dimensions. Unmindful observers would have had no cause for concern, but he was not among that fortunate number. Suspicion and trepidation were his passengers.

Instinctively, he braked the 1975 de Ville and steered into a grassy cornfield driveway. The sleek sedan's big tires crumpled ragweed, brome, clover, and wild Sweet Williams indiscriminately as it inched forward to a stop. He put the vehicle in park, leaving the engine running.

Bremer removed a .32 automatic from the glove compartment and waited.

His fancy luxury car stood out conspicuously in a rural environment saturated with Chevys and Fords—pickup trucks mostly. The Cadillac was as out of place as Lauren Hutton, donned in

16

lace and Chanel No. 5, feeding slop to pigs. Bremer, too, dressed in a gray three-piece suit, blue tie, white shirt, and Florsheim brogues, was a foreigner in a denim world.

He checked the gun's chamber. It was loaded. How did it all come to this? True, he had for many years lived a life that rounded curves too fast, failing to consider what was beyond the bend. It was almost as if he were compelled to push the pedal as far as it would go, hell-bent on getting past where he never dreamed of going.

A psychiatrist would perhaps trace it back to his boyhood in Little Rock. He was the smallest kid in his class—from grade school through high school. He was the guy that all the other guys could safely beat up. They called him "Little Pete" or "Beat on Pete" or worse. He could run fast, and his legs frequently carried him away from a prospective bloody nose or black eye.

Often, he would take refuge at his father's gas station, where he would do various chores, including attending the pumps. He was so small he had to stand on an orange crate to reach the cash register. Things didn't improve much at Little Rock High, where he was mostly ignored by other boys. He was always relegated to right field during PE softball games, a position that saw little action and generated less respect. It was the "last guy in" place, under a system that required everyone to get some playing time.

Peter was never good enough to make any varsity sport, though he considered track. Running—his forte and seemingly his lifetime role. Running as a child caught in his parents' quarrels. Running from a lack of close friends, running from diminutive stature, running from loneliness. Now running from bad decisions.

There had been two anchors in his life: his mom and Glenda.

In school he was skillful at math, which boosted his self-esteem and countered the shun factor. He, in turn, ignored most of the boys in his class and despised some. He took his satisfaction by socializing

17

with many of the girls. Some of them treated him like a cuddly bear cub, something cute that needed shelter. He savored the attention if not the associated belittling.

Even at Arkansas State he had few male friends, and those were fellows who, like him, were interested in economics and the general notion of success. Success as in making boatloads of money. He embraced business books about sales cultivation and personal growth like a Wall Street tycoon fondles the bottom line and stock options.

And now look at him. Even his old grade school antagonists would have to acknowledge his achievements.

But at what price.

The Cadillac's air conditioning kept the car cool inside, an oasis on a ninety-degree day. The dot in the distance had multiplied in size, and the dust column behind it grew accordingly. Whoever was responsible for stirring up the mixture of gravel and grit was plodding along in due deference to the rough surface.

A delegation of crows swooped out of the steamy corn rows, presumably headed for a watering hole that fostered the lofty, relaxing reaches of a willow or sycamore tree. If only life could be so simple, Bremer thought, that he could fly up and away from troubles, leaving potential harm adrift in its own cloud of confusion.

He was thankful for one thing. Glenda, his wife, was not with him. He didn't have to explain to her the reasons for driving on a gravel road rather than a paved highway, parked in bucolic central, worried about whether he would see the sunrise the following day. She was back at their hotel suite in Cedar Rapids—oblivious, he thought, to the intricacies of his financial dilemma.

The approaching vehicle was now a mere 300 yards away. It seemed like a slow-motion scene from the movies. But this was no chase. Neither was the pursued hiding from the pursuer. Bremer was out in the open, unshielded by brush or trees. The big black car was parked in front of a canvas of green, as vulnerable as proverbial fish in a barrel.

What was it his mother had always advised? She knew young Peter, unlike his brother, Bobby, was the target of bullies. "Never, never, never invite trouble," she counseled. Molly Bremer was a master at invoking prudence. "Trouble," she would say, "looks for a place to happen. So, don't tempt it." He should have paid more attention to his mother.

She, too, had no knowledge of what he did or how he did it. And Peter wanted it to stay that way. God only knew she had suffered enough from her husband during those years after the honeymoon wore off in Little Rock. She had had enough abuse at the hands of Peter's father and certainly did not need any more anguish from the reckless actions of her oldest son.

Peter Bremer, like so many who wander into the perilous companionship of avarice and extravagance, wished many times in recent months to have his imprudent actions erased. While they may have preached forgiveness at the Baptist church of his youth, leniency and compassion were not part of the credo of the crowd he'd been associating with in the last year.

He was all alone in this fight, just like most of his life. Glenda didn't know. His mother and siblings didn't know. For that matter, he didn't even know where his younger brother lived. Bobby was in and out of jail. His sister married and lived in Rochester, Minn. He had also lost track of his father, a situation that caused him neither worry nor grief. He remembered his father as being devoid of love and care—a pathetic paranoid bent on dominance.

Bremer had delayed marriage for more than a year, afraid of commitment. However, after he moved to Cedar Rapids, the long-distance relationship with Glenda bloomed, and they surrendered to a love beyond passion. They married in St. Louis nearly two years ago.

Yet in all this time, vanity and shame trumped love and blocked his ability to confide in her.

Neither did area farmers and local business associates, investors in Riverside Packing Co., have any idea of the perils he faced. None had become his close friends, but he knew many by their first names. This was especially the case for coworkers at Riverside, where he was president and chief operating officer. He was on his way from the company's offices in Cedar Rapids to the slaughtering plant in the small town of Chelsea, forty-five miles to the west.

Bremer was alone with his predicament. Alone, especially in time of trouble, is not a nice place to live.

The vehicle and its dusty aftermath were almost upon him. In a matter of seconds, his future would be determined. He burrowed his small frame deeper into the leather seats, his eyes peeking out the side window. He was ready to shoot or ram any assailant with two-and-a-half tons of steel.

Bremer pointed the pistol upward in readiness.

He waited.

Chapter 2
1952, Kansas State Penitentiary, Lansing, Kans.

The guard closed the prison cellblock door, a squeaky prelude leading to the inevitable clank. It was not Bobby Bremer's first time in jail. Would incarceration change him this time? Or perhaps the real question was, did Bobby Bremer want to change?

"Lookie what we have here, boys. Fresh meat. Fresh, tender meat. And ain't he so pretty."

Hogg Mulder glanced at the other inmates in his block at the Kansas State Penitentiary, assigning himself as the man in charge. To say Mulder was odious would render the term deficient several times over. He was utterly repulsive, inside and out, the kind of human that only a mother might suffer. But in Mulder's case, no one would take bets on that.

His dull gray prison garb was highlighted by spilled food stains. His dirty hands matched the limited vocabulary of his foul mouth. It appeared he had not washed or combed his hair since Roosevelt's first term.

"Who wants to go first with this little sweetie? He looks tough, so we may need several fellows to hold down his fuckin' delicate ass, but that makes the process even more attractive and excitin'."

Three weeks after his birth in Medicine Lodge, Kans., Mulder's parents recorded his name as Clemency Kiowa Mulder. The *Clemency*, his father told others, was in honor of a great grandfather, and *Kiowa* was intended to give the newborn the bearing of the Kiowa Indian. The tribe considered the Medicine Lodge area sacred. The Mulders were self-proclaimed atheists, a declaration that in ensuing years was much appreciated by local churchgoers.

In 1947, Judge Ansel Q. Blakeman of the Kansas District Court sentenced Mulder to fifty years in prison for the rape and near-death beating of the teenage daughter of a Presbyterian minister. Many claimed that the trial, other than a fulfillment of the law's guarantee of judgment by peers, was a waste of taxpayer's money. Mulder had bragged to several alleged friends, "I had my way and more with that chick."

That announcement spread like a prairie wildfire. The threat of public reckoning was thick as Kansas wheat. Mulder's inability to post a huge bond saved him from harm. Judge Blakeman apologized to the victim's family for "suffering such a heinous crime," but angry Kansans said the death penalty would have been a more appropriate expression of regret.

"If ever there was a person who was misnamed, it is Clemency Kiowa Mulder," the judge said in open court. "He displayed no clemency to this young woman. And if the Kiowa Tribe wants to petition to have its name removed from this despicable beast, I will duly consider it."

To aggravate matters, Mulder had been drinking the night of the crime. His attorney argued for diminished capacity, but the judge scoffed at such a defense, accepting instead the testimony of a bartender who said Hogg was in his tavern for no more than fifteen minutes. Yet Blakeman, a rock-solid Methodist, took the occasion to expound on the evils of alcohol.

"While I don't believe for one second that this vermin was intoxicated at the time of the horrible act, alcohol may have incited him," the judge said. "And this kind of behavior in the very town where Carrie Nation launched her campaign against the results of fermentation."

Hogg, thirty-four, was assigned his nickname by other inmates of cell block 15 because of his unusually grimy appearance. It was a moniker he savored as a pig takes to mud. "Just spell it with two g's for emphasis," he ordered when the term was first bestowed. And then he grunted his formal approval.

Mulder's six-foot, 210-pound frame generated a lavish amount of body odor, indicating his scant familiarity with soap. He circled Bobby Dominick Bremer, twenty-two, like a hungry wolf. Some inmates, intimidated by Mulder's size and boorish nature, moved in concert toward Bremer while others acted as lookouts for guards. It had all the marks of jungle savagery. The only chink in Mulder's tough-guy makeup was a high-pitched voice that sometimes skipped into a squeak.

Bremer grew up in Little Rock, Ark. He had a rap sheet almost as long as Lana Turner's inventory of ex-husbands. His grade school mischief added to the trials of his mother, Molly Bremer, who was forced to raise three children by herself during the war years after her alcoholic husband ran off. He was a regular visitor in the principal's office, then juvenile court. He never finished high school.

His latest run-in with the law was an appropriate summary of his history: He stole a car, robbed a country bank in Kansas, and, when arrested, punched the officer in the face. Those capers, when added up, netted him five years in the Kansas State Pen. It would have been more, except his court-appointed lawyer successfully argued that the young Mr. Bremer did not have a gun at the bank heist. Instead, he had stuck his right index finger in a black sack and feigned possession of a weapon.

Bobby, it seemed, was born with a distaste for authority at any level. His older brother, Peter, was svelte by contrast and determined to fight his way through the thickets of the business world.

Now Bobby Bremer faced someone a lot more menacing than the schoolyard bully. He was no shrinking violet, slightly taller than Mulder and with less fat around the midsection. Lansing prison wasn't Bremer's first stop on the jailbird junket. He had physical disagreements with fellow prisoners before and had left his mark. But this was different. Mulder seemingly had a badass committee behind him.

Mulder stepped cautiously toward Bremer, hoping his menacing eyes would inject fear in his prey. Bremer had his back to the wall, physically and metaphorically. That meant he could see all his would-be attackers. He did not budge. His intimidating glare held Hogg in place. The others stopped too. Bremer motioned with his right hand for Hogg to come forward. His left hand curled around his back as if he concealed something.

"Ah," Hogg croaked. "Such a big shot. I'll bet your plump ass still has red marks on it from when your mommy spanked you. I know all about you, have the complete dossier on your miserable life. Your daddy was a no-good drunk who beat on your mommy. You were always in trouble, too dumb for schoolin'. And your brother and sister were always favored by your mommy."

Bremer retained his pose.

"Boys here tell me you were lucky to get Ds during your so-called education and that you were still readin' Dick and Jane books in high school." Hogg, a certified numskull, snorted at his humor attempt. "They figure you majored in dumb. With a pedigree like that, it's my guess girls shunned you like roadkill. I'll bet you've had more contact with wardens than with girls.

"You left out the part," Bremer said without a blink, "where I beat the crap out of a scumbag fatso at the juvenile farm who must have been your twin brother. Except he didn't stink as much. He claimed to have been born indoors. I expect your mother dropped you in a pile of pig shit, and you haven't improved since."

"Why, then it's true. You are a spoiled and snooty asshole," Hogg shot back. "A brat in need of spankin'. We can do that and more."

24

"It's Mr. Asshole to you," Bremer said without hesitation, his glare unwavering.

It was the kind of ping-pong moxie that sought credibility in the often-uncivilized realm of prison politics. It is a place where survival is the first item on the agenda. And the second item. It is not unusual for inmates to seek coalition, no matter how unstable that might be. The enemy can be the guy across the table at meals, the guard who ignored his training, or a lowlife like Hogg Mulder.

For most, a challenge behind survival—and one especially difficult for Bremer—was loneliness. Even though he seldom displayed it, he loved his mother. His was an inhibited rapport, short on expression and long on seclusion. He never felt close to his siblings, and he hated his father. Now the absence of family gnawed on him. He would never acknowledge that. Such was the deformity of his character.

Lack of pluck was not one of his shortfalls.

"I don't understand," Bremer said as he motioned to the half-dozen or so inmates behind Hogg, "how your supposed buddies here can stand to be in the same county as your stinkin' ass, much less follow you around as if you were part of the human race. They all look smarter than simply being sheep following a skunk. And I apologize to the skunk for using it as a likeness to you."

Clearly that stretched Hogg's underwear. He stood erect, searching for a comeback. His alleged cohorts registered a look of reassessment.

"I've changed my mind about you," Hogg addressed Bremer after a few seconds of deliberation. "On closer examination, you're not so pretty. Tender, maybe, and certainly you have a cute mouth."

His tenor voice skewed into a Tiny Tim falsetto on the words *cute mouth*, and Hogg's standing suffered with it. He coughed to clear his throat.

"But I think you need surgery." He fought to regain ranking. "Maybe a carving on one of your butt cheeks, a brandin' perhaps. Whaddia think, boys, a tiny *K* for Kansas?"

If there were a movie critic on the penitentiary newspaper, he would have found Hogg's retort on the lame side. It had none of the puff of his opening threats. The entire scene was a study in social metamorphosis.

Suddenly the atmosphere of prison politics readjusted, if ever so slightly. Bremer translated the change in body language like a seasoned parliamentarian. The looks on the faces of some of Hogg's troops became more benign, and Hogg himself visibly swallowed as to signal a withering of bluster. It had become a virtual standoff, an amazing achievement for an outnumbered target.

The ball clearly was in Hogg's court. His blowhard bubble was leaking, and he knew it. It was decision time: proceed or back off.

Hogg lunged at Bremer with a shiv he retrieved from the back of his belt, fully aware that a declarative statement was in order—an attempt to reassert his standing. Alas, his fighting style did not match his rage. Belatedly he underestimated the savvy and brawling aptitude of Bobby Bremer.

Bremer grabbed Hogg's wrist, the hand holding the shiv. Its ragged edge turned into the backside of Bremer's hand and produced blood. With his left fist, Bremer aimed and successfully landed knuckles on Hogg's nose. More blood. He twisted Hogg's shiv hand with such force that Bremer was quickly behind his assailant. The shiv was now penetrating flesh on Hogg's back. And then there was more blood.

He bent Hogg's arm with all his strength, a hammerlock that would have gained raves on Saturday Night Wrestling. The smelly one's eyes began to water—a result of the pain—and Bremer's eyes smarted from the blend of body odors radiating from his foe. He considered silently whether part of Hogg's attack plan was his stench. This unattractive dance went on for more than a minute.

With a shout that guards were approaching, the prospects of stalemate, and the burgeoning perils of an assortment of body bouquets, Bremer released Hogg with a stiff shove. Hogg stood with the convicting shiv still in his hand as guards entered the area. His stature as the self-appointed cell king disintegrated like souring milk on a hot summer's day. Hogg was hauled off by guards with a promise of solitary confinement.

"Is everyone here OK?" one of the guards asked. There was mumbling of answers that he interpreted as a yes. Hogg's brief tenure as pack leader was over, and prison protocol determined that none of the inmates were going to make like witnesses and provide testimony about anything.

"Hey, young fella," the guard moved toward Bremer. "It looks as if your hand is bleeding. What happened here? Want to talk about it?"

"Cut myself shaving," Bremer replied.

Everyone got the message, and Bremer quickly elevated himself in the pecking order of cell block 15.

Whether or not his successful confrontation with Hogg was Bobby Bremer's informal indoctrination into the prison canon, it certainly was the latent baptism for his future. He casually strolled past the other inmates and felt their newly granted respect as surely as if they had cast ballots for him. It provided him the kind of regard he believed he had never received in school, at home, or anywhere in the outside world.

Growing up, Bremer was afflicted by the notion that, as the youngest sibling, he suffered the least attention rather than the customary most. He inherited some hand-me-downs while his older brother, Peter, mostly got new things. He was troubled by the belief that his father regarded him as a tag-end burden, an extra kid who further stretched a limited household budget. His father essentially ignored him, the worst affront.

Molly Bremer sensed his hurt and tried to compensate for it. But she could not repair the deep emotional scars left by slaps along Bobby's head, strikes administered when her husband's alcohol-stewed temper ran out of control. A mother's salve goes only so deep. At school, too, he believed he was largely discounted, a factor in his disinterest.

When he was not in trouble of some kind with authorities, young Bremer held several odd jobs. Longest was his work at a pawnshop, where he learned the craft of deal-making and became familiar with guns. Many guns brought to the owner's shop, especially pistols, were suspected as stolen. Their value was thus reduced, and they were resold at a discount.

The pawnshop tutored him in one other skill: the art of opening a safe. Then he met a young man with a matching attitude and proclivity for trouble. Ignoring his mother's pleas, Bobby expanded his beer drinking to the point of weekly bouts of being sozzled. One Saturday in June 1952, the pair hot-wired a 1950 Chevy near a tavern where they had been drinking and departed for unknown parts with three cases of Schlitz beer.

They wound their way through the Ozarks, repeatedly paying tribute to the beer that made Milwaukee famous. Half out of their hops-soaked heads, they impulsively decided to wobble into the Baxter Springs, Kans., Merchants Bank and, with slurred instructions, asked a teller for money. The savvy bank employee stepped on an alarm and handed Bremer a bag of a couple dozen dollar bills and a stack of blank deposit slips.

The robbers gleefully departed only to be met by a committee of law enforcement officers outside the bank. As the debacle unfolded, a police officer who immediately deciphered the abundant ineptness of the two drunks began to laugh. Bremer caught him with a left uppercut. He was arraigned, tried, convicted, and sentenced by the end of July.

"Mr. Guard," Bremer called as he headed down the hallway a few days later. "Could I make a telephone call to my mom, let her know that I arrived here in one piece and that I'm OK?"

Courtesy to a guard is almost as rare as a sirloin steak served by the warden. It turned out to be one more element of Bremer's prison education, his growing encyclopedia of how to get along on the inside—what to do, what not to do, who to associate with, and who not to. His previous jail time was cut short by good behavior. Being polite did not come naturally for him. The surprised guard led Bobby to a phone booth near the visiting room.

"Ma. It's Bobby. I just want you to know that I'm OK up here in Kansas."

His mother was astonished. Her mind was a mixture of gratitude and disbelief that her son was considerate enough to call.

"Oh, Bobby," Molly Bremer joyfully sang. She wiped her hands on her worn apron and pulled a kitchen chair to the telephone stand. "I'm so happy you called. It's wonderful to hear your voice. They never let you say much during the trial. I know you didn't mean to hurt that policeman. You—"

"Ma. It's all right. I did what I did. I ain't makin' excuses. I'm sorry for again causin' you grief. This Lansing prison isn't such a bad place. While it's been less than a week, I'd say the food is better than at the other places, but not like your collard greens and sweet tea. Your cooking is the best, Ma," he said softly. "And I found out they have a nice library."

She was pleased with Bobby's apparent change.

"Gee, Bobby. I wish you were back here in Little Rock. I'd serve you roast beef and mashed potatoes with those collard greens. And right now, I'm baking your favorite: cherry pie." She began to cry.

"Ma, please don't cry. If I knew you were going to cry, I wouldn't have called. Things will be OK. I can take care of myself. I'll write to you in a couple of weeks. They don't allow many phone calls here."

"You won't forget?"

"I'll write, Ma. I've gotta go."

"Be sure to brush your teeth, Bobby."

"Yeah, Ma. Goodbye."

"Bobby?"

"Yes, Ma."

"Be nice to the people there. Try to make friends."

"Right, Ma."

"I'll try to come up and visit you some time. It's not that far from Little Rock."

"If you say so. I'll let you know about visiting times."

"Your sister is doing fine. She is dating a boy from Minnesota. Guess she couldn't find one in the whole state of Arkansas. So, she's seeing this northern guy. Met him in school. He seems nice."

"Mom, someone else is waiting for the phone."

"They won't mind. Tell him you are talking to your mom. He'll understand. Peter is still at Arkansas State. I think he likes it there. Says business is his thing, so I hope he does well in that. He plans to take some additional courses after graduation.

"I hope you're not bothered by that persistent sore throat. You've always been prone to sore throat, Bobby, more so than your brother and sister. I should send you some goose grease to rub on your neck at the first signs of a sore throat. Do they have Vicks VapoRub up there? That's good too. Try to stay out of drafts. Do you have enough covers on your bed?"

"Ma, the guy wants to talk to his girlfriend."

"OK, then. I guess girlfriends are more important than moms. You be sure and write now."

"I will. Goodbye, Ma."

"Goodbye, Bobby. I love you."

Bremer turned over the phone booth to the fellow waiting and decided to stop at the prison library before it was time to eat. He thought again about his mother back in Little Rock. She was alone now in that little house on Cumberland Street. She had friends from work, and of course her parents, who lived nearby. But he suddenly formed a glimpse of what goes on inside a mother.

He stopped in the hallway and stared at nothing. A fissure of a smile interrupted his granite-like face. It was one of those situations where life sometimes unfolds in a way that even surprises one's self. His grandfather, ever the subtle one, would have inquired if he was having a brain spasm.

Bobby Bremer, in a matter of seconds, realized for the first time the complexity of mothers.

Chapter 3
1942, Little Rock, Ark.

The Mobil gas station was not unlike others in Little Rock. The snakelike air hose slithered through the driveway and tripped a bell when customers drove in, signaling to those inside the need for service outside. The attendant not only put gas in your car's tank but checked the oil and washed the windshield as a matter of routine. And at no extra cost.

If you needed air for a low tire, you would just pull around to the office side, and it would be dispensed for you, free of charge. And behind that were restrooms and a water fountain for white people. Negroes had their own drinking and restroom facilities on the other side of the building.

Rust along the rooflines signaled deferred maintenance and trying times. The priming of the economy, orchestrated by President Franklin Roosevelt, had not trickled down to the hinterlands and Little Rock to the extent it had in bigger cities. There were some WPA projects in Little Rock, like the Robinson Auditorium, the city zoo, and the museum, but not the kind of bounty bestowed on urban centers in the east.

The great majority of people in Arkansas and the entire Midwest were struggling to keep their heads above water, although the economy—buoyed by a buildup of war materials—had mostly shucked off the effects of the Great Depression. If good times were on their way back, it was at the price of wartime blood.

The pall of World War II—Adolph Hitler and Kamikaze pilots, who set Pearl Harbor ablaze and formally thrust the United States into combat—transformed life into perpetual worry and fear. It touched every family in some way. Yet the matter of going on, simply existing each new day in the shadow of war's upheaval, was its own challenge.

Jack Bremer usually was up to his elbows in grease or oil as he repaired the transmission, brakes, or some other deficient car or truck part in one of the two bays adjacent to the small office of the Mobil station. The truth was he made more money fixing vehicles than pumping gas. It was joked that, after Bremer scrubbed down and flushed most of the pervasive grime and grease from his face and hands, few people in town recognized him.

It was also said that Jack Bremer could be a mean son of a bitch, especially when he was off the wagon. Liquor expanded and emboldened his surly demeanor, and those closest suffered the most. It was not unusual for Molly Bremer to confirm his violence with a black eye or bruises. She had threatened to leave him. But like many abused women, she was trapped by the love of her children, raw economics, and the culture's credo of shame.

Bremer's Mobil station, with the flying red horse, was nothing out of the ordinary—unless you consider the spectacular corner azalea bush, flagging its showy magenta flowers, elevated in eye-catching magnificence by the dead and rotting wood of the nearby bottlebrush. The station was not fancy like Magnolia Mobil in the better part of town, with its white stucco walls set off by a red baseline, red gas pumps, and red tile roof. What was different down at Bremer's station was the diminutive figure who handled gas sales on many days.

Peter Bremer was just a boy, and small for his age.

Now twelve, he had been pumping gas for the last two years. His father could not afford to hire anyone, so young Peter was the man—all four feet and two inches of him.

Peter stood on an orange crate to reach the cash register. He hauled out a small step ladder so that he could check the oil and reach the windshield. He got to know, just by looking, if a tire was low on air. He was the opposite of his father in many ways. Peter was polite, helpful, and uncommonly social for a boy whose father was a stranger to courtesy and caring.

And he was a promoter. Frequently he would convince a motorist, especially the young ladies, to purchase a Baby Ruth or something else from the candy rack. He sold more new tires than his father. Once, he dispensed an entire set to a matronly looking woman who could not get over his "blazing brown hair and nub of a nose." His strict father would never acknowledge it, but Peter had accumulated customer-relations savvy that would make a Watkins salesman envious.

Dealing with the public came naturally to him, unlike his younger brother, Bobby. Bobby Dominic Bremer was a remake of his father—a year younger than Peter but four inches taller and a hundred times ornerier. No one pushed Bobby around at Jefferson Davis Elementary, whereas Peter often ended up at the bottom of a boys' scrum.

Bobby never offered to help at the gas station, and Jack did not want him there. They were too much alike. Bobby was the tough-guy kid, his impulsive and unfeeling nature embodied by the slingshot that was his permanent back-pocket companion. It was his Tom Mix six-shooter. He enjoyed swaggering with his pals on the way home from school, picking off birds for the joy of it. He bragged to his brother that it was more fun when the bird wobbled off with a broken wing or leg.

Peter read books and collected baseball cards. He especially liked *The Cat Who Went to Heaven,* a story about a poor artist. Twice he had seen the Little Rock Travelers baseball team play the Southern League powerhouse Atlanta Crackers. His prized possession was a

Tris Speaker baseball card published by Goudey Chewing Gum. Speaker played in Little Rock in 1908.

Bobby lounged at Squirrely Ahearn's comic shop, perusing the latest episodes of Tom Mix, Red Ryder, and the Cisco Kid until asked to buy something or leave. He usually departed with an affronted scowl. Molly took them to see the movie *Meet John Doe*, with Gary Cooper, a story about ordinary people helping their neighbor. Peter enjoyed it. Bobby pronounced it as "a foolish story." He said people "are mostly for themselves."

"A few are selfish," Peter argued, "but the majority would help others if possible. I think you are just a sourpuss," he told Bobby. "You think your way is the only way."

"Maybe I am a sourpuss, Petey, but you are a sucker and let other kids shove you around. I say if you give people an inch, they'll take a foot. Nobody is gonna tell me what to do."

"Nothing new there, Bobbsey," Peter shot back. "Nobody can tell you anything."

"I told you to stop callin' me Bobbsey. I hate that name."

"Then stop calling me Petey."

"OK, both of you. Stop it."

Molly declared a truce, and in motherly fashion ruled that both had valid points.

Peter liked running the gas station better than going to school. On too many occasions, he skipped a school class or two—feigning illness—in favor of life at the gas station. That would upset his mother, but it was OK with his father. If given half a chance, Peter Bremer had a promising future in the business world. For him, the challenges and excitement of learning on the job transcended any benefits of school.

"Hey, Pissant! Didn't you hear the ding-dong? Get your butt out there and wait on that black Buick," his father yelled. "Whatsa matter? Your ears gone bad?"

It was not like Peter to ignore a customer and the beckoning bell. His attention had been misdirected by the scantily clad Miss May, strutting her stuff on the back wall calendar. His mama would never know, but the truth was he enjoyed staring at the risqué calendar pictures of unknown women, whose bodies were displayed in not-so-discrete locations of many gas stations around the country. Miss May's curves eclipsed those of the 1941 maroon Pontiac two-door sedan that she leaned on, and she stirred his young body.

The Mobil Oil representative had dropped off several of the 1942 girlie calendars, and Peter planned to sneak one home to show Bobby.

"I see the customer, Dad. I was studying my arithmetic and didn't notice right away."

He rushed out and greeted Mrs. Buick, a youngish, good-looking, fully clothed customer whose smile grew as she viewed Peter, his service cap slightly askew. He gave her a sales-selling, welcoming smile, speculating silently that she may be a relative of Miss May.

"Sorry for the wait. How can I help you, ma'am?" he asked in his still-boyish voice. "That sure is a nice lookin' car you're drivin'," he beamed. "Someday I want to own a Buick." If she had been driving a Mercury, he would have said Mercury. That is simple sales language.

"Well, well, young man. Aren't you the urbane, precocious fellow?"

She handed out a smile that went from ear to ear and exposed perfect and brilliant white teeth. Peter did not know what urbane and precocious meant, but he translated the white teeth into money. He had been to the dentist once. His crooked teeth looked as if they had been tossed into his mouth by a baseball pitcher who lost his control.

Baby teeth fell out on their own or were yanked by his dad. Cloves were his mom's recipe for a toothache.

"Do you need a fill-up, ma'am?"

He guessed she was about thirty years old. He wondered if she had taken a wrong turn, perhaps had meandered over from the Quapaw Quarter and its fancy Antebellum mansions. The station was in a working-class neighborhood, and most customers were grinders like his father. Financial survival was a paycheck-to-paycheck dance. Many, just like his dad, ran tabs down at Bubba's Tavern.

"Yes, ah do," she purred. "But y'all are kind of small to be running a business." She bestowed her charm in profuse portions. A puff of spring breeze billowed her blond hair and transported a trace of perfume past Peter's nostrils. "Ah must say, y'all are just the cutest gas station attendant ah've ever come upon. My gracious, have you been in business long?"

She chuckled and extended her slim, bare arms in a graceful gesture, then tossed her petite nose skyward—not in haughty dismissal, Peter thought, but in friendly, beguiling, unspoken conversation. Peter soaked it in like the budding adolescent that he was.

In addition to someday owning a Buick, Peter's inner consciousness also recorded the desire to someday have a sweet-smelling girlfriend with blond, flowing hair.

"Well, ma'am, I'm just helping my father. He runs the business. I pump the gas when I'm out of school, and he does most of the mechanical repairs and lube work. Would you like regular or hi-test?"

"Honey, ah need hi-test for this big ole machine. It slurps up gas like my daddy consumes Jack Daniels. But then, y'all wouldn't know about that. You know what they say about a Buick. They pass everythin' 'cept a gas station." She giggled, tossed her head back, and the blond locks went flying.

Peter turned the pump handle to erase the previous sales numbers. The sales indicator now displayed zeros, and above that, the price of ethyl—twenty cents a gallon. He squeezed the nozzle handle, and gas began to flow in jerky spurts. His eyes surveyed the chrome strips on the Buick's front and back fenders, which bestowed style and speed. The back swooped graciously to dainty rectangular taillights.

Another ribbon of chrome extended from just below the vent window to the back taillights. This Buick Special was decked out with fender skirts and white wall tires. Peter's saliva thickened as he pondered its sleekness. Suddenly gas belched from the overflowing tank. He released the handle, hung up the nozzle, and grabbed the oil rag from his back pocket to wipe the dripping gasoline. She had not noticed, and he released a sigh of relief. Some car nuts would have filed a lawsuit over spilled gas.

"There you go, ma'am. The tires look fine but let me check the oil for ya."

Peter scampered to retrieve his little stepladder, plunked it next to the fender, and popped the car's hood. He scurried up the steps, pulled the dipstick, and wiped it with his rag. He reinserted it and withdrew it again. It showed full. Down the steps, dipstick in hand. He presented Mrs. Buick with the viscous evidence.

"Oil looks good!" he said.

"Oh, my," she exclaimed as she touched up her lipstick. "Aren't you the efficient one. Ah do appreciate your service mah young man." She rubbed her lips together with sensuous flare, parceling the bright red evenly.

He quickly put the oil stick back in place, locked the cap, and closed the hood. Next, he wiped the already sparkling windshield, headlights, and side-view mirrors. He glanced at the pump, then at the lipstick.

"Is there anything else, ma'am?"

"Ah think not, little man. Y'all have done a marvelous job. How much do ah owe you?"

"That'll be $2.40, ma'am."

She handed him three one-dollar bills.

"Ya keep the change for wonderful service with such a pleasant disposition," she tweeted in birdlike soprano. "And don't y'all be telling your daddy about the tip." She tossed her blond tresses in motion, waved, and slowly ushered the big Buick out of the station. Peter watched until the car was absorbed by street-side shrubbery and general traffic.

He looked up at the blue sky, which was unblemished by clouds. This certainly beat studying history in a stuffy classroom. What a magnificent combination—Business, Buick, and Blond. He decided to treat himself to a cold bottle of Coca-Cola. The nickel clunked into the bowels of the Coke machine, and out popped a seven-ounce bottle of ice-cold soda.

Peter could feel the cold beverage caress the full length of his esophagus. He closed his eyes, oblivious to the world around him, including the widening war in Europe and the Japanese rampage in the South Pacific and China. He knew of the war if not its dimensions. He knew men were being drafted, and some volunteered to fight. He realized some would not come home.

Only now dribbles of news were seeping out about the Doolittle Raid on Tokyo in April, which did little damage but boosted America's morale after the devastation at Pearl Harbor. Peter and his grade school friends heard of the Doolittle bombing, but made no assessment of it. There was no discussion of the war in school and little at home.

They also knew about the reopening of Camp Robinson some nine miles outside of town. It was among the many new military stations where young men underwent basic training before being thrust into the horror of armed conflict in some unknown place on the other side of the globe. It seemed far removed for a twelve-year-old. However, World War II would soon come to Peter and his dad.

Seventeen eastern states had already instituted gas rationing, and the others would soon follow. Automobile factories stopped making cars and converted production to tanks, planes, howitzers, and other war machinery. The fact was that gas was plentiful, but there was a shortage of rubber. Rationing gas saved rubber.

Ration cards were issued. Class A drivers were limited to three gallons a week— factory workers, eight gallons. Police, doctors, essential war workers, letter carriers, truck drivers, and politicians were not restricted. It introduced Peter to math, history in the making, customer whining and bargaining, and wartime politics in one swooping lesson.

"Pissant!!" his father yelled in his usual debasing style. "Stop daydreaming! Get in here and fetch me a one-inch box-end wrench. You know where they're at, and don't take all day."

Chapter 4

"Peter? Did y'all finish your homework? I know you had numbers to work on, and spellin'. You ain't foolin' me none. You skipped school this afternoon so's you could go down to your father's service station. I wish you would pay more attention to your schoolin' and less to makin' like you was some sort of business operator."

Molly Bremer rubbed her hand through Peter's dark brown mane. She felt something hard, probably petrified transmission grease. She doubted if his hair had been combed all day, maybe not for several days. She sighed inwardly.

She had to admit Peter was considerably better than young Bobby at grooming and keeping his clothes halfway clean. Bobby generally opted to do the opposite of what anyone instructed him. Contrary was a natural gear for him, it seemed, and the only shift to obedience involved his father. He knew that not minding him invited a whack alongside his head.

"Ya leave the boy alone," Jack Bremer yelled at his wife. "He's needed down at the station, and you know that. What little school he misses won't hurt nothin'. I expects he learns more about life and practical things pumping gas than he does from books. Ya just leave him be and fix dinner. I'm hungry."

How Molly Price, thirty-four, met and married Jack Bremer is not an unusual story. They attended the same Baptist church, and as teens, both attended Little Rock High School. Molly graduated; Jack quit after his junior year. School functions led to future dating, and back then, Jack had a modicum of manners. Nevertheless, they let hormones dictate—intimacy went too far, and Molly's parents insisted on marriage. A daughter, Hattie, bolstered their bonds. Peter followed three years later, and Bobby the year after that.

Three children in five years will test any marriage, and while Molly was up to the challenges, Jack faltered. He doted on Hattie at first and mostly ignored the boys. As Peter took an interest in his dad's business, frequently tending the gas pumps, Jack cast favor on his older son.

The small, rented bungalow on Cumberland Street became the source of yelling and fighting that frequently drifted into the neighborhood, especially when disputes spilled out to the front porch. The verbal abuse over the years swelled to physical violence, and more than once, Molly considered taking the children and putting Jack in the past. But go where? With what financial means? And at what social cost?

"I'm fixing your favorite, Jack," she said, wiping her hands on her apron. "I know how you like fried chicken, mashed potatoes and gravy, and collard greens." Molly tried to modify his disposition via the stomach. It sometimes worked, but this night Jack had too many draws from an unlabeled amber bottle of cheap hooch that Molly suspected came from some back-hills distillery. It fed his growing addiction and low self-esteem.

There were those years when Jack maintained a likable disposition. He paid adequate attention to his appearance then and could even be funny. More importantly, he occasionally spoke pridefully of Molly and his young family. But money pressures, aggravated by liquor, altered him inside and out. He was only thirty-five, but his red and pocked face, expanding gut, and permanent scowl, instead depicted an angry and troubled fifty-year-old.

Molly once suggested he apply for work at one of the Arkansas ordnance plants. The pay was decent, overtime was available, and there were no worries about business overhead. He rented the service station building for seven years, financially unable to save enough money to purchase it. And tools were expensive. But he was his own boss, which fit his loner personality. Instead of giving thought to the ordnance plant idea, he exploded into a juvenile tirade about her lack of confidence in him and his business abilities.

"Why do you keep harping about the boy working down at the station?" he barked, ignoring her menu recitation. "Unless you want to drag your ass down there and pump gas in his place, just leave the goddamn situation alone. Or maybe you'd like for me to pay a hired man and cut your household account by half. Is that what you want?"

Alcohol abuse poisoned him. It even infected good news. Hattie had received a Student of the Month award in March, but Jack dismissed it with derision.

"That supposed to make my day?" he mocked. "Send me jumpin' over the moon? Any money come with your big award? Or just a piece of paper?"

Hattie ran off crying.

"What I thought. Just a piece of paper."

Molly desperately wanted to say something, tell him how terrible it was to make a child feel worthless and crush Hattie's dignity. She wanted to shout that. Shout it to the whole neighborhood, the whole block, the entire world. But that would not cure his wounded soul.

She had learned in recent months that arguing, or even responding in an even manner, were not ways to answer her husband, especially when he had been drinking. Silence was the route she usually chose. As a dry wind gradually saps the Earth and everything on it, so the roots of marriage whither without caring love. And that's where Molly and Jack were—in the middle of a desert.

She once proposed that he check with AA, but that cost her a lacerated lip and bruised arm. Molly was too ashamed to take her problems to her parents. They had their own health issues and were already burdened by having to raise her younger sister's daughter. The sister was not sure who the father was, and two years ago, ran off with some ne'er-do-well from Conway, Ark. They had not heard from her since.

And for some reason—and maybe she was to blame for it—neither she nor Jack had developed any closeness with neighbors. She envied the circle of friends her parents had in the area where she grew up. People there relied on one another for big things and little things—a comfortable environment. It was as if you were a hand wave away from help or a cup of sugar.

Pastor Jimmy Clendon down at Good Neighbors Baptist Church seemed like a friendly person, someone willing to listen, but she was hesitant to consult him. And God only knows what hostility and meanness would generate in Jack's paranoid mind. Every day she felt her spot in the world growing smaller, the painted corner of her life shrinking, leaving her with nowhere to go.

"You didn't answer me," Jack shouted.

"I'm sorry," Molly replied meekly. She forgot what they were talking about—or what he was talking about. "What was your question?" She lifted the collard greens to sprinkle some chopped bacon and salt into the pan.

"What was my question?" Jack sputtered and fumed. He got up from his chair, slammed his pacifier hooch on the table, and walked over to the stove. He twisted her around, knocked the pan out of her hands, spraying hot water all over her left arm and sending the collard greens flying across the floor. She screamed.

"When was the last time you listened to me, really listened?" He was preaching himself into a lather.

"Why do you treat me as a lowlife, someone beneath your high and mighty opinions?" He cranked up his rail. "What was my question? Goddammit, you just ignore me like I'm some piece of junk advertisin' from Montgomery Ward. Hell, you'd probably give that promotion crap a second look—but not me. You don't ever hear what I say, Molly."

Jack's face was aglow with anger; his lips quivered with insecurity. His throbbing gut danced with his wildness and flailing arms.

"Jack, don't hit me," she murmured in fear, tossing up her arms in self-protection. "Whatever you say is fine."

"Daddy, don't hit Ma," came a loud command from an unlikely source. "I promise, if you hit her, I will someday kill you," Bobby blurted. His voice conveyed a calm certainty and almost business-like bearing. He sat down then as if the confrontation had been settled and his decree pronounced over the entire household. He pulled out his slingshot and fondled it as if it were a .45 pistol.

Peter was astounded by his brother's bluntness and courage. Or was it stupidity? Hattie, as usual, had departed with the first sign of trouble.

For Jack Bremer, it was like the time in high school when he tried to score from third base on a squeeze bunt, only to be confronted unexpectedly by the smiling catcher, ball in hand. He stopped—had no place to go. His own son Bobby, the kid who didn't do a damn lick of work at the station, was trying to tag him out! The little prick!

A strange thing happened.

Rather than run over that "little prick" and beat the hell out of him instead of his wife, Jack Bremer dropped his fist. He turned and scowled at Bobby. Then he swung his right arm wildly, as if aimed at Bobby, only he struck the potato bowl. More food went flying. There would be no fried chicken with gravy and mashed potatoes.

In the next minute, everyone departed, leaving Molly to clean up the mess. She also faced anew the question of where this troubled family was headed.

Chapter 5

Morning's wake-up light beamed through the tattered curtains of the Bremer bedroom. An open window admitted a light breeze, which en route fashioned a gentle sway in the magnolia tree out front. Its white flowers were long gone, deferring honors to its glossy green leaves. The tree grabbed nearly all the proximate light and sun power, leaving little for the spotty lawn beneath.

Molly was not surprised to find the other side of the bed vacant. It was not unusual for Jack to sleep on a cot in the garage, or even down at the station. It all depended on his mercurial mood and the degree of his descent into booze. And last night was one where he cuddled with alcohol. She was relieved to note his absence. She stretched, rose, and slowly walked over to the dresser mirror.

She looked at herself and cried.

What happened? What went wrong? Was it something she did or said somewhere, someplace, that set them on separate paths? She almost always deferred to his wishes, whether it was on family matters or bedroom intimacy. She may not have been a candidate for *Good Housekeeping* magazine's Homemaker of the Year, but her house was clean, her family well fed and healthy and never without clean clothes. She did her best with what they had—more than a lot of women could say.

It was not as if her wardrobe was bulging with clothes. She did not have a cobbler's closet full of shoes. She wore scarves instead of hats, anklets instead of nylons. She darned the holes in family socks and patched the ripped places in the boys' overalls. Her kitchen was a combination of cabinets and appliances that her mother once had or that Jack bought used. Nothing was new.

Molly wiped her tears with the sleeve of her pajamas. She ran her fingers through her dark, shoulder-length hair with an involuntary comb-like sweep. Time to put on a good face for the kids and get them ready for school. Not that they were unaware of the problems their parents were having. That was again portrayed by last night's spectacle.

There was not another woman. She was quite sure of that. She still had above-average looks and a nice figure that weathered three pregnancies. But she could not compete with his morose moods, the paranoid Jack who took company with alcohol. What to do?

It was 6:45, time to shake off the questions and face the day's practical realities. She slipped out of her pajamas, put on a bra and underwear, and pulled the one-piece cotton housedress over her head. She tied it at the waist and stepped into some frazzled flats, which had accumulated more than a few miles.

"Time to get up," she said softly as she opened the door to Hattie's small bedroom. Her daughter grunted in protest, and Molly knew it would take a second prodding to dislodge her from bed. She made no attempt at gentleness when she turned the knob on the boys' door, walked in, and shook Bobby from his slumber.

"Time to move," she ordered. Bobby grumbled, rose like a spellbound zombie, and stumbled to the bathroom.

"Where is your brother? Already up?" Molly asked the half-asleep form trying to line up in front of the stool. His aim was initially off target—another cleanup job for his mother.

"Did you hear me? Is Peter already dressed and ready for breakfast and school?"

"I don't know, Mom. Petey is not my responsibility. How should I know where he's at?" He rubbed his eyes, and the new day came into focus. "I think I heard him get up."

"I wish you would be a little like Peter," Molly said. "He's more dependable and less sassy. Get dressed now."

She left him and headed down the short hallway to the kitchen. A small living room fronted the bungalow. The kitchen had a dining area. There was a pantry toward the back door. Her eyes first concentrated on remnants of collard greens that she had missed in her cleanup the night before, but her consciousness quickly turned to a room devoid of sound and movement.

"Peter? Are you out here?"

She looked to see if he had plopped down on the living room couch to extend his sleep. He had done that before. No one was there. Next, she walked toward the pantry room, which also doubled as a storage area and place for coats and shoes. In one corner were the washing machine and ironing board. Jack's work clothes were hung in the garage, where he also kept some tools.

"Peter, are you hiding somewhere?" She opened the back door, noticed it was unlocked, and stepped on the dandelions and broadleaf plantains that passed for a lawn. She ducked beneath the clothesline and walked to the side of the house. The backyard was just as quiet as the kitchen. Where could he have gone? Usually they lock the back door, but she could not remember doing it last night.

Maybe—for whatever reason, she thought—he's fooling around in the garage. Molly looked past the cot, lawnmower, shelves, and tools, but her scan produced no Peter. There was no car in the driveway in front of the garage, the place Jack always parked their 1937 Ford. That did not surprise her. He seldom left the car for her to use. She either took the city bus or caught a ride with one of her parents.

"Peter." Her voice picked up in volume and anxiety. It was simply not like him—Bobby, yes—to play games or wander from routine. She mechanically rubbed her right hand across her brow and returned inside. She went immediately to Bobby and Hattie, seeking answers from drowsy sources, again checking rooms automatically on the way.

"Hattie, are you up?"

"Yes, Mom."

"Have you seen Peter this morning?"

"No," Hattie responded quizzically. "I haven't seen him or talked to anyone since last night." She was awake enough to read apprehension in her mother's question. "Did you check the closet and look under the bed?" She was half serious and half attempting to lesson her mother's unease. "Mom, he's around the house somewhere. He didn't just disappear into thin air."

Perhaps not literally, but to a mother's instincts and fears, it improbably seemed to have happened. She was convinced Peter was not in the house or yard, leaving the possibility he was on his way to school or, more likely, down at the service station with his father.

"Bobby, are you sure you didn't hear Peter get up this morning? Get dressed? If he had gone to the bathroom during the night, you would have heard him. Right? Or gotten up for any reason?"

"I don't know, Mom. I may have heard some shuffling, but I sleep kinda hard. I just don't know for sure. Maybe, he got up."

"OK, both of you, get dressed quickly and come down for breakfast. Else you'll be late for school."

Molly redirected her attention to the needs of Hattie and Bobby, postponing the search for Peter, even though that was all that occupied her fearful mind. The children ate their oatmeal and toast and swished it down with milk. They grabbed their pencil cases and books and were ushered to the end of the block, where Molly waited with them for the school bus. It was Wednesday, an early dismissal day because of report cards. But all that gave way to Peter.

The bus came and left. Now her worry quickly slipped to panic. She had to contact Jack. Perhaps Peter was with him. Maybe instead of going to school, Peter decided to play morning hooky since there were no classes in the afternoon. That was it, and her alarm turned into fury. She made up her mind to walk the seven blocks to the gas station, grab Peter's ears and pull him home, screaming all the way. To hell with what Jack would think.

Once at home, Peter would get a paddling with the yardstick that would bring him within an inch of his life and leave a permanent impression on his mind and rear end. She was sure he was at the station. She returned to the house, grabbed a sweater, and briskly took off down Cumberland Street for Bremer's Mobil Station. Her thoughts alternated between angst and anger.

Molly was oblivious to everything around her and, at one street crossing, was almost struck by a milk delivery truck. After five blocks, she turned the corner and started to run toward the gas station. It was just beyond the stop sign ahead. She could see the flying red horse emblem. Her lungs heaved. Her heart pounded.

Her eyes probed the outside apron of the station. There were no cars being filled with gas, no one seeking service of any kind. The big doors to the bay areas were down. She raced to the front door and grabbed the greasy knob.

It was locked.

She cupped her hands over her eyes to see better through the front plate glass window. No one was there except for Miss May and her ample curves.

Molly sat down and cried.

Chapter 6
1975, Iowa

The vehicle that produced profound apprehension in Peter Bremer's brain sped on down the rural gravel road past his big Cadillac refuge. No shots were exchanged. The pickup driver presented neither a gun nor aggressive behavior.

To Bremer's astonishment, the man glanced toward him and smiled. He honked the horn of his Ford truck and delivered a demonstrative wave as if he were acknowledging a familiar neighbor. He graciously shared the dust with Bremer and his shiny black sanctuary.

Bremer watched as the vehicle proceeded eastward, still uncertain if it may turn around; its devious occupant resolved to do him harm. Such is the mindset of a person beleaguered by distrust and unadulterated anxiety. It was—if he were focused and forthcoming—a creation of his own actions. Sadly for him, there was no cure for either internal fear or outward reality.

The farmer driving the pickup was oblivious to Bremer's predicament. His effusive wave and relaxed manner signaled a frame of mind unburdened by the troubles that beset the dapper businessman with the messy and shrouded record. He was reluctant to confide in Glenda. He refused to tell his family or business associates, and he certainly could not disclose his problems to the authorities.

He suspected the FBI and IRS were already delving into his history. On top of all that, there were problems at Riverside Pack. Some shareholders with significant investments and loud voices claimed Bremer was spending company money as if it were his own. They charged him with trying to purchase other companies when Riverside Pack was still in its infancy. An enterprise that began with hope was suffering from a severe case of skepticism among some investors.

It was several minutes before the grip of alarm abated, and rational comportment assumed a foothold in Bremer's bearing. There was no one in sight as he backed the big car from its roadside spot and proceeded westward, picking up speed gradually. He had been on this country road before and knew that the Seville's suspension system would neutralize its washboard surface.

Incredible, he thought. Several miles to the north, he could be traveling on the straight and smooth concrete ribbon known as Highway 30—the Lincoln Highway. Who knows? Maybe it would be safer for him to use the busier Route 30 than some remote county road. He was satisfied that the back roads were his best option—the best option to stay alive.

Bremer was still thinking about the waving farmer and his gregarious manner, envying such a carefree life. He wished he could trade places, but that would be unfair to the farmer. He was not the one who provoked danger, the one who dangled promises into the deal-making den of rattlesnakes. But survival ignores fairness. It seeks circumvention. It searches for any way out.

When one gets pushed into a corner, any escape measure is fair unless, of course, you are strong enough and confident enough to push back. Peter was not. He was not snively like his father, but he was not formidable either. As push came to shove in his relations with the underworld, it was a mismatch that had Peter Bremer mad dashing like a hunted fox. Running.

Iowa's rural road system runs on a one-mile grid, except where rivers and old farmsteads impose barriers. Bremer was unaware he was on E-58 when he came to the junction with Iowa 21. Instead of turning north toward Irving, he swung south, then west on E-66, the route familiar to him. More back roads led him into the small town of Chelsea, Iowa.

His composure improved, and his apprehension diminished as the black Caddy rolled into the vast parking lot of Riverside Pack. Friendly territory, as it were. He pulled into the up-front parking spot marked "President and CEO." Bremer readjusted his blue tie, which had become as disordered as its wearer.

Riverside was strategically located on the Chicago and North Western Railway line, a double track all the way into Chicago and Denver markets. The shallow Iowa River meandered nearby but, while prone to flooding, offered no channel for delivering meat products.

"Good afternoon, Mr. Bremer," a muscular man, dressed in white coveralls and a yellow protective helmet, said with a deep, gravelly voice. "How are you doing on this hot summer's day?"

Bremer looked around at the one-story plant layout that was crisscrossed with electric lines, telephone poles, and water conduits of various sizes. The gentle breeze transported an amalgam of odors that emanated from the killing station and waste doors of the place that produced steaks, rump roasts, and hamburgers.

"Just fahn, Elmer. Just fahn," Bremer responded. He didn't say "fine" with a long *i* as Iowans say it. He still pronounced his *i*'s with the Southern flavor that he learned in Little Rock. And it was the requisite "just fahn" that conveniently masked his profound troubles.

"It's a great day to make hay while the sun is shinin', and it's a great day to make some money in the meat market."

Plant Manager Elmer Anders chuckled appropriately to his superior. Anders was just under six feet tall and weighed over 200 pounds and had a booming laugh to complement his girth when the occasion demanded. Bremer's line did not qualify for any belly-bending whoop. Anders swiped his clean-shaven jaw with his calloused hand.

"Price could always be better," Anders replied. "But business is good, and we are not only meeting the payroll but hiring. Just out of curiosity, how come the big sedan is so dusty? Looks like you drove through a flour mill getting here."

Elmer laughed, but Bremer did not. This time there was more wallop in Ander's whoop.

"I can have one of the boys give it a quick wash while we talk if you want."

"No, Elmer. It runs just fahn with a layer of grime. Maybe it doesn't take the corners as fast."

He ignored Anders' question about the car's grunge. The Cadillac looked out of sorts among a lot full of pickup trucks. Dust was the only common denominator.

More than 300 people were employed by Riverside Pack. They had decent-paying jobs in a town that was starving for employment and jilted by a previous company, which promised to re-open the slaughtering plant that suffered a revolving door of owners. This time farmers and businessmen injected their own hard-earned savings into the operation. It provided the perfect formula, many believed, where beef raised in Iowa was processed by Iowans at a plant owned by local investors.

Riverside Pack, to a great degree, was born out of desperation. Farmers and packinghouse workers in the area, disappointed and abandoned in the past, were holding their collective breath again. And for good reason. If Riverside and its investors could overcome the 1975 storm clouds of high interest rates, declining farm values, and drops in farm exports, a miracle was in the making.

There was renewed hope. The divisive Vietnam War had ended in late April. President Ford proposed a tax cut that Congress expanded to $23 billion. It spurred growth and checked the economic recession. Stagnation and 12 percent inflation earlier in the year seemed to be reversed, although the national jobless rate clung to a stubborn 9 percent.

Chelsea, like its Massachusetts namesake, was a working-class community that struggled economically for years. Unlike the Boston suburb, it was isolated in the middle of farm country and had no industrial fat cats living on nearby hills. It had been on the decline for years. Its population peak came in 1925 when it was a few souls short of 600. By 1975, the population had dropped to about 380. The town had a strong Czech heritage, part of the glue that held it together.

The biggest challenge for the community was that much of its incorporated boundary lay in the flood plain of the Iowa River. The river's meandering manner and tendency to overflow chased many out of town. The joke, albeit a poor one, was that if it rained an inch, the town would be flooded. Rock and dirt berms gave some protection to the packing plant.

This was fly-over country to the wheelers and dealers of Wall Street and Washington. Most did not know an Angus steer from a Holstein heifer. Nor did they know much about the area's struggling economic status. But the residents of Tama County, Iowa, population 19,533, inherited resilient genes. These were strong people who, like all farm communities, had survived the vacillations of weather and markets. Nearly half the plant workers were farmers too.

It would seem that if you lived in a place that has the richest farmland in the world, set in one of the most favorable growing seasons, making a living would not be such a challenge. The rural axiom—that farmers who fail to save up in the good years are likely to pay the price in the bad years—had many adherents.

Anders knew that up close and personal. Despite a degree in agriculture and business from Iowa State College, he was forced to abandon farming in early 1966. He had plenty of company. He rented out the few acres he owned and took a job at Wilson & Co. in Cedar Rapids. Then the job at Riverside became available.

"Look at these orders from West Coast grocery combines," Anders turned another page in the sales book and used his stubby index finger as a pointing stick. "We are doing surprisingly well in the San Francisco area, in the heart of fish country. What's the explanation for that, Mr. Bremer? I don't get it."

"Well, I've made some contacts out west," Bremer explained. "I guess some of them are starting to pay dividends. Shipping costs to the west coast are our biggest problem. Bigger volume will help that, cutting unit costs. Even the sophisticates of California like the marbled beef we raise in Iowa. Beef produced here is more flavorful and tender than range critters with harder muscle. You taught me that."

"True enough," Anders said. "You can't have a juicy steak without marbling and some fat. Range cows exercise too much. I want you to look at production costs while you are here. Floor guys are making $5.60, about average, but some of the supers haven't had raises since we started. Where can we save to keep margins steady? These are all things you may want to talk about with the board. Overall, I think shareholders will be pleased."

Bremer appreciated Anders's knowledge of the slaughtering business and his ability to get along equally with workers at all levels. However, Bremer's mind and attention seemed to be pulled to external issues, matters beyond Riverside Pack, mostly on how to avoid the people who wanted their money back now—an amount he could not deliver. Loans have a way of coming due.

None of his options were realistic. One was irrevocable. It caused him to take back roads. It had a finality that would cause anyone to shudder. Anders noticed the distant look in his boss's eyes but had no idea of the perils that generated it. He was aware of the uproar among some investors—published charges that Bremer was leading directors on the board rather than the other way around, but he wanted no part of that skinning.

"One other thing we should consider in the upcoming weeks," Anders guided Bremer away from his dark thoughts to a less noisy area of the plant. "Those damn bone saws produce enough racket to make them rock 'n' roll bands sound soothing. We need to purchase better ear protection for workers." They walked closer to the office area, beyond the blood and guts.

"You are right to be concerned about shipping costs," Anders continued. "I'm sure you are aware that the Teamsters contract expires next year, and I can guarantee you drivers will want a hefty raise. The trucking companies will pass that along."

Bremer nodded but did not respond.

"By the way," Anders added, "I noticed in the Cedar Rapids paper that Jimmy Hoffa, the old Teamsters boss, is missing. What do you make of that?"

James Riddle Hoffa was president of the International Brotherhood of Teamsters from 1958 to 1971. He secured the first national agreement for truck drivers' pay in 1964. Under his leadership, it became the largest union in the country. But his alleged connection with organized crime led to his downfall and, some now believed, his disappearance.

Bremer shrugged. He was unaware of the news about Hoffa's disappearance. Nevertheless, it was a topic that would not mix well with his own apprehension. Anders was no psychiatrist, but his natural savvy told him there was more on Peter Bremer's mind than shipping costs. He read the man's face like a soothsayer.

"Something bothering you, Mr. Bremer? If you gotta question about the plant, don't hesitate to ask it. Hell, I may not have an answer, but I won't lie about it. Worst thing a man can be is a liar— or someone who frosts things over to not look like a lie."

Bremer was surprised by Anders's forthright talkativeness. No one ever accused Elmer Anders of being a gasbag, one to clog up the conversation lanes. He was not shy or distant, but his words were measured. They were uttered with genuineness and in no need of an interpreter.

"No, Elmer," Bremer responded with a breath of hesitancy and a hint of ambiguity. "Why do you ask?" His screened vagueness was compounded as he looked down at the cement floor and made circular patterns in the sawdust with his expensive wingtips.

"Well, to be honest, Mr. Bremer," Anders looked him straight in the eyes. "You wear your worries on your face. You appear troubled. If I've done something wrong, or if there is a problem here at the plant, tell me straight out. I'm sure we can work it out."

Before Bremer had a chance to assure Anders that the two had no issues, that the perceived worries were external, the plant manager added his own philosophy about zooming in on the truth, how to avoid dancing with the facts and get down to the substance of a matter.

"I've always been a big fan of Harry Truman," Anders said. "Harry sought honesty without any coloring. He knew you couldn't pick up a piece of shit by its handle," referring to a phrase often attributed to the president. "He abhorred pomposity no matter the source. He had this big disagreement with General McArthur, who Harry figured gave orders to God. Not on Harry's watch."

Anders shook his head as though he were assuming Truman's determined mind.

"Elmer, as far as I can see, everything at the plant is going fine," Bremer injected. "I just have some other issues to work out."

Chapter 7
1942, Little Rock

"What seems to be the matter, ma'am?" came a voice that echoed from behind her.

Molly Bremer, with her head down and hands covering her eyes, had cried until her body was nearly void of any more tears. She had left home without washing her face or combing her hair. Nor had she put on a clean dress. She wore the same smock that had been soaked in collard green spray the night before. Appearance was not on her mind.

She was still sitting on the step outside her husband's gas station, not knowing what to do or where to go.

"Ma'am!" the man said louder. "What's the matter here?"

Little Rock Police Sgt. Ernest Shadron was on his way to work when he saw a woman sitting in an empty gas station lot with her head down, appearing out of sorts. He had been a cop long enough to sense that something was wrong, that a person may need help. Molly was unaware that Shadron had pulled into the station. She was lost in a haze of fright and indecision.

"Ma'am!" Shadron all but yelled in her ear.

Molly's head jerked up, and her hands fell upon her dress in an automatic gesture of modesty. She was shocked to see the police officer standing before her. It was as if she had been on some obscure trip that was part of a terrible dream, and now she gradually gathered her senses to recognize reality. She slowly rose and gazed foggily into Officer Shadron's eyes.

"What seems to be the problem?" he asked softly.

"I don't know," Molly said, her voice shaking. "I don't really know."

"Are you lost? Where do you live?"

Molly turned around and pointed in the direction of the family's house.

"That way. We live that way."

"What's your name and address, ma'am?"

Molly looked around as if searching for her identity. She glanced upward at the leafy trees, then at the sunlight that cut through the woody openings. What should she tell this police officer? That her husband abused her? That he was a drunk? That their lives were in shambles, that the world seemed to be coming to an end?

"My son seems to be missing," she said nearly inaudibly.

"What do you mean he seems to be missing?" Shadron asked.

Molly was unsure what she meant. Her mind was a jumble of thoughts and words that resisted arrangement into a comprehensible sentence. Somehow, she had to work her way through a muddled mind and talk sense. She was about to stand when her legs wobbled and her body wavered. Shadron caught her mid-fall.

"Ma'am, why don't you come over and sit in the squad car?" he suggested.

Molly did not resist. The officer opened the passenger door of the black and white 1940 Ford and took her arm. She rested her feet on the running board while holding onto the door with one hand. He boosted her into the seat. She took a deep breath and stared into the officer's eyes, this time with a clearer head.

"My name is Molly Bremer," she said slowly. "I haven't had breakfast and may be a little light-headed. I ran down Cumberland Street. You see, I can't find Peter—my son, Peter. I walked to the bus with Hattie and Bobby—our other children—and then I raced here to look for Peter. He wasn't at home this morning, so I thought he may be with his father here at the gas station.

"My husband runs this Mobil station. But the place is locked up. I don't know what to do."

She furnished other details: Peter's age, his height, a general description of what she thought he would be wearing. And she mentioned her husband's business and that Peter frequently helped his dad at the station. She omitted any reference to last night's uproar at the Bremer household.

"Ma'am, I'm Sgt. Shadron. Is it possible your son left early for school? Or maybe he got a ride with someone else? There is the possibility he came here, and his father drove him to school. The chances are he is in class. What's the name of the school? We'll drive over there and check things out. Is that OK with you?"

"Oh yes, Officer. That would be most kind of you." Molly was grateful and relieved at the same time. What he suggested, one of those possibilities, was probably true. It was unlikely for Peter to run off without a word, she thought—or without at least leaving a note. Bobby would do that, but not Peter.

"I will call into the station and let them know I will be a little late," Shadron informed her. He closed the door and radioed headquarters. Molly's uncertainty failed to dissolve as the police cruiser headed toward Jefferson Davis School. While Jack's tirade last night was not the first, the entire episode seemed to carry extraordinary dimensions. She was unable to define it. It was a fearsome feeling.

Shadron pulled into the school visitors' parking area, and the two proceeded to the office. It was nearly 8:30, and classes had already begun. Hallways were clear except for stragglers. The woman at the office reception desk was on the phone and motioned for the visitors to take a seat. The presence of a police officer did not seem to hurry her conversation, but Molly stood at the counter and conveyed a look of urgency. It worked.

"What can I do for you?" the woman said, placing the phone on its cradle. Shadron stood and joined Molly.

"I want to check on my son," Molly said sheepishly. "I want to see if he is in school."

"What's his name?"

"Peter. Peter Bremer."

"What grade is he in, and who his teacher?" asked the receptionist.

"He's in seventh grade, and his teacher is Sandra Tegland."

"OK, one moment, please. Susie," the receptionist called to an office aide, "will you please run down to Mrs. Tegland's room and see if Peter Bremer is in class? This is his mother, and she's concerned whether he's in school."

Molly sat down and watched as Susie dashed down the hallway. In two minutes, she returned, and Molly could read her face.

"Peter Bremer is not in class this morning," Susie said to all those in the small front office.

"Mrs. Bremer, is there something more you would like us to do?" the receptionist said. "I can call the principal if you want."

Molly looked at Officer Shadron. No answers were forthcoming.

"No, thank you," Molly replied. She and the police officer left.

"I'll drive you to your home," Shadron told Molly. "If you don't hear from your son by noon, give me a call, and we'll talk more about it. We can put out a missing person bulletin at that time. Is there anything more you would like to tell me that might help in locating him, other places he might go, or if he is with his father, where they might go?"

"I don't know, Officer," Molly brushed her hand through her hair. "I don't know where else he might go. "Home, school, and the gas station are really the only places Peter goes. He has never gone down to the playground during school hours. He is small for his age, Officer Shadron, often picked on and unlikely to go places where that could happen, places where there are no adults around. I just don't know."

Shadron swung by Bremer's Mobil Service on the way just to make sure Peter had not shown up there. Nothing had changed. The door to the business was still locked. There was no one around. He took Molly home and went to the police station. He reported the incident, even though it started as an unofficial stop on his way to work. It had the aura of "unusual" wrapped about it, and he feared for Molly and Peter.

She washed her face, combed her hair, and put on a clean dress. She made herself a bowl of Quaker oatmeal and topped it with brown sugar and a splash of milk. But it was Peter's face that was a constant companion, no matter where she looked or what she did. A tear slipped down her face and into her oatmeal.

Looking back, it was like a storm emerging on the horizon. All the wishing, all the hoping that things might turn in a different direction, were washed away by the building forces that could not be changed. Now Molly had to deal with the aftermath. She gazed out the kitchen window. Her moist eyes blurred the stirring leaves of the sprawling white oak.

She decided to call her parents.

The phone rang six times before there was an answer. It was her mother.

"Hello."

"Hello, Mom. This is Molly. How are you this morning?"

"I'm fine, Molly. What's wrong?"

Mothers have a way of reading between, through, and around the lines in a fashion that would dazzle a veteran fortune-teller.

"Mom, Peter isn't over at your house, is he?"

"No, what do you mean? Isn't he in school?"

"No, Mom. He wasn't around when I got up this morning. Nowhere in the house. He wasn't at the station. Neither was Jack. The station is locked up. We checked at school. He isn't there. I don't know what to do. I don't know where he could be."

"What do you mean 'we' checked at school? Who is 'we?'"

"I walked down to the gas station to see if Peter was there. A policeman saw me sitting there alone and stopped. He took me to the school. I guess he sensed I needed help."

Price, Molly's mother, had never been a major trumpet player on Jack Bremer's small bandwagon. For one thing, she believed he blew his own horn too much and never sang praises of her daughter. He was good-looking all right, but too often at parties—before and after he and Molly were married—he would strut around like a peacock in search of action. That ruffled Aliza's feathers.

"Maybe Peter went with his father to the zoo or some other place for the day," she answered her daughter. She sidestepped what was really on her mind: *I warned you plenty of times about Jack Bremer, but you ignored my advice. He has always put himself first. Now you have three kids, and you still don't have a husband. It's a bad situation that I can't fix.*

"Molly, they may have just gone to some supply store, you know, pickin' up fan belts or batteries."

"Mom, I think Jack took off with Peter."

"Took off!" she said in a flabbergasted tone. "Took off where? And why?"

"We had a big fight last night. Jack was worse than usual. He had been drinking. He knocked a boiling pan of vegetables out of my hand. I fixed a nice meal, but he didn't stay to eat. He was gone all night, and this morning Peter was gone too. I think he came back and took him."

"Why would he do that, honey? And leave Bobby and Hattie behind? That makes no sense."

"I'm afraid it does. You don't know him. Jack has become so difficult, so moody and paranoid and half the time drunk that he would grab Peter and run just to hurt me. He likes Peter. Bobby is too much like him, and Hattie has grown out of her daddy's little girl role. But Mom, Peter would be scared to death. He is smart but not as gritty as Bobby."

"I'll come over, Molly. But I think you are jumping way ahead of yourself. What did the police officer suggest?"

"He said to wait until noon, and if we don't hear something by then, he will put out a missing person report on Peter."

"That sounds like good advice."

Molly said goodbye and walked to the front door and opened it. She peered up and down the street through the screen, hoping beyond doubt that a small figure would miraculously appear from behind the parade of azalea bushes and oak trees. The only movement was the flickering leaves, showing their underside as a foretelling of rain.

A tear trickled down her cheek.

Chapter 8

The summer of 1942 was one of the darkest times in Molly Bremer's life. Often she internally compared her situation to that of parents who were mourning the loss of a son to the war. There were more and more people like them as the United States expanded its fight against the Japanese in the Pacific. Grief over her son's disappearance made her almost immune to outside events.

Arkansas and all America were blanketed with gloom as the Japanese took over Guam, Wake Island, the Philippines, and parts of China. German U-boats sunk American ships in the Gulf of Mexico, in the St. Lawrence Gulf, and the Atlantic. German mines were found in the Mississippi River Delta.

While the US Naval victory at Midway lifted spirits, there was soul-shaking anxiety as American forces launched the Guadalcanal campaign in efforts to grind out beachheads in the South Pacific. On the Eastern European front, the German Luftwaffe began bombing Stalingrad, ultimately reducing it to near rubble. It sent a chill far beyond the Russian front. There was a genuine fear that Hitler would order the German invasion of the United States.

The minimum draft age was lowered from twenty-one to eighteen.

Cumberland Street in Little Rock was especially shadowed by sadness and despair. In more than two months, there had been no word within the family and no official information concerning the vanishing of Peter Bremer and his father. While Peter may still be alive, his mother's heart struggled to acknowledge it. She was convinced her husband had abducted Peter.

No amount of comfort from family and neighbors could extract her from sullen depths. Peter's absence consumed her. There was news that a young navy man from down the street had been killed in the Solomon Islands, which added to the neighborhood anguish. The Blue Star banner in the front window of his home, a sign that a serviceman lived here, was replaced by a Gold Star flag, denoting his death.

Molly did not blame the police department for failing to locate her son. They had investigated the matter, put out missing person bulletins throughout the state, and even made calls to authorities in cities where Molly believed her husband might have gone. But after a month, new police matters took precedence. As June edged toward July, it seemed to her as if Peter and Jack Bremer had fallen off the earth.

Arkansas laws on kidnapping and abduction, Molly discovered, were like those in many states—about as definitive as midnight fog. She was told that her case was not a matter of kidnapping since the son was with his father, and ransom was not an issue. The Arkansas statute on abduction, she was informed, only addressed females under the age of fifteen.

Busy lawyers shunned arguing a vague law on behalf of a mother with little money.

Her mother tried to redirect her attention to Hattie and Bobby and life in the moment, but such logical advice did not fit into a maternal perspective on optimism and possibility. Molly's memory was one dimensional and not easily amended. Her mind was saturated with images of Peter, and no amount of solace and counsel could rub them out. When the screen door banged as Bobby or Hattie exited, it was Peter's semblance that preceded it.

The truth was that Bobby needed direction and correction. Molly's preoccupation with Peter's absence obstructed parental attention to the other children. She was finally awakened when a police officer knocked on the front door with Bobby in tow. The cop had caught him trying to break into a car just down the street from the school.

That was only the beginning of additional heartache for Molly Bremer. Over the next several weeks, Bobby was in and out of trouble to the point where he had become a household name at the precinct station. She had begun work at the government munitions plant and was unable to keep track of him all day. She caught rides with other employees and was grateful for it, but coworkers had no prescription for an aching heart. She sometimes sobbed in silence, and it was embarrassing.

Crowning all that was a brutal and perpetual beating of herself. Why had she failed as a mother? What should she have done differently? Why had she failed as a wife?

Her soul was bloated with ambiguity.

———————

Jack Bremer down-shifted the Ford into second gear as he slowed to make a left turn into the depths of Mississippi.

"Where are we going, Daddy?" Peter asked, fidgeting in his car seat and gawking at the tall pines. His thoughts were a jumble. He was not scared, being with his father, but there was a peculiar discomfort circulating in his mind. "Are we going fishing? You said one time the two of us would go off by ourselves and, like Grampa says, 'talk back to those largemouth bass.'"

His father remained silent, eyes fixed straight ahead.

Peter knew fishing was not on his father's agenda. The absence of fishing gear was not the first clue. You do not toss clothes in a suitcase on orders of your father, tiptoe out of your own house at 6:00 a.m., and do it all in a rush if you are headed on a bass-fetching expedition. Yet, he had no inkling of the dimensions of what had just happened and what was ahead.

"So, I can skip the last week of school?"

Jack Bremer had uttered barely ten words the entire trip from Little Rock to Gulfport, Miss. Young Peter had slept much of that time. How do you tell a twelve-year-old that you are not on a fishing trip, but on a trip fishing for direction in your life? How do you explain to your own flesh and blood that, in truth, you are a parent running away from family and responsibility?

How do you look at your son and inform him that he is along to hurt his mother, that he is part of an exercise in vindictiveness?

"We may go fishing, Pete," he replied in hopes of concealing his guilt.

"Daddy, I'm hungry. Can we get something to eat?"

Bremer was hungry too. It was nearly two o'clock, and they had not stopped to eat since Jackson. As they headed eastward, they discovered that most of the eating places along coastal Route 90 featured seafood. No Dixie Pig barbeque signs anywhere. He slowed the car to 20 mph. The shiny leaves of a magnolia tree slowly revealed a sign that advertised Hobson Road Stand, but when they got there it looked too elaborate and expensive—and busy.

The Gulf Coast, like most of the country, was abuzz with military buildup. Signs sprouted all along the highway and declared "help wanted" in the shipbuilding industry. The state, with financial assistance from the federal government, was already planning to widen Beach Boulevard, the local name for Route 90, to four lanes, especially with the construction of Keesler Air Force Base at Biloxi.

"Look for a fruit stand, Pete," his father answered after several minutes. "Would you like a juicy apple? Or a banana?"

Peter did not want to turn down anything to eat, but his taste buds were set on something more substantial. They passed through Biloxi. His appetite was suddenly diverted as the car rumbled across the Back Bay Bridge, which spanned the wide Gulf inland channel. It looked a little like the Mississippi River, except off to the right the sparkling water ran as far as one could see, interrupted only by outlines of big ships and barges.

Neither Peter nor his father had ever seen the Gulf of Mexico. For the stranger, it was a breathtaking view. Peter strained to absorb its expanse. The angle of the sun created billions of sparkling diamonds mingled with wave wrinkles, which reminded him of snow patterns molded by winter wind. While scattered, puffy clouds meandered over the mainland, the dome over the Gulf was clear and calm. At the horizon, the azure sky bumped into the water with only a hint of distinction.

"Welcome to Ocean Springs," a sign announced once they were on the other side of the bay. Seagulls flitted about, screeching their obnoxious objections about sharing the coastline.

"Dad! Look over there." Peter pointed out the right side of the car. "See that Coca-Cola sign. I'll bet they have hot dogs."

Bremer had cleaned out the gas station cash register and grabbed other money he had stashed in the house before they left Little Rock. Leaving his wife was not a spontaneous decision. The big fight at home tipped his fragile temperament and dissolved any remnants of affection he had for Molly or concern for the family. He took Peter's advice and pulled behind the Coca-Cola advertisement.

They entered the small restaurant and were greeted by a middle-aged woman with a greasy blue apron. Her mix of strawberry and gray hair, mangled into a bun clinging for survival, complemented her dull eyes and tired face. The air was a mixture of filmy cigarette smoke and the clean harmony of the Platters' number one hit song:

"Only you can make this world seem right; only you can make the darkness bright."

The jukebox volume consumed the small restaurant with leftover vibrations for anyone passing by. Bremer wished for less sound and better lighting. He and Peter occupied one of four booths. Maroon-colored shrimp sauce decorated the top of the uncleaned table. Peter could not find hot dogs advertised on the big menu signs behind the counter, but there was a wide variety of po'boy sandwiches listed.

"Dad, I ain't seein' no sign for a hot dog, just a lot of them po'boys. Are they for poor people?"

"I 'spect they're for anybody, Peter."

"When you hold my hand, I understand the magic that you do." The Platters tried to sing above the eatery din.

There were few people in the place, but they were talkative. The big noon crowd had mostly headed back to work in shipyards or wherever they were going.

Bremer's thoughts drifted briefly back to Little Rock and Molly. It was more like a brain tic, a spasm rooted in time. It was void of caring. There was no remembrance of holding hands and the romance of young love, no more recalling of good times. The magic mentioned in the Platters' song had withered away.

"Mister, what can I get you?" the waitress inquired. A green pencil dangled behind her right ear, propped by straggly hair that explained her day. Shrimp sauce seemed to highlight her apron too. It was clear that she had dismissed neatness and style for some time.

Employment could be found at any number of coastal companies desperate in need of manpower. Jack and Peter had to settle somewhere. But after eating, Bremer drove on through Gautier and Pascagoula. More large cranes poked out of the landscape and portrayed a country bent on flexing its muscle to defeat the Axis nations.

At Grand Bay, Ala., just east of the Mississippi state line, he turned right on an unimproved road for no reason than that it provided further distance from Little Rock—an even more remote place to hide from family obligations, memories, and perhaps the law. It quickly evolved into a more isolated spot than he anticipated, a place that cast the impression that civilization's end was around the corner.

The road was more like a narrow path. In some places, brush and wild azalea—blooms long faded—fought for space and scrapped up against the car as it squeezed past. The road's red dirt surface was baked by the cycle of frequent rain and hot sun. After a few miles, Bremer began to wonder where he was going—both geographically and in life. But at every turn, it seemed the paranoid and self-centered elements of his nature were too fixed to alter his direction.

They crossed a wooden bridge that rattled in protest at being disturbed. Approaching a curve, they were hailed by the open arms of a mammoth tree that at first glance appeared to be smack in the middle of the road. To Peter's imagination, it took the form of a fictional giant, a long-armed monster that hadn't shaved in many weeks. Long straggles of grassy, beard-like vines dangled from the tree's limbs.

"What sort of tree is that, Dad?" Peter asked.

His father did not respond; his mind was caught up in an unfamiliar place. The maps Jack had brought along had marked US 90 and some paved roads, but not a back-water trail like the one they were now traveling. Time soon solved the problem. The path intersected with a paved two-lane road. Arrows on a junction sign, peppered with bullet holes, pointed left to Mobile and right to Bayou La Batre, Ala.

Bremer turned right, past some fields of sprouting cotton. Ten minutes later they entered the town. Unsure of what to do next, he stopped in the parking lot of a white building that advertised oysters and shrimp. Peter pinched his nose as an antidote to the air's briny smell. He looked around, anxious as a fish out of water, his mind swimming with questions. He could sense his father's uncertainty.

Two hundred feet down the street, a large sign gave notice of the upcoming "Thank God Dinner." Jack and Peter had no idea what that meant, but from the size of the placard, it was obviously an important event. Smaller lettering invited everyone to the feast: Sunday, May 31, after the noon Mass in the parking lot of St. Margaret's Catholic Church. The menu featured boiled shrimp, crabmeat, oysters, and fish.

"Howdy, mister," a voice came from a man who had walked up behind the Ford, its motor still running. "Y'all look lost. Is there some way I can direct you?" He noticed the Arkansas plates on Bremer's car.

Jack, left arm arched from the car window, did not see the man approach and was mildly startled. He glanced back, looked at a fat face with a broad smile and a man with a watermelon stomach. At first glance he thought the fellow was connected to a nearby fruit stand—at least as a consumer.

"Good afternoon, sir," Bremer returned the greeting. "We just drove into town and are lookin' for a place to stay, get a bite to eat this evenin'."

"First off, mister, there ain't no sirs in Bayou La Batre. No royalty here, unless you count them royal red jumbo shrimp. Now, they have a high place in the hearts of every person in this here region." He laughed, and the watermelon bounced in agreement. "No, we's all just common, workin' folks.

"But, more to answerin' you'all's question. There's a couple of boardin' houses you might check, but places to stay down here are hard to come by. Believe it or not, because of all the war construction in big towns, we have families moved into the Bayou, and the men have to drive a hour to work in Pascagoula and Mobile. It's crazy, I tell ya.

"I wish't I owned a trailer court. Could make a lot of money and wouldn't have to get up in the middle of the night to go shrimpin'. That's hard work. You looking for work? They's plenty of jobs."

"Maybe," Jack said softly.

"This your boy?" the man asked. He was short as well as wide—a man, Bremer thought, who didn't miss many meals. His blue cap unintentionally matched his blue short-sleeved shirt, which escaped the left side of his waistband. His baggy black slacks, decorated with splotches of what appeared to be oil, were held up by overtaxed red suspenders.

"Sorry, I apologize to ya. Didn't even introduce myself." He stuck his hand through the car window in Bremer's direction. "My name is Clarence Salette. Came here from Louisiana almost twenty years ago."

"Howdie. My name is Jack Bremer, and this is my son, Peter. Glad to make your acquaintance."

"Ma pleasure, Mr. Bremer. I've gotta boy 'bout the same age. Name is Malcom, after some kin in the Missus's family, but we call him Sonny. He's a good boy, that Sonny. Where ya from?"

Bremer was reluctant to answer directly.

"Up north. Came down to, uh, to do a little fishin' maybe."

"Well, most of the fishin' down here is out in the Gulf, unless you go up to the top of Mobile Bay. Can escape the saltwater there."

"What's the name of the boardin' house?" Bremer asked.

"Bayou Overnite is one. Keep drivin' south. Go across the channel bridge and past the Catholic church. The channel is where many of the shrimp boats are moored. The street then angles to the left. I think it's about five or six blocks down from there. Left-hand side."

"Many thanks. What did ya say your name was? Clarence?"

"That's it. But most people call me Sal. That's Salette with the last part chopped off." He laughed, and his mid-section bobbed accordingly. He was one of those people whose persona seemed parked in the positive, and his rolling, thunderous laughter infectious. Even Jack Bremer leaked a smile.

"I'm half owner of a shrimp boat. I'm the half who does most of the work." He snorted again, and his belly followed suit. "If yer down by the channel"—he motioned in a southerly direction—"look for her. She's a pretty boat. White topped with red lipstick. Her name is *Sally*. Fella by the name of Wally, Wally Bankston, is the other half owner. Hence the boat's name. Sal plus some of Wally."

"Well, Mr. Sal. We're much obliged."

With that, Bremer waved goodbye and drove south. The town buzzed with business. "Now Open" read a sign on Hazel's Beauty Salon. They passed a bank, a grocery store, and several seafood outlets. Soon they approached the channel bridge. Peter was bug-eyed as he saw the endless lineup of boats—shrimp trawlers, barges, tugs, cruisers—on both sides of the draw bridge.

Route 188, marked as Wintzell Avenue in town, crossed the channel—except, of course, at those frequent times when the two ends of the drawbridge rose skyward to allow seafaring traffic to move through. The newcomers spotted boats pulling into docks and heard their toots and whistles as they maneuvered the highway of water. It was an immersion in maritime culture for Peter Bremer and his father.

They drove past St. Margaret's Catholic Church. The church's rear parking lot and a large grassy area abutted the ship channel. Bremer followed the street as it swung left past the Baptist Church, Alba School, and several seafood eateries.

"Gosh, Dad," Peter blurted. "They must have no hot dogs or hamburgers down here. Everything is seafood. 'Spect they do a lot of fishin' down here. Maybe we can catch some."

Just beyond a row of live oaks, Bremer spotted the boarding house sign that said Bayou Overnite.

"We'll pull in here to see if they have a room. Maybe"—he looked at Peter—"the boarding house lady serves hot dogs."

Chapter 9
Alabama

Luck was with them. A vacancy opened at Bayou Overnite just that morning. Moreover, Bremer learned from the boarding house operator that a filling station in nearby Coden was looking for a mechanic. He inquired the next day and took the job.

There was no fishing.

Some days Peter went with his father to the gas station, but he was not allowed to operate the pumps. Most of the time, he hung around the boarding house. Life became boring. He got to know Mrs. DeKnight, the operator, less formally known as Zelda. He even helped make the beds and swept some of the rooms. Almost from the beginning, she had a peculiar feeling about the circumstances surrounding Peter and his father. But she did not pry.

Rather, Zelda took on the role of a kindly aunt and teacher. She saw to it that Peter had his teeth brushed and hair combed, that he was occupied in some manner. She told him about her upbringing, where she went to school, and a little of the town's history, all in hopes it may dent Peter's shell and guarded attitude. He was reluctant to say much, but dribbles of his life began to surface.

The pieces of a fractured family emerged. Her immediate concern was his lack of social contact. He had no interaction with children his age. So, she took him to the town library. One day they stopped at the playground near Alba School, but Peter showed no signs of opening the door of his isolated self. Zelda became his sole aperture to outside life.

"This town sure has a funny name," Peter said one day after they returned from the grocery store. He calculated that the best way not to mess up the pronunciation was to avoid it. "Almost as funny as Little Rock. Far as I can tell, there ain't no big rock there or little one." It was a slip, revealing his hometown. But he did not worry about it, comfortable in feeling that Zelda would not cross-examine him about his circumstances.

They were sitting on a six-foot-wide swing anchored by heavy chains to the ceiling of the boarding house's wrap-around porch. The Spanish moss on the live oak trees across the street seemed to be sleeping, unperturbed by the breeze. Squawking gulls brandished their annoyance in complete indifference to the outside world. In the distance, pulleys begging for oil screeched as they ushered heavy cables and loads at the nearby shipyard.

"What kinda tree is that?" Peter pointed. "We saw one comin' into town. It looked like a giant with a beard!"

"That's a good description, Peter. It's called a live oak. I guess that's 'cause they keep their leaves nearly all year long, right through winter. We say winter, but it hardly ever freezes down here. Up-ta Mobile it sometimes freezes, but not down here in the Bayou. And that fuzzy stuff y'all call its beard? That's Spanish moss. Some call it a parasite, but it don't take nothin' from the tree."

The two-story boarding house was flanked by the live oak on one side and a magnolia tree on the other, with azaleas and bottlebrush scattered in between. The oak's wide waist and sprawling arms cowered other vegetation into submission. Peter was familiar with the magnolia, and it took his mind briefly back to his home in Little Rock. His thoughts were redirected by the clanging of bells.

"What's that?" he asked.

"I cain't rightly say," Zelda replied. "I just know it comes from the boats, and I s'pose it's some kinda signal." She looked at him and wondered about his roaming mind. "And I'll tell you about the town's name, which you think is funny."

She explained that "Bayou is a French name for swampy, low-lying areas, marshy places often next to bigger masses of water like the Gulf of Mexico here. Or along the Mississippi River. The town is a seafood center—claims to be the seafood capital of Alabama." She paused to collect her thoughts, redirecting them from this vacant, boyish face, which seemed to conceal burdens too heavy for his years.

Zelda looked upward, searching for direction. Perhaps, she thought, the mundane will bring solace to this worrisome soul. She did not fancy herself as a counselor. Her credentials, notably her warm heart, were shaped by life's lessons. She was orphaned as a teenager and raised by an aunt. Both of her parents died of complications from the Spanish flu. Around the Bayou, her reputation for goodwill and pleasant nature was matched only by her cooking.

"On hot summer days"—she again looked at Peter—"when there is little wind to clean up the air, the town can smell really fishy." She curled her nose to demonstrate.

Peter nodded in agreement.

"We must have had a warm day with no breeze when we arrived," Peter said, smiling, "'cause it sure was stinky."

"I have a friend," she chuckled, "who describes that smell as a combination of old crab and wet dog."

Peter failed to fully comprehend the comparison, especially the old crab part. He had been at a crab boil several days ago, and nostril memory from that experience was sufficiently fresh to provide a hint at her appraisal. Like all fishing ports along the sea, Bayou La Batre had a land, sea, and air identity, distinctively dissolved in its briny climate.

Zelda was the right age but the wrong size for the archetypal magazine auntie. She brimmed with attention for young people and was considerate of all. Physically she lacked the model of a squat, matronly woman whose mostly gray hair was hoisted in a bun. She had had no children of her own to stretch the midriff, so her figure was mostly intact. Her dark hair was short and styled with peeking strands of gray. If of a mind, she would not have to labor to catch the eye of a conscious man.

"Are there snakes here?" Peter asked. He hated snakes. Once he mistakenly picked up a garter snake beneath his mom's clothesline, thinking it was an apron string.

"There are," Zelda said. "But you don't have to be afraid in town. The bad ones are out in the swamp."

"What does La Batter mean?"

"It's *By-U La Bat-tra*," she annunciated. "Some shorten the Bayou part to By. The early French built a fort here, which in English was known as 'bayou of the battery.' *La Batre* is French for 'the battery.' Does that make sense?"

Peter nodded. He was fascinated by the town's history, and Zelda gave him a schoolteacher's full lesson, from native Americans to French settlers. "Some people in Mobile," she said, "think the world started up there, but we know the French landed here and on Dauphin Island in 1699. Pirates tried to run them out, but the French held on."

Zelda was pleased with Peter's rapt attention. It was almost as satisfying as when one of her boarders complimented her on her homemade cinnamon rolls.

"Then came the British, and in 1780 Spain took over. In 1810, a group of pro-American radicals exercised their muscle and formed the Republic of West Florida. Next, in 1861 with the Civil War brewing, came the Republic of Alabama. That lasted about a month before the Confederate States took over. When the war ended, we became part of the Union. That's a lot of different flags."

"We studied about the Civil War and slavery," Peter responded. "Did this area have slaves?"

"If you had enough money, you probably owned a slave," Zelda replied. "But there's lot of poor people down here, poor whites too. And poor whites didn't have slaves." She paused. "Mobile, up the road from here, was one of the largest slave ports on the coast. They bought and sold black folks, entire families, like they was cattle."

She talked about how black people were still treated as second-class people. Peter said he knew about that. There were no black children at his school in Little Rock. His worry-wart personality popped up again when she talked about hurricanes, especially how a 1906 storm all but destroyed the area. She assured him that hurricanes are rare and usually happen in late summer and fall. .

"Where's Dolphin Island? Are there dolphins down there?"

"It's complicated," Zelda said, turning up her eyes for emphasis. "It is Dauphin Island, d-a-u-p-h-i-n, not dolphin like the fish. It is named for the oldest son of the king of France, the heir to the throne, because the French controlled this area at one time. Do you understand?"

"I guess."

"But, yes, there are a lot of dolphins, the fish, there too. Dauphin Island is a long, skinny strip of sand about five miles south of here. People live there, but there is no bridge. They get to the mainland by boat."

"Wow, that would be fun."

May was about over, and school ended for the term. One day Zelda decided to give Peter a quiz on the area's history and other things they had talked about. For the first time since he left home, his smile was genuine. He was eager to take her test, and he produced the answers as if he were a Gulf Coast native.

"Good thing you didn't ask about spelling," he told Zelda. "I like math and history, but spelling words is tough. But"—he giggled—"I will never forget how to spell the word *geography*. My third-grade teacher gave me a formula for spelling the word *geography*. Do you know what it is?" He took delight in being the one with a question.

"'Fraid not," Zelda replied. "You'll have to be the teacher."

"Well, all's you have to do is remember the first letters for words in this phrase." He snickered again. "The phrase is 'George Edwards' Old Grandmother Rode A Pig Home Yesterday.' That's how to remember to spell geography. Get it?"

Zelda nodded, and they laughed together. That session cemented their connection. Peter's new life was slightly more tolerable.

Zelda's cooking talents quickly became apparent to boarders. They also discovered she was a stickler for promptness. Being late for supper was a mortal sin in her book, an insult, really. At the appointed time, without a roll call, she led a short prayer of thanksgiving, and the meal began. Her use of stoneware and cloth napkins made eating special.

"Now, I want y'all to meet our new guests," Zelda had said that first time Peter and his father joined other boarders for supper. The commingling aromas of fried shrimp, mashed potatoes, and corn on the cob wrestled for the attention of the hungry group. "Elroy, Shorty, Bugs—Shorty, please take off your hat—ah'd like you to meet young Peter and his father, Jack." And with that, the presenting ceremony was over.

Zelda was not only an exceptional cook but kept a clean place. No one came to supper without washing hands and putting on clean clothes. This was not just a place to hang your hat. Zelda wanted it to be home for her boarders. She delighted in showing nice things and presenting a comfortable atmosphere.

Fruity wallpaper topped the brown wainscoting that circumvented the big dining room. A border strip near the ceiling was laden with cherries. Her sleeping rooms were pleasantly decorated too. There were curtains on the windows, and each room had a closet and a large brown bureau. Feather pillows topped cushy beds. A lamp stood next to a rocking chair.

It was a pleasant place.

On the last day of May, the entire town celebrated at the "Thank God Dinner." Zelda took Jack and Peter, and the Arkansas natives discovered they loved shrimp. There was boiled and fried shrimp, fried and raw oysters, fried fish and stuffed crab, hush puppies, baked beans, and cabbage slaw. It was a seafood feast, and Peter's stomach groaned as it stretched to accommodate a full plate. Children raced around the grounds, but Peter stuck to his father's side.

It was a splendid day, the temperature in the mid-70s. There was no salty haze and sticky humidity, no tumbling black clouds that sniffed of rain. Rain was almost as regular in the Bayou as grits on a restaurant menu. The area had more rainfall than the Pacific Northwest. A gentle north wind swayed the hanging moss on nearby live oaks in a low dance.

The channel waters behind St. Margaret, which ran south to the Mississippi Sound and then onto the Gulf, were filled with shrimp boats decked with colorful pennants that fluttered in the soft breeze. The boats all had names: *Smooth Water*, *Deep Thinking*, *Ellie Mae*, *Net Profit*. Peter started counting them but quit at forty. They lined the narrow inlet like an armada on watch.

The boats' downriggers, tall arms that lowered the nets into the water in search of shrimp, stood at upright attention as revelers ate and traded stories of life on the sea. The Bayou was not only a seafood paradise but immersed in sea-going culture. The shrimp and oyster workers combed the nearby waters like Kansas farmers raked the wheat plains.

A burgeoning shipbuilding and repair business supported the floating machinery. However, most ship repair shops in the Bayou were short-handed because many workers had left for better-paying jobs in Mobile and Pascagoula where destroyers and LSTs were being assembled for the navy.

"Well, howdy to mah new friends, and to you too, Zelda."

Clarence Salette was in his Sunday finest—that is, a clean shirt and overalls and a big straw hat. He wiped his mouth with a napkin and extended his hand.

"Oh, Zelda. Ah didn't mean to imply that you're not a friend. You know you're a good fr—". She cut him off with a gentle wave.

"Hello, Sal. No explanation required," Zelda responded with a dash of intoned irrelevance. "Thank you for helping organize the big town celebration. This is quite a turnout," she said, gesturing over the grounds. "Oh, Sal," she gurgled. "You still have some shrimp sauce around your mouth." She pointed at the leftover condiments that decorated his chin. He grinned and made a repeat swipe of his face.

"And if mah brain recalls correctly, you two are Jack and Peter," he said.

"Nice to see you again, Sal." Bremer took his hand.

"Zelda here knows this fahn young fella with me," Sal gushed. "He be my boy Sonny. Malcom, if y'all inclined to be formal, which ain't too often in these parts. Handsome lad, ain't he?"

"Sonny is the spittin' image of you, Sal," Zelda heaped on the sweet talk. "And I 'spect those shoulders of his will bud out strong just like his daddy's. You've a right to be proud, Sal."

"Them's kindly words, Zelda. You know," he giggled. "If I wasn't taken, I'd be askin' you out for a date."

That produced laughter all around, even a broad smile on Jack Bremer's face.

"Did you get enough to eat, boys?" Sal inquired.

"I couldn't eat another shrimp even if it was a baby shrimp," Peter said.

"Good, good," Sal continued. "Say, why don't you two young-uns run off and see if you can find some pretty girls. And ah'll bet if you look hard enough you can find a confectionery booth somewheres 'round here. Ah knows they have some chocolate-covered pecans. Here's a quarter. Now, scat."

"That's mighty nice of you, Sal," Jack Bremer said. "I can see why you are well-liked here."

"Well, thanks, Mr. Bremer. Ah'm trying to convince the town and the pastor here to make this an annual event, like they do in Europe. Over there they have the blessing of the fleet and a big celebration every year. They have a boat parade, and the bishop stands out on one of the vessels and gives his blessing to all the shrimpers and their families. It's a big deal. Maybe next year we can make it an official blessing of the fleet."

"Sal, where's Irene?" Zelda inquired of Mrs. Salette. "Is she workin' the Bingo tent again?"

"Yep, that's where you'll find her. She loves Bingo. Loves workin' it. Loves playin' it. Maybe I should be callin' her Bingo." He pondered that a moment. "Then's when we get to arguin', I could say, 'Ain't I always right, Bingo?'!" He looked around, pleased with himself. "On t'other hand, maybe not."

He laughed—one of those belly tickles that builds from imagined resourcefulness into thunderous, body-trembling hilarity. They looked at Sal as he grabbed his sides to keep his 250 pounds from disintegrating. It was infectious. Zelda folded over in mirth.

With that, Salette took his one-man promotion stump to others in the crowd. Zelda purchased a ticket on a quilt being raffled by St. Margaret's Ladies Sodality. She also bought some baked goods for the boarding house, including an angel food cake at a stand operated by women from South Bayou Baptist Church. After introducing Jack to others in the crowd, Zelda headed back to the boarding house. Jack strolled the grounds and spotted Peter and Sonny laughing and pointing at something. Boy talk, he surmised.

Something like that. At Sonny's direction, the two focused their eyeballs on the derriere of a middle-age woman who clearly avoided any inclination to disappoint her appetite. Her walk, in the boys' evaluation, was an amazing demonstration of cause and effect. Each of her steps led to a symmetrical dance of buttocks, and what red-blooded boy could think of anything else at a time like that.

"Can you believe it?" Sonny pointed. "How many cats do you think are fighting under her skirts?

It was new territory for Peter's preteen tutelage. But no translation from Sonny was needed. He stared at the woman and choked with suppressed laughter. He looked away only to discover that the image was attached to his retina. Sonny, buoyed by his new friend's hysteria, started making cat sounds. Now the two had moved to a new level of mutual frenzy, laughing at each other in a contagious fit.

Again, to Peter, it was an antidote for loneliness. While he appreciated Zelda's adult presence and direction, it did not replace a mother's natural warmth and love. But Sonny was the remedy for a feeling of being alone and unattached. Like an impish cousin, Sonny quickly administered a sense of companionship.

The two sized up the girls. Sonny flicked his eyebrows in assent, and Peter smiled in quiet concurrence. They had no trouble discovering the sweets booth. On Sonny's motion, the pair inspected the entries for the gumbo cook-off and pretended they were among the judges. They plucked red royal shrimp samples and dashed off to one of the boats. There, Sonny escorted Peter aboard, where they examined nets and holding baskets.

"Ahhh, Peter," Sonny counseled. "Ah wouldn't mention the cat-fightin' to Zelda or your dad." Rumination produced more advice.

"'Specially Zelda. She may haul off and swat you."

Peter laughed and nodded in agreement. Just then he heard his father shouting for him to return.

"Hey, Sonny. Maybe we can meet someday down by the school and talk some more," Peter proposed. "Or we can go to the library."

"Seems OK by me," said Sonny, "but ah don't spend a lot of time at the library. See ya."

With that, Peter scurried off the boat and trotted toward his father. He had a good time tasting all the seafood and messing around with Sonny. The clouds of doubt and despair still circulated in his brain, but they were scattered and masked for a while. Likewise, the festivities in the small town by the sea dispersed the fears of a world in disarray.

Neither upbeat Salette nor anyone else had dampened the day with talk of the war and what dangers it posed to the Gulf Coast. German submarines prowled the Gulf of Mexico, and the government had ordered blackouts and beach patrols all along southern waters. There were restrictions on how far out in the Gulf fishermen and shrimpers could go.

None of these things crossed Peter Bremer's mind. His thoughts in early June descended into greater depths of why he was in Alabama in the first place. His father worked six days a week. There had been no fishing trips, and he suspected there would be none. Talk of visiting nearby Dauphin Island and taking the ferry never materialized. Zelda had told him some of the mysterious stories of the barrier island, but his dad's promise to go there evaporated over time.

Peter wanted to see Fort Gaines at Dauphin Island's east end. Zelda explained that it was the site of the Battle of Mobile Bay near the end of the Civil War. He had read about the naval clash in history books and remembered the famous words of the Union's Admiral Farragut: "Damn the torpedoes. Full speed ahead."

Zelda told him that some Union ships, sunk by mines and Confederate batteries, still rested at the bottom of the bay. Now the Army Air Corps was busy building a radar station near the old fort.

The next week, with his father's permission, he accompanied Zelda on the Mobile & Bay Shore railroad on one of her infrequent trips to Mobile for shopping. It was another welcome digression for Peter. But in the days after, the hollow feeling in his stomach became almost chronic. It was accompanied by a persistent notion that going back to Little Rock with his father was a fading wish.

He dwelled upon happier times, simple things, like when the family would gather around a small backyard fire, which his dad labeled "pretend camping." In those days, he was confined to his own horizons, but there were security and comforting warmth that complemented the radiated heat cast by the burning chunks of oak. He yearned for the haven of family closeness.

One day he and Zelda packed a lunch and hitched a ride down to the beach. It was a pleasant break from boredom. He ran barefoot through the fine white sand piled up like drifting snow and then on the hard beach next to the retreating tide. He chased herons and plovers and watched the gulls tracking fishing boats like hens pursue a feed bucket. Their quest was rewarded in the form of entrails dumped by men gutting fish.

"Once, about a half-mile down the beach"—Zelda pointed eastward—"there was a fancy place called the Rolston Hotel. It was owned by John Rolston, known 'round here as the cotton king. People came on big riverboats from as far as New 'Awlins to dine and dance. Place burned down in 1927."

Peter sat on the beach and let the gentle and rhythmic waves massage his feet. He remembered that first time he spotted the expanse of the Gulf of Mexico—its brilliance and ever-changing color—as wind and clouds collaborated in a precarious portrait. His life had shifted, too, with each passing day, more weighted by loneliness for home.

In the ensuing days, he met several times with Sonny Salette. Sonny proposed they hop aboard his father's shrimper headed out to the Gulf, but that was too adventurous for Peter. Sonny knew it would be OK with his father, but Peter doubted that his father would approve. He declined the offer. Instead, they walked down to the Mississippi Sound and tossed driftwood at gulls.

Sonny, like his father, was one of those gregarious fellows who was hard not to like. He did not brag. Neither was he envious. He possessed an inclination for the impish, but never in the sense of being mean or hurtful. He was extremely comfortable in his own skin.

Though a tad on the hefty side, he was not flabby. Sonny was street wise—that is, educated in the culture of the Gulf Coast. It was not his temperament to look for trouble, instigate an argument, or worse. At the same time, his friends knew he could be plucky, unafraid to face a challenge if necessary.

"Got in a fight down here," he told Peter on one outing on the beach. "This big kid from school smacked me in the jaw, and ah ricocheted backward like a busted anchor line. Hurt like hell."

"Why did he do that?" Peter asked.

"Oh, we had an argument over a fish."

"Why did you argue over something dumb like that?"

"Well, he said I smelled like a fish. A dead one. I said he looked like a blobfish that run into a prop."

"What's a blobfish?"

"Oh, just the ugliest thing on Earth. Won't find it around here, but everyone knows 'bout em. So, yeah. It was over fish."

"What did you do?"

"Kicked him in the pecans. He was too big to take straight on."

"Pecans?"

"Yeah. Mom says ah shouldn't say *testicles*—or worse, *nuts*—but if it was necessary to use that word, ah should say *pecans*." They started to laugh. "Well, pecans are nuts."

"Pecans it is," said Peter. The laughs turned to convulsions.

Suddenly Sonny dropped to his knees behind a huge log that had drifted up on the beach. His cap with the Alabama Crimson Tide logo flipped off his head. He grabbed it defensively, pointed at the Gulf expanse, and shouted at Peter.

"Get down! I think I see a German sub out there!"

No second warning was needed. Peter dove for the ramparts and squiggled down in the white sand. He had seen nothing out on the watery expanse, and palms up signaled his inability to detect German subs or any kind of danger. Sonny began to laugh again. Peter poked him in the arm and owned up to his gullibility.

"This here is a fun place," Sonny turned serious. "Lot of critters 'round here. The pelicans are mah favorite. They go after fish like a kamikaze pilot. Gulls are lazy complainers. They are bird bums, lookin' for a handout every day like it's their job."

He pointed out at the breakers, his mind floating like the clouds overhead.

"Ever wonder how far those waves travel?"

Sonny paused to cultivate his inspiration—this being the fisherman's son, who seldom went to the library.

"Standin' here, you can catch the breath of the sea and hear its heartbeat."

Neither boy recognized those days as the spawn of friendship, the launching of a connection that would run as deep as the Gulf itself.

On another occasion, they walked all the way to the north end of Bayou La Batre and checked the names on tombstones at the Odd Fellows Cemetery. On the way back, Sonny deployed his charm to solicit a small basket of strawberries from a lady at a fruit stand. They walked slowly down the street and munched on the sweet treat as Sonny proclaimed his way with women.

It was a budding friendship of opposites: the local boy acting out the senior role and Peter willing to accept the position as the understudy. Peter granted full latitude as Sonny strutted his hormonal declarations. He knew love was more than bullish mechanics but declined to preach about it. His father never discussed such matters, and so it fell to his mom to explain the full meaning of mature love.

"Did y'all ever grab a girl's butt?" Sonny burst with immodest swagger, strawberry juice framing his lips. Peter shook his head sideways. "Well, I can tell you that Alice Beaufort's derriere is a delight. What made it more delighter, she pretended with a frown that she was upset, but later Slim Willis overheard her giggling about it. Can't tell me otherwise. She liked my hand on her butt as much as I liked my hand on her butt."

Sonny showed him how to assemble a fishing line with two hooks and a dangling weight in hopes of catching sheepshead and whiting. They used dead shrimp for bait. Peter promised not to divulge the location of Sonny's secret cove. Neither recognized the depth of their association. Still, for Peter, the call of home in Little Rock was stronger.

Sitting on the boarding house porch weeks later, he listened to the repertoire of the mockingbird, which was content to pilfer every warble in the Bayou. Zelda had briefed him on the bird's song plagiarism, how it mimicked other species. Or maybe, Peter pondered, the mockingbird was weaving a medley of chirps into a new creation, its own rendition. Maybe he should think along those lines.

"When are we going home, Dad?" Peter asked one late June day as Jack was scrubbing oil and grease off his hands after work. What had been cloaked in reticence spilled into the open. "I want to see Mom, and Bobby and Hattie too. There's nothing to do here," he blurted.

"Soon, Pete. Soon."

To Peter it lacked the sound of sincerity.

That Friday night, Jack Bremer worked overtime to remove the grime and oily smells of a car repair shop. He put on a new pair of tan slacks and his best plaid shirt, combed his hair neatly, and applied some sort of smelly stuff to his clean-shaven face. Peter was old enough not to need an interpreter.

"You help out Zelda tonight," he addressed Peter as he took off. "I'll be home in a couple of hours."

Peter went to bed at nine and lay awake for two hours, thinking about many things before he drifted off to sleep. His father had not returned. The next day was a repeat. Peter liked Zelda, and she liked him, but they were an odd couple. Not family. Sort of friends, but not close. More like two people in need of companionship. Though she was not a mother, she sensed his inner turmoil.

He enjoyed his carefree days with Sonny and was unsettled at the idea of dismissing him from his life. But friendship, no matter how genuine, cannot replace family. He missed his mother, and while he would never disclose how much to Sonny, it was an overriding force.

Two months in the Bayou had acclimated him some. His nose had almost accepted the pervasive scent of briny air; his ears nearly attuned to the clanging and tooting of the shrimp boats. Zelda had provided botany lessons on plants ranging from the proliferous live oaks and bottle brush to swamp reeds. He had learned of the kamikaze feeding forays of brown pelicans and could distinguish a plover from a common tern.

More importantly, Zelda had given him attention and, maybe just as significantly, growing confidence. As much as Peter admired her, it was mostly external. There was no mistaking their rapport for familial blood.

Chapter 10

On July 23, Peter's thirteenth birthday, he launched his plan. He had stashed nearly eight dollars in change collected doing odd jobs. He informed Zelda, misleadingly, of his intention to spend Thursday morning walking along the Bayou shipping channel. He said he planned to check on oyster shellers.

She had served him hot cinnamon rolls and orange juice for breakfast and even placed a birthday candle on one of the frosted delicacies. His dad left for his mechanics job without saying happy birthday or anything else. He seemed to be less and less interested in Peter or Peter's well-being.

Jack Bremer's apparent withdrawal from fatherhood made Peter's decision easier—that and the long days. Time, when you are young and away from family and familiar things, plods unmercifully along. He had tried to keep busy; he worked briefly sweeping and cleaning restrooms at the gas station and even piled up shells outside the oyster docks. Zelda praised him, saying such motivation would render him profits in years to come.

"Tell them that you worked for me and earned some money clipping grass at the neighbors. I have confidence that you will find work along the dock," Zelda dispensed parental-like support as he left the boarding house. "I know your father will be pleased."

She gave him several suggestions of places that may take on a hired hand. "But don't forget—I plan to make you a birthday cake, and we'll celebrate tonight. This is the big day you become a teenager."

Neither did he reveal his intentions to Sonny, and that troubled him some.

Peter walked across Wintzell Avenue with all the motions of one headed for the shrimper channel. After two blocks, he circled back to the shed behind the boarding house where he had hidden his satchel. He then walked south toward the train depot in nearby Coden. He was familiar with the departure time. Trains, which made limited trips to the Bayou before, now ran six days a week because of war jobs.

He waited twenty minutes at the two-story Coden station before hearing the train's mournful whistle as it rounded the curve into town. Belching smoke and squeaking brakes heralded its approach. It was decision time for Peter. With the fifty-cent ticket to Mobile in hand, he could still change his mind and remain with his father. Boarding meant he might never see his dad again.

The whistle announced more than a departure from the station. His mind twirled in all directions like a train on a roundabout looking for the right track forward. He stepped into the lone passenger car and looked for a seat among an army of tired faces. Mercifully, side windows were halfway down, allowing the stifling mixture of cigarette smoke and body odor to find a way into the ether of southern Mobile County.

Peter stood in the back of the rail car, watching his life, southern pine trees, and other bayou flora pass by. The war had changed many things, many lives. Cotton was no longer king, gradually being replaced by synthetics. The seafood industry was still vibrant, even if distracted by the demands of war goods. The locomotive grumbled upward, away from sea level and his father, pulling people and fifteen freight cars.

An hour later, Peter stepped off the railroad car at the Government Street depot in Mobile. Immediately he was immersed in a sea of confusion and uniformed people. Military personnel were headed in all directions, many laden with the same apprehension that engulfed young Peter Bremer. They knew where they were going.

Peter was still unsure. For a moment, he thought of enlisting in the army. Too young and too short.

Across the street, a brass band, propped on a flatbed truck, blasted out a medley of patriotic songs, but Peter didn't recognize any of them. Nor did he understand that the five-piece group, sponsored by the Alabama Dry Dock and Shipbuilding Co., was drumming up support for the sale of war bonds.

Unsure what to do next, Peter shuffled off north and, after a few blocks, sat down on a bench in Mobile's Bienville Square. A short distance away he spotted two drinking fountains: one for whites, the other for Negroes. He walked to the one designated for whites, but it was out of order. He looked around, ambled to the fountain for Negroes, and gathered in its cool liquid.

It was 11:30 and too early to nibble on one of the sandwiches he had packed. Gulls and pigeons, sensing food like hungry hoboes, competed for a handout, but he shooed them away. Maybe it was Peter's diminutive nature and shabby-looking satchel that drew the Rev. Patrick Dunne's attention. He sat right next to the timid teenager.

"Good morning, young man," he said.

Peter responded with a shy "Hi."

"I'm Father Pat from Immaculate Conception Cathedral. It's the church just down the street. Right nice day to be traveling." He motioned toward Peter's satchel. "As for me, I'm out stretching my legs before finishing up on my Sunday sermon. This week's reading is St. Paul's spiel about women being subject to their husbands. That is always a risky one to be preaching on. But that's no concern to you. Where are you heading?"

Peter searched for words, but none came.

"If you are looking for travel help, the Mobile Welcome Center is just a block over on Dauphin Street." Dunne entered the void. He pointed up the street.

"Do they have maps?" Peter asked softly.

"Oh, I'm sure they do. How far you planning to go?"

"I lost my map to my grandma's house in Little Rock, Arkansas," Peter invented a story.

"I'm positive they can assist you. Is there something I can do for you? That's quite a long way for a youngster to go alone."

"I'll be fine. I better be going. Thanks for the direction."

The woman at the welcome center informed him which trains would get him to Little Rock and how much it would cost. She had bus schedules too.

"You can take the coast rail over to New Orleans," she said to Peter, "but that's a big city for a little fellow and, I might say, not a very nice place either for young people that are travelin'. My thought," she said in matronly overtones, "is for you to take the Gulf Mobile & Northern to Jackson, Tennessee, then cut west by bus to Little Rock. Closest and safest."

Peter looked at the material.

"Do you need any brochures about the Mobile area?" she asked. "Or do you plan on leaving today?"

"Thank you, ma'am. Y'all been very helpful," Peter said. He left the center.

The bus station was near the Mobile train depot. The train ticket to Jackson cost $3.25. The bus fare to Memphis and then on to Little Rock added up to $2.75. He decided on the bus. There was time to eat his apple before the bus departed at 2:15. He sat on an unoccupied wood bench, made smooth and shiny from the backside of waiting travelers and gaped at the surroundings.

It was midsummer, yet it seemed every light pole and downtown tree trunk was plastered with Mardi Gras posters. It was like seeing expired Christmas promotions in July. Peter wondered if anyone supervised the removal of these outdated placards. Sonny claimed Mardi Gras originated in Mobile and was like Christmas. Peter argued that nothing could compare to Christmas.

He tossed the apple core in the trash and boarded the bus, again with mixed feelings. He knew now his father had never intended to return home. Jack Bremer left Little Rock as the final break from a calcified marriage. The more Peter thought about it, the more he ached inside. His father's drinking, he decided, had led to the estrangement of his parents. How can that happen? Two people say they love one another and, after a time, they don't? It made no sense to him.

He also knew his father would not be alone for long.

The bus rumbled north through the towns of Deer Park and Buckatunna. He was squeezed next to the window by a wide body with stripes on his sleeve. The summer landscape, speckled with the white blooms of cotton fields, sped by the bus window like a movie scene. In other places, the pervasive rust-colored soil was barren and desolate. Near Waynesboro, Miss., dark skies portended a downpour but instead cast a mist that gave the countryside view a bubbly veneer.

Some navy fellows gabbed about outfitting the USS *Alabama* with sixteen-inch guns at the Norfolk Navy Yard and how "those big babies would remodel Jap asses." Other military men, one puffing on a Roi-Tan cigar and periodically flicking ashes in the aisle, traded vivid accounts of girls back home. All generously employed a word Peter had heard before, one his mother advised against as a sign of a poor vocabulary.

He still remembered the first time he heard the word. Bobby said it and laughed at Peter's lack of scholarship in crude terminology. His brother, then eight, uttered the word in all its deformity and conscripted Peter to join in the mischief. Their mother's harassed ears evolved into a tongue-lashing, and each received a remnant of bathtub soap to chew on. Peter could still taste the Palmolive bar.

Peter gave the boisterous troops and cigar smoker a disgusted glance and removed a peanut butter sandwich from his satchel. He savored the creamy treat as his tongue labored to keep his jaws from cementing. He wished for a glass of Kool-Aid to lubricate his gums and complement the tasty tidbit. He longed for the time when the whole family laughed together.

As the miles expanded, so did Peter's excitement. Contentment with the path he had chosen soothed his weary body. The rhythm of the swaying bus and its tires slapping against the roadway joints collaborated to infuse further sedation. Sleep finally captured him.

No one around him knew of the turmoil that churned inside Peter Bremer. Nor did they know it was his birthday.

Chapter 11
Little Rock

"Mrs. Bremer, please fill out these release forms."

The court clerk was courteous, professional, and empathetic. For her, it was a familiar process with familiar dimensions. A parent—apologetic, despairing, and disappointed over the misconduct of a child—faces the formalities and structure of the state's legal machinery, all the while praying that this scene will never have to be repeated.

"You fully understand that, based on the tribunal magistrate's ruling, your son is expected to make full restitution as a condition of his release?"

"I do," Molly answered in a whisper.

Molly, oblivious to the woman's bubble-cut hairdo and flowery smock, was consumed by Bobby's criminal behavior that inserted them into the Arkansas judicial bureaucracy. It was new territory for her, and it added another layer to her despondency.

"And, Mrs. Bremer, please remember the court's strong recommendation that your son, not you, must earn the $16.80 for repairs to the front door of Jim's Corner Grocery and the cigarettes that were stolen." Her eyes peered over horn-rimmed spectacles perched on the bottom of her nose, lending accent to her words.

"He can either work off the payment at the store or find some other jobs."

"I understand," Molly said.

"And Bobby Dominick Bremer, do you understand what the court is instructing you to do, that you must obtain a job or jobs to pay off the damage that you caused? Is that clear?"

It seemed that the grocery store break-in—and his arrest and prosecution in the juvenile justice system and attendant lectures and court ruling—had produced a hint of seriousness in young Bobby's mind. Molly's apprehension centered on the questions of regret and reform. It was the third time Bobby, only eleven, had been in trouble at school or with the police.

The court official was also aware that Molly alone was confronted with her son's delinquent tendencies and that she was struggling to maintain her household. It had been some two months since her husband and son Peter had disappeared. Those wounds and distress were now compounded by Bobby's aberrant behavior. She was unable to watch him while she was at work, and her daughter Hattie had no influence on Bobby.

Molly was not a forceful disciplinarian. She had relied on Jack to keep the boys in line. Hattie was a model child, but none of her common sense and comportment rubbed off on Bobby. A month earlier, when a police officer had Bobby in tow, Molly asked her father to talk with the boy. That translated into a lecture-scolding and a kick in the pants—not what she had in mind. She believed such rebuke only hardened Bobby.

"Mr. Bremer!" The clerk turned up her volume. "I asked you a question and expect an answer. Do you understand that what you did is wrong and that you must make restitution? This is a serious matter, young man. It is my strong belief that one more time in court and the judge will hand you a ticket to juvenile detention. Do you understand that?"

"Yes, ma'am."

"Yes, ma'am what?"

"Yes, ma'am, I understand."

Bobby was quiet the entire twenty-two blocks and one bus transfer home. His head was cast downward, and his eyes fixed on the floor—a posture suggesting indifference, anger, or possibly remorse. In the complicated mindset of preteen males, it was probably a fluctuating mixture of all. They had taken the bus because the used Ford sedan Molly had purchased was getting repaired.

Once home, Bobby ran upstairs to his room without a word. Molly, with strands of her hair dangling in defeated disarray, rested her head on her arms, folded on the kitchen table, and began to cry. She was amazed that she had any tears left in her emotionally spent body. Since Peter left with his father and the problems ensued with Bobby, she had lost eight pounds. More significantly, she had lost the hope and conviction that she could manage her realigned family.

How, she pondered, could Bobby be formed in the same womb as two other siblings and yet be so different? She had given them the same love. She did not consciously accord more attention to Peter and Hattie as the children grew up. None received financial favors. Had Jack's brooding and unpredictable behavior, fed by alcohol and marked by outbursts of violence, shaped young Bobby's character and wayward tendencies?

Her youngest son, like his father, seemed withdrawn. More than that, it was as if he constructed a wall around himself, isolated and unreachable by court threats or motherly love. The teens, she knew by her own experience, may be the toughest time of one's life, but Bobby carried it beyond puberty's normal struggles. Worse than just hiding behind his wall, he appeared comfortable there.

What, she begged and pleaded in inward prayerful fashion, could she do to change things? She was working steady hours at the munitions plant. While the minimum wage was thirty cents an hour, the plant started workers at fifty cents an hour with chances to earn overtime. She signed up for the maximum hours. After six months, employees received a ten-cent boost.

Molly had purchased new clothes for Bobby and Hattie in anticipation of the approaching school year. Her rent of $45 a month was fully paid, and after groceries she even managed to save a few dollars from her take-home pay of around $22 a week. There was no 1 percent Social Security deducted from her paycheck because she did not reach the $3,000 annual threshold. She paid no income tax. For as little as she had in financial security, it was the status of her family—an absent Peter and contrary Bobby—that preoccupied her daylight hours and tormented her sleep at night.

She spent part of the afternoon picking beans from her small back-yard garden. It was the only sunny spot in a yard graced with oaks and magnolia. Her mother called shortly before supper to ask about the court hearing. It was painful to discuss Bobby, whispering talk that Molly felt said more about her than her combative son.

"Would you like company?" her mother offered. "I am not busy this evening. Ah'm sick of hearing war news. Three more of our ships sunk in the Gulf of St. Lawrence. Vichy roundin' up Jewish people in France. Unbelievable, I tell ya."

"No, thanks, Mom. I'll be fine. Maybe today's experience will turn things around for him."

"Well, sure do hope so. Your father says Bobby needs more discipline, needs a knot tied in his tail. Talk again tomorrow."

She had unsettling doubts that things would change, but what else could she say? What else could she do? Hattie helped her make supper. In addition to fresh green beans and fried chicken, they warmed yams leftover from the day before. And, of course, sweet tea.

"I don't think I'll work overtime tomorrow," she informed her daughter. "I'm so tired."

Molly had worked Sunday through Thursday morning before coming home for the court appointment. It was not unusual to work six-day weeks. She hated to miss Sunday church services, but the government's war machine took no time off, and Molly needed the job and overtime.

"You deserve Saturday off, Mom," Hattie comforted her. "It's been especially hard for you since Peter and Daddy left. I just want to tell you that none of this is your fault. You've done your best, Mom. I want you to know that. You've done your best. Even Grandma says so."

"Oh, Hattie."

The two embraced in unspoken love. Their tears reinforced a relationship that overwhelmed Molly at a time when she most needed strength. Hattie had a natural gift to comfort. Second-hand news that her own mother placed no blame on her boosted her resolve—and her esteem.

"Go call your brother to supper," she said, dabbing her tears.

Molly awakened the next morning to the solemn intonations of Gabriel Heatter. The Mutual Broadcasting icon was updating the war in a rebroadcast from the night before, but it was all news to her. She had fallen asleep on the porch daybed not long after the dishes were washed and the house picked up.

The night before, she had clicked on the little Firestone radio in the kitchen shortly after nine. She was exhausted. The last thing she heard before drifting off was the soprano strains of sultry Frances Langford singing "I'm in the Mood for Love" over the Armed Forces Radio Network. Molly was in the mood for rest uninterrupted by life's shadows.

The radio stayed on all night, pumping out a combination of white noise and intermittent static. Most stations signed off after the 10:00 p.m. news. Transmitters were turned on again at six the next morning.

"Today," Heatter droned in the Arkansas morning, "in the horror known as World War II, Nazi Germany continued its systematic deportation of Jews from the Warsaw Ghetto, sending hundreds to a concentration camp at Treblinka, Poland, sixty miles away. Men, women, and children are reportedly rounded up like cattle and placed on railroad cars."

Molly rubbed her eyes, reached for a nearby blanket, and attempted to focus on the kitchen clock. It showed ten minutes after six. She shook her head in disbelief that it was already morning. She nestled back in the sagging curvature of the old couch. Outside, the annoying chirp of robins splintered the calm of a new day.

Heatter continued: "Meanwhile in the United States, the government has ordered nationwide compulsory civilian gasoline rationing because of wartime demands. Most drivers will be limited to three gallons of gas per week." His signature pronouncement of "good news tonight" fit nowhere in the broadcast. Molly had no worries about gas rationing. Everyone employed at defense plants would have all the gas they needed.

Local news and weather had replaced Heatter by the time she woke up a second time, now approaching 7:30 a.m. Even with nearly nine hours of sleep, her body felt like it had been run over by a tank. She stumbled over to the chrome-legged kitchen table, sat down, and rested her head on folded arms next to the salt and pepper shakers. How could she be so tired? Maybe she should see a doctor. Was it pure physical fatigue, depression, or a combination?

She planned to make coffee, but heavy eyelids foreclosed such faint intentions. Her semi-conscious mind roamed the conflicts of her life. There, spread before her subliminal landscape, a dark, insurmountable wall emerged, a predicament so overwhelming as to obscure any rational path of resolution. It was as if troubles pursued her into a boxed canyon of her mind.

Her languid state took over.

It seemed like only minutes when an awareness of human presence penetrated her drowsy body. She stirred as a gentle hand touched her shoulder. It radiated a reassuring comfort as if some angel gently administered a healing potion. The touch dispatched an unexplained rebirth of solace.

Molly breathed a relaxed sigh, grateful for her daughter's love and maturity. She pictured Hattie's flowing hair, caring smile. She always knew when a touch of love was needed. Honestly, Hattie was the last shred—though a solid one—of constancy and normalcy, and she was thankful for it.

"Oh, Hattie."

Molly lifted an arm to touch the hand on her shoulder.

"I don't know if I could retain my sanity without you. You strengthen me in ways unaware to you. You are growing into such an outstanding young lady, and I am so proud of you. I love you so much."

The hand on her shoulder shifted to her neck and was finally joined by a second one that clasped her forehead and administered even deeper relief.

"Mom." An almost-whispered supplication fell on her ears. "Please don't cry, Mom. I'm home. It's Peter, and I'm home."

Molly could not believe her ears. Was she hallucinating? Had the devil now joined the badgering brigade, the unrelenting list of disappointments? Yet there was authenticity in that squeaky, soprano-like sound that signaled Peter's unchanged voice box. She could distinguish the voices of her children like a mama bird discerns the unique tweets of her offspring.

"It's me, Mom," he chirped. He let the earnest intonations sink in. "It really is me, Peter. I've come back home."

Molly raised her head slowly, still afraid that it was all some fantasy, like the mirage of a desert oasis. She succumbed to growing excitement and confidence that it really was her son, but did such wonderment happen outside the movies? She had to take the chance.

She had to push through the doubt and defeat that had saturated her life and search for respite in the form of a small boy.

She turned and looked.

Suddenly July became Christmas and every other calendar highlight of the year. Molly's disposition and outlook on life turned a somersault from melancholy to exhilaration. She gazed at his frazzled cowlick and seemed hypnotized by his collection of freckles. His eyes dazzled like a lighthouse beacon, transmitting a kind of palliative peace that only the presence of love can convey.

Molly cried in the grasp of her thirteen-year-old son.

It was the sort of joy that only a mother can fully grasp.

It was the delight and discomfort of pregnancy, the pain and wonder of birth, the apprehension and admiration on the first day of school, and all the other ups and downs of a child growing up, rolled into one great sigh of happiness and relief.

"Let me look at you." She drank in his presence. "Peter it is you!!"

Molly yelled for Hattie and Bobby. Hattie bounded into the kitchen, aware of the urgency in her mother's voice.

"Oh, my gosh!" Hattie yelled. She threw her arms around Peter's neck. "Where have you been? What have you been doing? Tell us everything. I can't believe it. You look wonderful. It's exciting to have you back home."

"Hi there." Bobby greeted his brother in a vivid lack of enthusiasm. Ya don't look like ya growed much."

They laughed.

"Did ya run into Miss May anywhere in your travels?" Bobby asked.

Chapter 12
August 1975, Iowa

Peter Bremer, curiously, was relieved by the rows of beef cadavers hanging from conveyors. A psychologist may find symbolism in that. Rather than seeing himself as a victim of bad decisions and the target of gangland enforcers, the slabs of meat shifted his attention to the business of making money for area farmers and Riverside Pack.

Hidden beneath his shield of denial was raw fear, but the parade of split-open carcasses presented no foreboding to him, assigned no allegory.

Bremer took pride in building Riverside from an idea to a successful business, one that, for the moment, was returning a dividend to investors and providing a slaughtering outlet and market for Iowa beef farmers. As he toured the operation, his mind—at least temporarily—was diverted from dusty roads and threatening goons.

"Yer doin' a helluva job here, Elmer," Bremer stroked his plant manager. "We both know that my knowledge of running a packing house is about the same as my ability to milk a cow."

The two laughed.

"Hell, down in Arkansas we knew plenty about wild hogs but little about corn-fed beef." Bremer, by habit, adjusted his tie as if he was strolling through the Drake Hotel in Chicago's Loop. He sidestepped a spray of cow shit. "Oh, like everyone else, we savored a juicy steak down there but had no idea which end of the critter it came from. And in St. Louis they claim to know their beer, but not much about prime beef."

Bremer was the main pitchman and CEO of an undertaking some dubious observers had branded as "prime bull." He buttoned his white butcher coat and proceeded down the processing line like a general reviewing the troops. The carcasses gave rigid attention, legs splayed in a semblance of salute. Here was a man, trained in finance, who bounced around the insurance and investment arenas, now up to his neck in hides, briskets, and low-margin balance sheets.

Indeed, it was an unlikely place for tailor-made suits and alligator shoes. There is nothing pretty about a slaughterhouse operation, yet here was Mr. Bremer, bounding along with a three-carat ring and an outlook befit of a Fortune 500 company. He was oblivious to reality, comforted by the legions of hanging bovine that, for the moment, kept him safe from financial issues and worse.

It was like Richard Nixon whistling Dixie past the Watergate hotel, ignoring investigations and front-page stories as so much Washington wind. It was only a year ago that the president was forced to resign in shame after the wind became a gale and exposed the truth to the point that disavowal was blown asunder.

Reality finally finished first.

Bremer subscribed to the Nixon coverup strategy, painting everything rosy while in full dodging gear, taking cover wherever it was available.

"No, Elmer, the day we hired you away from Wilson Foods was the day Riverside turned the corner," Bremer continued to lather his top plant official. "You understand the finer points of an operation like this, and when we celebrate ten years of financial success, you, Elmer, are going to be the one taking the bows. You will be the one deserving the center cut of acclaim."

Elmer Anders was no rookie. He worked with bullshit every day. He needed no translator, but when the boys in suits make their prerequisite visits, it was part of his job to escort them through the blood, guts, and balance sheets. He was an amiable man, one who took pride in knowing the business and the people who worked the lines.

People—friends and neighbors—are why he took the job. Like most small-town Iowa residents and farmers, he had a deep respect and sense of kinship for men and women immersed in the daily grind of making a living. He was one of them. Riverside employees didn't see him so much as plant manager but as another fellow struggling to make ends meet.

While Peter Bremer knew poverty, and never wanted to see it again, he and Elmer Anders were now men of different worlds, ran at different speeds, and circulated in different lifestyles.

"You are supposed to wear one of these." Anders handed Bremer a safety helmet. "I don't want to get in trouble with government inspectors and our own safety director," Anders added, punctuated with a belly laugh.

It was not Bremer's first excursion through the killing corridors. He had never requested a barf bucket. It was close when he witnessed a 1,200-pound steer struggle with the .22 bullet implant on the kill floor. And his lunch struggled to stay down when he first observed a workman, whose shoes and clothes looked as if he were painting a red barn, thrust his knife into the dead animal's throat and jugular to launch the process of bleeding out.

Like a committee of surgeons, some workers remove the hide while others swing knives to extract the viscera. Head and limbs are removed, and the remaining carcass is quartered. The operation moves along a disassembly line much as Henry Ford drew it up for automobiles headed in the other direction. Only, in the Ford factory, the horns were an important element.

Once acclimated to the gory routine, Bremer marveled that this flailing of knives transpired like an orchestrated violin section. He was fascinated by the detachment of the packinghouse crew to the business of butchering. Workers dismantled the parade of carcasses and simultaneously discussed—sometimes vigorously—sports, politics, and religion.

"We're processing about five percent more beef than we did several months ago," Anders explained. "You said you found some new markets on the West Coast?"

Bremer danced around a pool of blood.

"Well, not only the West Coast, Elmer, but I've managed to make a few deals in the Chicago and Midwest area too. I'd really like to expand that market because shipping costs are much less. The more sales we can make in the Midwest, the better our margins, but then, that's what the other guys are thinking too."

Small operations like Riverside had to compete with the big boys, packers that had thousands of employees and thousands of incentives for retail grocery chains. Competition was mostly corralled by the Big Four—Armour, Cudahy, Wilson, and Swift. It was a reality that Bremer quickly discovered after taking over the reins at Riverside.

"So, we have sought special arrangements."

Bremer did not elaborate. "Special arrangements" was the euphemism for a herd of sins, including deals with shady Chicago front men and their cousins in shipping and handling. The menu was engrained in Chicago commerce, and the prime cuts usually went to the bosses in Cicero and Chicago Heights.

It wasn't Bremer's introduction to the south side of honesty. He was well acquainted with the history of the quick buck and savvy investment schemes in certain quarters of St. Louis. From the Pendergast era of the 1940s to the infamous law benders of the 60s, St. Louis was like a little crime brother to Chicago.

Bremer, always the front-office type, had dabbled in insurance, investments, and loans ever since leaving Arkansas State. He converted his math and economics proficiency into a blueprint for financial comfort, making numbers jump around like magic on financial sheets. That he colored outside the lines occasionally did not weigh on his conscience.

Until his position with Riverside Pack, his only significant job outside finance-related jobs was a five-year stint as a fashion advisor for men's suits at the St. Louis-based Goodman Clothiers. There he met Glenda Goodman, whose father owned the business.

Bremer's confident style, persuasive smile, and dapper attire opened sartorial doors up and down the Mississippi Valley. He worked river towns with the cockiness of an agile, muscled barge deckhand. Always looking like a member of the chamber of commerce ethics committee, he frequently resided on the periphery of dishonesty. At one time he provided damage and liability insurance to a dummy warehousing business run by the mob.

Those connections gave him passage for marketing Riverside beef. One informal agreement covered shipping, refrigeration, storage, and distribution, with unsavory elements claiming its cut all along the way. Certain side deals led to windfall benefits for Peter Bremer and others. Unwritten entanglements with snake-like operators incorporated the formula for poison.

It was his failure to satisfy financial obligations of some addendum transactions, born in avarice and arrogance, that now pursued him like an angry divorce lawyer. He had borrowed money from a loan shark source tied to the Mafia to cover an investment in Middle East oil exploration. Repayment on the loan was in arrears. His neck was on the line, and he felt someone breathing on it.

If conscience is a person's moral compass, Bremer seemed to have a knack for ignoring it.

Until now.

Chapter 13
1942, Little Rock

"Mom, you're choking me!"

Molly Bremer engulfed her son with hugs of unrelenting delight and indescribable joy. If she had more arms, they, too, would have suffocated him like a maternal octopus.

Tears flowed down her cheeks in unrestrained ecstasy.

She kissed him and swayed with him from side to side in a motherly sit-down dance that no outsider could understand. It was like the day of his birth, perhaps even more wonderful, more spectacular. For the unexpected had taken shape, a regeneration of her flesh and blood into the powerful force of the family.

Peter was home.

"Mom, I'm going to fall." Peter attempted to loosen his mother's grip, but it only caused her to hang on tighter. "Mom, it's me, Peter, OK? I'm happy to see you too. I really missed you and home. I missed our family." She squeezed even harder. "You can let me go now," he said. "I plan on staying. Do we have anything to eat?"

"Peter, if it's really you, answer this question. Remember when you wanted a puppy, but your father said dogs were too much trouble and expensive? Remember? You even had a name picked out for the puppy. What were you planning to name him?"

"Mom," Peter replied with exasperation. "I'm hungry and tired."

"I know," she laughed, again pulling him close for more proof of his existence. "Just tell me what name you had chosen for the puppy."

"We didn't get a puppy." Peter tried a new form of extraction.

"I know, but tell me the name anyway, of the puppy you never got."

"*Dizzy*, Mom. *Dizzy* was the name I had chosen."

Molly rose from her chair, grabbed his hands, and fashioned a different sort of dance, this time around the kitchen table with its Formica top and chrome legs serving as the epicenter of a bizarre romp. Dishes in the cupboard rattled and joined in the frolicking as she skipped along. Peter stumbled along with her, a strange look on his face.

"Dizzy was the name. Dizzy was the name," she sang. "Thanks be to God. Dizzy was the name."

Finally, at about the third nonsensical stanza, she stopped singing and dancing and sat down. Again, she drank in his total being.

"Oh, Peter. I can't tell you how overjoyed I am to see you, to hold you."

"I think I understand, Mom."

"You know what?" she gushed. "We are going to have a special dinner tonight. We're going to invite your grandparents, other family that can come, the reverend, some of my friends at work, and you can ask anyone you want too. You name the menu, Peter. Your wish is my command."

"Could we have breakfast first?" Peter said. "I'm really hungry."

Molly, slowly and reluctantly, came down from her heavenly perch. She moved toward the refrigerator in search of ham and eggs, fingering her hair mechanically as to organize any snarls. The entire day was an eruption of frivolity and joy. She telephoned her mother and other family members. She called friends at work and Pastor Clendon.

Once she ran out to the back yard looking for neighbors to release the unbelievable news that consumed her entire being.

At dinner that night, the festive time fed on stories that recounted Peter's short life. Someone remembered the time when a mouse ran up his pant leg in the garage. Or, when he yanked out all the Brussels sprout plants thinking they were weeds.

"How 'bout just last year when Peter congratulated Norma Lee Brown on the impending birth of her child?" Grandpa Orval snickered. "It was after church. 'Member the look on her husband's face? Turns out Norma Lee was eatin' too many chocolates and things."

"Or—" Grandma Aliza started laughing before she launched into her embellished yarn of Peter's love for toy trains. "He was about two or three, and we were at the toy section of this downtown department store." She chuckled and stroked her wiggling stomach.

"Grandma, just get on with the story," Bobby enjoined, half to speed the issue along and half in a pique of envy at all the attention being lavished on his brother. He was tempted to bring up Peter's fondness for Miss May.

"Sure, sure," a complying grandma said without any signal of offense. "Peter," she said, pointing at him across the mashed potatoes, "stood there watching these toy trains tooting and running in every direction, through tunnels and around curves." She regained her unrestrained mirth and snorted at the image forming in her mind.

"He watched and watched, mesmerized, so long that he ignored the need to go potty. Slowly"—she transferred one hand to her mouth to subdue her mirth—"a puddle began forming on the floor beneath him."

Everyone had heard the story before, except Pastor Clendon. His laughter boomed over the collective hilarity. Molly's cousin, Velma Hughes, was surprised at the reverend's unrestrained merriment. She had thought he was a bit stuffy. Being not one of his biggest fans, she claimed to friends that his sermons "had a great ability to instill boredom if not slumber."

Velma was generous with her opinions, especially about the pastor and church affairs. She and Molly frequently disagreed on such matters. Molly often wondered if members of other churches had the same tendency to "pound the preacher," as she called it. But this day, Velma kept her tongue in repose.

Peter was the focus of everyone's love, and no one asked him where he had been or how he returned home. Those were matters for another time. The business at hand was rejoicing in the presence of Peter and one another. Molly could not remember a time when she was happier.

"We share your joy," Pastor Clendon said, offering Molly a handshake and forgoing a hug. "We all wish you the best of luck. It won't be easy raisin' the family by yourself. Havin' no father around is like a town full of churches where half the bells are broken—like a house with two walls. But if anyone can do it, you can."

It was not the sort of affirmation Molly wished for, and after the pastor left, Velma uncorked an uncensored harangue that would have curled his cassock. While tuned up, she took the occasion to blast his "insufferable inclination to quote chapter and verse from the Bible like nobody else has ever heard of Jeremiah and Ezekiel. He can't go two minutes without introducin' us to another of his personal acquaintances in the Scripture."

Molly's mother was finally able to steer the gathering back to Peter and the rest of the family. She convinced Velma that it was the wrong time to unload her dislike for the pastor—no small conversion in itself.

Peter did not invite anyone. When his mother suggested the idea, the only person who came to mind was Sonny Salette, his pudgy buddy from the far south of Alabama. It was not a name or memory that fit the occasion. Sonny, too, would be a topic for the future.

The weeks that followed were equally joyful. It was a different household—as if the entire place had received a new coat of paint inside and out, and everyone was bedecked in new clothes. The tension of an abusive husband and emptiness created by a missing son no longer dominated Molly's existence.

The only dents in her life were the occasions when Bobby turned sour. And then there was the news that a second young man from the neighborhood was missing in action, this time a sailor aboard the USS *Tucker*. The destroyer hit a mine in the Pacific and sank.

In Europe, the news grew even more depressing. The Germans advanced quickly into Crimea and Russia and all along the eastern front. Horrible accounts of German atrocities against Jewish people trickled into the West. Thousands were executed in Poland. Jews from all over German-conquered regions were sent to concentration camps.

By 1942, with years of barbaric experience in administering concentration camps, the Nazis were experts in inflicting misery and death. Dachau, outside Munich, had been the first. Opponents of Nazism and Adolph Hitler, especially Catholic priests and socialists, were among the initial prisoners. Yet it took Pearl Harbor to thrust the United States into the conflict, and now it was a national enterprise.

Molly and munitions factory employees everywhere in America gave up their Labor Day time off and worked to build the war effort. Few blinked an eye when President Roosevelt authorized the removal of all Japanese Americans to internment camps. There was some comic relief from the war news. Molly and her coworkers laughed over the antics of a new radio duo Abbott and Costello.

And *Fibber McGee and Molly* spun ridiculousness on NBC Red Radio. McGee's never-ending closet of junk that exploded into a living room crash when he opened the door was a routine for laughter. Velma was a big fan and took delight in informing anyone who would listen that the "McGees," Jim and Marian Jordan, were natives of Peoria, Ill.

"I heard you talking the other day with Bobby about a Sonny somebody." Molly approached Peter one day in September. "Both of you were giggling, so I suppose he must be a new acquaintance."

The giggling, as she described it, was more like snickering over Miss May and the eleven other shapely women on the 1942 Mobil calendar. Bobby had it hidden in his closet.

"Is he someone you met at school?" She had a suspicion that was not the case, that Sonny was a person who lived in the "lost weeks" of Peter's life, as she described those days. Angling the question through school, she believed, would be less unsettling.

Peter was not anxious to talk about those ambiguous days with his father, the forced trip south and being away from home. Eventually, he felt compelled to say something about Sonny. Moms have a way of ferreting information, wearing either the hat of a probing district attorney or assuming the role of an affronted parent who is denied crucial information.

So out of the blue one day, he told her.

"This Sonny Salette was a guy I met, Mom." She put down her thread and needle and the overalls she was mending and gave him her full attention. "He showed me around the town we were in, told me about the Gulf of Mexico and shrimpin'. He's kinda chubby and has a weird sense of humor, but a nice guy. He—"

"What town were you in, Peter?"

Now he wished he had never brought up Sonny's name.

"What difference does it make, Mom? You asked about Sonny, and I'm telling you about him. He was really nice. We chummed around. He took the time to explain things. He—"

"What things, Peter?"

"Things. Like how shrimp boats lower their nets. He took me on his Dad's boat and showed me. And how others harvest the oysters in the brackish water. It takes brackish water, the mixture of fresh water

119

and salt water to produced good oysters. I found out I don't like oysters, but Sonny eats them raw. But I like fried shrimp, and I like fish, 'specially them red fish."

"You were down by the ocean?"

"Mom. I've gotta go now."

Chapter 14

The low winter sun poured in the kitchen window like a heating lamp, pushing past the drawn curtains and streaming over a small fern drooping from a round wooden table. The rays massaged Molly Bremer's back and neck with penetrating comfort. Her eyelids dropped in a serene response; her hands clutched a steaming cup of Folgers coffee.

Molly's mind brimmed with joy, and some apprehension, as she contemplated a new year and a different life. It was the first time in months that she felt free of stress, no longer pulled in many directions at work or home.

Hattie was her usual thoughtful and obedient self. Bobby was moody but behaving. And Peter was back into a comfortable routine. Her happiness meter was off the charts. Peter's return had turned her completely around from being a despondent, heartbroken mother whose entire being was headed south to someone with newfound purpose and a semblance of contentment.

The children were at school. She had a rare day off from work at the munitions plant. The rent and utility bills were paid, and so was the charge for fixing the clutch on the Ford. A neighbor had given her a recent issue of *Look Magazine*, the one with Lt. James Stewart, the actor, on the cover. She was searching for the inside story on Hollywood stars who had been drafted or volunteered for the military service when the phone rang.

"Molly," the cheerful woman said. "How are you this morning? Are you still up to do some shopping? Or at least looking?"

It was Madeline from work. Molly needed nothing for herself, the children, or the house, but it had been a long time since she had headed to a store just for fun, for the hunt. Looking would cost nothing, and it would also be an avenue for socializing, exchanging factory gossip.

"I'm doing wonderful, Madeline," Molly answered, running a hand through her uncombed hair. "Just savoring my third cup of coffee. You OK?"

"Oh, yes. It's just nice not hearing all the hammering, screeching, and yelling of the factory floor. I never thought I'd be involved in such a commotion, pouring out sweat next to a guy who is fifty-five and too old to be dropping the bombs we're making. I'm tired of looking at fuses."

"I know what you're saying, Maddie," Molly chuckled. "Look on the bright side. You could be working in sheet metal and riveting. You could be Rosie the Riveter, donning that blue shirt and red bandana. Now, that's a noisy place."

"Yeah, yeah. We're the lucky ones. Long hours. Short breaks. Hot lights and cold lunches. Kids with dripping noses and no men to snuggle with at night. Sure. We've got the life, toots. Are you going shopping or not?"

"Yes, yes," said Molly. "I'll pick you up about ten. See you." Clank went the phone back in its cradle.

She finished her coffee, brushed her teeth, combed her hair, and slipped into a white blouse and yellow skirt that featured rows of small and large roses. Fifteen minutes later, she pulled into the grassy, unpaved driveway leading to the side of Madeline Houston's two-bedroom bungalow.

Before Molly could turn off the engine, her coworker popped out with the screen door banging behind her. Madeline was slightly less stylish, wearing rolled-up denims and a gray shirt that blared "Buy War Bonds." Absent was the picture of Uncle Sam.

"Hi-de-ho, Miss Fancy. I didn't know we were supposed to dress up," Madeline said, opening the car door. "Are we headed to Cohn's

Department Store? I can't afford shoes from that uptown place. I need to stop at Sears." Molly backed into the street.

M.M. Cohn's, on Main between Sixth and Capitol, was the biggest store in downtown Little Rock. A trip to Cohn's was more than mere shopping for necessities. It was a place to fantasize in fashion, dance the impossible dream, and just stroll without any intention to purchase. It was a place to be seen.

The act of buying there said, *"You won't see me in a bread line."*

"No, we're not stopping at Cohn's. I really don't have to buy anything. Why Sears?"

"I need to buy new work boots," Madeline replied. "Mine are on their last lap. I don't know if you listen to the news, but they are talking about rationing shoes."

"Shoes? What's next? Milk?"

"This is also a pretty fancy car, Molly. You must be working a lot of overtime, or did you borrow it from some good-looking fellow?"

"Y'all kiddin', right? It's mine—paid for and, oh yes, it's fancy. Has a brand-new clutch, the kind that operates the way a clutch is supposed to. People are so impressed and say, 'that's such a nice-looking clutch.' The color and texture are so fine. And I'm sure you noticed the continental kit and whitewall tires." Both laughed.

"Where are the kids?" asked Molly.

"Mom came and picked them up. They are always glad to go to her place where they're subject to all sorts of chores and discipline."

Madeline's husband, Ted, had enlisted in the army. The draft required all men age eighteen to forty-five to register. His father had served in the military. Many of his friends enlisted or were drafted. He believed it was his duty to join in the fight against Hitler and Hirohito. Madeline opposed his enlistment only to hear him quote President Roosevelt: "There can be no appeasement with ruthlessness."

She was unsure, but she believed his unit was in North Africa.

By the early months of 1943, the once-reluctant and -neutral United States was deep in World War II. Dwight Eisenhower had been named supreme commander of Allied forces in Europe. In the Pacific, US forces defeated the Japanese in the Battle of Guadalcanal. It was a turning point in reversing Japan's aggression but a long way from total victory.

Like every other corner of America, life in Little Rock had changed. The war caused shortages and higher prices. It seemed the only thing not rationed was bad news. But the human toll was heaviest. Many homes had absent sons and husbands, and a growing number of them had family members who had been killed, wounded, or taken prisoner. For them, President Roosevelt's fireside chats provided little comfort.

Ironically, Molly had become an island in this sea of anguish, her personal despondency transformed into distinctive bliss. It made her uncomfortable around those who worried about family members in the military, especially friends like Madeline. She refused to hide her uncommon delight for Peter's return, but restraint was required.

What could she say that cloaked her buoyant feelings?

"Have you heard anything from Ted?" Molly asked as they headed downtown.

"Not in five weeks," said Madeline. "Not since they left some place in England, I think it was. How are your kids? How is Peter?"

"They're fine. How are Ted Jr. and Missy? Do they ask about their Dad?"

"They have, but I tell them he is on a business trip. I don't know if they understand that. Do you think that's OK, Molly?'

"There is no good answer, Maddie, and your explanation is as good as any. These are hard times."

"Nice to have a day off, finally, from work and the kids." Madeline wound up her chatter motor. They were a good match. Madeline could pitch talk like Dizzy Dean tossed baseballs, fast and furious. Molly was a good listener, sometimes amused at her friend's ability to spit out words while taking little time to catch a breath.

"Sometimes I wonder where all these bombs are going. It's really amazing, don't you think, Molly, that we have all this stuff coming in one door, and after a little bending and grinding and grunting, it all goes out the other door as bombs and bullets. I wonder how long it will all go on. I wonder how long before Ted comes home."

They rode in silence for less than a block.

"Do you like your work, Molly? Would you rather be working in a store? Do you ever wonder about who is killed by the stuff we make? I mean, I know we are at war, but it's all so terrible. We spend all our money, time, and effort to kill them while they spend all their time, money, and effort to kill us.

"Why, Molly? Why is it so difficult to get along?"

It was a question that mankind posed to itself since the beginning of time, and Molly's silence suggested she had no answer. She briefly thought about her personal situation. Jack was not a bad person, just someone who had surrendered to drink.

"Molly, have you ever thought of dating someone?"

The abrupt twist in topics almost caused Molly to miss the turn onto Scott Street. Dating, with all its ramifications, had not even registered on her "sometime in the future" list. Neither had she given serious thought to what her absent husband was doing or where he went.

"Madeline!"

She glanced sternly at the younger woman, who believed it was an innocent inquiry, then quickly back at the traffic ahead. "I've got my hands full raising three children, maintaining a house, and working. I have neither the time nor inclination to be thinking about dating. Why bring up the subject?"

"I'm sorry, Molly. I didn't realize you had such strong feelings on the matter. As a friend, I just thought that, at some point, you may have considered getting a divorce from Jack and continuing your life. It's hard making it alone. I can tell you that."

"I didn't mean to bark at you."

Molly slowed to angle park down the street from Sears' front door.

"My mother suggested I consider divorce. But for what reason? It costs money to hire a lawyer and go through all that paperwork, and I have no intention of remarrying. I believe my job in life is raising Hattie, Bobby, and Peter. Maybe that's narrow, but that's where I am at right now."

They exited the car and headed for Sears.

"I admire your courage, Molly. Really, I do. I admire how you have been able to accept what happened and adjust. You don't need to apologize to anyone for what you decide. Independence and dedication to one's kids—that's a good thing." She paused. "But I miss Ted."

They entered the store.

"Maddie. I must confess. I had been in the grip of gloom. Even before Peter's return, I began to realize that I was the only one who could extract myself from despair and let in hope. Sometimes you have to convince yourself to move on. You can't just give up. I almost did. Peter's return became emancipation. I was freed from the hole in my heart."

That was the most she had revealed to anyone about what went on inside her. Even with her mother, Molly had always taken a more artificial approach, skating around the truth. Her candor even caught her talkative friend off guard.

"Now I worry about Bobby. Hattie is fine, and I think Peter will make a success of his life. But Bobby seems to be always unsettled."

"Where are we headed?" said Madeline. "Oh, yeah. Shoes."

"Motherhood is an amazin' thing, Molly. You're a stronger person than I am. Don't mind me. I just like flappin' my lips."

Chapter 15
August 1975, Iowa

Peter Bremer tossed his white butcher coat and protective helmet on a table in the break room, then adjusted his tie. He automatically pulled the cuffs of his shirt so that they extended a half inch beyond the suit sleeves. Touring the Riverside Packing plant was a comforting relief from office hubbub and, more pointedly for him, menacing loan collectors.

Without prologue, he shook hands with a dozen or so packinghouse workers. His dapper dress framed him like a pristine island in a sea of sweaty blue-collar working stiffs happy to wind up another day of grappling with knives, saws, and beef slabs. Work at a slaughter plant is taxing labor.

"I want to personally thank you men for your hard work," Bremer told the group as he pumped calloused hands. Plant Manager Elmer Anders was surprised that the company president had taken the time to acknowledge some of the workers. "I was telling Elmer that we have had satisfactory sales, and I think that will continue. But we must fight increasing costs, especially for shipping. If we could control that, we could bump up wages."

No one said anything. They liked Anders and trusted him, but people who get their hands dirty on the job are always suspect of those who don't. Still, a job was a job, and Riverside wages were as good as any around rural Iowa. They all knew the pay fell short of the union scale at Wilson's in Cedar Rapids or at other Midwest plants.

Inside, each of them appreciated Bremer taking the time to visit with them and even talking about a pay raise if other costs could be controlled. But none were likely to express that appreciation to someone in a suit, and they sure wouldn't acknowledge it in the presence of a coworker. Right or wrong, that's just the way it was.

"I was thinking," Bremer looked down at the floor. "Maybe I'll suggest to management that you all get an extra paid day off on Labor Day weekend. Maybe the Friday before, giving everyone a four-day holiday. We've been able to keep up on orders. What do you think, Elmer? Would that work out? Can we do that?"

"Well, Mr. Bremer," Anders rubbed his chin to reflect his puzzlement. "You are management. I'd imagine if you recommended it, the rest of us would be happy to go along."

That brought a shout of approval from workers. Bremer smiled and waved goodbye. He felt good about his visit to the Chelsea, Iowa, plant, but even as he walked toward his dusty black Cadillac, he pondered the real or perceived dangers of his trip back to Cedar Rapids company headquarters. August had not surrendered any of its heat and humidity, creating a dog-day haze that accompanied his nervous mindset. Anders walked him out to the parking lot.

"That was a nice gesture back there, giving the men an extra day off," Anders said. "They will remember your visit. It makes my job easier. It makes everyone feel more like they are a part of the team, have an interest in making this place successful." They reached Bremer's car. "Are you sure you don't want to run your vehicle through the plant wash? It won't eliminate all the grime but rinse off some of that heavy dust."

"I'd better be heading back," Bremer said. Anders could sense his boss was preoccupied with more than the cost of shipping. Little did he know of the complexity of issues racing through Bremer's brain—the intertwining dilemmas of unpaid personal taxes and the more frightful consequences of unpaid loans from informal and racketeering financiers.

The last letter received from Chicago contained ominous language.

And the follow-up telephone call from someone named Rusty Ragno was enough to shake anyone's back molars. Bremer did not know and had never met Ragno, but the phone introduction was no Chamber of Commerce overture. In crime circles, Ragno was known as "The Hook," which was an acknowledgment of his ample nose and strong-arm method of attaining goals.

Ragno presented, in distinctive Chicago lingo, his credentials as the representative of Adrian Koffmann. Bremer had met Koffmann briefly at O'Hare Airport when the loan was approved. He was among the fading Chicago cadre who were still successful at skimming, embezzling, and loan sharking, even though the US Justice Department had made crippling inroads in eradicating mob influence.

Koffmann's underworld history was well known among federal investigators. Some within the FBI and their snitches silently suggested that Koffmann may have been complicit in the assassination of Sen. Bobby Kennedy in 1968. Kennedy, as US attorney general, hounded the Mafia and the Teamsters' boss, Hoffa, who was then an alleged business contact of Koffmann.

The Chicago Outfit had its fingers deep in the rich Teamsters Central Pension Fund. The fund was a ready source for much of its loan shark business. Now there was speculation that Koffmann may have also had a hand in the recent disappearance of Hoffa. The relationship between the union and the underworld was well known, but also a tangle of suspicion and duplicity.

Hoffa was convicted of fraud, bribery, and jury tampering and sentenced in 1967 to thirteen years in prison. However, he won release late in 1971 in a pardon deal sanctioned by President Richard Nixon. The well-publicized deal barred Hoffa from union activities until 1980. Bremer was aware of that history and that Hoffa had mysteriously disappeared less than a month after Koffmann okayed Bremer's $75,000 loan.

The idea that Koffmann and the mob may be even remotely tied to Hoffa's disappearance made Bremer shudder. Removing someone as notorious as Hoffa from daylight would make Bremer's disposal from the land of the living look routine. What made matters worse is that Koffmann had already granted an extension to Bremer's promissory note.

Bremer stilled owed $65,000. The loan extension was for another three months, which meant he had eight months to pay off the debt, but at a boosted interest rate of 14 percent. That put Bremer's scheduled repayment, including interest, at more than $9,000 a month, an agenda too rich to accommodate his heedless spending habits. He was two months in arrears, and Koffmann's correspondence shunned any Emily Post touch.

"Dear Mr. Prick," Koffmann's enlightening and subtle letter began. "This is to formally inform you that your repayment pattern is grossly negligent, something that is frowned upon by our board of directors. It is our custom to receive payments on time. We seldom send courteous follow-up notices. Collection, you should know, ultimately takes a different form."

It didn't require a Harvard lawyer to read between the lines. The letter and the phone call, which was less ceremonial than the letter, had added wrinkles to Bremer's forehead and migraines to the area behind it. The combination had caused him to take the awkward route to Chelsea. Now he had to decide if the threats required taking a similar circuitous road back to Cedar Rapids.

He waved goodbye to Anders.

Security is one of the things that you acquire when you drive a car the size of a Cadillac. Bremer headed north out of town, the big sedan surrounding him like a down comforter on a freezing night. It warded off Chicago's chilly threats, at least temporarily. He drove up County V18 and shortly turned east on Highway 30, the Lincoln Highway.

Am I running from myself? It was among things racing in his head as he speeded up his return trip. *Have I been diving off the deep end of an empty pool? Imagining too much? Fearing my own bad decisions?*

It was the sort of philosophical soul searching that Bremer seldom did. His compulsive nature afforded scant regard to contemplation. These were loaded questions he asked of himself. It was more of a motherly inquiry, one designed to trigger self-evaluation, a suggestion to think things through before acting. Or, as Molly Bremer frequently cautioned her children, "Look before you leap."

At his boyhood church, his pastor may have called it a "come to Jesus" reckoning. However, Bremer had long ago dismissed the need or importance of consulting any deity. Still, as the big car hummed eastward, his thoughts pulsated with the notion of change and, more precisely, what he could do to extract himself from a dangerous predicament. His extravagant lifestyle had to be modified.

He drove on. The undulating hills of Tama County yielded to the loam-rich fields of Benton County, which trumpeted the tasseled corn and lush soybeans that defined Iowa's agricultural wealth. Bremer's troubled mind was a stark contrast to the placid countryside. Even cars the size of army tanks cannot erase unambiguous images painted by mob agents.

What a journey, he thought, from growing up in poverty in Arkansas to investment success and wealth-building to being president of a company. He knew his mom had been proud of his achievements, but she would not be happy at his ill-advised spending and borrowing. She had worked hard to help pay for his college costs, not to mention the price of keeping his brother out of jail.

His mother still lived in the same house in Little Rock. She never remarried. After the war, she left the munitions plant and took a job at the new Timex factory. She retired two years ago. With all of Bobby's problems, the last thing he wanted to do was add to her worries and woes. She was unaware of his self-inflicted torment.

"Oh, my dear Peter. President of a company? I never dreamed you would be so successful. No matter what you do, I will be so proud," she had said in their last telephone conversation. "I still remember that day in 1942 when you returned home. My little boy. Back from who knows where. It was like a miracle. It was one of the happiest days of my life."

Would she be happy if she knew about his avarice-induced distress?

Bremer entered west Cedar Rapids. He had wanted his mother to move closer to him, maybe even to Cedar Rapids. He felt an obligation to her well-being. But that idea conflicted with his financial woes, especially with threats to his own safety. Moreover, she was content in Little Rock.

He swung the sedan onto Sixth Street, toward Riverside headquarters. The parking lot would be mostly empty as office employees departed at 4:30. His stop at the office was prompted by the need to double-check inventory records to make sure his promise of an extra day off for the Labor Day weekend would not cause order snafus for the last big cookout of the summer season.

Where did the money go? What did he have to show for it? He and Glenda never settled down like most couples, never purchased a home, started a family, or took vacations. He had a small amount of money in CDs at Merchants National Bank, but much of his stock portfolio had been sold and reinvested in Riverside shares.

Some of his money, including that borrowed from Chicago sources, had evaporated in a horrible, "can't-miss" Middle East oil venture. His attorney had warned him against it, but Bremer's appetite for get-rich-fast schemes overwhelmed prudence. Now the due day had arrived.

Bremer swung into the left turn lane to the Riverside Packing office, yielding to a trickle of traffic entering the large Hawkeye Downs complex just across the street. The Downs was one of the premier stock car racing venues in Iowa, and events there attracted more fans than minor league baseball games. The first event was still more than an hour away.

Bremer's mind raced for answers. How could he meet the loan payments?

Based on his financial history, the bank was reluctant to lend him that kind of money. The CD investment did not command the kind of cash he needed quickly. Perhaps one of the other Riverside investors would loan him at least some of the money he desperately needed to keep the Chicago wolves at bay.

He pulled into the parking stall designated "President" and turned off the engine. He failed to see the other car approach. Suddenly, out of thin air, it was behind him. Where did it come from? Its driver drew up tightly, so bumpers touched. He was hemmed in like a victim before a firing squad.

In a panic, he scanned the lot for other vehicles, but it was empty except for a pickup truck with a flat tire by the back fence. The entrance to the building, and his parking spot, were at the side far away from busy Sixth Street.

It was a predicament that theretofore had only revealed itself in Bremer's worst nightmares.

A swarthy man of fullback proportions jumped out and ran toward Bremer's car. Another man remained in the gray van that suddenly had been converted into a two-and-a-half-ton steel barricade. There was no time to reach for his gun, no time to take evasive action, no time to think.

In a flash, the big man yanked open the door of Bremer's car and grabbed him by his suit coat lapels. It was not a move designed to straighten his tie.

Chapter 16

Peter Bremer's body vaulted out of the car as if propelled by a cannon. His 155-pound frame seemed like an insignificant bother to the boorish enforcer from Chicago. The top of his head nicked the door frame in the process of his unsolicited exit, and within seconds his entire being lay in a chastened crumple on the blacktop surface.

"Mr. Bremer," the goon feigned politeness. "Would you kindly remove your Hart Schaffner-draped ass from the ground and stand up like the spineless loan-dodger you are? Please? Before I lose my gentility."

Bremer stood instantly and came face to face with a human being he guessed was the delegate of mob loan king Adrian Koffmann or possibly the spear carrier known as the Hook. He soon discovered that hoodlum hierarchy was practiced with sacred exactitude. The scowling muscle bag was an envoy of the distinguished Rusty Ragno, the Hook.

He was the advance man, the warm-up goon.

"You are not with Mr. Koffmann?" sheepish Bremer uttered just beyond a whisper.

"You guessed right, Mr. Bremer. Mr. Koffmann has more important business than taking out the garbage. You may recall the name Ragno, or the Hook? He is the gentleman sitting in the van, pouring over loan documents and payments made thereon—or, in your case, non-payments. He is not a happy person. Rusty Ragno hates bill collecting. And he hates collecting bills out here in the middle of corn country."

The Mr. Nice Guy routine faded.

The designated clout commissioner, solidly arranged on a six-foot-two frame, clasped his persuasive hands to Bremer's cheeks and squeezed. The president of Riverside Pack looked like a squished fish out of water, lips coiled in muted suppression. The bruiser adjusted his subject's face upward, toward his own menacing countenance, and positioned himself for a full flow of cigar breath, a loathsome preface to his main message.

A tattoo of a scantily clad woman on his right bicep, just below where a black t-shirt sleeve left off, danced in rhythm to his flexing. A matching dark ball cap portrayed him as a Bears fan. Sunglasses concealed his hostile eyes and complemented an unshaven face. The formal meeting was about to begin. He uttered his discourse with force and gruffness.

"First, Mr. Asshole, it is not important that you know who I am— except for my position, that I am here to introduce you to Mr. Ragno. By the way, it may interest you to know that Ragno is another name for 'spider.' He has this peculiar hobby of collecting spiders. He usually keeps a couple in his briefcase."

Guttural satisfaction filtered through his hairy face. Bremer noticed saliva seeping out the corners of his mouth.

"Mr. Ragno, for your edification," he spewed, "is also a classical pianist. You could say he is a specialist with piano wire. He loves the opera and is a big fan of the late Ezio Pinza. And, get this, he fancies Shakespeare. I think you will enjoy his twists on things. Or maybe not."

His dressing down was equally a drooling down.

"Think of me"—he now softened to a counterfeit smile—"as a midwife. I make things happen when necessary. I witness the loans and other obligations as they flow through the gestation period. If the process is normal, I monitor with benign attendance. If there are complications, I am called to recommend resolution. If need be, I assist in delivering the loan's repayment on time."

He paused.

"Capisce?"

Bremer was at a loss for words, unable to readily translate the euphemistic run-on. He was relieved that the mass of muscle had released his vise-like hands from his face. His pinched cheeks felt as if the goon's fingerprints were still there. But it was brief deliverance as Peter stood naked before the reality of his recklessness. In a split second, he felt a slap in the face that pirouetted him like a ballet dancer. He almost ended up on the ground again.

The man grabbed Bremer's blue tie, yanked it like a noose, and nearly lifted Bremer off his feet. Then he administered a fist to Bremer's midsection that exploded his lungs and caused him to gasp for replacement air. He bent over only to be greeted by a knee to his jaw. Traces of blood dribbled from his mouth.

So this is the price of delayed payment.

Now the "midwife" walked away and, in tag-team fashion, yielded the message-delivery arena to the man who likes spiders. Bremer had no time to wonder why this individual, dressed in a gray suit and burgundy bow tie, was known as the Hook. His only thought was when the nightmare would end.

Ragno's approach was deliberate. He casually pulled on nylon gloves, and his manner suggested he may be less brusque than his advance man. He walked slowly, measuring his steps with a malevolent blueprint. He stopped, looked at Bremer, and in mocking fashion, lightly brushed off Bremer's suit, straightened out the lapels, and adjusted the tie. In a manner befit of jujutsu formality, he bowed.

The Hook, with strands of his curly hair escaping his black leather ivy cap, came on like a runaway train. He stomped on Bremer's left foot. His military-style boot crushed bones and conveyed a message of pain that shot from toe to head.

Bremer slumped in anguish. The Hook yanked his face upward.

"Look at me, you piece of phony crap. You are a work of art, a forgery from top to bottom. As a friend says, your six-shooter is minus six rounds. You may be able to dispense a load of bullshit out here in the cornstalks, but whatever made you think you could cheat on Chicago loan institutions? You are even dumber than I thought. It's your type that gives banking a bad name."

Again, he pretended to brush lint from Bremer's suit.

"You really should pay more attention to your grooming, Mr. Bremer. A man of your position should not look so unkempt, or how do the French call it, *echevellee*? A man of your stature should not look so bewildered. But then, a man of your esteem should also pay his debts in a timely way."

He toyed with his delinquent client.

"Do you know any Shakespeare, Mr. Bremer? Ah. Perhaps not." He paused, looked up, and assumed the role of announcer. "I believe, as the dutiful Katherine articulated to the other women in *The Taming of the Shrew*, you have no respect for your lord. You take your benefactor for granted. Or, as she so delicately put it, 'Too little payment for so great a debt.'"

Ragno, who savored flipping his character, returned to the role of urbane mobster.

"You are aware of how big your loan is, aware of how much you have repaid, aware of conditions. We didn't advise you on how to spend the loan amount, only that it had to be repaid in accordance with our schedule. It wasn't a recommendation. It was a prescription for good health." Another pause for dramatic effect.

"You haven't followed contract requirements. Now other steps must be taken."

He grabbed Bremer's hands.

"Are you right- or left-handed?"

Bremer was not sure if he heard the question correctly. He didn't understand, which was a common and repeated shortcoming in his wayward financing. His feeble shrug substituted for a verbal response.

"In other words, Mr. Bremer, do you write payment checks with your right hand or your left hand?"

Bremer still failed to get the drift of the inquiry.

"I don't understand what you mean. I'm right-handed, but—"

"All I needed to know," Mr. Hook said.

He dropped Bremer's right hand and, after a full survey of the left hand, gripped its middle finger. Squeezing like a vise in two places, the Hook snapped the finger as if it were a twig. Bremer forgot that the thug had tramped on his foot. The fingertip dangled on his hand like a broken tree limb following a storm. He wanted to scream but feared it would invite more torture.

"That, Mr. Bremer, is not in lieu of a payment on your debt, but an all-caps, boldface notice that worse is on the way unless you follow the payment agenda. Do you understand?"

Bremer nodded his reply.

"Here's an addendum to our final notice."

The Hook reached into the pocket of his suit jacket and removed a small plastic case. As if handling a rare specimen, he meticulously removed a black spider, careful not to crush it between the two fingers of his right hand. With his left hand, he clutched Bremer's lower jaw, forced open his mouth, and stuffed the spider back so far as to trigger a gagging swallow.

Bremer's eyes popped in disbelief. The thought of a spider working its way down his esophagus overwhelmed the pain of his foot and hand.

"One parting piece of advice, Mr. Bremer. You are challenged with some serious reorganization of your priorities. I recommend development of a binding blueprint for your future, with line one devoted to repayment of this loan. Remember, cadavers do not make plans. Is this perfectly clear? Tell me what you learned here today."

Peter Bremer's brain, reflecting agony from several parts of his body, fumbled for a response. Physical assault, spiders, and now this guy wants to conduct a quiz?

"I guess," he began, breathing heavily and holding his stomach as to reorder his intestines, "I guess that paying on a regular basis is good, something I should do."

"You dumb son of a bitch!" Ragno boomed. "Saying repaying your loan on time is 'good' is like saying water is good. Making your payments as specified in the agreement you made with Mr. Koffmann, on time, not a day late, is more than good—it's lifesaving.

"And one more thing. Loan enforcement has expenses. Your next payment, as a minimum, is $20,000."

Ragno, a veteran button man for the Chicago Outfit, took pride in the execution of his craft. Lifting his shoulders in a satisfying gesture, he exhaled and returned to the van. The two men drove away. The leader of Riverside Pack stood outside company headquarters, shaking and alone.

Chapter 17
1943, Little Rock

"Oh, my goodness! Notify the principal!" she pointed at one of the older boys. "First have them call the police and ambulance! Hurry! The rest of you students, move along."

Marge Steen, an eighth-grade teacher at Little Rock's Jefferson Davis Elementary, had seen plenty of fistfights, boy-type wrestling, and girl hair pulling, but this was the first time she had witnessed the aftermath of a stabbing. The student rushed her orders to the office, and Marge kneeled next to the victim in the hall just down from her homeroom.

Immediately, she could tell this was more than a surface wound. There was a rip in the boy's shirt and evidence of a major gash, the source of the seeping blood. She removed the shawl from her shoulders, pressed it against the wound, and hoped that would slow the bleeding. She thought the boy was Travis Ellis.

Ellis was not one of her classroom members, but when you are in a school system for eighteen years, you get to know most of the students and their families. She looked up and down the hallway after she had discovered the scene and saw a group of shocked students gathered nearby. No one was running away.

"What's happened?" asked a breathless custodian who ran up next to Mrs. Steen.

"Do you know this boy, Harold? He's been stabbed, I believe."

"Good night! Stabbed, you say? Why, that's the Ellis boy, Travis Ellis. His dad sometimes helps move the track barriers before and after races. Ellis is a pretty good runner. Oh, this is terrible. Who would do this?"

"Right now, we have to get this young fella to the hospital," Mrs. Steen counseled. "Harold, please check at the office to see if the ambulance has been called."

The custodian quickly departed. At that moment, the boy began to stir. His groans turned into crying as he reached for his chest area.

"Are you Travis Ellis?" Mrs. Steen asked softly.

He nodded, his crying advancing to a wail.

"You've been injured, Travis. We have called the ambulance. It will be here shortly. Try to lie still. You will be OK."

She was unsure about her diagnosis but believed it was the best thing to say. Teachers need to be everything—consolers, advocates, boosters, nurses, referees, parent substitutes, and sometimes even educators.

"I am Mrs. Steen, Travis. Try not to move too much. We will help get you medical care."

It seemed like it was taking forever for help to arrive. Why does time assume prolonged dimensions in a crisis? The boy's breathing seemed regular, and he was not coughing. Finally, she heard approaching footsteps.

Principal Chad Worthington raced beside her.

"Can I help you, Mrs. Steen? I heard what happened."

"Well, Mr. Worthington, I think the best we can do is try to keep the bleeding to a minimum. I want to maintain pressure on the wound until the ambulance people arrive. They will know precisely how to react." She was grateful to have learned first aid while with the Girl Scouts. "Thanks for offering to help, and thanks for your company."

In fifteen minutes, the medics arrived. Young Ellis was taken to Baptist Hospital. While the injury was serious, luckily no vital organs had been severed. Loss of blood was the biggest concern, and once transfusions had taken place, the emergency room doctor gave an encouraging nod to Ellis's parents.

After the ambulance left, police checked the school scene and talked to Mrs. Steen and several students. It was certainly the biggest crisis at the school since the beginning of the fall term. There had not been such a student attack since 1938 when a rival school group triggered a melee after a basketball game. Four were injured then.

"No one witnessed the altercation and stabbing," Principal Worthington told a police officer, "at least that I'm aware of. This is terrible. I can't imagine a stabbing here. Someone obviously brought a knife in their gym bag or some other sack and, I would guess, kept it in a locker."

Police found few answers to their questions from students or staff. Some of Ellis's classmates speculated on the identity of the knife wielder. However, most of those assumptions were based on an exchange of harsh words between Ellis and two other classmates competing for top spots in the high hurdles. Conjecture evaporated when a detective interviewed Ellis at the hospital.

"Yeah, I know who stuck me," Ellis told Officer Ben Jenkins. "It was Bobby Bremer. The two of us were talking about this one girl when he pulls this knife out of a sack and starts swinging. I dodged but slipped and fell. That's when he got me. If I could have run, he'd ate my dust. Bobby is not much of a runner. More a waddler, like a duck."

Jenkins asked Ellis if he had provoked the attack, by words or action.

"He came up to me. Ah'm supposin' he planned it all along because he picked a time when no other students was in the area. Nobody. Bobby's not smart, but he ain't dumb in some ways." Ellis shifted in his bed and uttered a mild groan. "Kinda smarts here," he placed his hand on a layer of bandages.

"You didn't answer my question, Travis. Did you say anything or do anything that would have caused this?"

"Ah don't know what difference that makes. Guys get into arguments and discussions all the time, but no sane person pulls a knife. Bobby Bremer is slightly nuts, if you ask me. I expect his dad beat his brains out once or twice. Or maybe he's 'shamed of that roll of fat around his belly. And he knows that just about anyone in school is smarter than he is."

"And you told him that?"

"No."

"Well, what did you say?"

"He says this one girl likes him and that ah shouldn't be talkin' to her, as if the Constitution and freedom of speech is all of a sudden tossed out to benefit him. Hell, she's nothin' to look at. Ah just said hello to her. Ah says to him, maybe she admires the ripple 'round his belt, or it could be she has poor eyesight. Nex' thing I know, he's flashin' this blade around."

Jenkins took his notepad and headed for the phone booth in the downstairs lobby. He checked with the precinct desk sergeant, and they agreed he and another officer should visit the Bremer home immediately. The two met on Cumberland Street, just outside the Bremer residence. Jenkins rang the doorbell.

Molly Bremer's rearranged world, mostly upbeat and settled after the return last year of her eldest son, Peter, instantly took on the shades of despondency that gripped her life before. Policemen at your front door create anxiety, which in her case is grounded in experience. Bobby was her first thought.

"Mrs. Bremer?" Jenkins inquired.

"Yes. I'm Mrs. Bremer," she said, brushing a strand of hair from her eyes. "Could I help you, please?"

"May we come in?"

She opened the door without saying a word, and the officers entered.

"Mrs. Bremer," Jenkins said. "There was a stabbing at Jefferson Davis School this afternoon. Travis Ellis is the victim, and while the wound was serious, doctors at the hospital believe he will be OK."

Molly did not look up; her fears were racing ahead in anticipation of what she would hear next. After a few seconds, Jenkins continued.

"The Ellis boy identified your son, Bobby, as the one who knifed him. We will have to take him into custody, Mrs. Bremer. Is he here?"

Molly's hands mechanically covered her mouth, restraining an urge to scream in anger and frustration. Again she resorted to reviewing what she may have done wrong, how she may have treated Bobby differently than her other two children. Did Bobby somehow feel left behind? Was it poor self-esteem? Did he have a learning disability?

Silence filled the room.

Jenkins was about to repeat his question when Peter walked into the front room.

"Mom. What's the matter?" he asked. "Why are policemen here?"

"Is Bobby home?" Molly looked at Peter.

"Yes. He was reading an Archie comic book in our room. What's going on?"

Molly struggled to make words come. She looked at Jenkins, then at Peter. The emotions collected until she could no longer keep them from turning to tears.

"Mom?"

"Peter," she sobbed, "the officers want to talk to Bobby. He's been involved in a fight at school."

Molly accompanied Bobby and the officers to the precinct station, then to court. After an initial appearance before a magistrate, Bobby was sent home. A formal hearing the following week authenticated the delinquency charges stemming from the school fight. Bobby admitted to the stabbing. A date was set for sentencing.

When you hear a judge, albeit in Juvenile Court, pass your son along for detention consideration, it shakes your insides in unimaginable ways. This was Bobby's fourth trip before Little Rock authorities—and by far the most serious. The continuing problems, capped by physical harm to another person, is the sort of record that causes the most lenient of judges and magistrates to shake their heads.

Certainly Molly Bremer understood the seriousness of her son's troubles and the authorities' fast-depleting patience. But she fought the notion that Bobby was at a crossroads with disaster, that he was some sort of deviant destined for a career of breaking up rocks. A mother does not think that way. A mother's hope for a child may be challenged but not terminated.

Bobby Bremer was twelve, old enough to be considered for detention but not subject to adult penalties. Another thing in his favor was that he drew a different magistrate than the one who handled his last appearance in court. While he looked at a summary of young Bremer's troubles, Homer Hollins noted that he came from a home without a father. And Hollins had been down this road before, always hoping that such a young person should be given one more chance.

Magistrate Hollins had some alternatives. He could send Bobby to a youth detention camp for up to two years, given that a personal injury was involved. He could hold him in the detention section of the city jail for a short period. Or he could release him with a stern lecture about a persistent life of lawbreaking.

"I will again attempt to impress upon you the kind of future you can expect if you don't change your actions and attitudes," Hollins addressed Bremer and his mother. "You, at some point—stand up straight—at some point you will be incarcerated, either as a juvenile or adult, unless you change your ways."

Bobby pulled two marbles from his pocket and rubbed them together as if to expect some genie to save him from his difficulties. He made no eye contact with the magistrate and, for all Hollins knew, heard nary a word of what the court official had said. Even for an indulgent person, that sort of disregard can quickly swell to contempt.

Hollins took his gavel and rapped it on the desk as hard as he could. His aggressive reaction would have surprised his colleagues. It even surprised him.

"Let me tell you, young man," his mood began to curdle as he interrupted himself. "Look at me! You look at me and pay attention, or by golly you will be spending this night in the lockup. Give me those marbles, and then give me your full attention."

Bobby looked up, showing the interest of a boy at a quilting convention. He handed over the opaque marbles and sat down, on his hands, on the front-row bench. He stared at the floor.

"Stand up," Hollins bellowed. "You stand up straight, hands by your side, and look at me."

Bobby complied.

"I want to tell you first off young man, that I am making a special note in the record that if you get into trouble again, I want to personally handle your case. That's to make sure your con game is not perpetuated. In other words, Bobby, if you come before me again, you can count on doing jail time, juvenile detention."

Hollins paused to gather his judicial posture. Mr. Nice Guy had metamorphosed into Mr. Hanging Judge in the flash of a gavel. Bobby Bremer had that sort of bizarre, provoking power.

"Do you think you understand what I have just told you?"

"I think so, sir," Bobby answered.

"Good. In that case, I want you, as part of these proceedings, to go home and write—twenty-five times, in your own words—what I just told you. I want you personally to deliver that essay to me in one week. Beyond that, I sentence you to six months in detention with probation. That means if you obey your mother, obey school officials, and act like a civilized human, you won't have to spend time in detention."

Hollins breathed a huge sigh and looked at Molly.

"Now, please leave me."

He had second thoughts.

"I'm sorry, Mrs. Bremer."

Chapter 18
1975, Iowa

"Mr. Bremer! What happened to you?"

Charlie Draznek exited a side door of Riverside Pack headquarters in Cedar Rapids and was shocked at what he saw. He seldom ran into the company president—not his social circle—but had bumped into him in corridors, never in a situation like this.

"*Sakra*. You look hurt! Oh, excuse the language. I'm Charlie Draznek, one of the custodians. Do you want me to call an ambulance? Or the police? What happened, Mr. Bremer?"

"I know who you are, and no, Charlie, I don't need an ambulance. I'll be all right. Don't call the police."

"Well, what happened? Sure as heck the wind didn't rip your suit coat like that. And your face! Looks like you were in the race warmups at Hawkeye Downs and your car overturned."

"No. It was just a little misunderstanding between me and this other fellow," Bremer said, still holding his aching abdomen. "He and his misunderstanding were a little bigger. I'll be OK. Thanks. See ya tomorrow. Do you need a lift somewhere? I don't see your car."

"Thanks, Mr. Bremer. The missus, she will be along shortly. We're headed to the Kozy Inn for supper. Got the crave for one of them pork tenderloins, don't you know."

Draznek was unschooled in management affairs, but he knew that the bottom line here was that Bremer had more than just a bad day at the office. Peter's explanation would not have convinced a rookie office boy. His vagueness was exceeded only by his intent to conceal. Draznek considered calling someone but decided it was none of his business.

He did not need the custodian job at Riverside offices, but neither did he want to sit around at home.

After retiring from Wilson & Co. and a two-week walleye fishing trip to Park Rapids, Minn., Draznek joined the janitor crew at Riverside. Work was a social event for him. He was good at fixing things but better at "shooting the breeze," as he called it. He walked away, worried by what he had seen.

Charlie was among Cedar Rapids' extensive Czech population, who were respected as sociable, caring, hard-working family people. Nearly 20 percent of the city's residents had Czech or Slovak ancestry. He was among those who for years pushed to organize a National Czech Museum in the city. Last year he and his cohorts were successful.

Peter Bremer limped to his Cadillac. Slowly he inserted his battered body behind the steering wheel and drove off, forgetting the reason he returned to the office. He was at the intersection of truth and vanity. Glenda would ask the same questions Draznek did, only with more probing and alarm. He pulled into a Sinclair station and hobbled to a restroom. There he wiped off streaks of blood, combed his hair, and generally rearranged himself. There was nothing he could do about the torn lapel.

Strangely his broken finger was less painful than his stomped foot. And in a twist of physiological consequence, his bodily distress was overwhelmed by mental anguish.

Vulnerability shook him. It rattled every inch of his slight frame.

Fear, initially delivered by letter, then a phone call, and now in person, clearly had grown like a cancerous tumor. It had metastasized throughout his body and seemingly set every cell on a trembling fit. His immediate aim was to find some prescription to control the shaking. He should have driven to a hospital. His elected remedy caused him to shudder more.

It was no surprise that Peter Bremer shunned alcohol. At an early age, and many times thereafter, he vowed not to follow the destructive path that his father had taken. He had seen how it affected his father's physical and mental well-being, led to the abuse of his mother, and eventually ripped their family apart.

He managed to fend off the taunts of beer-guzzling college friends. Once in St. Louis, at a gathering of business associates, he tried a Budweiser. His initial refusal was read as an insult to the entire institution of beer brewing. He was not afraid of becoming an alcoholic. More pointedly, he disliked the taste of beer or whiskey. Even more, he detested the stink of cigarettes.

That was then, before he found himself facing the fangs of evil. Instead of driving directly to the upscale hotel suite he and Glenda were renting, Peter pulled into a parking spot near the Fox & Hounds Lounge. He removed his coat and tie and shuffled in. Fortunately, there was a booth in the back. He recognized no one in the going-home crowd, and he was glad for that.

"Jack Daniels on ice with a spurt of water," he said in response to the young waitress's question. That recipe for relaxation was copied from a friend. "Please make it a double. Oh, and bring me a bag of Planters nuts." He promised himself that, effective or not at calming his system, one drink, albeit a double, was it.

"Are you OK?" the waitress asked. Ordinarily, by house rules and server convention, the trials of customers—evident or otherwise—are not matters for inquiry. But Bremer looked like he had been shot from a cannon into a brick wall. "You seem to be in pain," she said with accuracy.

"No, no." Bremer again declined attention and assistance. "I'll be fine. I think my ulcer may be acting up. That's probably it. Just needs a little balm. It'll calm down." He faked a smile. She went to get his drink.

Bremer, was one of those rare mid-forties men who escaped the belt-line rolls that seem to aggregate naturally. He did not exercise on a regular basis and attributed his slimness to an inherited metabolism. His parents were not ever overweight, and his mother maintained an attractive figure, even at sixty-seven.

No doctor had ordered him to monitor his sodium intake, so he chewed on the salty nuts and then drenched them in Jack Daniels No. 7. He savored the combination, and the second sip of whiskey tasted sweet and without any repulsive aftertaste. For a minute or two he lost himself in the mixture of humanity and wondered what all of them were hiding from.

He fingered with the evening menu, which shortly drew the waitress's attention. He held up his hand in a gesture of disinterest in eating. A few minutes later he returned to his medicine. Gradually the quivering eased. The alcohol was performing its sedative powers. Peter took another sip of the drink and, in looking around, half noticed the bantering display of one-upmanship and blue smoke rolling out of competing nostrils.

I think I am good to go, he pronounced after a quick self-examination. He inspected his hands. They were steady. He pushed the remainder of No. 7 to the side, left a tip, and departed. He would have to tell Glenda the truth, but at least she would not go crackers over his trembling. The four-block drive to the hotel was like a trip across a marsh; his thoughts pulled through a swamp of stress, struggling to formulate the best account to a woman he loved.

He had worked for Wide Plains Insurance a little over two years when he met Glenda in St. Louis. She was an inch taller than Peter—something few noticed. Even a disinterested eye was pulled to her significant attributes. Her long legs propped a well-proportioned body topped by gorgeous, well-coiffed blond hair.

Her blue eyes were kind and summoned those she met with gentle magnetism. Peter was pulled in like a heap of helpless metal shavings. He reveled in his vulnerability. On their second date, he pegged her "magic," and it became her private nickname, his go-to love tag.

Glenda was not the manifest dumb blond. After graduating from Washington University with a degree in art history, she decided to work with her father. Her decision, she believed, was prescribed by events following her mother's death from breast cancer. She was not going to abandon her father. So she discarded her ambitions and worked in company public relations.

That was eight years ago. Her adoring father had taken to uttering not-so-subtle suggestions that she become more "sociable," a euphemism that matured to outright counsel that she consider dating.

"I appreciate your generous attention to me," he told her, "but the time has come to pay more attention to yourself."

In those years, Glenda became the face of Goodman Clothiers, in commercials and community events. She even greeted customers at the headquarters store. It was significantly due to her efforts that Goodman expanded from three to ten stores in the Midwest. She charmed potential women customers. "Our lines," she would recite in TV ads, "are designed to enhance your lines."

After college, Bremer held jobs in accounting and insurance. He sold Glenda's father a $10,000 term life insurance policy. Glenda, an only child, was the beneficiary. Howard Goodman was impressed by Bremer's urbane approach, business acumen, and dapper attire. But mostly he became absorbed by Peter's uncanny salesmanship. He offered him a job, first in buying men's apparel, and Bremer took it. He quickly advanced, as did the paycheck, to men's fashion advisor.

Those were good days, Bremer pondered, sitting in his car outside the restaurant lounge. Should he tell the unvarnished story to

Glenda? It would be the honest approach, really the only one for someone you cared for. His weakness and proclivity to water down the truth and genuine desire not to frighten Glenda argued in the opposite direction.

He remembered the night Glenda invited him to her home in St. Louis. She lived with her dad. The three watched the Apollo 11 moon landing, listened to the intonations of CBS anchor Walter Cronkite, and finally the immortal words of Astronaut Neil Armstrong: "One small step for man, one giant leap for mankind."

What was emblazoned on his mind, as history unfolded, was the way her eyes sparkled when they exchanged looks. They intended to share wonder at the overwhelming, futuristic events taking place in space, but instead they succumbed to the age-old sirens of love. It was the kind of magic that far exceeded anything he had tucked in his sales repertoire.

Equally amazing was the speed of time. Those enchanting memories were six years old.

He needed such magic now, a formula to unravel his self-generated tangle. Why had he shunned his lawyer's advice to stay away from oil speculation, especially the slippery slope of Middle East ventures? Plain old Arkansas common sense was trumped by avarice—and then the stupidity of borrowing money from the shady side of the lending street.

Maybe he wasn't beset by the lure of alcohol, but Peter Bremer was beholden to the muse of the quick buck, the deal that could not fail, the kind of horrible investments posted as warnings in the college business textbooks he once regarded as the bible. He had been the victim of his own sales knack. He could sell a product but apparently lacked knowledge on what not to buy.

When Wide Plains Insurance offered him a position as vice president for development, he took the job. It was an opportunity to make more money and save face should his bad investments and lending sources come to light—that is, become known by Mr. Goodman and his daughter Glenda. The company asked him to open a new office in Cedar Rapids, Iowa. That added distance to his coverup of truth.

Glenda was crushed by his decision. Peter, too, realized their relationship had advanced beyond friendship. It was a dilemma that his business bibles had not covered. It pitted the desire to escape, run from an honest confrontation with reality, against the powers of affection. Bunkum, the old dazzle-them-with-your-dance routine, was part of sales tradition. He proposed a solution.

He would get established in Cedar Rapids, with the new office up and running and living quarters found, and Glenda could join him later. He would come to St. Louis on some weekends; she could visit him in Cedar Rapids on others. She bought the deal. Within a week of moving to Cedar Rapids, he signed a two-year lease for a three-room office suite in the ten-story Stevens Building. No outskirts lean-to for Peter Bremer.

The Stevens Building is a handsome Chicago school structure, built in 1918 in the heart of downtown by the late Maynard Stevens. Stevens, a contractor, was part of the city's power structure. Bremer's office was perched on the fifth floor, surrounded by lawyers and investment dealers, the kind of pedestal where he felt comfortable. The street level housed an upscale women's clothing store.

For two months he lived at the Montrose Hotel. It was considered a fine accommodation by most—but not quite what Bremer wanted on his business card. He rented a suite at the Roosevelt Hotel, the swankiest domicile in town, outside the old family mansions and estates.

After a year of a shuttling romance, they were married.

Bremer had informed his mother of the engagement. He told her about the $2,100 princess-cut diamond by Etsy he purchased for Glenda. "Nothing is too good for my Magic," he told his mother. Molly Bremer was more interested in traditional Baptist behavior before marriage and counseled him accordingly. Soon after, Glenda and Peter were married by the pastor of Christ Episcopal Cathedral at the Goodman home. It was the Goodman family church.

Molly had suggested a Baptist ceremony but bowed to Peter's argument that it was what Glenda desired. He fortified his case by noting that Glenda wanted "some spiritual aspect" to their wedding, but not in a formal sense. It was a small affair. A few Goodman relatives attended, as did Peter's sister Hattie and her husband. Younger brother Bobby was in prison.

Now Peter faced yet another sales challenge. Postponement was no longer an option.

He pulled into his Roosevelt Hotel parking space, exited the sedan, and nervously looked in all directions as he entered the elevator. He pushed the button for the twelfth floor. Maybe he could tell her that one of the men at the packing plant took exception to a comment about management-employee relations, hence the cuts and bruises.

It was another shallow ruse meandering in his mind. He hated himself. He stepped out of the elevator, walked the short distance to the suite, and immediately noticed the door was ajar. He always stressed to Glenda to keep the apartment locked. Not only was the door open, but splintered wood lay scattered on the floor.

He heard a mumbling of voices. A different kind of fear engulfed him, a fear centered not on himself but the woman he loved. For the first time, Peter Bremer, in the gut of his business and personal processing, realized the importance of adhering to a contract.

He raced inside, panic pushing him like a hunted animal.

Chapter 19
Little Rock, 1945

"What do you think, Pastor Clendon?" Adora Mae Marston probed outside the church after services. "Was the president right in dropping the atomic bomb on Japan? How does that line up with the sixth commandment, 'Thou Shall Not Kill?' Lot of innocent people dead. Isn't all human life sacred?"

Adora Mae was not noted for discretion or inhibition. If there is a pot to be stirred, Molly Bremer's dad Orval Price frequently pronounced, "Adora will be first in line with a big spoon." She headed several church groups at Good Neighbors Baptist, including the finance committee. According to Molly's dad, that gave Adora "mistaken authority to shoot off her mouth."

"Now, Adora Mae. You assume there are just two answers to your question, either black or white, when there may be a dozen shades of gray," piped Dick Thornton, a member of the church council and operator of a dry-cleaning business. "Yes, many civilians were killed, but many may have been saved from a prolonged war."

"Good gosh, Dick." Adora stiffened. "That is rampant speculation, the kind of fluff that comes out of your laundry driers. You must be on Truman's re-election committee. It's quite possible Japan was about to surrender anyway." Her look alone would have stopped the Japanese in their tracks.

Pastor Jimmy Clendon reached beneath his vestments and pulled out a white handkerchief. The hot mid-August sun and the ardent political subject tossed in the middle of church decorum produced beads of sweat on his forehead. The blotting of perspiration allowed him time to summon ministerial memory regarding conciliation. He concluded the time had come to step in with a response before the just-ended Christian services progressed into un-Christian hard feelings.

"It's fine to have discussions about government policy," Rev. Clendon offered, "even military policy. But there is one thing we can all praise God for, and rejoice to the heavens, and it's that the war is over. The end to shooting and bombing and killing is over. Our sons and daughters are coming home." He waited for a response. "We can say Amen to that?" he searched. And with that, the undeclared truce had been formally blessed, and life in Arkansas could resume without casualty.

Everyone nodded and mumbled the prescribed Amen. Adora abstained.

Orval Price sniffed skyward as if some mysterious ill wind had drifted upon the churchgoers. He knew full well the source of the pungent bouquet. It was Adora's generous application of toiletries, powder, and related essences. He began sneezing and coughing out of editorial expression only to have Aliza Price send him a sour look. She read him like a veteran psychic.

Molly Bremer was not only grateful the war was over but that the pastor had stepped in strategically to prevent another conflict between her father and Adora Mae Marston. Orval Price was poised to go nose to nose with Adora, sharing his own opinion and all the information collected at the American Legion.

"I'm proud of you, Dad," Molly said to him as they walked to the car.

"What the hell are you saying, Molly?" Price sputtered. "That woman is so full of herself I'm surprised crap isn't oozing out of her ears. Why she—"

"Dad, calm down. I'm proud of you because you didn't say outside of church what you just said now. After all, we just finished praying for all people, and that includes Adora Mae."

"Maybe your prayers include that crone. Mine don't!"

"Now, Dad." Molly sought a palliative approach. "Adora can be as loving as her name is charming." The tactic fell short.

"Charming? Right," he said sarcastically. "Charlotte is a charming name too, and she was a spider. I know about Adora. She is a master at crocheting opinion and sees no holes in her fabric. Moreover, if you get in her lane, she'll run you over." He took time out to gather the balance of his assessment.

"I'm glad no one shook her hand," Orval said, provoking puzzled looks. "Well, she was so perfumed up that a shake of her hand would have pumped talcum powder all over town." His audience repressed their sniggers.

With that, Molly, her three children, and her parents gathered at the Big Stack Pancake House, their second religious stop on many Sunday mornings.

Price served in the Marine Corps. He never saw combat, but Marines have their own blood type. It runs thick, it runs loyal red, and it is not prone to run away from a fight. Like others at the Legion Club, Price applauded President Truman's dramatic gamble to end the war and killing of more Americans.

All over the country, people celebrated the Japanese surrender and the return of peace. Little Rock was no exception. Even small towns planned to have welcome-home parades. It was just a question of timing, how to include the most returning servicemen and women. It was also the end of fear and the eventual end of rationing.

Some servicemen, including a resident on Cumberland Street, had already been discharged. The Bremer boys, among others, knew the neighborhood army veteran had been wounded by a sniper's bullet in the North Africa campaign. They pestered him until he revealed the scar that now hid the specter of death and heroics of a medic.

Manufacturers of ships, aircraft, and tanks were already retooling for anticipated orders of family sedans and farm tractors. Molly wondered what would happen at the munitions plant. Eventually the entire war machine would be geared down to peacetime levels. Rumors, a by-product at any factory, were flying like Howitzer shells, and most were centered on cutbacks.

Molly was thirty-seven. The boys were in high school, and Hattie was a freshman at Little Rock Junior College, contemplating a degree in music. Peter was on the high school debate team and was earning an A- report card. Bobby was adhering to the restrictions prescribed by the court and, to his mother's surprise, was maintaining a B average. Her primary worry was keeping her job.

Peter found a part-time job bussing dishes at a downtown restaurant, and Bobby cut lawns and split wood for stoves. That helped meet budget demands, but it failed to boost Molly's meager savings and financial security. Her father offered help, but she declined, knowing that her parents had their own money struggles.

On this Sunday night, Molly planned to relax. She turned on the little Firestone radio, stretched out on the living room couch, intent on getting lost in the mysteries of *Ellery Queen*. Few people owned a television set. The manufacture of televisions had been banned during the war. There were fewer than two dozen US TV stations, and nearly all had shut down in 1942.

"Will one of you kids get the phone?" she asked, silently hoping it was one of their friends. "Please?" she said after the fifth ring. It was Hattie who responded.

"Mom, it's for you. I think it's Madeline Houston."

Molly sighed, hoisted her legs from repose, and shuffled to the phone.

"Girlfriend, don't tell me you were snoozin' already. You have to get a life."

"Hi, Madeline. I wasn't snoozin'. I was getting ready to listen to *Ellery Queen* in a few minutes. What's on your mind?"

"Won't keep you then. Just wanted to ask if you heard about Timex opening a new plant in North Little Rock. Maybe we could make watches instead of Kraut eggs and Howitzer hooters. Whaddia think? Story in the *Arkansas Gazette* says Timex will be taking job applications down at the junior college next weekend. I'm going to apply. You're welcome to ride along."

"Sounds interesting," Molly replied. "Maybe I will come along. Have you heard from Ted? When is he coming home?"

"He expects he will be in the hospital over there for another month. I am so anxious for him to be home. I don't know how soon he'll be able to work, so I'm hoping to hold on to a job. Let me know one way or t'other. Toodaloo."

Molly and Madeline took jobs at Timex. It was their good fortune. Arkansas, unlike other states, did not experience the post-war boom that had been pent up in deferred buying. The state's population declined in the years after the war as military posts and ordnance factories reduced operations or shut down. Some people moved away. Nearly one hundred thousand black people left the state.

New Timex and Westinghouse factories gave Little Rock some stability, and Molly assumed that steadiness. By spring of 1948, life settled into a comfortable routine. She had no luxuries. Neither did she have worries of want. Her health was good, and she celebrated her family and a small group of friends.

She could see Jack Bremer's features in her children, but Jack Bremer the husband was a faded memory. Life moved on. Several years had passed. The wounds of war were salved by reunited families. The Bremer household fell into the comfortable march of a renewed country.

Hattie was now a senior at the University of Arkansas, and Peter a freshman at Arkansas State. Bobby, a high school senior, told his mother he was not interested in college. He enjoyed carpenter shop, working with lumber, and Molly could see him seeking a job in construction. He was good at math and liked to build things.

All of that splintered one Saturday night in early May 1948.

This time there were no more court lectures for Bobby Bremer. Molly appealed to the judge, arguing that Bobby was basically a good boy and had stayed out of trouble for several years. But the court's mercy was not to be found, and a mother's plea was buried by judicial vexation.

Bobby's involvement in a break-in and robbery at a North Little Rock malt and ice cream store was the last straw. His criminal mischief record had reached the tipping point. He would not graduate from high school. He would spend the next ten months at a juvenile detention work farm.

Molly cried. She felt so alone. What happened would be a nightmare for a mother and father. A single parent absorbed all the pain and disappointment, and in Molly's case, all the perceived blame and shame. There was no one's shoulder to cry on, and once again she had to fight off despair. Again she took refuge in Peter and Hattie, promising herself—ordering herself—not to give up on Bobby.

He looked so empty to her. Her thoughts mingled with sniffles as the judge shuffled and signed papers. *My son is the victim of robbery*, she thought with motherly measurement, flipping the facts in reverse. They took his school clothes and exchanged them for the washed-out orange uniform of an offender. They stole his identity. They transformed him from student to criminal. The trip from free teenager to ward of the state was quick but long on anguish.

Despite his five-foot-ten, 175-pound frame, Bobby looked so little, so scared, standing before the judge like a shivering ram waiting to be sheared. Did they have to place him in handcuffs? Did the judge have to sound so gruff? Is he a father? Are his kids perfect?

"You will spend the next ten months at the juvenile facility at Alexander, Arkansas," the judge informed him. "You will have the opportunity there to continue high school studies. You will also have the chance to learn about the law and being a civil person." As it turned out, the seriousness of the case kicked the matter out of juvenile proceedings and into adult court. It was little solace that he was not subject to the short fuse of Magistrate Hollins.

"Mrs. Bremer," the judge said, looking at Molly, "are you aware the boy with your son had a gun, a pistol?"

She shook her head in the negative. *It seems*, she thought, *that he's blaming us for that. Bobby had no gun.*

"That, Mrs. Bremer, makes the matter more serious. Court dismissed." He slammed the gavel.

A man from the sheriff's department juvenile office came forward and took Bobby by the upper arm. He did not speak, but his precise action needed no explanation. He looked at Molly, and after their eyes met, he ushered Bobby to his mother for an unexpected detour. It was a bend in procedure in favor of compassion, which surprised the grateful mother and released her emotions.

Molly sobbed as she hugged Bobby and said goodbye. He showed no emotion. He avoided her eyes; his face was a portrait of indifference. She stuck a slip of paper into his side pocket after showing it to court officials. Scribbled on it were her telephone number and home address. Would he write or call, this youngest of her flesh?

"I will write you often," she said. "Did you hear me, Bobby? And I will call." With that, he was taken away.

The May sun, already climbing and beaming its seasonal essence, angled its way into Molly's kitchen. However, it was accompanied by a cold north wind, which chilled the pretenses of oncoming summer. She was alone, and the house was cold. The kitchen table, the centerpiece of family life in so many homes, was again her retreat, a place to lean on as she appraised the latest chapter in her life.

She decided to have a talk with herself.

In a recent sermon, Pastor Clendon talked about the need to keep one's head up in the face of hardship, and he alluded to the four difficult war years. Personal adversity, too, he had said, at home or in business, can bring a person to the "rim of ruin." He said: "We must reject the suggestion of Henry David Thoreau that 'the mass of mankind lead lives of desperation.'"

The first thing, she silently promised, is to never think that life is too embarrassing, that it's not worth plodding on. She once had been mired in that muddle when Peter was gone, but that path was one she now despised. Neither would she sacrifice Bobby on the altar of statistical reasoning, the notion that she had been successful in raising at least two of her three children.

Molly vowed never to abandon her youngest or succumb to the view that Bobby is not worth a mother's love and worry or that, in some warped way of thinking, he is inferior to Hattie and Peter. She fought the heartache.

A tear slipped from her right eye and trickled across her cheek. It landed on the table, soft and quiet. There, glistening in the middle, was the image of Bobby.

Sure, he could be frightfully callous. Yes, it seemed impossible for him to show love. Most children are prone to bend the rules, but Bobby was more inclined to ignore the rules. However, there was that one time when he wasn't the usual Bobby, and it was that person she saw in the wet spot on the table.

"Mom," he had said after one of the several visits to the principal's office. "I'm sorry." And then he handed her a slip of paper. She was surprised by what he had written: "I didn't mean to make you cry." That, she told herself, is the real Bobby.

Chapter 20
1975, Cedar Rapids

"Stop right there! Put your hands where I can see them!"

Cedar Rapids Detective Lt. Louie Byrnes yanked Bremer inside the hotel suite in a not-so-much "welcome home" greeting. Byrnes scanned the hallway to see if anyone else was present.

"What's going on here?" Bremer pleaded, markedly flummoxed. "Why are you here?"

"The better questions are, Who are you and what are you doing here?"

Byrne released his grip. He was a no-nonsense cop who was long on savvy and experience but short on patience. His size and gray-speckled crew cut added credentials if not charm.

"I am Peter Bremer and I live here."

"And you have identification? Perhaps a driver's license?"

Bremer suddenly realized his disheveled appearance was not likely to persuade even a rookie cop of his claimed identity, much less a veteran like Byrne. He removed his wallet and feebly handed his driver's license to the officer. Byrne gave it a thorough look.

"OK, Mr. Bremer." He returned the license with a puzzled look and a shake of the head. "Did you just come back from a bad experience with a pit bull, or is that your normal dress?"

Byrne regretted that his cynicism had jumped ahead of professional courtesy and training.

"I'm sorry for that," Byrne said before Bremer could respond. "It's just that your appearance is unusual under the circumstances."

"I understand," Bremer said, readjusting his clothes and smoothing his hair. "What's happening? Why are you here? Where is Glenda? Where is my wife?"

"Glenda is sitting in the bedroom. She is fine. I am Lt. Byrne, and we responded to the hotel's call minutes ago. Seems as if someone broke into your apartment this afternoon. They wanted to get in awfully bad"—he pointed to the shattered door—"but the funny thing is the lady says nothing seems to be missing. She came home and found this," he said, again gesturing at the disarray.

Byrne rubbed the mole on his cheek as if it held answers to the mysterious.

"In my experience in police work, when a culprit goes to the bother of making a mess like this, he will walk away with valuables of some kind—jewelry, money, artwork. Since that's not the case here, I would surmise, Mr. Bremer, that the bad guy, or guys, was looking to do harm to a person."

There was a calculated pause.

"Would that person be you, Mr. Bremer? Or did they already meet up with you?"

My God! Bremer thought. *He is a quick read.*

"Could I see Glenda? I want to make sure she is all right."

"Come on in," Byrne said. "She discovered this situation, she said, after returning from a shopping trip." They walked through the suite. "Here she is."

Bremer rushed to her and hugged her, relieved for her safety. But shame quickly flooded his mind. He had put her in danger. He had exposed her to the consequences of his mistakes. And perhaps worst of all—he shuddered as he pulled her closer—was that she was innocent and ignorant of his shadowy life. How does that fit with love?

His many wrong turns had finally merged in the last place he wanted—Glenda's doorstep.

"I don't understand, Peter," she cried. "What's happening? Why has our suite been broken into?"

"Are you OK, darling?"

"I'm fine. I found things this way." She gestured toward some scattered books and a broken piece of pottery. He looked at the shattered Acoma jug that he had insisted they purchase on a trip to New Mexico.

They held one another and sobbed in a miniature dance, propelled by waves of emotion, electrical impulses that bounded freely like a nuclear reaction that was unsure of its destiny.

Byrne asked some additional questions and made another sweep of the suite. Minutes later he returned.

"Excuse me, folks," he said. "My assistant will make a few notes and take some pictures, and we'll be gone. Do you have any idea who would break into your apartment, any enemies?" The officer looked Bremer squarely in the eyes, reading every nuance of reaction. "It's my opinion that they were looking for someone rather than *something,*" Byrne repeated. "Not finding that someone, they wanted to leave a message."

Bremer looked at Byrne and then back at Glenda.

"It may have to do with a business matter," he said. "I think it will work out."

Byrne read it as a signal that no more immediate information would be forthcoming. He also sensed this was not the end of Bremer's troubles. In Cedar Rapids, Iowa, this did not look like an ordinary business dispute.

"Well, if there is anything more you want to add to our report, just give me a call at this number." Byrne handed him the PD information card. "Are you sure you don't need medical attention for those cuts and scrapes?"

"Thanks, officer. I'll be OK."

Byrnes left. The police technicians were done in ten minutes, and a hotel maintenance man showed up to examine the damage. He hammered a temporary fix and promised a full repair and a new lock before he went home.

Peter and Glenda sat in silence on a living room divan, holding each other and a jumble of questions. It was one of those situations where a lot was being said without a word spoken. She had soaked a washcloth in warm water and was dabbing at the cuts on his face, careful not to provoke bleeding again.

He looked at her and then out the huge north window of the apartment. The silos at the huge Quaker Oats plant testified to Iowa's breadbasket standing, but Bremer saw only despair and a future famished of good alternatives. But the bigger contrast, one that slowly came into focus for him, was the deep love he had for Glenda and his lack of honesty with her.

Truth confronted Peter Bremer.

She began to sob again.

"Sweetheart." She looked pleadingly into his eyes and gently touched a mark on his cheek. Her warm caress sent a shiver of guilt through his body. "I don't under—"

"Glenda, my Magic, please don't cry." He held her closely, the only obstruction being remorse. "Listen, I've done some foolish things, terrible things. I've made some horrible decisions." He told her the entire history of his investment debacles—born of greed—and involvement with unsavory characters from Chicago's underworld.

When he told her of the deadline set by mob agents, whom he depicted as sleazy businessmen, and their explicit manner of persuasion, her weeping swelled into shaking and shrieking. His litany of mistakes took several minutes, and her digestion of them lasted longer. They sat entangled in a blend of fear and profound love.

"One of their henchmen accosted me this afternoon outside the office," he confessed. "I think he broke one of my fingers." He omitted mention of the spider.

"Let me see," Glenda gasped, examining his finger. "You should see a doctor."

"It doesn't really hurt much. Maybe we can just fix a splint, try to immobilize it. Do we have some sort of small wooden brace we could tape to the finger?"

"I know what may work," she said. "I'll break one of my emery sticks in two. Let's try that."

The idea worked.

"Why don't we ask my father for help?" Glenda sniffled. "It's not too late. I know he would help you."

Bremer said nothing. He just looked at her, inhaling her beauty and discerning the elements of her character he had never focused on—grace, intelligence, compassion, unconditional love. Clearly there was more to this woman than mere eyesight revealed. How could he have been so shallow, so stupid? Was he much different from ogling friends who beheld her physical assets and disregarded her person?

It angered him when someone called her a blond bombshell, a moniker that carried a suitcase of undertones. And yet he had been blindly attracted more by her physical appearance and natural charm than by her deeper virtues. Was that the curse of all men? Or was that more of his addictive rationalization? Her eyes sparkled with sincerity but also glistened with distress.

"I am so sorry, my love," he whispered.

Again, when she tried to speak, release the words that held her many questions, he placed his finger on her lips in a plea for forbearance.

Here I am holding an incomparable treasure, he thought, *while up to my eyebrows in financial trouble.* The irony. A rich man who is poor. Or, he played with words, a poor man who is rich. He smiled. Her eyes brightened.

This was a woman who once decided her father was more important than her personal career. She cared for him, helped operate the family business, and was flesh-and-spirit present with him as he worked past the death of his wife, her mother. Glenda was an exceptional daughter. She was strong—another trait he had overlooked—maybe as strong as his own mother, who also did what circumstances demanded.

And integrity ran in her family. Howard Goodman was not among the elite of St. Louis, but he was notably generous and well respected among local retailers. He did not boast his philanthropy but preferred to recognize the charity of others. He seldom missed Sunday services at Christ Episcopal and once invited Bremer to accompany him and Glenda. But Bremer was too full of himself to find room for religion.

Other than his church, Goodman's favorite beneficiaries were the American Cancer Society and Salvation Army. He even rang bells at Christmas. Sure, Bremer reflected, Mr. Goodman would bail out his daughter's spendthrift husband, but that would require humility and complete disclosure on Bremer's part. Vanity covertly stepped forward.

"I have also been a fool in how I've treated you," Bremer said softly. "I want you to know that our love, my love for you, is the most important thing in my life. I would do anything to protect you."

It was sincerity and affection unlike she had sensed before from Peter. His vow to keep her safe had dimensions still hidden to them. Again her tear ducts opened, this time in joy and love rather than fear and doubt.

"I love you too, Peter," she cried. She waited for the sniffling to abate. "I have been waiting to hear that. I know we can work things out together."

"Glenda, will you forgive me?"

She kissed him and then hugged him with no deference to his injuries. Her warmth and genuineness dissolved his physical pain. Her radiance left him speechless. They embraced as if closeness was the only remedy, the only escape from the ominous dilemma that Bremer had created. After minutes of rapturous relief, Glenda leaped from the davenport like a schoolgirl and skipped to the telephone.

"Let's celebrate our love and resolve to survive all this," she said excitedly. She dialed hotel services. "We can eat right here. I'm ordering cabernet, two bottles, and two Riverside Pack steaks." Her eyes melted the last of his rooted guile. He was finally able to speak past his overwhelmed senses.

"Glenda, darling. You are amazing. Here I am, traveling aimlessly down places I shouldn't be, and you steer me straight. What a lost soul I have been. Thanks for loving me enough to straighten me out."

They enjoyed wine and dinner, talking as if they were honeymooners. When words ran out, they stumbled like exhausted dancers to the davenport and fell asleep.

Their love was secure, but their future was not.

Chapter 21
Cedar Rapids

"Mr. Bremer. There's a gentleman in the lobby waiting to see you. He seems upset about something."

Anna Drahos was the receptionist for a bank of offices at Riverside Pack. She no longer carried the full bucket of water that secretaries are expected to tote for their bosses. She had done that for twenty-five years at one of the biggest law firms in the city. By the time she left, she knew as much about the practical side of the legal business as some of the lawyers there.

"How do you know he's upset?"

"Well, I just jumped to the conclusion that his constant whacking of the rolled-up newspaper over his knee wasn't a sign that all of his stock shares jumped in value this morning. And his low-level mumbling wasn't a good sign either."

Anna, not one to suffer fools, wrinkled her forehead and held the palms of her hands upward, a combined gesture that suggested his question was on the superfluous side.

Bremer laughed. He needed that sort of honest kick in the corporate caboose—for several reasons. He had told no one about the break-in at his hotel apartment. No one asked about the mark on his cheek or wrap on his finger. Nor did he mention anything about Mr. Ragno's parking lot shakedown. Only Glenda knew about his horrible investments and reckoning deadline with underworld elements.

"Did he give his name?" Bremer asked.

"It's a Joe Schuman. Here's his card. It says he is CEO of Eastern Iowa Pipe Installers. Also owns Schuman's Office Supplies. Seems that is an unlikely combination. Pipes and paper? I guess it must work."

"Thanks, Anna. Please show him in. I think I know him. If I remember correctly, he is one of our investors. One of those people who always has a question at the annual meeting."

"OK. I'll go get him." Her black ponytail, sprinkled with strands of gray, swung like a clock pendulum gone wild as she turned to leave. "At least he doesn't have a section of pipe in his hand."

Though Schuman launched, nurtured, and still managed two companies, he was not the kind of businessman who thought a necktie and fancy jacket defined who he was. He usually wore a blue chambray shirt and tan slacks. His shirt pocket bulged with two ballpoint pens, an agenda ledger, newspaper clippings, and a world map.

His wife frequently reviewed his pocket anthology for ink stains. Friends needled him about carrying the world on his shoulders and whether he was worried about getting lost. Joe took the ribbing in stride, and when someone raised a question about geography, he would whip out his mini atlas and show them. He knew the capitals of every state and most countries. The pocket's outside displayed the company logo, a big *S*, superimposed on a map of Iowa.

Joe was an avid newspaper reader and no stranger to the "Letters to the Editor" column. More than once, former presidents Johnson and Nixon had been his letter targets for the "mismanagement" of the Vietnam War. Other issues that stimulated his blood pressure were perceived arrogance, no matter its source, and Schuman's intense aversion to "folderol," his term for anything he regarded as fluff or without practical application.

He belonged to Elmcrest Country Club, where he had fun tweaking his Republican friends, but dogmatic Democrats suffered an equal dose of his censure. He proclaimed moderation to be the path to all success. The local newspaper, too, was called out when he believed a story or coverage lacked balance or suffered inaccuracy.

"Good morning, Peter," Schuman said, entering Bremer's office.

"Hello, Joe. Please take a seat. What's on your mind?"

"I don't have much time," Schuman said unceremoniously, "and with what I have to say I may need a head start dashing out of your office." He remained standing.

"As they say, Joe, it's a free country. And your shares in Riverside Pack are the only ticket you need to say your piece."

"You don't say," Schuman reacted with some surprise. He shifted his stubby frame closer to Bremer's desk. "And that coming from a man all tailored up and reading the *Wall Street Journal*." He pointed to the gray broadsheet opened to the Dow Jones averages.

"As you well know, this company was started on a shoelace, with money coming from family businesses and area farmers." Schuman got down to business. "I don't think J. Paul Getty and Howard Hughes are listed among the shareholders of Riverside Pack. These investment dollars were hard earned, and for many it was like starting a new church. They put their faith in you and Riverside."

"You are correct, Mr. Schuman. Although I wouldn't be averse to accepting investment money from Mr. Getty and Mr. Hughes."

"That's where you and I differ, Mr. Bremer. This is an Iowa company with Iowa investors and local loyalty. J. Paul Getty would have this little operation sold off and shut down as a tax loss quicker than snacks are consumed at a dieter's convention. But that's beside the point. This is the point."

Schuman opened the Cedar Rapids paper to its business pages, where he had circled a story in red. He spread the newspaper over Bremer's desk, trumping the *Wall Street Journal* and its stories on high interest rates, high inflation, and still unsettling unemployment. It also smothered Bremer's fresh cup of coffee.

The story Schuman had marked was about the upcoming annual meeting of Riverside Pack, this time slated for the Roosevelt Hotel's

Excelsior Room following a company-sponsored luncheon. According to the story, Bob Schieffer, the highly respected reporter for *CBS News*, would give the keynote address for the meeting. His talk would focus on the status of the economy.

"For two years we've managed just fine to hold our annual meetings right here in the auditorium," Schuman said. "It's not fancy, but neither is slaughtering beef. What in the hell are we doing renting the Excelsior Room downtown, where there is no parking and the stairwells have never seen a shred of cow shit?"

"Now, just take it easy, Joe."

"For God sakes, Peter, you'd think we are rolling in cash itching to be spent? I see the books. I see the margins. We have done well in a tough business. Truthfully, we have been more successful than I expected. And you and management, but mostly our workers, can take credit for it. But this"—he thrust his finger at the red-circled story—"is not the standard for frugal operations."

"Joe, this is just a small way to say thank you to our investors, to acknowledge that together we have made Riverside Pact viable. It is—"

"What it *is* is folderol," Schuman interrupted. "It's unnecessary expense. The Roosevelt Hotel doesn't hand out luncheons that feature cold-meat sandwiches and a bag of potato chips. And Bob Schieffer, who I believe is one of the more trustworthy reporters in TV news, isn't going to come out here free of charge because he likes how people in overalls are snapping their suspenders."

What Schuman didn't know—and perhaps saved him from a heart attack—was that Bremer had initially planned to take the annual meeting to Chicago's Palmer House Hotel. He wanted to show the capital of meatpacking that Riverside could butt heads with the big boys and blow smoke at Swift, Wilson, Armour, and Cudahy. Luckily he had listened to Glenda's father, who advised against it.

"Joe, are you sure you don't want to sit down?"

"Damn it, Peter, be serious. This is extravagant spending, and more than that, it spells attitude. It tells me that frosting and champagne are creeping into our management style, and that bothers me. Look what happened to *Collins Radio*, and it is a well-managed company. Unexpected things happen. Business forecasts sometimes run off the road."

Collins Radio of Cedar Rapids, considered the Cadillac of communications and avionics, was forced to sell to Rockwell International when business slumped and experiments in mainframe computers fizzled. Thousands were laid off, and the city's No. 1 employer struggled to regain its footing.

"Should we cancel plans to hold the annual meeting at the hotel?"

"No. That would send another kind of signal. I simply want to advise you and others that in the future, Riverside-produced hamburgers, potato chips, and soft drinks served buffet style right here in our own auditorium will serve our needs and stockholders just fine. And that's assuming we are still making a profit. And we don't need no damned open bar. You didn't think I knew about that, did you?"

Schuman gathered his newspaper.

"Thanks for listening. I apologize if I sound gruff and patronizing. My wife says I can be preachy, and by that she means ineffective." He looked directly at Bremer. "I really want Riverside to succeed, to stay afloat. Hell, I only purchased a couple thousand shares when this got started, ten thousand dollars' worth, so maybe I've said more than my allotment. Best of luck to you and this company."

"Joe, never apologize for suggestions made in good faith. Thanks for coming in. I have your card, and please know that I believe your thoughts are constructive. I may call you for advice as we move forward."

No one ever accused Peter Bremer of being antagonistic or unbecoming. His long suit was portraying civility and confidence. He had no misgivings about his dapper dress and impeccable grooming, convinced that appearance lent credibility. He did not insist that others in Riverside management, including its lone female vice president, wear formal business attire. He did rule out jeans.

Unlike his brother Bobby, Peter was naturally sociable. His mother was gentle and respectful. Her admonition, delivered with a wagging finger, was "Be considerate and polite; it never cost anyone anything." His father was more than the opposite, not just bad mannered but often sullen and mean.

Joe Schuman was the least of his problems, he thought. Front and center was Rusty Ragno, the Hook, the man who liked spiders. Somehow he had to come up with $20,000, a minimum payment to keep him alive through September. That message finally sunk in like the gash on his cheek. It was not something he could put off like the professional procrastinator he was.

One option, selling some of his Riverside stock, could trigger anxiety in the company. Perhaps he could borrow the money somewhere, using the stock as collateral. But Merchants Bank was not likely to warm up to any loan requests, and he had no savings at other banks. Howard Goodman, Glenda's father, would have no problem loaning him the money, even without security. Glenda would urge that too. However, for Bremer pride was quickly being subdued by necessity.

Bremer walked to the queue leading to the coffee vestibule, exchanged greetings with employees, and after a short wait thrust his cup beneath the spigot of the fifty-cup Hamilton Beach urn. One sip told him that Charlie Draznek was the architect of this brew. Charlie, the custodian, had a reputation—ranging from terrible to wonderful—for making extra strong coffee. His alleged preferred recipe called for coffee strong enough to hold a spoon upright.

"Mr. Bremer! Do you like my coffee?" Charlie shifted his mop bucket handle to the at-ease position. "Look. It's half gone and not even ten o'clock yet. Either the coffee is extra good, or people don't have enough to do." He laughed, and Peter did too.

"You look much better today," Charlie continued. "I was worried about that bruise and cut on your face. You looked like you went a couple rounds with Mohammad Ali." He laughed, but Bremer did not. "But I guess it wasn't that serious."

"I'm doing fine, Charlie," Bremer responded. "But thank you for your concern. See you around the building. And, Charlie, maybe back off a few spoons on the coffee."

"Naw, Mr. Bremer. That would spoil the recipe. *Dobry den pro vas.*"

It was Charlie's stock "have a good day."

Bremer was surprised others did not inquire about the bruise. Then again, maybe they thought it was none of their business, that it was the outcome of a domestic dispute. That thought produced a smile as he recalled last night with Glenda. Back at his office, he was confronted with an unopened letter he had automatically tossed on his desk upon arrival. Glenda, in the high-low mixture of the previous day's events, had forgotten to give him the letter until this morning. He had stuffed it in his coat pocket without a second look, but now the sender stood out like a neon billboard.

The letter was from the Internal Revenue Service.

Bremer needed another poke in his well-being like President Ford desired another question about Dick Nixon. Once opened, the contents temporarily redirected his attention from Rusty Ragno.

After the usual salutations and introductions, the terse document converged on the salient issue.

"We would like to ask you some questions concerning your tax returns for the years 1973 and 1974." What the hell are they talking about? Bremer mumbled to himself. He did a quick self-audit of those years and thought he knew the sources of his income, but he could not assure himself of total compliance. He had turned all that financial stuff over to a tax preparer and never thought about it again.

"Would you please come to the Internal Revenue Service offices to review this matter?" And the letter noted a proposed date and time and the location of the Cedar Rapids office. "If this time is not convenient, please give our office a call." The number was listed. "However, be advised of the need to give due diligence to the issues involved." The letter was signed by Don McKenster, the chief investigator for the Cedar Rapids IRS office.

Bremer was unaware of it, but the IRS was giving him the benefit of the doubt regarding his willingness to cooperate and answer questions. It was more common, especially if there was any threat of flight, for the IRS to hand over its findings to the US attorney. From there, evidence would be presented to a grand jury, and if an indictment was returned, the subject would be taken into custody by police or the federal marshal.

Even though he did not read courtesy or compassion into the IRS letter, Bremer was mindful that the agency had long arms. He decided to cast off procrastination and dialed the listed number immediately. He would meet with the IRS late next week. Then he contacted several financial advisers about raising the $20,000 payment for Ragno. One suggested approach left him $5,000 short, an amount he decided, after a deep chastening swallow, he would borrow from Glenda.

Clearly with the personal attack and break-in at the apartment, the time for delay had passed. He called Glenda, and she was delighted he had involved her in keeping the mob wolves at bay for another month.

Bremer, always one to bet on the odds, figured he had at least a week to come up with the money. Still, as August moved toward September, the noose around Bremer's neck slipped tighter.

Chapter 22
1952, Kansas State Penitentiary

In two months at the Lansing, Kans., lockup, Bobby Bremer's chameleon nature had thrust him from a tough-guy state prison rookie who savored conflict into a trouble-free inmate who greeted guards with respect. That, and the use of the library, would have shocked and pleased his mother.

The confrontation with Hogg Mulder was a bad memory. His discontent on the outside and seemingly satisfied posture on the inside would have given a college psychiatry major enough to ponder for a thesis.

He even confided to a prison counselor that he was wrong and sorry for punching a police officer when he was arrested for bank robbery. He and an accomplice stole a car in Little Rock and then drove 280 miles to the small southeastern Kansas town of Baxter Springs. Spurred by alcohol and a lack of common sense, they robbed the bank. Bremer feigned the use of a gun, and the absence of a real firearm was successfully argued by his court-appointed lawyer as a reason for leniency. He received a five-year sentence.

It was one more bump in the road for a young man who seemed to detest a smoother path. The time he served at the juvenile farm in high school carried no lessons.

Bremer, twenty-two and in the prime of his life, had the physical and mental qualifications for the draft and potential service in the Korean War, but the military doesn't give a second look at young men in trouble with the law. His older brother, Peter, had also escaped being called into service by route of college deferment. He was a senior majoring in business at Arkansas State.

Not serving in the military did not keep Bobby Bremer awake at night. His alcoholic father had not been in the service, although his grandfather, Orval Price, was in the Marine Corps and active in the American Legion. None of that rubbed off on Bobby. He was not opposed to military service but had no interest in it. Prison made the issue moot.

"Bobby," a slightly built young man yelled down the corridor of cell block 15. He was dressed in a short-sleeved blue-and-white checkered shirt buttoned at the neck. His blondish-brown hair was leveled off into a flat top. It seemed to Bremer that either the fellow's head was too small or his ears were too big. They protruded like side-view mirrors on a Ford delivery van. His cleanly shaved face, neat appearance, and kindly manner gave him the look of a librarian, which he was.

Clearly he was not one of the prison's confined guests. Closer examination would also suggest he was a nervous novice on the penitentiary staff. Indeed, Felix Forsythe was one year out of the library science program at Emporia State. While short on confidence, he knew book categories and filing mechanics the way Einstein comprehended math formulas.

Forsythe and Bremer had a growing friendship. Bremer's self-esteem was boosted by Forsythe's attention. Conversely, Forsythe gained sureness in that he coached an unlikely student to gain an appreciation for poetry. The off-setting respect was sweetened when Forsythe brought cinnamon rolls to their makeshift classroom.

"Those books on poetry you wanted have come in," Forsythe sing-songed in his tenor voice as he noticed Bremer heading for noon dinner. "They're the ones on writing structure and selected works of Walt Whitman. You may pick them up any time." He worked mostly alone in the prison library, which had its advantages but also an uneasy side if one considers its environment of lawbreakers, some of whom have violent records. Guards would sometimes visit the library to chat, and the Protestant chaplain occasionally helped with restacking.

"That was fast—all the way from Leavenworth in a week's time? Thanks, Felix, for getting those," Bremer said. "I really appreciate your runnin' down Whitman's *Leaves of Grass.* I've heard a lot about him and been wantin' to read the entire works for some time."

Forsythe worked with a Leavenworth librarian to create their own book exchange program.

"I guess Leavenworth ain't that far, perhaps figuratively as well as distance," Bremer said.

The Kansas State Penitentiary is a mere six miles south of its big-sibling slammer, the federal prison at Leavenworth. Leavenworth is nationally known as a place with bad actors. It had its birth as a military post and prison. In 1895, it was turned over to the Federal Bureau of Prisons. A new penitentiary opened eleven years later. As construction proceeded on the new complex, it looked more like a museum than a prison.

Leavenworth, the nation's largest maximum-security federal prison, quickly and convincingly gained the reputation as being escape proof. It may have looked like an art gallery, but its thick walls, barbed fences, and guard stations created a fortress-like picture. Except for the matter of Frank Grigware and friends. Grigware and five others in 1910 smashed the prison gates with a hijacked yard locomotive. They literally drove a train through the front door.

While the others were quickly recaptured, Grigware escaped to Canada. In 1916, in a convoluted unfolding of history, he became the mayor of Spirit River, Alberta. The Royal Canadian Mounted Police and the FBI finally caught up with Grigware in 1933. In another twist of life, serious doubts about his original conviction led the US to drop its extradition request in 1934. Grigware never returned to the US.

"Oh—Bobby, I don't know your poetry preferences, but you might also consider the works of Carl Sandburg. He won the Pulitzer Prize last year for his collection of poems, and in 1940 he won a Pulitzer for his biography of Abraham Lincoln. He has more awards than Truman has quips. He's a Midwesterner, too, born in Galesburg, Ill., and I believe when he was a man our age he worked as a farm laborer in Kansas."

"Sounds like a downright ordinary guy," Bremer replied. "Y'all perhaps would save me some of his writin'? Ah'd appreciate it. And speakin' of President Truman, ah was as surprised as a June bug on a lizard's tongue when I heard he wasn't gonna run for reelection. Too bad. I like ole Harry. Tells it like it is, or at least like it oughta be. I guess Ike will do OK."

"Yeah, guess so, Bobby. Course prisoners can't vote. You know that."

"I know it. See ya 'round, Mr. Librarian."

He picked up the books after a lunch of cold beans and rice with hamburger chunks and bread. Water was the *boisson du jour*.

Bremer quickly learned the geographical dimensions of the Lansing prison. His section was routinely referred to as the Hill. The unit perched on the facility's high point and gave inmates a good view of the surrounding area. "How long you been on the Hill?" became part of conversations. The prison was built by inmate labor in the 1860s. And part of any inmate's introduction to Lansing was vital demographics. The Dalton gang and a cohort of Machine Gun Kelly were once among its notorious occupants.

After his initial confrontation with Mulder, who was serving a fifty-year sentence for the rape and near-death beating of a teenager, Bremer avoided the scumbag like a moldy sardine sandwich. That was made easier when prison officials moved Mulder to the other end of the slammer. No one in cell block 15 protested Mulder's exile. And while Bobby had backed Mulder into a corner of inmate ignominy during that dubious welcome confrontation, he did not assume any jailbird royalty. But dehorning Mulder bought him peace among the inmate community.

He was also collecting skills in the prison building shop. Carpentry was the one class he never skipped while in high school. The shop, which was responsible for most routine maintenance around the prison, also had wide-ranging metal works that included the massive task of providing Kansas drivers with vehicle license plates.

By October, cooler weather had moved down from the Nebraska, Iowa, and Dakota tundra. The chill in the air reminded him that he had not written his mother since July. She faithfully wrote most weeks. A ripple of guilt flickered through his body. Just as quickly as he began his letter to her, the feeling melted. He reread her last letter:

My Dear Bobby,

The weather has been rainy in Little Rock. As my father says, you can almost smell winter in the air. Dropped down into the 40s the other night. I suppose it's colder in Lansing. Madeline and I take turns driving to the Timex plant. This week is her turn. She hasn't changed much. Talks more than a cricket on a hot summer night.

Her husband, Ted, is doin' fine, no lingerin' problems due to his war injuries. He got a job in dispatch with the Little Rock Police Department.

Hattie is doing fine, she tells me. Wouldn't surprise me if she marries that Minnesota fella. Peter is Peter, engrossed in his business books. He will graduate next May and hopes to make lots of money, doing what I don't know. Exciting news here is that we're finally gonna get a TV station in Little Rock. They say. Believe it when I see Howdy Doody's nose.

It's lonely without my children. It's difficult to explain, especially I think to a boy, but maybe that's wrong thinkin'. For one thing, you are no longer a boy. You're a man.

I trust this finds you well, no sore throat, warm enough, and that the food is edible. Maybe they'll serve roast beef and collard greens occasionally. Ha! Your grandparents are doin' fine. Your grandpa is still arguin' with Adora Mae over politics. And at church, too. Those two may believe in God, but they must also believe that politics and religion mix.

Are you makin' any friends? My heart aches when I think that you are all by yourself, without family. Try to get along with others, Bobby. I know that you sometimes become impatient, but remember the golden rule. What are you workin' on? How do you pass the time? Do they have church services there?

Well, it's nearly 9:30, and I want to tune into Fibber McGee and Molly. He makes me laugh, especially with that junky closet. I guess it's only natural I'd feel sorry for Molly, puttin' up with his shenanigans. Haven't heard from you in a while. Always remember, Bobby, I love you and think of you. Please write.   Mom

Bremer obliged. He wrote his mother about his newfound interest in poetry and new friend at the prison library. He knew she would be pleased about both. He also told of his work in the carpentry department. In none of his rare letters had he mentioned a word about the inaugural fight with Mulder.

"*Mom,*" he wrote, "*I think poetry, like a song, takes words and gives them new shades of color, deeper meaning.*" He told her what he was reading.

Molly Bremer's calloused hands had never opened a book of poetry, but she was pleased that Bobby had found a new pursuit.

Perhaps, she thought, it was also a sign that he was mellowing, that whatever wounds were festering inside of him were beginning to heal.

Sure, Mom. We get the best food here. As everyone says, it's like the country club, as if I know what they serve at the country club. Really, it's not bad. Not a lot of roast beef and collard greens, but it's pretty good when you consider they have to feed nearly 1,500 prisoners every day. Don't know if the guards eat here, but that would be another 120. They have a farm here, and some of the inmates work there, but I'm not interested. I haven't been out there, but others say the farm produces all the pork and milk used in the prison. Lot of vegetables, too.

I helped on some construction projects, including building of a new soap factory. They make all kinds of soap, from barber's lather to laundry varieties. It's amazin'. We supply soap for state institutions all over Kansas. I guess nobody around here should go dirty and stinky. I know a few, and not just inmates, who are badly in need of something to improve their body smell."

Since he avoided religious services at the prison, he disregarded her question about church. The Protestant and Catholic chaplains held Sunday services at Lansing and at the Kansas Industrial Farm for Women.

I'm happy about the cooler weather, although the cell block area is kinda damp. Fellas complain of cockroaches. One guy keeps talkin' about his pet cockroach. Says he named it Harry S after the president. Guess he must be Republican. But this beats the 100-degree heat. Sometimes during hot spells, it was hard to get to sleep. No breezes like at home.

Thanks for writing, Mom. Lots of guys never hear from their family, so I appreciate your letters. I'll try to write more often.
Bobby.

Surprisingly Bremer was one of only four convicted bank robbers at the Lansing prison. Grand larceny and burglary made up nearly a third of the inmate population, with just over a hundred in for forgery. Seventeen prisoners were convicted of murder. Nine were lifers and two were hanged for murder in 1952. Nearly 400 were first-time offenders. Bremer was among those with two convictions in adult court.

He wrote to his mother more frequently in subsequent months though not weekly. Peter and Hattie would telephone Molly but never wrote letters. Both were home that Christmas, but there was no indication they planned to visit Bobby. Molly suggested a trip to Kansas, but neither had the time. It took nearly ten hours to drive to the penitentiary.

After arrangements with prison officials, Molly and her parents, Aliza and Orval Price, drove to Lansing on the second Saturday following New Years. Visitation was allowed only on weekends. They left at 5:30 a.m. and arrived at the visitor's center about 3:45 p.m. The prison's stark gray outline against the sullen winter sky could not suffocate Molly's excitement for seeing her son. The high barbed wire failed to puncture her anticipation.

It was another forty-five minutes after check-in procedures before they saw Bobby. Molly and her parents were escorted down a long corridor by a muscular, bald-headed guard wearing a sweat-stained shirt that broadcast body odor. He motioned them through a barred gate and into a small room. The ceiling, floor, and walls were painted alike, a boring tan. The only variation was where whitewash covered up words and drawings deemed inappropriate for outsiders.

Bobby was sitting at what looked like an ordinary picnic bench. There was no other furniture. The guard relocked the gate and left without a word—except for the statement made by his stained shirt.

Molly kissed the back of Bobby's neck and then sat next to him. His grandparents wiggled in on the other side.

"Hello, Mom," Bobby said. "It's good to see you."

Molly's loving smile cut through his crusty character. A shiver, a strange sensation to him, worked its way down his system. She patted him on the cheek.

"Oh, Bobby. I've waited for this moment so long, to see you and touch you and just be with you. I think of you every night. I pray for you every night."

She peered deep into his eyes, a mom look that, in a few seconds, incorporates a child's lifetime, from slippery newborn to clumsy adolescent and independent adult. Bobby looked down, unable to return such profound love.

"And it's good to see you too, Grandma and Grandpa. Thanks for coming."

It was a tearful reunion for Molly. She leaned over and held him tightly without saying a word. It was as if she was drawing him back into her womb, safe from the evils of the world, safe from his own bad decisions. Finally she broke her grip.

"Bobby. Bobby," she said softly.

Again she looked into his eyes. Her own were clouded with a misty mixture of joy and sadness—joy in having her third born next to her, sadness because of their surroundings. *How do I fit into the reasons he is here?* she thought. *What could I have done to alter his situation? How could I have kept my Bobby from getting into trouble, from rebelling against his surroundings?*

"Bobby. I tried my best. I tried to love all of you the same."

"Mom," he said in a whisper.

"No, please, Bobby. I have to say this."

She took his hands in hers and looked at them, thinking of the time when his entire little body fit into her caring hands. Then she revisited his eyes.

"Bobby, a mother's heart has room for all of her children." She paused, searching for a positive, responsive light in his face. "And the rooms are all the same. There isn't more love in one room than another. But sometimes a room needs special attention, and while the heart is everywhere at once, the body and mind cannot be. When Peter was gone, my mind was in his room, and I had so little time for you and Hattie." She began to cry. "I'm sorry."

"Mom. It's not your fault. It's OK. I'm here because of what I did, not what you did. Or didn't do. Please don't cry."

They sat in silence.

"Mom," he said, glancing above her eyes. "I like your hat."

She squeezed his hand harder. It was a navy pillbox, certainly nothing pretentious. It was the first time ever that he commented on her apparel.

He looked at the clock. They had little time since visitor hours ended at 5:00. He stood and placed his hands on her shoulders. They were big hands, the same hands that tossed the oatmeal dish defiantly on the floor as a two-year-old. Now they were hands bound by his seeming inability to manage the realities of life.

"Are you doing OK, son? Are you feeling OK?"

"Mom, I'm getting by. A couple of years and I'll be up for parole. As for feelings? This place doesn't allow much for feelings." There was an uneasy silence. "I think we have to go now, Mom. Visiting is over in a couple minutes."

"We'll be back in the morning," his grandfather said. "We can talk more then. You can catch up on the news back home. I'll fill you in on all the wild ideas of Adora Mae," Orval said. "That woman, I swear, is a Communist. I wish she would move to Moscow."

"Orval, just take it easy," Aliza advised. "Take one of your Adora pills before we go."

Aliza, like many wives, knew exactly how to modify her husband's blood pressure. Bobby laughed. They all welcomed relief from the pressures of prison's unequivocal confinement.

On Sunday they attended church services with Bobby before returning home. The prison chapel was nearly full, a surprise to Bremer and Molly. *There is comfort and hope here*, she thought. She was even more consoled after the clergyman's sermon.

"And so I would like to conclude," the minister said, "with a word of advice that St. Paul had for the people of Corinth. There was discord and a lack of hope in Corinth, just as there is today, and Paul tried to reassure the people that better things will come.

He said, 'So we do not lose heart. Though our outer self is wasting away, our inner self is being renewed day by day. For this light momentary affliction is preparing for us an eternal weight of glory beyond all comparison, as we look not to the things that are seen but to the things that are unseen. For the things that are seen are transient, but the things that are unseen are eternal.' Have faith, friends. Believe in the unseen."

Molly's family walked back to the visitor's center. The clanking of the various steel doors and gates spoke in no uncertain terms. Molly mustered her courage, determined not to leave a sobbing image. She forced a smile.

"I know you are on the right track, son." She resisted drawing out the goodbye. "I love you. Be sure to write."

"I think you will be fine," Orval Price told Bobby. He slapped his hand on Bobby's shoulder in reassurance. Hugging another man, even if a grandson, was not part of Orval's makeup. "If hope can survive here, then I think there is also hope for Adora Mae Marston," he said in parting.

Bobby Bremer had a newly found understanding of the depth of his mother's love. It was far beyond words. Love projected from her eyes and was transmitted by her touch. The mere act of visiting him in prison was a statement that needed no elaboration. Even his grandfather's words nourished his spirit.

He was also pleased to learn that the chaplain was one of the volunteers at the library. *Hope* was more than just an expression.

Chapter 23
1956, Goshen, Ark.

"Slow down, damn it," Bobby Bremer instructed. "You drive like Marilyn Monroe is puttin' on a swimsuit show in two minutes over at the beach."

Bremer's disposition was as curdled as two-week-old milk left standing in the sun. Since his parole from the Kansas State Penitentiary at Lansing two months ago, his temperament had regressed to the surly status of pre-prison days. He returned to his short-fuse demeaner, an attitude that suggested he would rather be on another planet.

"What's with you?" Jimmy Jones replied. His words mingled with the blue haze output of his Chesterfield cigarette. "All week you've been actin' like you have a burr in your underwear. Ya keep like that and you'll puke in disgust over your own sour self."

Jones, twenty-five, was a year younger than Bremer. He had worked for Mountain Landscaping in Goshen, Ark., ever since graduating from high school. He enjoyed the job, mostly because it allowed him to breathe the fresh air of the Ozark Mountains in northwest Arkansas. And it gave him regular access to white bass fishing at the well-known Twin Bridges.

He was shorter than Bremer, but the outdoor labor had filled out his muscular framework, which gave support to an attitude that surpassed his stature. He was not one to side-step a fight, not to prove something but because of a slightly warped idea of righteousness.

Goshen had two main industries, tourism and catering to the well-off administrators and coaches from the University of Arkansas. Many of the educators lived in Goshen, which is a mere twelve miles from Fayetteville, home of the Razorbacks. The town was once known as College Grove, a nod to its proximity to the university and its snug location among the oaks, hickories, and pines of the Boston Mountains. The Boston range is part of the Ozarks.

The biggest single employer was the sawmill, where soft- and hardwoods were hewn into various uses—from pallets to cabinetry. Jones lived in an old trailer just outside town, a happy retreat from Fayetteville, his birthplace and one of the state's largest cities. While the Fayetteville area was growing slightly, most of Arkansas was losing population.

"Watch for the Y in the road and then Horton Street," Bremer directed as they drove up a dirt road off the Blue Springs Highway. "That's where we pick up this Dobbs guy. He's probably a little shit who knows less about the workin' end of an axe than Elizabeth Taylor. And why do we have to be his mama, teachin' and guidin' like this was the Boy Scouts?"

It was easy enough to get lost in the backwater of the Ozarks. Roads twisted like a gossip's tongue at a chinwag convention. Drivers were hemmed in by tall pines that admitted only filtered light. Dust from the red baked soil, riled by passing vehicles, caked vegetation. Jones was careful to slow for the narrow concrete bridges, which spanned snaking streams.

"I swear, ya gonna get us killed," Bremer repeated his critique of Jones's driving. "Are you sure this doesn't lead to the end of the world?"

"For starters," Jones retorted, "I know a damn sight more about the roads in these parts than Little Rock hot shots like you. Secondly, this Dobbs 'little shit,' as you put it, is six-six and built like a fuckin' Ozark brick shithouse. He's a little slow in thinkin', so we need to help him out. We're pickin' him up because the boss asked us to. Ya also might do well to remember that he's the boss's nephew."

There was a moment's pause in this upland dressing down.

"Lastly, I understand you've taken a liken' to poetry, which isn't exactly the prescribed background for learnin' how to wield an axe."

"Don't piss me off!" Bremer gave him a lightning look.

"Piss you off? Hell, you've been in that goddamn sulky pond since we left the office this morning. If ya ask me, your outlook today seems to be as wicked as skunk piss. Can't figure what's botherin' y'all."

"Well, nobody asked ya to figure anything."

Bremer spent a week with his mother in Little Rock before reporting to work with the landscaping company in Goshen. Having a job was part of the parole arrangement. Though he enjoyed his visit home, he chose not to live in Little Rock. One of his juvenile parole officers found the job in Goshen.

He was unsettled. Leaving the controlled environment of the Lansing penitentiary produced conflicting emotions. On the one hand, freedom to move around without major boundaries like barbed wire fences and high walls was enlivening. Yet he missed the ordered life of prison, especially the quiet of the prison library, a place where he could immerse himself in his newly discovered passion—poetry.

Freedom, of course, also meant he was responsible for feeding his face, and Bremer liked to eat. There were other expenses. He rented a room at a boarding house on the outskirts of town for $1.50 a day, and last week he purchased a 1946 Chevy pickup, with minor rust along the front fenders, for $250. His mother co-signed the loan. He was determined to be independent. Gas was $0.22 a gallon. He was being paid one dollar per hour, the minimum wage.

Working meant he had less time to peruse and explore various kinds of poetic formulae. He was pleased that the Goshen town library was open until 8:00 p.m., even though its collection was limited. Slowly he advanced his understanding of poetry. At first, his concept of poetry was limited to rhyming. Eventually he became fascinated by metrical patterns, imagery, and the numerous other devices employed by poets.

Bremer, while at the prison, also became attracted to articles and essays about frontier freedom, a concept of unrestricted life and autonomy unencumbered by government rules. He became absorbed by agrarian populist groups and sovereignty proponents who believed that state and federal officials were antirural and aloof to the plights and rights of struggling people.

He was pulled to stories in newspapers and magazines that told of bankers foreclosing on small businesses and farmers—mostly in isolated hinterlands. He knew how his mother had labored to pay bills. That was a natural incubation for brooding notions of banking and financial injustice. And all the while the government and its agents were abetting the bankers.

Bremer, the essence of virility, quickly sensed while in prison that poetry was not of major interest among inmates. It was best, he determined, to tell inquiring inmates that his library focus was on Zane Grey and western adventure or tales of mob violence. And that was not entirely a lie. He enjoyed *The Riders of the Purple Sage,* but less than the works of Robert Frost. He was amused by Frost's ponderings of how he "sweated though the fog." Though Frost was describing the task of writing, Bremer felt that the line summed up his life.

"There's Dobbs standing up ahead," Jones said. "God, he's big. Stick a few leaves in his goddamn overall pockets and he'd look like a ten-year-old oak tree."

"You sure swear a lot," Bremer said. "Is that a lack of vocabulary or didn't your Mom teach you any better?"

"Well, Mr. Poetry. I suspects it is a little of both. My Mama had her hands full just feedin' us since my goddamn Paw was nowheres around. She didn't have much time for schoolin' us. Truth is, I think she kinda liked my colorful language. She suggested I enlist in the navy. No matter. How I talk is no skin off your ass."

He slowed the Mountain Landscaping dump truck and pulled up next to Dobbs.

"Hop in the back," he yelled at Dobbs. "It's too tight for the three of us in the cab, and we don't have that far to go."

Dobbs dutifully jumped into the truck box, using the dual wheels as a ladder. The three were headed for a private residence where the owner wanted some brush removed from his back yard. It would take most of the day to clear out a patch of multiflora rose, a thorny bush planted some years ago in place of fencing. Imported from Japan, its popularity as a hedgerow had withered to scorn. Now plant specialists were labeling it a "fast-spreading invasive perennial" that should be removed. Jones turned down a rutted gravel lane that led behind a small barn and the hellish target.

"This is it, the garden of hell," Jones announced as he braked to a stop. He fired up another Chesterfield. "Out behind this barn is a row of multiflora rose, a bush that's meaner than the devil himself." They all jumped out of the truck, grabbing large cutters, shovels, and axes. "I think it would be better if we just bulldozed it." He pointed and scowled at the fiendish enemy. "We're taking the long and hard road against this stuff."

Jones knew that the wiry scrub, whose thorns flaunted a sharp, curved tip, could seemingly reach out like a rattle snake seeking flesh. Once before, he had submitted his innocent body to the covert mugger only to finish the day looking like he had raced through a grove of razorblades. This time he wore leather gloves that extended halfway up his arm. He handed similar protection to Bremer and Dobbs.

"Be careful with this crap," he warned. "It hides behind its rosy name like a whore at the county fair, but there's nothin' beautiful about it. Cut it off branch by branch, piece by piece, and don't try to knock it down with your feet. If you go wadin' into this shit, it will crawl up your pantleg and grab your nuts like a starvin' squirrel. I'm tellin' you, fellas, it makes blackberry vines look like balm handed out by the Watkins man." He paused briefly in his shrubbery bombast. "The guy who planted it should have to sleep in a bed of it."

Dobbs may have had mental challenges, but his common sense trusted Jones's advice. He handled the thorny invader like a surgeon removing a tumor. He did not need a job, but his wealthy uncle believed work would have both social and self-worth benefits. More than that, the uncle saw the strapping twenty-two-year-old as a human being as worthy of life and happiness as anyone else.

The uncle never formally adopted Dobbs but assumed responsibility when the boy was three. He was unmarried, and Dobbs was like the son he never had. Dobbs's mother, spoiled by the family's fortunes, chased after whiskey and men. She had not seen her handicapped son in ten years. Dobbs's father was an even a worse scoundrel. He left right after conception.

"Ouch!" Bremer yowled. "You weren't kiddin' when you said this pack of thorns has a mind of its own." He retreated from a chopped vine that seemed to twist back at him in revenge. Blood trickled down his arm, just above the elbow. "It's like a prison guard who reaches out with his baton and raps you in the back of your legs for no reason. Jones, I should've heeded your advice."

"Yeah, it's nasty stuff, Bremer. And after you cut it off, toss it on the truck. The owner wants to pile it and burn it. Says it's only way to drive a stake through the heart of this filthy bush." Jones tried to bite his tongue, but the scalawag in him prevailed. "Let's see, Bremer. You, the poet of Little Rock, are bleedin' while Dobbs, the handicapped guy, is unscathed, nary the worse for wear. Somehow there's a message in all that."

Jones was unable to restrain laughing at his cleverness. When he looked at Bremer, he detected the slimmest suggestion of a smile.

Bremer scolded himself for his natural inclination to scorn advice or direction. It had been at the root of his problems for years, and he did not know why. He tried to discuss the matter with his mother after his release from prison, but pride filtered and twisted his intent, ultimately defeating it. Confronting his obstinate tendencies was a challenge.

"Ma," he had said meekly at breakfast one day, eyes cast toward the floor. "Why didn't Dad like me?" His voice sounded wounded, strangely higher pitched than usual.

"He never talked to me much, except to yell at me, give me hell. Never invited me to come down to the gas station and help like he did Peter. I was just an obstacle in his path, someone to slap around. Before he started drinkin' bad, he showered love on Hattie and was nice to Peter too. But not once did he say a kind thing to me. It was like he didn't want me."

Molly was unprepared to answer though not totally surprised at what she heard. She had always feared that Bobby nursed feelings of being left out. When Peter was gone during that horrible summer of 1942, taken by his father on that fake adventure to the Gulf Coast, she had all but ignored Hattie and Bobby in her depressed state. Hattie understood, but Molly feared Bobby saw it as one more example of finishing last.

"Bobby"—she paused, looking for words—"I am sorry if you've ever felt alone when growing up." She looked across the table, but his unreceptive eyes concentrated on the gray linoleum with splotches of yellow flowers. "Bobby, please look at me." She waited.

"Please?" Her doleful request slowly pulled his head upward, though his eyes continued to avoid full engagement.

Weeks later, leaning on his shovel and staring at the thorns of a bush he had never heard of, his mother's soft pleas echoed in his mind. Was he as gnarly and unbending as a rogue bush? Why was it necessary for his own mother, for God's sake, to virtually get on bended knees to seek his complete attention? He wished he had not made her wait in misty compassion.

When his eyes had finally met hers, he saw the bubble of a tear tracing down her cheek.

"I cannot speak for your father," she had said. "He was an honorable and even a lovin' man when we were first married, but I guess life and liquor turned him sour, made him someone else. I can't explain that. I don't know how a human being tosses off love and responsibility and just walks out the door. I don't know why he treated you differently."

She paused and took a deep breath.

"I can only tell you, Bobby, and I mean it sincerely, that I loved you—and still do—the same as Hattie and Peter. Parents don't play favorites with their children, Bobby."

She had tried to explain that when she visited him in prison.

"It may seem sometimes that one child is getting special attention, but I can assure you that all evens out. And one other thing. Just because you are an adult doesn't mean I don't care about your life, worry about your well-being, and love you with all my heart."

As he replayed her words, Bremer vowed again to confront his contrary nature, to bend his attitude about life, for her sake if not his own. Somehow he had to wipe misfortune from his face, toss off whatever it was that colored his temperament. He loathed the thought of being a copy of his father.

"Hey, Bremer. You OK? Daydreamin' ain't no way to attack multiflora rose. It'll rise up, dig into your flesh, and turn into a nightmare when you're not lookin'."

The trio was almost finished with the bramble business. Jones sensed a more relaxed Bremer. Not that he converted to a Sunday school teacher, but at least he had shelved Mr. Malcontent for the moment.

"We'll dump these blood suckers over in that ravine, douse them with gas, and send them to horticulture hell," Jones said, outlining the final steps.

"Hey, Jones," Bremer shouted with a proposal.

He looked around and then amended his idea.

"You too, Dobbs. When we're done here, let's stop at Sammy's Roadside Still for a cold one."

Chapter 24
September 1975, Cedar Rapids

"Mr. Bremer," his secretary buzzed. "Line four. It's your wife. You asked me to call her."

Bad news seems to beget bad news, and the run of tribulations for Peter Bremer was piling up like a blizzard of banana peels on a frozen pond. He was skating on thin ice and groping for a way to keep his balance.

"Glenda. Hi. This is Peter."

"Hello, darling," she cooed. "How is your morning going?"

"About as good as President Ford's," Bremer lamented. "Both the unemployment rate and inflation are over 9 percent, and then this morning—did you hear—some nutso named Squeaky Fromme tried to shoot him, out in California."

"How awful," Glenda replied. "Is the president OK?"

"Yeah. He's fine. Her gun clip had four rounds, but none were in the chamber. That's cutting it close." Bremer could have been thinking of himself.

"Honey, those ideas from financial advisors to raise money fell through. We're back to square one. I don't know what to do. Somehow I need to come up with $20,000 in a few days."

"Well," Glenda said as though she had been pondering the idea for months, "if you won't let my father help, and if you won't sell any Riverside stock, what's the possibility of asking a licensed stockbroker for a loan against your shares? Don't they do that, darling?"

There was silence like the kind when ideas bounce around in your head and look to develop roots.

"Peter," she said after nearly a half minute. "Are you there? Peter?"

"Yes. I'm here."

He was embarrassed that he, the one with the finance degree, failed to think of such a solution. He loosened his tie.

"I knew there was a reason I married you! Glenda, my Magic. You're the greatest. I'll check it out immediately."

Her suggestion simultaneously lit another light bulb in his head. *That*, he said to himself, *may be one of the reasons the IRS is hounding me.*

Some years before, Bremer had been so successful during his time with Wide Plains Insurance, selling policies to Cedar Rapids area farmers and businessmen, that some of his clients came to him with an idea. Would he organize an effort, they proposed, to raise capital and breathe new life into the defunct packing operation in Chelsea, Iowa? Farmers were desperate to open a new market for their beef.

Likewise, a group of merchants and other Midwest business leaders, savvy to the notion that success on the farm meant success in the city, had been impressed—if not mesmerized—by Bremer's suave manner and sophisticated sales technique. If this monumental undertaking had any chance to succeed, Peter Bremer would be the man who could pull it off.

Selling stock was not new territory for Bremer. At one point, before his stint with Wide Plains, he had passed the exam in Missouri and obtained his broker license. However, after a short time with a St. Louis trader, he followed other business opportunities. It was not that difficult to become licensed in Iowa. Bremer accepted their challenge. Attorneys filed the necessary paperwork, and he was off on a new dance with financial escapades.

As part of the process, he formed a new company, Rapids Securities, which he envisioned would become as recognized as an Angus steer throughout cattle country. It was exactly the sort of venture, the dash off into unknown territory during a bad economic storm, that business college students daydream about.

Bremer was churning with excitement and anticipation. His business risk juices were primed like those in a fine steak.

Would he, could he, they had asked, sell one million shares of Riverside stock at five dollars a share?

That was like dangling a red flag in front of the dapperly dressed Peter Bremer. The boyhood gas station salesman in Little Rock with high-octane ambition put his foot to the pedal.

It was an amazing ride. In a less than three months, he had oversubscribed the goal by nearly twenty-five thousand shares. Bremer had raised more than $5.1 million, and Riverside Pack was back on the track to slaughtering beef. Capital in hand, he closed Rapids Securities.

It was as if he had started out in a rusted Nissan Datsun and raced over the finish line in a sparkling Ferrari, a half lap ahead of Al Unser Sr.

That was spring of 1971. By late fall, enough Riverside plant improvements had been made to allow startup hiring to begin. The hope was to have a line running before the end of the year. Joy abounded in all corners.

Bremer was ecstatic. He had been given a $25,000 payment up front and another $15,000 for organizational expenses. His newly formed securities company was paid three cents commission per share, which put $30,000-plus in his pocket, and the jubilant Riverside board voted a bonus to Bremer of 3,000 shares in Riverside stock. Earlier he had sold himself four thousand shares, using borrowed money and part of the $15,000 organizational advance to pay for it.

With investors seemingly in a rainbow euphoria, the sky was the limit for the ambitious and unchecked Bremer.

In the fall of 1971, he reaped further financial fallout from his successful relaunching of Riverside Pack. The board of directors elected Bremer president of the company, with annual compensation that included another thousand shares of stock. By 1975, his holdings stood at an even nine thousand shares. Share price had moved little. Directors, reluctantly, deferred dividends again, opting instead to put available cash into plant improvements and reserves.

Now, as Bremer meditated on his predicaments, it added up to good news and bad news. Raising cash by borrowing against his Riverside stock was extremely good potential news that would allow him to temporarily get the mob off his back. At the same time, his tax problems were likely entangled in the fees and commissions associated with stock transactions from several years ago.

Adding to that monetary muddle were losses he had declared on past tax returns dealing with investments in Middle East oil ventures. Bremer's avarice and risk appetite caused him to bite into a drilling scam that produced little more than embarrassment and lawsuits. It was not the only dead horse he had bet on. He had risked cash, made promissory notes, and leveraged stock to buy into other sink-hole deals. To clear up all the webs of his weaving would tax a Harvard lawyer with a Wharton business degree.

Then, of course, was the bailout money he had surreptitiously and irrationally obtained from a mob-controlled Chicago lending agency. That was the fire that needed immediate attention.

Bremer called his Cedar Rapids lawyer. Which licensed securities firm, he wanted to know, had the best arrangement for borrowing money against his stock value? By midafternoon, he had an answer. A firm dealing in over-the-counter equities would loan 50 percent of the stock value, or in Bremer's case, about $22,500. It was like manna from heaven.

He retained ownership of the stock, but if its value fell below a certain margin that pushed the loan amount, the agency could issue a call order. He would then have to pay up in cash or stock. Bremer had no interest in all the ifs, what might happen down the road with the deal. He wanted the loan money. It was his ticket to safe breathing for another month.

"Let's go to the Lighthouse for its famous rack of ribs," he telephoned Glenda in a celebratory mood. "I received the loan, just as you suggested. We need to toast your ingenuity, your business acumen. Are you sure you didn't major in finance? Oh, Glenda," he sing-songed. "This is wonderful."

He danced around his desk as if Rusty "The Hook" Ragno had been hit by a truck loaded with frozen beef slabs. Bremer lived for the minute, and he had just drawn a get-out-of-jail card—reprieve from the Outfit. As soon as the loan on Riverside shares could be processed, he would wire $20,000 to Adrian Koffmann, Ragno's boss.

"Mr. Bremer." His secretary leaned her head around the open door. She had heard his chanting and shouting. "Are you OK?"

"Excuse me, Glenda." He cupped his hand over the phone mouthpiece. "Yes, I'm fine." He looked at his secretary. "More than fine." He waved her in dismissal. "Glenda. I'm back. Maybe I should hire you as VP of finance." He gushed in delight. "I think it's a sure thing. You couldn't fail."

He had images of Glenda sashaying into a board meeting, waving sheaves of paper carrying spectacular news of profits.

"Would you like that, Glenda? And, as a side benefit, you would get to sleep every night with the president of Riverside Pack. Whaddia think? A deal?"

"Oh, Peter," she said, her soft voice tutting a lyrical charm that would rival "The Lorelei." "You are so cute, and you have the nicest way with words. Let me think," she said in teasing tones, tossing her blond hair backward. "I don't think I'm interested in the first part of your offer but very interested in the last part. Perhaps," she said, boosting her lilt, "you could come home now and give me a demonstration of benefits."

The thought of Glenda's proposition sent shivers through his body. He stopped his pacing and sat down behind his desk lest someone else would observe his excitement. He poured a glass of iced water and took a big gulp. It cooled his blood flow and triggered his memory. He had an appointment with his tax attorney to prepare for the IRS meeting.

"That sounds inviting, Glenda, but I'm locked into an exciting meeting with a lawyer to talk about taxes. You know. The letter that came the other day."

She remembered and offered a raincheck.

"I understand that barbequed ribs have enchanting qualities and are adorably messy," she proffered in a sultry soprano pitch.

"The Lighthouse it is," he said. "Better run now. See you later."

It was an appropriate place for Bremer to cap off a memorable day in which, once again, he stayed one step ahead of disaster. Indeed the Lighthouse was a celebrated supper club famous for great food—especially steaks and ribs. It regularly featured an excellent jazz combo that lifted the spirit while not stepping on the eardrums, allowing patrons to dine and visit in peace.

But more than that, in Bremer's case, the Lighthouse legacy fit his journey into storied settings. It was said that Al Capone once ate there, but then Al Capone ate at most every restaurant from Chicago to Denver. Perhaps of greater veracity was the claim that John Dillinger sat in a booth just to the left of the entrance, where "his gun went off and left a hole in the wall."

Chapter 25

"Peter. What's this transaction with Red Sea Exploration?"

David Etting dug into a box of legal documents with one hand and extracted a hand-written paper with the other. The lettering on it looked more like the scratching of a nervous chicken.

"I know you miscalculated on the oil venture," the tax advisor sighed with understatement, "which was with Dubai Drilling." Bremer had lost a barrel of money on contaminated oil holes, a venture that had all the marks of a slick Middle East scam. Greed has no perspective. In his case it turned out to be the mother of all avarice.

The veteran lawyer adjusted his glasses to rest on the tip of his nose and waved the document like a caution flag. "But what role does Red Sea Exploration play in all this?"

Etting was more than just a tax guru and highly respected lawyer in Iowa. He was a CPA with a law degree from the University of Iowa. He had been given numerous professional awards. More importantly he had years of successful litigation. He had represented heavy hitters and minor leaguers, people in tight scrapes and those with routine matters, but Peter Bremer was a client who comprised a legal puzzle that had more twists than an octopus selling a truckload of pretzels.

Integrity was Etting's calling card. His tailored gray Cosani suit from Holley's Menswear, conservatively punctuated by a dark blue bow tie, lent his slim, six-foot-plus frame even more stature. Some lawyers shout. Some try to dance with rhetoric. There are those who employ body language as effectively as Sophia Loren. Etting's recipe included a full sense of the law, an astute mind, a confident demeanor, a civil tongue dipped in bass timbre, and a keen wit.

That he exercised his legal prowess on behalf of a client with a muddied past and shaky future, to say nothing about flimsy finances, was further defining. It was important to Etting to keep Riverside Pack and its players afloat. His fierce Iowa loyalty and desire for Riverside to succeed was as much his motivation as Bremer was.

Etting did not own a single share of Riverside stock. Curiously, though he admired risk-takers, his conventional nature shunned such adventure. Once during a lawsuit that centered on an invention that turned sour, he quoted Teddy Roosevelt's strong preference for a man who fails over one who never tries. He also sensed that Bremer's enthusiasm and knowledge of the meat industry was pretentious if not spurious.

The two accidentally met at Emil's Café one noon hour. In truth they were aware of each other before that chance encounter. Their Cedar Rapids offices were in the same block. Bremer became an overnight star in downtown quarters, first with his thriving insurance business and then in his over-the-moon sale of Riverside stock. He had been invited as a guest speaker at Downtown Rotary—an informal knighting by the power structure. Etting had been a downtown fixture for years.

Later, when Bremer made his formal Riverside stock pitch to Etting, sales had already surpassed the goal. The ever-courteous Etting declined buying into Riverside, but congratulated Bremer on the successful revival of the company. He hoped Riverside would prosper to the benefit of the shareholders, some of whom were his clients, and Iowa.

On the advice of a downtown merchant and Riverside shareholder, Bremer went to Etting for his legal questions and tax problems. Now the two faced each other over a cardboard box of business records that had all the organization of a Phyllis Diller hairdo. The battered container could once have been a grocery carton that had been run over by a delivery truck.

"I'm sorry for this mess," Bremer confessed, pointing to a hodgepodge of folders that gave filing a bad name. "Guess I didn't pay much attention to the importance of record keeping over the years. For a long time, I didn't have—couldn't afford—a full-time secretary. I know. I know. That's no excuse."

"You are correct on that count," Etting said evenly. "But we must try to reconstruct your business activities from the documents here. Is this everything?"

"It's all I could find."

"OK, then. About this Red Sea outfit. How does that fit in? All I find here is some scribbling about payments for long-term equipment leases, signed by you and some Middle East potentate, whose name is mostly illegible."

It was the kind of record keeping and business disorderliness that would gag the average lawyer, but Etting had the professional demeanor and experience to stomach such disarray. In the past he had encountered plenty of rough business contracts and misnamed balance sheets.

Bremer loosened his tie and consulted his conscience. His knack for ducking and dodging, bouncing between the strictures of truth, sought an explanation that would satisfy the question regarding Red Sea Exploration.

Etting read his client's mind like a master psychic.

"I want the complete story, Peter. What you fail to have in documentation must be appended by truthful recollection. I need to know everything. I can guarantee you the feds have enough records on you to paper the courthouse walls. I must have every deal you've been involved in, every investment, every loan, every profit and loss."

He paused and waited for Bremer's eyes to reach his.

The files stacked in Bremer's plain brown box, torn and struggling to remain intact, contrasted visibly with Etting's neat library and conference room decor. The room was appropriately guarded by encircling shelves of seemingly every law decision and theory handed down since God issued Genesis. Fat books waited patiently to be consulted.

A vast, shiny oak table, surrounded by chairs with red velvet cushions, held the cardboard box with the same regard as it had given hundreds of expensive leather briefcases. Its reflection on the lacquered table was not as defining as what first glance might tell. It was not the Pauper meets the King. Rather, it held the story of the plunger, the reckless gambler and speculator, who meets his own reckoning.

"I must see your soul's balance sheet," Etting said.

Bremer did not need a translation.

It was an auditing shakedown that he never read about in a college textbook. He knew Etting was right. The walls of his world were slowly but surely moving inward, leaving him less room to wiggle. The mob was approaching with a single purpose. The IRS sought justice for the federal treasury. Riverside investors expected honesty and a return on their money. Only Glenda stood with him, sharing his anxiety with unconditional love.

Etting stood with him too but unbending as an oak tree in collecting every splinter of information on Bremer's business life. The scheduled one-hour meeting lasted three. A canopy of ventures was outlined, and in many cases it was clear Bremer had climbed out on a financial limb.

It seemed to Etting that his client's last sure footing had been on that orange crate where he stood as a boy to reach the cash register at his father's gas station.

There was one goal in this tax matter: try to see both the forest and the trees.

Bremer surprised his moral barometer as he also informed Etting of his wildly imprudent loan from the Chicago underworld. Like an adolescent who wrecked the family car, he held his breath, waiting for a scornful look and scalding sermon. None came.

"How much did you receive from them?" Etting asked in emotionless form. It was not his first experience with stupid. The tax lawyer paused a second to digest such nonconforming business behavior and held his eyes on the box of papers that would somehow have to be organized and shaped into a credible and understandable case for presentation to IRS agents and eventually the US Attorney and federal court.

Bremer sheepishly outlined the $75,000 loan from one Adrian Koffmann, the mobster formally listed as chief financial officer of Chi-Cero Investments, and the belated and recent $20,000 payment to him. That loan covered indebtedness from other ventures, including the busted Mideast oil deal. Somewhere in the box, the entrails of his entire glut of business indigestion had to be reconnected and arranged to make sense. It was a daunting task, even for Etting.

"You asked about Red Sea Exploration. As I understand it," Bremer said, "it was an independent entity that ran tests for oil deposits in advance of actual drilling. We had to pay them for geological examinations and the search for hydrocarbon deposits. It's a necessary first step before you get into the expensive business of actual drilling."

"Peter," Etting said evenly. "Did you verify that Red Sea Exploration was truly independent, that it had no connection with other investors in Dubai Offshore Drilling? Did you check with anyone in this country or anywhere about the reputation of these companies, about their track record?"

"I guess I didn't look close enough," Bremer replied.

Etting declined to pursue the obvious.

The three hours were a plodding that would strain a tax expert with the patience of a cloistered monk. The documents were placed in calendar sequence. Copies were made and assembled according to companies involved. Etting noted the transactions that had tax consequences. He questioned Bremer in an attempt to stitch structure and fill holes in this lace of commercial muddle.

Piecing Bremer's domestic transactions, which were as circuitous and entwined as hillbilly genealogy, was a walk in the park compared to maneuvering and reconstructing the paper trail of the bumpy and dubious Middle East deals. Etting not only had holes to fill but a mountain of evidentiary challenges created by the absence of corroborating witnesses.

He scratched his balding head, as if that would stir up more answers.

"Please, let me look at the letter from the IRS again," Etting requested. "I want to double check. The meeting is next Monday at ten, right?"

"That's correct," replied Bremer, as he handed the letter to Etting.

"The Labor Day weekend has pushed things around," Etting said, half to himself. "I want to review the documents you gave me today and your personal notes, then meet one more time before the session with the IRS. Can you be back here at eight o'clock Monday morning?"

Bremer agreed.

"And check your memory for other records or other persons who may have information pertaining to your financial information,"

Etting advised. "We will need those missing returns from two years ago. You must understand, Mr. Bremer, that the IRS will have many of these records. And with records come questions. We need to be prepared, assuming they will know everything since your first squawk in the delivery room."

Etting, usually confident of his footing on even the slipperiest of legal challenges, had a gnawing feeling that his case for Peter Bremer may shape into a web of thin ice. He was particularly worried about the unknown, the perils of unrecorded payouts and receipts and undocumented agreements, the business hidden outside the big, brown cardboard box.

There was no dancing with figures. They were black and white evidence of what happened, and sometimes an astute lawyer could color in a faint of gray in their meaning. But Etting knew that waltzing with tax laws and the IRS was like courting a slide rule. He would play it straight and hope for the best.

———————————

"Don, do you believe there is intelligent life on Mars?"

Don McKenster looked out the west window of the Federal Building in downtown Cedar Rapids, chomping on a tuna fish sandwich lathered in mayo. It was not unusual that the veteran IRS agent brown-bagged his lunch, especially when the caseload took a jump. Two other agents, Dick Maloux and Norb Welton, were assessing tax returns and other information pertaining to Peter Bremer, the president of Riverside Pack.

"I'm not sure there is intelligent life on Earth," replied McKenster, the short, stout chief investigator on the case, who displayed evidence of not always choosing diet-smart menus. "Why, Mr. Maloux, are you curious about life on Mars? We have enough unanswered questions right in this office."

"Just wondering. NASA launched that Viking probe to Mars a couple of weeks ago," Maloux explained. "It's supposed to reach the planet a year from now and maybe we'll find out if there are any Martians up there."

"Well, if there are Martians," McKenster rejoined, "it would be just our luck they owe back taxes."

Maloux and Welton had already loaded up on calories at the Butterfly Café. They delighted in the special, a hot beef sandwich topped with mashed potatoes and gravy, and failed to resist the butterscotch pie. The combination was so gastronomically satisfying that an IRS agent may be tempted to overlook any unreported tips.

Outside, along the west side of the Federal Building, the Cedar River flowed steadily southward, unaware and unconcerned with the trials of man at a time when unemployment and inflation were on the rise. The river had one goal: gather the flowage from streams as far as southern Minnesota then join the Iowa River to deposit the consignment in the Mississippi River.

The Classical Revival style federal building, completed in 1933, housed nearly every federal agency in the city, including the US Post Office. Its three levels, plus a basement, followed a familiar template and, with ground-level parking, consumed a full block. Much of the third floor was given over to US Courthouse functions, including the ornate courtroom, the judge's chambers, the clerk and probation offices, and the US Marshal.

Just west, parked in the middle of the Cedar River, city hall rises skyward with all the illusions of a towering battleship. But the focus of McKenster & Co. this day was Peter Bremer, the up-and-coming executive of Riverside Pack.

McKenster uttered a silent thank you to his wife, Wilma, for packing his lunch. He peered downward from the second-floor window at the murky water, which mixed with eroded, rich Iowa bottomland and leeched nitrate fertilizer that farmers applied to boost corn production and feed the nation. Life flowed on within the halls of justice and the walls of rivers.

"You won't find any answers to these tax puzzles by gazing out the window," Welton said. "This is a labyrinth of confusion mixed in a mishmash of invention. I've never worked such a case." He looked over at McKenster. "And here you are, calmly digesting your usual tuna sandwich with a dill pickle on the side."

"Actually," McKenster replied casually, "I was just thinking how lucky I am that this tuna fish wasn't caught in the Cedar River. "I wonder, Mr. Maloux, whether there are rivers and tuna on Mars."

"You fellows have been working too long on this case," Welton diagnosed. "After reviewing these documents and returns several times, I think Mr. Bremer must be a demented magician."

"All the reason to go over all the figures one more time," McKenster said in slave-master style. "I believe we have enough information, enough background and raw tax evidence, that we can present this matter to the US Attorney with fairly strong assurance of success."

That produced a chuckle from Maloux.

"What?" McKenster asked with a puzzled look.

"I was just thinking," Maloux said, smiling, "how these curvy little symbols we call numbers can bring down the biggest of big shots. Shifty crime bosses have met their undoing because of tax violations—fat-cat country clubbers humbled by undeclared foreign income. Not that Peter Bremer's indiscretion on taxes is national news." He paused. "It's akin to the troubles some men invite when they try to manipulate the curvy figures of the opposite sex."

"Careful there or you'll be the subject of an Ann Lander's column."

"I wonder," Maloux said, continuing his musings, "whatever happened to Jimmy Hoffa? Here's a fellow who, after four years in prison on bribery and fraud charges, was pardoned by President Nixon. That was several years ago, and what, last month, he disappears from the face of the Earth. I don't think he's buried under any taxes. More likely it's concrete. That's the rumor."

"Well, in Mr. Bremer's case, I think we've done what we can," Welton said. "We've been auditing his returns, collecting documents, and interviewing people for more than six months. This case boils down to omitted income, disguised transactions and overall screwy reports. I've not worked on a tax case with this many turns on dead-end streets in twenty years with the IRS."

Welton continued, "The crowning gem in all this is the large deduction he took on his tax return two years ago for what he claims was a church donation. Now, I'm not saying Mr. Bremer is not a believer or that he doesn't go to a church. But $15,000? To a tiny church here in town? That would have been a right generous sum even for Howard Hall when he was alive, and he probably had more money than anyone else in Iowa."

"Well, you interviewed the lady at the church, the part-time secretary," Maloux added. "You said she may have looked ninety years old, but her memory was sharp. She was positive Mr. Bremer didn't donate $15,000 to the church. And she has the records. You described her as stern looking, white braided hair in a bun and dressed in a brownish housedress. She will make a good witness if need be."

"I remember her saying 'absolutely not,' when I asked if he gave that much money," Welton said. "Her eyebrows were arched in disbelief. She said they received less than $30,000 all year from the entire congregation. They could only afford a part-time preacher."

"But Bremer's name was listed on the donor rolls?"

"Yes. There were periodic Bremer checks of $20 or so, but not $15,000."

"You know what he's going to say?" McKenster said. There were agreeing nods. "Misplaced zeros created from illegible records."

"And, when you described him to her, did she have any recollection of such a fancy-dressed fellow?"

"Well, Dick, she confessed she didn't go every Sunday."

Chapter 26

October 1957, Garden City, Kan.

"Fuckin' John T. Moses. Did you hear that!? The Russians put a satellite in space. Circling Earth like the damn moon."

Jimmy Jones stroked his sprouting black beard and waited for a response. None came. He took another draw on his half-burned cigarette. Smoke filled the tiny room, and ashes were sprinkled on the floor like powdered sugar.

"They call it Sputnik. Damn, that puts the Rooskies in the space race lead. Bet that squeezes the testicles of old Ike."

Bobby Bremer's attention was buried in a magazine article on C. J. "Buffalo" Jones, the first mayor of Garden City, Kans.

"What do you think, Bobby? Hey, Bobby. Are you listenin'? Don't you ever pay attention to the news?"

Jones was not exactly a news junkie. It was a rainy Saturday night, and he had flicked on the radio in hopes of tuning in the Grand Ole Opry. Instead of hearing Patsy Cline's mournful rendition of "Walkin' After Midnight," he heard the news about Sputnik from CBS reporter Daniel Schoor.

"I wish you wouldn't use that word," Bremer finally said. "My mom don't like it."

"Whoa! Guess who's still sufferin' with a logjam of gaseous materials trapped in the twists of his bowels. Too much sauerkraut last night?"

There was another pause in Jones' rambling, and then his tongue caught up with his thought processes, which frequently was unfortunate for everybody within hearing distance.

"So your mom doesn't like the word *testicles*? That's funny. Guess I could have said *gonads*. Tell me, Bobby, would Harry Truman say *testicles* or *gonads*?"

"You know what word I'm talking about, and it ain't *testicles*."

Bremer and Jones shared an apartment on Hackberry Street in Garden City, having moved from Goshen, Ark., several months before. Like many young men before them, they were motivated by adventure and the appeal of trains clacking west. Equally compelling was the desire to make more money than they had been receiving at Mountain Landscaping Co.

In violation of parole, Bremer drove his truck from Goshen to Coffeeville, Kans., and sold it. The pair then rode a connector railroad north and hooked up with the westbound Santa Fe Super Chief. They had no plans except to go somewhere else. It was a quest for the unknown with the famous Santa Fe railroad as their escort. "Unknown" turned out to be the dusty and smelly little town of Garden City.

Soon they found work at much better pay. Both signed on at the Great Western Feedlot, a burgeoning cattle operation just outside Garden City, bounded by the Arkansas River, Santa Fe Railroad, and the old Santa Fe Trail. It was the twentieth-century version of feeding and herding cattle, minus the lawless days of wild cowhands and open ranges.

The land in this section of middle America, where the horizon has no end and dust storms turned day into night in the 1930s, was once again changing the very nature of Garden City. Irrigation gave life to the feed grains, which replaced the waning sugar beet industry. And grain nourished the cattle-feeding industry. Kansas outlawed free-range cattle in the late 1800s, once crop farmers gained enough political clout and built enough fences. Feedlots helped cattle regain a major footprint in Kansas, just like in the old days, and spurred the development of meat processing.

Bremer and Jones found themselves in the middle of a cultural transition with the railroad still being a main player. There was talk of large slaughtering plants and big payrolls, lured to Garden City by thousands of cattle and the transportation power of the Santa Fe.

"I heard the news about Sputnik," Bremer quietly replied.

"You know what grinds my molars," Jones filled in the quiet. "Old President Ike—and Bobby, Eisenhower is old—didn't have the foresight to invest in the future. Now he's the target of Nikita Khrushchev's laughter. Hell, with all them German scientists we inherited after the war, we should be first in space. Don't you have an opinion?"

"Whatever you say, Jimmy."

"Really. Eisenhower could have spent the money he squandered sending troops to Little Rock—what, to force Negroes to go to a white school—on space research. I still can't believe he did that. Tell us how to run our business down in Arkansas. Pushin' Negroes to attend a school they don't want. Everybody would rather be with their own."

"Whatever, Jimmy. Seems you finally got to the bottom of what's hurtin' your molars."

The apartment the pair shared was sparsely equipped. It had two bedrooms. There was a small chrome dinette in one corner of the kitchen, offset by a wood cooking stove that also provided heat. A small living room—more a sitting area—had a worn blue couch and a bulky brown armchair flanked by two wobbly lamp tables. The upper part of the living room window, which served as the final resting place for a half-dozen flies, was also the exit for the chimney of a seldom-used oil heater.

There was no TV. Television was still a luxury in Garden City. Unlike Bremer, Jones was not a reader except for western comic books. Tom Mix was his favorite. And he regularly listened to the Liberal, Kans., radio station and the broadcast sagas of the Lone

Ranger. Some of his spare time was spent at the local pool hall drinking beer and playing spots and stripes.

"You ought to read more, Jimmy. Find out some history on Garden City. Take this geezer, Buffalo Jones, the first mayor. Maybe he's a relative of yours. 'Course, he had better things to do than shoot pool. He was once warden at Yellowstone Park. Then he tried to raise buffalo commercially on his ranch. It says here that he helped bring the railroad to town, but he gets more attention in this article for planting dozens of cottonwood trees up and down Main Street. But not many of his trees survived the drought of 1879."

"None of your business if I play pool," Jones replied.

"Get this," Bremer continued his semi-lecture as if Jones were an attentive student. "In 1914, this Jones fellow, now seventy years old, goes to Africa and ropes a gorilla. He gave lectures on his escapades until he died in 1919. Hell, Zane Grey has written about him."

"Who is Zane Grey?"

"Shit, Jones. Don't you even know who Zane Grey is?"

Silence meant Jones had no clue.

"He was billiards champion of Kansas back in the early 1900s," Bremer answered his own question without looking up.

"Really," said Jones. "Guess I'll have to study up on him."

"Interesting town." Bremer lumbered on with his verbal history tour of Kansas, knowing he was mainly talking to himself. "They've had terrible weather over the years—cold, heat, torrential rain, drought. Just last March a record blizzard hit this area."

"Well, if you ask me there's too damn many Mexicans here."

"Jimmy, you got a problem. Try to see people for who they are. That's what Mom always said. If people work hard, take care of their family, and mind their own business—like most of them Hispanics do—why get all in a lather? They were in this town long before us. Get over it."

"You sure been thinkin' a lot about your mama lately, Bobby. Are you homesick or somethin'? And you, a graduate of Kansas State Prison? I'm startin' to get worried about you."

"Yeah, I think about my mama. So what?"

Jones could get on his nerves, but Jimmy had become a good friend. He had misjudged him at first, just as a lot of others had misjudged him. Jimmy had his prejudices, but who didn't? Bobby really hated Jimmy's smoking habit, mostly because the cigarette stink attached to everything.

The northwest wind kicked up a howl that preordained winter's lurking deep in the calendar. Autumn was a beautiful time of year with the vivid colors of oaks, hickories, and maples—and the temperatures that caressed rather than fried. Yet it had this menacing backdrop, this behind-the-curtains bogeyman called Winter. Jones rose from the couch and closed the kitchen window.

"That's cool. I ain't sayin' bad things 'bout mamas," Jones said. "But comes a time when youse have to pull away too, know what I mean? I know my mama loves me, but that don't mean I have to be thinkin' 'bout her half the day. My dad I hardly remember."

Garden City, if you could eliminate half of the wind, is a good place to live. But the wide-open spaces, while invigorating to the inner yearning for freedom, also can leave a soul unstable—tottering on the edges of a perpetual horizon unbroken by hills and stands of trees. The Great Plains slope without detection as they fall away from the uproar of the Rocky Mountains.

"My old man was mean. I believe he hated me. I don't know why, but I believe he hated me. Maybe that's why I think a lot about my mother. I know she loves me. God only knows I've given her plenty of reasons not to, but she still cares for me."

Bremer continued his brushup on Garden City history. A bored and squirmy Jones lit up another cigarette and slowly twisted the radio knob in search of something more palatable than news.

"You gonna get another truck?"

Bremer was annoyed by yet another interruption of his reading.

"I don't know. I doubt it. We can always hitch a ride with one of the other workers."

He looked down at a sepia-tinted photograph of a bearded Buffalo Jones. Bremer was fascinated by how a man could change so much. In this case, the flamboyant Buffalo Jones, once an avid pursuer and killer of range bison, had transformed into a defender and preserver of wild buffalo. Maybe he, Bremer, would someday be a county sheriff. With his record, maybe not.

Monday morning found the two filling cattle lot feeders with hay, replenishing salt blocks, and shoveling manure. They cleaned leaves and other debris from livestock watering tanks. Next on the agenda was rounding up unvaccinated yearlings, those without the ear tags, for brucellosis shots. Neither said anything, but if one could read their minds, one would have discovered similar thoughts: Why the hell am I scooping cow manure when I could be working in the serenity of the Ozark Mountains?

Despite the activity, neither felt overheated in their light flannel jackets, which would soon give way to coveralls and winter gear. The fickle plains weather was already showing its face. The week's discomfort grew as a biting, cold wind flowed down from Nebraska. The weatherman labeled it a "Canadian air mass."

"I sure ain't looking ahead to freeze my ass off out here the middle of nowhere," Jones blabbered past a toothpick held in the corner of his mouth. "Guess what I'm sayin', Bobby, is that I'm not all that sure I'm cut out to be a cowboy. I don't mind workin' with these bovines, but I ain't excited eatin' dust."

"Hell, we ain't seen nothin' yet, Jimmy. Wait 'til the snow is piled up deep as your back pockets out here in these pens. Then you'll be shoveling shit and snow. And your fingers will tingle with frost."

"Ya sure gotta way with words, Bobby. I feel better already."

Friday night found both of them down at Lefty's Pool Hall while most of the town was out at the high school watching Garden City take on Holcomb in football. Bremer sat at the bar, nursing his third Falstaff. Jones, pool cue in one hand and beer bottle in the other, circled the green-matted table like an over-confident coyote eyeballing a newborn calf.

He placed the beer on the side of the billiard table and picked up the chalk to smooth out the cue tip but, just as much, to give him more time to prance his mojo. He lifted his straw cowboy hat and scratched his head in one motion. The dilemma seemed to be whether he should aim for the 10 ball, with the 8 ball lurking behind it, or play it safe and put the 11 in a sure-shot position next time around.

His opponent, a tall fellow with black hair snarling out of a sweat-stained western hat, was chafing at this ponderous pretense. He signaled his growing irritation by tapping the handle of his cue stick on the chrome legs of his bar stool. It had all the clicks and clatter of Morse code that spelled trouble. The Pall Mall dangling from the corner of his mouth glowed anew, and then blue smoke drifted from his nose.

Jones understood.

"What, Jose, you no like my style?" Jones said in his impulsive manner.

The question had a ring of sarcasm and challenge, and Bremer and a half-dozen others in the pool hall heard it clang loud and clear through the room's murky setting. In the ordinary scheme of things, the question would have produced a snide response of equal or harsher intensity, and the billiards game would have gone on.

Not now. Not this time. With beer and pride fueling young egos, Jones's remark produced a reaction that would have surprised even a chemistry professor. There comes a time when insults catch fire from the smallest spark. One by one, Hispanic young men sauntered toward the pool table, beer bottles in their hands, dignity on their minds, and expectations on the upswing. No one had to say more. The air changed like an atmospheric disturbance ahead of an oncoming thunderstorm.

Bremer disliked the dawning flareup. He quickly walked over to Jones, grabbed him by the arm, then looked at the other young men.

"My friend didn't mean to start anything," Bremer offered. "His mouth sometimes gets ahead of his cabeza." And he pointed to his head. It was one of the few words he remembered from high school Spanish. "He can sometimes be rude, and his mama wouldn't like it."

Where did that come from? Talk about the pot criticizing the kettle.

"What are you doin'?" Jones jerked his arm away from Bremer's grasp. "I didn't say anything wrong. And you leave my mama out of this. Go away and consult your own mama."

Bremer felt like slugging Jones himself, and that could have been the antidote to the brewing melee. He didn't. And then Jones lit another fuse.

"Look, Bobby. If you want to get pushed around by these wetbacks, that's your business. But I ain't afraid of them."

Ten minutes later, two Garden City police officers and an off-duty Finney County sheriff's deputy knocked enough heads together to end the fight. An intuitive bartender had called authorities even before the first punch was thrown. Jones was admitted to St. Catherine Hospital, where a one-inch gash to his left cheek, administered by a broken beer bottle, was sutured, and binders were wrapped around his chest area to keep a broken rib immobile. A patch covered his blackened right eye.

Bremer had a bleeding and busted nose. Once cleaned up, he, Jones, and three of the young Mexican combatants had a weekend's free lodging in the Finney County Jail. Judge Wesley Staker was not about to disrupt his Saturday pheasant hunting trip to allocate justice to a group of cretins. Their collective court appearances were set for the following Monday.

As it turned out, the fight was a routine rumble for a town with a colorful history of law breaking, a good deal of it ethnically motivated. Sometimes the cause was residual rancor between grain growers and free-range cattlemen. To put it another way, as long-time police dispatcher Margaret Meiffert once told a *Garden City Telegram* reporter, "I like the unpredictability of the job."

Newton J. Earp, older half brother of the more famous Wyatt Earp, served as the town's first marshal. However, Lee Richardson was the area's most notable lawman, serving as both town marshal and later as Finney County Sheriff. He solved bank robberies, put an end to the murderous Fleagle Gang, and had a shoot-out with the killer of a Dodge City police chief. Little wonder the town named the zoo after him.

The pool hall wrangle was not so routine for Bobby Bremer, a detail that should have taken precedence over impulse. He was convicted of assault and battery, disobeying a police officer, and violating parole. All of which earned him a trip back to the Kansas State Penitentiary at Lansing.

Chapter 27
Kansas State Penitentiary

"Yes, Mom. I should have known better."

Molly Bremer sniffled her way through a litany of disappointments and what-did-I-tell-you reminders.

"Yes, it was stupid to leave Arkansas without informing my parole officer. Stupid not to tell you I sold the truck and not make payments. And it was stupid to get involved in a fight that I knew after the first punch would send me back to prison. Mom, you don't have to tell me what I already know."

"If you already knew it," she lamented, "why are we having this conversation?"

She tried to stifle her sobbing. Lord knows, she had been down this path too many times before with Bobby, but a mother's tear reservoir never runs dry when it comes to children in trouble.

"Mom. Crying won't change things."

Bobby called her immediately after the court hearing in Garden City. He did not want her to learn of his latest skirmish with the law from some other source. Not only was his parole revoked, but the Garden City judge added another year to his incarceration. Once again, meals and confined housing would be on the tabs of Kansas taxpayers.

"I was hoping you would be home for Christmas," Molly said softly. "I guess that's now out of the question."

"I can't be home, Mom. That's just the way it is. I'm sorry. I should have known better. I didn't mean to cause you more grief."

"Oh, Bobby. I know that. I know that you wouldn't intentionally hurt anyone. Please understand that my love for you hasn't changed. I wish I could be with you. Maybe we can get up to visit you again at Lansing."

"That would be fine, Mom. I must go now. Goodbye."

At Monday's sentencing, Judge Staker had dispensed with the law's necessity about waiving a formal hearing, then proceeded directly to sentencing. He perused Bremer's rap sheet and shook his head in dismay. Staker was not a member of the Benevolence Society. It may as well have been Jessie James standing in the courtroom before him. The judge was wound up and delivered a lecture worthy of a WCTU preacher.

The judge recited Bremer's record line by line—a list of transgressions since Bremer first soiled a diaper. Bremer's court-appointed counsel was wordless.

His Honor, becoming exhausted by his own verbosity, punctuated his sermon by informing Bremer that he would be in prison until the end of 1959.

"And I'm recommending no parole. That means we will be nearing a new decade before you see free air, assuming you keep your nose clean behind bars. Do you understand that, Mr. Bremer?" he asked. Bremer nodded, was given a chance to speak on his own behalf, declined, and it was over. The next day he was in a prison van carrying customers back to Lansing.

Jimmy Jones, after his trip to the hospital, was sentenced by the same judge. He received a six-month term in the county lockup. Two others involved in the fight received the same treatment and became Jones's neighbors in a cell down the hall. That, and the judge's pronouncement that the brawl participants would be equally responsible for reimbursing Lefty for damage to his pool hall, concluded the episode.

That was the last time Bremer saw Jones. He had a letter from him a month later in which Jones lamented the isolation and cold of western Kansas and the boredom of the Finney County Jail. Bremer chuckled at that, wondering if Jones expected the jail to have a pool table. Jones added that he was anxious to get back to the Ozark hills.

"You got lucky bein' sent to Lansin'," he wrote Bremer. "This county jail is a real shithole. Guy in the cell next to me is crazy. Water seeps in the corner near his bed. He often sits on the floor. Says he watchin' the silverfish wiggle around and thinks how he might rig up a pole to catch some. Guy is crazy.

"I got hold of a calendar from Rusty's Auto Repair Shop. They let me hang it on the wall of my cell. I'm crossin' off the days on the bottom portion while enjoyin' Jayne Mansfield's picture on the top. I'm tellin' you, Bobby, that is some hot woman. It's about the only heat we have in this place. It's amazin' how often some of the deputies visit me, if you know what I'm saying'."

He also posed a question to Bremer.

"Bobby, how the hell are we supposed to repay Lefty for damages when we have no job? Or does the judge expect us to make payments when we get out of jail? Always wonder about that."

Bremer never answered the letter. By early 1958 he was again immersed in life at the state prison. He managed to land an assignment to the prison library, where he happily assisted the young librarian, Felix Forsythe. Forsythe rekindled Bremer's interest in poetry and steered him to the adventures of Jack London and Louis L'Amour.

On his own, Bremer was drawn to various articles featuring certain adherents of *posse comitatus*. At first, he reflected on a core idea of the movement, that is, citizens coming to the aid of local law enforcement. The notion of a sheriff's posse helping round up bad guys is engrained in western history and lore. However, his personal history and natural disposition repressed any desire to aid the police.

Over months of reading, Bremer became fascinated by the idea of people risking an ordinary and innocuous life for a cause. He discounted the details and motives of certain posse adherents and drifted to a more hard-minded view of group action. He looked past the notion of common good and became absorbed on achieving a narrower goal, one that sometimes incorporated sinister and hateful righteousness.

"What do you think of this posse comitatus idea?" Bremer asked Forsythe one day, out of the blue. It was one of those questions that whisk away any lingering cobwebs in a mind dedicated to a totally unrelated task. After enough time for his thoughts to shift gears, Forsythe settled on a response. He looked directly at Bremer, which underlined his opinion.

"Not much," he said. His tone conveyed a degree of revulsion.

"From what I know—I should say, from what I've read," Forsythe said with a measured voice, "the idea of posse comitatus has been corrupted by those who fancy themselves as protectors of the law but, in reality, are vigilantes." It was not exactly an affirmation of Bremer's thoughts. Neither did it deter his fascination with the movement.

Molly and her parents visited Bobby that following summer, and life for him at the state prison settled into a routine. He made a few acquaintances in his cell block section and a couple on the prison grounds crew, but Forsythe was his only friend. When he was not trimming shrubbery, cutting grass, or involved in other landscaping chores, he was in the library. He began writing poetry, simple lines that at first reflected his expanded interest in what he saw as injustice among the poor of the plains.

Life seemed to level out in comfortable symmetry for Bremer, as contented as the prison environment can be. He did what was expected, followed the rules, and avoided confrontation with other inmates and prison staff. Though he made no close friends, neither did he create any enemies. But the inevitable obstacle, which in

Bremer's case always seemed to mushroom from a molehill into a mountain, popped up unexpectedly in the fall of 1959.

He was walking across the prison yard. It was a gloomy late afternoon, with days getting shorter and the first hint of winter getting stronger. Uncertain clouds pushed each other around, wrestling to cover up any tiny specks of blue sky.

"My goodness sake! Who do we have here?" The loud voice came from several paces to Bremer's rear. "Is it really my ole sweetheart, the tough-guy poet of Little Rock? I reckoned you would have been on the literature staff at the universitee down at Lawrence by now. My, oh my!" he snorted. "What did happen to curtail your professorial ambitions? Maybe one of your poems had a criminal ring to it."

Bobby had not seen the man approach. He was tired, hungry, and needed a shower. A northwest wind dispatched shivers across his sweaty body. The last thing his disposition wanted was a poke in the ego. He kept on walking, ignoring the voice by not looking back. But he knew. Even after seven years. He knew.

"That it? The judge give you more time for lousy poetry?"

The man waited for a reply and received none.

"Bless my soul. You have no rhyme or reason for being here? Get it, oh bard of the slammer? Rhyme or reason?"

By now the voice had moved along Bremer's right side. Both were approaching a group of other inmates near the cellblock entrance. Most of them puffed cigarettes. Mumbles and smoke mingled. Later none claimed they saw what happened.

"What, the cat got your courage?"

"I recognize your voice," Bremer said softly, still avoiding eye contact. "I remember you and your stench. I bet you haven't taken a shower since the first time I met you and kicked your ass. The last I recall you were crawling around on the cement floor like a bleeding turd." He kept on walking. "I don't recall your name, so I'll just refer to you as your Royal Reekness."

Mr. Reekness moved closer. His hand reached inside his right pocket.

"My suggestion," Bremer said evenly, "is that you return to your personal shithole and write a letter to your mother apologizing for your existence."

The shiv dug into Bremer's right side. It was deep enough to provoke a stream of blood. He instinctively swung with his left hand, which struck Hogg Mulder's fending right fist. The shiv fashioned a second slice on Bremer's body, this time carving a one-inch gash on his left arm. But the bleeding arm grabbed Mulder's head and yanked it downward. At the same time Bremer's right knee rose like a launched catapult.

It was a crunching encounter.

Mulder tried to counter, aiming the bloody shiv at Bremer's retreating knee, but the pain from his rearranged teeth and the torn tip of his tongue deflated his plan of attack. His yellow teeth were a mixture of blood and shredded tongue tissue. After Bremer deposited his right fist deep into Mulder's soft belly, adding breakfast and noontime repast to his involuntary lurching, the fight was over.

Mulder, a slow learner who suffered at Bremer's hands at their first meeting, now lost round two. The only unanswered question was if Bremer would walk away from his defeated challenger or unfurl his full wrath. He kicked Mulder's right hand, sending the shiv flying like a wayward field goal. He slammed his fist into Mulder's head, sending him writhing to the ground. Next came a pointed boot to Mulder's left ribs, a blow that compounded pain and produced pleas for relief.

Bremer aimed a follow-up thrust at the attacker's head, but his conscience interrupted. After about fifteen seconds of deliberation, he backed away from the pathetic figure coiled in a fetal position, coloring the red soil of the prison courtyard an even darker red.

Guards grabbed Bremer. A pair from the medical station hoisted the unconscious Mulder on a stretcher and hauled him to emergency care. Bremer's sense of justice was bruised in that it seemed to him more attention was given to the perpetrator of the fight. No questions were asked, and no information was volunteered. No one stepped forward to outline the origin of the clash or give details. Other prisoners acted as if they'd been in China. The scene was saturated with indifference.

Bremer was taken to a first aid station where it was determined he needed stitches on both his rib cage and left arm. Both wounds were cleaned, and steps were taken to stop the bleeding. After a forty-minute wait, a young physician administered local anesthetics and sutured the lesions. Two days later he was called in by the block superintendent to talk about the fight.

Without witness input, Bremer had the gut feeling that it was going to be his word vs. that of the mangled and voiceless figure known as Hogg Mulder. The last he heard Mulder was still in the infirmary. He feared the mere appearance of a battered body contrasted with his two cuts would be strong testimony against him. As it turned out, Mulder was the least of his worries.

There are prison rules, which are mostly black and white, and then there are inmate rules, which have context but are subject to personal interpretation. Bremer had sufficient experience and knowledge of both for day-to-day survival. But when issues become cloudy, when a neutral agent is void of independent testimony, adjudication can run off the road. That's where Bremer landed.

Mulder regained his voice in several days and quickly mumbled claims of being jumped and beaten as he was innocently walking through the prison yard. He carried his story of being the affronted one like a veteran movie actor. At the hearing, Mulder said he was unaware of who Bremer was until after the confrontation began. He said he then recognized his "assailant" as "one who had given him trouble before."

Bremer gave his version, that Mulder had been the instigator of both fights and that he was defending himself. But he felt like he was spitting in the wind, fulfilling the record's need for a counter story that would be lost in the oblivion of disinterest. The bare table in the hearing room, pocked with cigarette burns and coffee stains, enhanced the perception that this was elementary justice.

The hearing officer summoned several inmates who had been in the area at the time of the fight, but no one could give evidence about its initiation. Eyes that were normally cued to every prison nuance saw nothing. Neither did anyone see Mulder pull a shiv, nor could they explain why Bremer ended up with gashes to his side and arm. Curiously the shiv was never recovered. Bremer was flabbergasted by the superficiality of the proceedings.

The upshot was that both men were placed in confinement quarters for sixty days. In addition the hearing officer recommended that any parole considerations for Bremer and Mulder be postponed a year beyond any scheduled proceedings. To Bremer, it was injustice at its pinnacle, the kind all too often administered by incompetent overseers whose primary interest was quick resolution.

Bremer was handled as a "special management" case; he was not placed in solitary confinement, but neither did he have the freedom to associate with others and participate in any prison pursuits. It meant the loss of library privileges and work with the landscaping crew. Even worse, it became a breeding place for duplicity, a haven where an ill wind could fan the spark of distorted ideas.

It was the wrong place for a man whose psyche had been battered by an abusive father and who had delusions of being the kid always left behind.

Chapter 28

September 1975, Cedar Rapids

There is nothing upmarket about the furnishings of a regional Internal Revenue Service office. The table and chairs are a sturdy dark wood, standard issue from the General Services Administration during the Lincoln era. Tabletop basics are the ubiquitous pitcher of water and enough glasses to go around. The GSA is the landlord for the government.

Generally any posh leather chairs and ornate desks in federal buildings and courthouses are issued to judges based on their political status and longevity—or their ability to persuade. Moreover it would seem inappropriate to have an upscale setting at an agency like the IRS, whose legitimate goal is to make sure you pay your fair share of taxes.

The Cedar Rapids IRS office had no pictures of political and bureaucratic bigshots. The only other fixtures in the small room were a coat rack and a bare three-foot flower stand near the window, noticeable only for its series of ring blemishes. The window was adorned with a yellowish shade, half pulled, which appeared to have absorbed moisture from a leak somewhere.

A single light fixture with two bulbs hung overhead, and the plastic covering featured a sizeable crack.

Peter Bremer and his attorney, David Etting, walked into the Cedar Rapids Federal Courthouse on First Street, strode past the bank of Post Office service windows and around the corner to the elevator opposite Floyd's Snack Shop. Floyd was nearly blind, but no one seemed to worry that he would put too much mustard or alfalfa sprouts on their sandwiches. Nor were they concerned that he would deliver the incorrect change.

Floyd was much beloved and as much of the building's human fixtures as the senior judge.

Etting punched the second-floor button. Once there, they wound their way past the congressman's suite, the offices of the FBI and ATF, and then to the west side IRS. After a minute or so, they were ushered into the main meeting room with the sturdy table and chairs, the faded window shade, and the cracked light fixture.

"Good morning. My name is Don McKenster," said a man who was five foot six in height and certainly no embodiment of a menacing IRS agent. "I'm the chief investigator in our office, and this is Norb Welton, a lead investigator. Agent Dick Maloux may be along shortly." McKenster extended his hand to Bremer and Etting, who introduced themselves as the preliminaries were fulfilled. Seats were taken.

Welton was taller and thinner than his colleague, whose head was hair challenged. Unlike his associate, he made regular trips to the YMCA gym. McKenster explained the nature of the meeting, a preliminary session based on information regarding Mr. Bremer's tax history. It was an opportunity, he said, to provide explanations to inconsistencies, unexplained voids in documentation, and conflicting records. Information would be recorded and become part of the official report of Mr. Bremer's tax case. McKenster rattled off the IRS case number, the date, and other essentials in order to dot the i's and cross the t's.

Etting submitted the standard reply of an attorney and noted that Bremer had come to the meeting voluntarily. He asked the agents to accord his client the legal considerations due anyone undergoing an investigation, including the presumption of innocence. He added that the ordinary citizen is not a master at comprehending the complexities of federal tax law.

McKenster further outlined that the meeting could result in a follow-up session, or the matter could be referred to the US Attorney for review. From there the case could result in formal charges presented in Federal Court or appraised by a federal grand jury. The agents proceeded to ask rudimentary questions about Bremer's job and residential history.

It took a mere fifteen minutes for Welton to address the elephant in the room. And it had nothing to do with the complexities of Middle East oil investments, life insurance perks, or Riverside Pack bonuses.

"Mr. Bremer, would you please explain this $15,000 gift and subsequent tax deduction made to the Prairie Church in Cedar Rapids?" Welton inquired. "The contribution is listed as being made in 1974 and reported on your tax return filed earlier this year. Do you have receipts or other information from the church attesting to your contribution?"

Etting looked at Bremer, clearly invoking insight or some sort of rationale for such a significant and palpable matter. It quickly became obvious to the attorney that this involved some of the missing documents in recent tax reports Bremer had provided. Bremer struggled to lift his downcast eyes. He seemed equally bewildered. Finally his head turned upward, and his gaze pulled to the bright sunlight streaming in from the west window above the empty stand.

For a few seconds his mind, like the pedestal, was blank, spellbound by the dust mites that were dancing through the light.

"Mr. Bremer, are you or were you a member of this church?"

"Yes. Glenda and I have attended services there."

"Have you provided financial support to this church and to the extent indicated on your tax return?" And he pointed to the document in question.

"We have given money to the church."

"$15,000 in 1974?"

Bremer was wedged between black and white figures, the kind of absolutes the IRS works with every day, and his chronic need to explain. Etting leaned over and whispered in his ear: "Is this part of the missing paperwork on recent returns?" Bremer nodded.

"Mr. McKenster, Mr. Welton. Could I have a few minutes with my client?" Etting requested. He hid his disgust and maintained an evenness akin to a client just pleading guilty on all counts. McKenster nodded an OK. Etting and Bremer left the meeting.

The client-lawyer room down the hall was more like a jail cell. It has a small desk and two chairs. The room has no windows except for the small transom above the door where a small fan, thanks to taxpayers, had been installed. The standard-issue light fixture with two bulbs, adorned by a plastic covering without cracks, was decorated by a collection of dead bugs.

"Peter, do you think there may be any more tax documents at your apartment? Any additional records will show your good faith to the IRS. Perhaps we could call Glenda and ask her to look again. One other thing. What tax preparing company handled your returns?"

"Well, Mr. Etting. Our tax returns were put together by a fella down at the office. He works in accounting and needs the extra money."

Internally, Etting again questioned why he took this case. At every intersection was an accident waiting to happen. Sometimes, he lectured himself, the wise thing would be to examine the downside of a potential case with as much scrutiny as any ancillary community good. But limiting oneself to sure winners did not fit his idea of lawyering.

"Tell me," Etting requested, his impatience leaking, "your friend at the office is an expert in taxes related to foreign investment? He can sense a dry hole in a Mideast oil scam and know what to do? He knows how to treat depreciation on equipment and balance gambling losses with winnings? Is able to compute base values on appreciated real estate? Is savvy about what deductions are legal and what is not? Able to spot and question a $15,000 gift to a church?"

He stopped, exhausted by his own exasperation. Seconds passed.

"I'm sorry, Mr. Bremer," Etting said. "That was unprofessional."

"No, you're right. I have been foolish. In many ways." He brushed his hand through his hair, then recombed it with his fingers, adjusted his tie. "My judgment, okay, my moral and ethical compass, has been off center for years—except for Glenda. That was a right decision."

Etting was unsure where to go, how to save his client.

"Let's call Glenda," he said. "Perhaps she can shed some light on something."

They walked down the hall to a pay booth. Bremer dialed and Glenda picked up on the fourth ring. He asked about other records and the $15,000. Etting could not hear what Glenda was saying, but his interpretive skills led him to believe that little news was forthcoming. Bremer nodded at the dialer as his way of communicating. He hung up after a few minutes.

"Glenda says we've been over all this before. There are no other tax records at the apartment. Everything was turned over to Harry down at the office. As for the church donation, she believes an error was made on the return, that it's more likely we gave $150."

The balance of the hearing lasted nearly two hours. Etting knew the church donation was merely an opening song in the IRS repertoire. Most of the hearing focused on foreign investments, treatment of bonuses, and gambling losses. Bremer's responses seemed to be a range of off-key dissonance.

A week before Thanksgiving Bremer was served a notice that he was to appear for arraignment in Federal Court on Monday, Jan. 12.

Chapter 29

May 1963, Kansas State Penitentiary

Bobby Bremer stood before the parole board for the second time since his fight with Hogg Mulder. Again he explained the circumstances of the clash, that it was Mulder who came up from behind and ignited the confrontation. He recounted the history between the two and that he had had no trouble with other inmates in the institution.

Molly Bremer and her father drove up from Little Rock to testify on his behalf. She again recited her son's situation in facing the difficult teen years without a father. If he was paroled, she said she would gladly have Bobby live with her, that there was plenty of room at her Little Rock home.

Prior to the hearing, she had even managed for Peter to call his brother and wish him success in being paroled. Unfortunately Peter spent most of the time talking about his new "executive" position with a St. Louis company and how much money he was making. Life was good in St. Louis.

Outside the Lansing prison, life bloomed too. Trees, bushes, and lawns throughout Kansas and the Midwest were coming alive from winter's hibernation. The energizing smell of springtime and the lure of open spaces infiltrated even tough places like a penitentiary. Freedom was in the air. Blacks in Birmingham, Ala., led by Dr. Martin Luther King, marched for an end to segregation. King would end up in jail.

The hearing room was not far from the library. Librarian Forsythe took time to testify, telling how Bobby volunteered there and had taken an interest in poetry. No one else attended. The smiling countenance of Warden David McNabb, confined to a gold-rimmed picture frame, looked down on the proceedings from the back wall. He was flanked by the Kansas and US flags.

It was a simple room with adequate lighting and enough space to accommodate five times the number attending. If there was anything to complain about, it was the strong odor of the freshly applied varnish to the wooden floor. The lacquer's polyurethane was seeking to escape its chemical incarceration, not unlike the designs of every inmate in the place.

"Mr. Bremer," a parole board member asked, "do you see yourself as ready to re-enter the outside world? In your short life, you have kicked over the traces many times, as a juvenile and as an adult. What makes you think you have had sufficient time in prison to contemplate your sins against society?" Not once did the man look Bobby in the eye. It seemed he was addressing a piece of paper on the desk.

Bremer knew he was not up for sainthood, that his record was full of bad decisions. He also knew a price had to be paid, but he believed he had done that. Authorities read the fight with Mulder all wrong. He was the one accosted. He was the victim, merely defending himself as anyone would do. But none of that gained a foothold. The official process saw only two inmates fighting.

Bobby looked at the questioner. He was in his fifties but already losing hair by the comb full. His bold red tie was so snug that the veins in his neck protested. The Adam's apple below his pointy chin bobbed with every word. His face was flush with ambiguity to the point where it was questionable if he wanted to be there. He fidgeted inside his light blue suit coat and rebuttoned it. His left hand stroked his forehead, but he steadfastly avoided eye contact.

Does this guy see me as only an inmate? Bremer wondered. *Is he aware that I am a human being, just as subject to injustice as anyone on the outside? Did he hear what I had to say about Mulder? Does he even care, or is he merely fulfilling an appointment made as a result of a donation to the governor's campaign?*

"Mr. Bremer. Did you hear my questions?"

"Yes, sir. I'm right here. Would you look at me, please?"

"I beg your pardon?" the parole board member mumbled, his head still down.

"If you looked at me," Bremer said softly, "I would feel better. I would feel that you are really interested in my case."

The request was ignored.

"You are correct about one thing, sir," Bremer said. "I've had a lot of time to think about things. I have made mistakes. Defending myself against Mr. Mulder was not one of them. We all make mistakes, sir. I'm sure you have made mistakes. The one thing I can say without reservation is that my mom has stood by me through all of this. Her love"—and he looked at her in the public section of the small room—"has never wavered.

"If I have acquired any remorse for what I've done, it's because of my mother. Nothing is due the state of Kansas." Perhaps, he thought seconds too late, he had gone a bit too far. But that was the story of his life. His actions were always slightly ahead of his calculations. "Yes, to answer your question. I think I am ready to be released, ready to live as a regular citizen."

He remained in place to answer any other queries. None seemed forthcoming.

"I'm sure your mother has forgiven you for your mistakes," Bremer told the official.

"I have just one question," said another parole board member who fussed with his ample white beard. Bobby was grateful that the man looked at him, granted him the status of presence. "Why do you say the prison has not helped you, has not in any way changed you?"

It was a worthy question, Bremer thought.

247

"Perhaps I spoke hastily," he answered, hoping to regain some ground he may have lost earlier. "The library here is a wonderful place. Your librarian has given me an appreciation for poetry and has recommended wonderful authors. And by working with the landscaping detail, I have gained skills that perhaps will help me get a job on the outside."

That was the end of the questioning. The parole board chairman said nothing beyond a prepared statement outlining the purpose of the meeting and the appropriate statutes that governed it.

Thirty minutes later Bremer and his family received the word. Parole had been denied a second time. He was not surprised. Molly cried, and her father shook his head in puzzlement. They left for Little Rock the same day.

Bremer returned to his work with the prison landscaping and grounds crew and spent the balance of his days in the library. He read more poetry and books by Jack London, Robert Louis Stevenson, and James Oliver Curwood. Most of all his mind thirsted for stories about plains injustice and the people of posse comitatus. In nearly every situation, Bremer cast himself as the aggrieved party, the target of unfairness.

It was a strong likelihood that he would not receive another parole hearing until early 1965. Under the procedure, he was supposed to be granted another opportunity to air his case within eighteen months, but that schedule was less devoted to rules than the convenience of officials. Bremer's outlook was not hopeful, and more than once he hinted that to Forsythe.

To satisfy his mother's wishes, he attended Protestant church services on a Sunday in June. He then called her. They talked—mostly she talked—for twenty minutes. She planned a visit during the summer. His grandparents were doing fine. Her father still argued with Adora Mae. "I don't know what's keepin' Hattie and her husband from havin' children."

Monday was rainy. The landscaping crew could not work. Bobby glanced out the prison's library window and saw an unending blanket of gray sky. He thought the bleakness was an appropriate metaphor for his life. June is not supposed to be like that. According to singer Shirley Jones, June is supposed to be bustin' out all over. He had seen the movie several times. That's what he felt like—bustin' out.

"Felix, who is the most famous prison escapee?" he asked the librarian as they were restacking books.

"What? What's that you say?" he stammered.

"I asked, who is the best-known person to escape from jail or prison?"

"Well, I don't rightly know. Let's see. Just a year ago, and you remember the news, two brothers escaped from Alcatraz. Newspapers said they somehow snuck through the prison drainpipe system, worked their way to the waterfront, and used an inflatable raft to leave Alcatraz Island. They were never seen again. No one knows if they really escaped or drowned trying."

He looked at Bremer and wondered what was going through his mind.

"I suppose some people would say John Dillinger," Forsythe said. "He made escaping jail a pastime. Often his gang would spring him. It was said he escaped from a prison in Indiana, near Chicago, by using a fake wooden gun he had carved and blackened with shoe polish. That's what the newspapers said, if you can believe them. That's pretty good." He chuckled. "Maybe a wooden nickel isn't worth anything, but a wooden gun will buy your freedom. Crazy stuff."

Bremer said nothing.

June weather improved, and the rest of summer was almost ideal. Both temperatures and humidity were below average for eastern Kansas. Bremer's work in landscaping left him little time at the library. For the first time, the grounds crew anticipated making money for the prison. License plates would not be the only profitable prison commodity. Seedlings of fir and spruce trees planted ten years ago had reached the magical height of Christmas trees.

All through the summer, the crew pruned trees and maintained the ten-foot fences around the two-acre field in efforts to keep out hungry deer. They also nursed shade tree saplings and ornamental shrubbery in what had developed into a gardening enterprise. A prison guard Buck Jackson, who acted as sort of a foreman for the group, became so enthused he recommended that a horticulture education program be started.

The question Jackson posed shortly before Thanksgiving was how to sell the trees—to individual customers at the prison entrance or by the truckload to outside vendors. That was quickly settled by the administrator of prison occupational services. The trees would be sold in bulk to dealers who have retail lots throughout the area. That would expand sales opportunities and keep inmates inside the walls.

Henry Bexler, known around Cold Springs, Kans., simply as Bex, was something of a plains philosopher. The stocky farmer intermingled complaints of "lousy" grain prices and "terrible" weather with the "oppression" of government. His grandfather was a native of northern Germany. Hence his father, like many German descendants, suffered insults and worse during World War I. Those scars were handed down to the son.

He was drafted by the army in 1942 and fought in the North African campaign against Rommel. The inherited anti-German wounds were smothered by his determination to show his American colors. He became more anti-German than those who loathed his grandfather. His basic training memento was a tattoo of Uncle Sam punching the likeness of Adolph Hitler.

Bexler was a crack shot and earned an expert badge firing the M1 rifle. In the years after the war, he won shooting competitions in Kansas and Colorado. He never married, and acquaintances confided to one another that that was probably for the good of both Bex and any prospective wife. He would not be comfortable in any fifty-fifty arrangement.

Some detractors called him "Shorty," typically those who disagreed with his politics, but that was really a misnomer. Bexler was five-nine and built like a corner post. He had the patience of a stepped-on rattlesnake. Though he lived alone on a 670-acre spread north of town, he was not a recluse. He drove to town at least once a week for groceries and a resupply of beer—and, of course, a chance to complain with other "victims" of the system. The day would include a stop at Keil's Tavern, where he played euchre and drank stubbies for several hours, all the time dispensing his latest opinions about the "government's attempt to control how we breathe."

He claimed not to benefit "one dime" from taxes he paid. He bragged that the rural school he attended for eight years was better than "town school" but never recognized that taxes paid the education bills. Ornery as a mule with a toothache, he refused to link taxation with the good gravel road that brought him to town or the county fire department that helped rescue a calf from a sinkhole.

"I'll play it alone," he informed his euchre partner. Bexler picked up the right bower in hearts. "If you have more than three trumps," he addressed the opponents, "you've got me. Otherwise give us four points. That puts us out—what's that? —five games to one," he boasted, knowing the tally full well.

He usually played it alone in life. The exception was gab sessions with several men in the region who commiserated about life's "tribulations," especially taxes and the use of the law in enforcing payment on bank loans. It rubbed him wrong that banks, as he put it, lent other people's money, including his own, and "make ungodly sums on it. And then they send the sheriff to collect on some poor soul."

Ultimately Bexler joined the Prairie People for Less Government, a loosely organized group that met with no regularity and usually in the winter when farm work was slow. It had several "town people" as members too; fierce independence was the common core. It seemed they talked more about the "evils" of banking than the "evils" of government.

A specific case heightened their dislike of bankers, and they asked Bexler to write about the "injustice." A farm couple's barn had been struck by lightning and burned. They managed to save their animals. However, the money intended to repay a bank loan was used to rebuild the structure. Bank officials did not see the wisdom in delaying satisfaction on the mortgage and, after several warnings, began foreclosure.

Bexler's article pitting the plight of the farm couple against the power of bankers received wide distribution among Kansas and Colorado weekly newspapers. The *Leavenworth Times* republished the item on its op-ed page. That's where Bobby Bremer read it. He wanted more information on Bexler's group. To him the foreclosure case smacked of the injustice he believed he had been subjected to. No credence was given to background circumstances, be it the fire that the farm couple didn't set or the fight he didn't start.

Bremer knew that prison personnel read inmate letters, those received and those sent. It was part of the security process, the prevention of contraband or any other devious objective. He wrote a letter to Bexler, but mailed it to the attorney in Garden City, Kans., who had represented him in court, and asked him to forward it. Ordinarily mail sent to inmates' attorneys was not censored. He asked Bexler to send any replies through the lawyer.

The exchange of correspondence began in July, and by late fall Bremer had a good picture of the Less Government group. He became aroused to the notion that citizens must be government watchdogs, especially at the local level where they could do something about the way laws impacted life. He liked the ideas forwarded by one Jacob Spietz, who argued that it is sometimes necessary for people to take "affirmative action."

Autumn was as gracious as summer; its shorter days were busy painting trees on a clement canvas. The mild weather extended into November, a reprieve from the normal winter prelude sent down from Nebraska. Then, in the midst of bright fall skies, the entire nation went dark. President Kennedy was assassinated in Dallas. A numbness permeated life. A man, a shooter, was arrested. Was he a pawn? Did he act on his own because of some disagreement with policy?

These were questions with unusual poignance for Bremer. He had no political party loyalties. He heard the anti-Catholic polemics before the election. And while Kennedy's father had been a kingpin in Boston financial circles and operated on the edge of honesty, the president was more like Franklin Roosevelt, Bremer thought, someone interested in the plight of the small guy, conscious of injustice.

Bremer and Forsythe talked about all these things. Was it ever right to take the law into your own hands? The country's forefathers seemed to think so. Didn't they endorse a home militia? Was that the same thing, though, as some mob gathering up broomsticks and shotguns to interpret justice as they saw it? Isn't that the job of law enforcement? Keeping order in a society of clashing opinion? The alternative is chaos and anarchy.

Late November cooled quickly. Two inches of snow decorated eastern Kansas and the prison tree farm. It converted the collective mindset from pumpkins and hayrides to winter and Christmas. The firs and spruces of the tree farm also underwent a metamorphosis, from a battalion of evergreens at parade rest to stand-alone adornments "just right" for someone's parlor. They were cut down, pruned of deadwood, and stacked in piles of twenty.

As the month proceeded, vendor trucks of all sizes arrived. Many vehicles had wooden racks. Trees were loaded and secured by large tarps. The inmates at the nursery—with their usual drab green prison garb, augmented by heavy gray coats, gloves, and boots—filled as many as a dozen vehicles a day.

During the second week of the rush, on a late Friday afternoon, the landscaping crew was faced with five trucks waiting for trees. Among them was a walk-in van, rented by the Kiwanis Club from Reno, Kans.

Overhead lights in the prison compound began to trickle on as the sun faded and December shadows slipped in place.

There was an overflow of human impatience by both vendors and tired inmates. Trees were being tossed helter-skelter into trucks. The Kiwanis van looked as if it were gagging on green clumps. Bremer jumped into the back of the van and stacked trees to make the best use of the space. Finally the van was full.

"That's it," he yelled at another inmate, who then moved down the line to load another truck. Bremer looked around and saw no one. A growing amazement seized his mind. He had a feeling not unlike that of a poor chap who answers the front door and is greeted by a beautiful woman who hands him a million-dollar check.

He pulled the rear doors shut, crawled to the front of the van, and snuggled beneath the forest of Christmas trees. He held his breath. There was talk outside. Among the mumbling, the driver acknowledged the receipt of an invoice. And then the pair wished each other a Merry Christmas. The van started up.

Two minutes later the big gates swung open, and the truck convoy exited.

It all happened so quickly and instinctively. He was like a baggage handler who stowed away on a nonstop flight to Hawaii, his mind filled with grass skirts and Mai Tai drinks. Bremer had pondered escape. He was not a lifer, not a dangerous killer, yet the thought of escape gnawed at him like an ulcer, fed by a besieged perception of having been wronged.

Just like that, the Kiwanis vehicle and Bremer were headed west. No one apparently had noticed. He could not believe it. Escape was a dream. But dreams seldom come pine scented. Opportunity had dressed up as Christmas trees. The Kiwanis van was the open door.

It was a ride that came with mixed feelings. Elation. Apprehension. Joy bursting to be heard. Fear pressed into silence. The sensation of undetected presence. The anguish of ultimate discovery. Gears shifted. Brakes screeched. At every stop sign, Bremer expected the rear van doors to fly open and the warden himself to search the vehicle pine needle by pine needle.

The van rumbled on—five miles, ten miles. Eventually, he would have to consider the next step. What happens if the driver opens the back doors? When will they unload the trees? When do I jump out and what do I do? Where do I go? But for the moment, he relished escape.

There was no running past guard towers. There was no hail of bullets, screaming men. He didn't have to swim through waste flowing from the sewage system to gain freedom. No raft necessary to bounce through choppy waters. He didn't even suffer a haunting glimpse at the prison bastion, standing there naked in the dim light of early winter.

The simplicity of it, Bremer thought, would have made John Dillinger proud.

Chapter 30

1963, Kansas

"You fucking idiot."

Buck Jackson stared at the floor, hands held outward and upward in perplexed dismay. He looked like the poor soul who just drove through a red light with the cop car stopped in the opposite lane.

Jackson, the guard who supervised the Christmas tree loading operation at Kansas State Prison, was given a dressing down that nearly ripped off his uniform. He claimed he conducted a head count at the prison nursery after all the trucks had departed and inmates returned to their respective cell blocks.

Clearly his reckoning was flawed.

The bottom line in his miscalculation was that one man, Bobby Bremer, was missing at evening supper's regular check.

Life can be cruel. As a senior in high school, Jackson was not in the running for class valedictorian. Yet had there been an award for modest goodwill, he would have been selected. He did not excel in sports but rather in sportsmanship. He believed others, gave them the benefit of the doubt. Perhaps those are not the best credentials to bring as a prison guard.

Trust inside a penitentiary is unwise, like petting a Doberman guard dog.

Jackson was the type who would hand a dollar to the town drunk after the blotto promised to spend the money on "a hot meal." He could have been the poster boy for adherents of the "I Told You So" guild or the "No Good Deed Goes Unpunished" fellowship.

"I suggest you take a course in counting," the night supervisor advised. That was after a litany of cuss words and unflattering adjectives. "We haven't had a prisoner walk away from Lansing in years. And now some guy makes like a pine tree and fades into the forest? This is not a pretty picture, Jackson. Perhaps you should update your resume."

Cameras at the gate led authorities to focus on the only enclosed vehicle that left the compound. The van, records showed, was driven by a volunteer from the Reno, Kansas, Kiwanis Club. Telephone calls produced no answers. An APB was issued, and deputies fanned out on state and county roads in the thirty miles between Lansing and Reno.

Bremer did his own math.

As the van rumbled west on a two-lane blacktop, he first estimated how long it would take to discover he was missing. That, he decided, could be anywhere from a few minutes to an hour. He knew Reno was no more than an hour away. It was supper time. The van driver may be hungry. Would he stop? It was unlikely the trees would be unloaded immediately.

He tried to visualize when and where the driver would stop. At some Kiwanis lot? Drive-up restaurant? His residence? Reno was an unincorporated mishmash of mobile homes, gas stations, fast food, and dead-end streets, all cohabitating with the busyness of the nearby Kansas Turnpike.

After ten minutes his equations hit an abrupt bump in the road. The driver stopped. Was the halt voluntary or provoked by flashing red lights? He heard the driver exit. There was mumbling, but it was not a conversation. The man was talking to himself. Then the rear van doors burst open. The driver continued to verbally review the matter at hand.

"I could tell by the rattle they weren't closed tight," the van driver said aloud to himself. "I should have checked them before I left rather than depend on that dumb-ass inmate."

He slammed the double doors shut and turned the levered bar. Bremer relaxed, only to suffer a twitching of the nose that was about to advance into an olfactory explosion. Pine needles collaborated to stimulate a looming sneeze. His only antidote was to bury his face into his thick winter coat. Again, timing was his comrade. The noise of the truck gaining speed muffled the spasmodic revolution.

As the van continued, Bremer reassessed his immediate plans. Should the driver stop again, he would jump out. Maybe. If he could discern that the driver was walking away to someplace, any place, leaving the van was a sensible choice for him. Besides, the pine tar perfume was building into a powerfully unattractive essence. But then what? He pondered options, envisioned the unexpected, and drew up countermeasures. Spontaneity would be in play.

By the time the van stopped again, some forty minutes later, his mind was a web of indefinite strategies. He heard traffic, big trucks grinding and moaning in a symphony of chaos. Shrill horns issued warnings. Hydraulic brakes announced intentions. It had all the elements of a truck stop. Bremer heard the meek beep of what he interpreted as a Volkswagen frantically maneuvering to avoid a restyling from a semi. There was a perpetual coming and going.

In seconds the van's driver got out, closed the door, and walked away. This was it, decision time. Bremer slowly worked his way out of the thicket of trees, groped for the inside lever, pushed forcefully upward with his right palm, and carefully opened the left-side panel. No one was close by. He stepped out and closed the door, vowing never to become intimate with a spruce tree again.

His eyes adjusted to the irregular lighting of what was obviously a major truck stop. Diesel fumes replaced the pine spores in his nose. There was a wispy mist that took on a greater magnitude in the amber glow of overhead lamps. It hastened the steps of visitors and dampened idle chatter. Bremer walked casually between the assembly of trucks, their motors humming in idle content. He looked at everything, but nothing in particular.

Then, inside a vacant cab, he spotted a faded red coverall hooked on a peg behind the driver's seat. Bremer confidently stepped up, opened the truck door, quickly grabbed the garment, and walked away. He strode along a row of trucks and stepped in between a Peterbilt and Kenworth, angry-looking monsters that seemed geared for a rumble. He removed his heavy jacket and slipped the coveralls over his washed-out green prison suit. He folded his blue jacket in his arms and assumed the persona of a big rig operator.

So far, so good.

On second thought, Bremer decided to avoid any pretense of being a trucker. That could lead to questions he was unable to adequately answer. Rather he would become what he once was, a hired hand at a western slaughterhouse, a man whose car broke down and who was looking for a lift to the end of Kansas.

Yes, handling cattle can be rough work. No, ah worked in the yards and not the cutting floor. The car? An old Dodge Coronet, a junker on its last leg. A rust bucket. Yeah. Cars can grind your patience, if you know what ah mean. Livestock haulers? Really? Fellows taking cattle from the KC stockyards west, you say? Thanks for the tip. Ah'll look around.

She was a pretty little thing, punching a cash register probably to earn money for college. And it never hurts to employ a perky, good-looking young lady to soften up the pocketbooks of grumpy Teamster Union members and other steering wheel wrestlers whose dispositions have been curdled by sore posteriors. Bremer lied and told her he had already eaten and was looking for passage west.

He stretched his legs in the aisles of the truck stop store, inspecting everything from beef jerky to girly magazines. Mostly he wanted to remove the chill from his bones and reset his short-term compass. Recalculate. The Kansas Turnpike, part of the new I-70 four-lane highway across mid-America, was one of the nation's busiest roads. A section just west of Topeka, opened seven years ago, was the initial part of the interstate system. There were patches of finished I-70 from Maryland to the Colorado border.

"Good luck in findin' a ride," she cooed as he exited the store.

There were many cattle trucks in the big parking lot, but most were empty. They must be heading east. Bremer knew there was another option for moving on. Somewhere in the vicinity of Lawrence, Kans., railroads headed west, and he thought one might be the Santa Fe. He could hop a freight. That had its perils too. Cold and railroad cops.

His ears perked. He turned his head into the drizzle, aligning his hearing position like a rotating TV antenna. The sound, though muffled by the heavy air, was familiar. Was it mooing? Or the wind singing a cold refrain? He followed the reprise. It became louder. There, near the end of the lot, a load of White Face steers sang undirected lows, mournful solos of portended fate. He gazed at them as if he were in an art gallery, sizing up a Julien Dupre painting.

"Howdy, young feller."

Bremer jumped like a roped doggie about to be branded.

"Whoa. Whoa," said a gravelly voice through a bed of white whiskers. "Sure as hell didn't mean to startle ya."

Bremer raised his hands in understanding.

"Just lookin' at this load of cattle and thinkin' maybe theys headed for one of the packing houses out west. Name's Jeb Mossman," said Bremer, greeting the man with his right hand. "Some nasty night."

"Oh, could be worse. I've driven in blizzards and on roads slicker than a Chicago con artist. Nice to meet ya, Jeb. Wayne Norman. I drive for whoever pays me the most. Right now, that's an outfit called Great Western. They run a feedlot in the far end of the state. You guessed right. These here pretty bovines will make fine steaks."

Bremer was as shocked as a newborn baby. Did he suddenly open his eyes to an opportunity for a ride west? Had a ticket away from Lansing just been plunked into his hand? He had to calm his hopes, act muted, and not appear like a nervous defector from the halls of justice. He coaxed himself into the role of unassuming drifter, a hard-luck victim who was willing to work hard if he could find any work at all.

"Damn car broke down. No big loss. Hopin' to get a job at one of them new packing plants out west in Kansas or Colorado. Hear theys hirin'."

His opening declaration, with a hint of supplication, drew no response. Wayne Norman, he supposed, was no road novice. A man of average height, who clearly missed no meals, Norman presented a weathered face that was full of savvy. He also guessed Mr. Norman was content to have himself for company and not someone dependent on social interlocutory.

"You probably know the lay of the land out there. Job prospects good?"

"Where ya from, young man?"

"Little Rock," Bremer replied. "Arkansas. Originally."

"Travelin' pretty light," he said without drama. Norman readjusted his cap in a habit that accompanied questions in the making.

He caught Bremer flat-footed, short both a suitcase and immediate response. He scratched his capless head in search of a reply, then pulled up the coverall collar around his neck to disguise the starkness of his chilled silence and any telltale sign of prison garb. There is no manual detailing the perils of prison escape and how to be ready for them.

"Ah don't have a lot of clothes or possessions of any kind," Bremer said with a sheepish look. He paused, searching like a struggling playwright brooding about the next line. Only he worried about creating a web that would trap himself. He looked the trucker in the eyes, bent on adding genuineness to his story.

"After ah quit a job in Sedalia, that's over'n Missouri, ah thought ah'd go west again for work. Know a fella out near Goodland, so ah packed up summer clothes and a few other things and sent em ahead. Glad ah did send stuff ahead after the old Dodge broke down. Ain't got the money to fix it. But ah don't mind hard work. Ah'll get back on mah feet."

"That right?" the trucker said, more with acceptance than questioning. Bremer sensed the trucker had a good ear for sorting out truth from babble. "Mr. Mossman, if that's your name, I don't know what yer runnin' from, and it ain't my business. But your eyes don't line up with your story. I hope your lookin' for work. Everybody who can work should work."

He reached under his open jacket, hitched up his belt, then rubbed his beard as if it somehow housed the answers to difficult questions.

"It ain't my custom," he said soberly, "but I'm offerin' you a ride part of the way. I cut south before Goodland. I'll let you out at Oakley, if that's all right. It'll be darn near breakfast time by then. What'd ya say your name was, Jeb?

"Yep. Jeb it is."

"Well, if you say so, Jeb. Here's a buck for breakfast."

"Golly, that's kind of ya, Mr. Norman. Ah just don't—"

"Save it, Jeb."

Five minutes later Bremer was turning west onto I-70 with the trucker and thirty-eight head of steers. He looked back through the semi's large side mirrors. There were several vehicles with flashing red lights entering the truck stop.

Chapter 31
1976, Cedar Rapids

"All rise!"

The bailiff shouted the familiar order, and everyone in the ornate Federal Courtroom stood as a slim yet obviously fit man entered from the door from behind the bench. He took one step up, sat down in a high-backed, black leather chair, grabbed the gavel, and slammed the session to order. Those present then sat down.

Judge Maxwell Mullin, labeled as "Move It Along Mullin" by some attorneys, peered at the paperwork on his desk through eyeglasses perched on the tip of his nose. This was routine for him; he'd been a federal district court judge for fifteen years. His habits seldom changed. He tugged on his left ear lobe, pulled back the sleeves on his black robe, reshuffled his papers, and looked out at the courtroom.

"This is the matter of the United States Government, more specifically the Internal Revenue Service, vs. Peter Benjamin Bremer," Mullin bellowed loud enough, Peter thought, for the entire block-long building to hear. He was surprised at the use of his middle name. *The IRS does its homework. They don't want to be confused with some other turkey named Peter Bremer.* He nearly forgot he had a middle moniker. Benjamin was his grandmother's maiden name.

"This is trial case No. US1975-493005 for the Northern District of Iowa, January 6, 1976. Cedar Rapids, Iowa, brought under Title 26 of the Federal Code. Mr. United States Attorney, are you ready to proceed?"

"We are, your honor," said Everett Schrader.

"And let's see"—the judge looked down at his paperwork again—"Mr. Etting, the attorney for the defendant, and Mr. Bremer, are you ready to proceed?"

"We are, your honor," Etting said.

Judge Mullin could be as stiff as a banker's collar on board meeting day, and he was often procedural to a fault. But he was highly respected as a no-nonsense jurist keen on the law. That is not to say that he did not, like many judges, have idiosyncrasies. He steamed when parties in a case were not present at the appointed time, though he was sometimes late—occasionally because of a long golf game. He could be grouchy, affable, or benign, sometimes all within the span of one hearing.

"This matter will be held before the bench, that is without a jury, as heretofore agreed upon. Mr. Schrader, you may proceed."

Except for court officials the only other people present, aside from the principals, were Glenda and a reporter from *The Gazette*, the local newspaper. Tax hearings ordinarily are painfully boring and ignored by the news media, but this procedure involved the president of Riverside Packing Co. That elevated the news significance.

It was akin to the newspaper's policy on shoplifting. Such a charge was too insignificant to take up valuable newsprint unless the mayor or some other notable was involved. The formula follows the "man bites dog" standard of news.

Mrs. Bremer was not charged—either due to prosecutorial discretion, benevolence, or the fact that the entanglements of the matter focused on her husband. She sat, alone, in the first row of seats behind the courtroom's wooden divider rail. She was directly back from the defense table where her husband and his attorney pondered stacks of legal paperwork.

Glenda removed her fur stole, suede gloves, and red winter coat but not her matching pillbox hat. She surveyed the courtroom. Her exploratory face revealed that she was in unfamiliar territory, one with the potential for life-changing consequences. She wriggled to find a level of comfort on the wooden seat.

Bright sunshine sifted through window shades and drapes on the courtroom's west side, illuminating justice and all present. However, no light was strong enough to reveal the historic murals above the room's wooden paneling. The paintings, products of the Great Depression starving artists' program, had been covered with whitewash. They depicted all sorts of prairie history. Some segments, sketches of vigilante justice and other behavior believed inappropriate, doomed the entire mural.

The five-and-a-half-foot-tall mural, commissioned in 1936, spanned the entire 216-foot circumference of the courtroom. It alternately received praise and reproach from an ambiguous audience. A judge ordered it covered up in 1951. Ten years later, the whitewash was removed. In 1964 it was painted over again. The yo-yo paint job would have given lead artist Francis Robert White a brush with abject despair.

None of that retouched antiquity concerned Bremer. He was fixed on the present, charges of income tax evasion, filing fraudulent and false statements, and failure to provide required tax documents. The penalties upon conviction ranged up to a $250,000 fine and three years in prison. It is the kind of prospect that will tighten your necktie and make the toes in your Florsheim wingtips tingle.

Schrader monotoned the essence of the case as formally described in the wherefore and whereas nomenclature of the law. It was during the outlining of possible penalties that Bremer began to stir in his chair next to attorney Dave Etting. As usual the defendant was dapperly dressed and groomed, undeniable evidence of his status but of no importance to the US tax code.

Don McKenster, the chief investigator for the Cedar Rapids IRS office, was the first witness called by Schrader. He outlined the broad scope of federal tax law, how it applied in the case at hand, and pertinent information regarding the investigation of Peter Bremer.

Etting asked questions of form and one that raised the specter of selective enforcement. McKenster denied that people of Bremer's stature were targeted. On re-direct questioning by Schrader, McKenster outlined numbers of tax evasion cases brought by the local office "without regard to the prominence of the subject."

As Etting expected, when Schrader got into the meat and potatoes of the IRS case, the emphasis was on bonus payments received by Bremer from several sources, his alleged losses connected with the complicated Middle East oil deal, figures regarding gambling, the murky use of stock options, and a laundry list of other income and deductions over the years. Prairie Church and the purported $15,000 donation by the Bremers was an afterthought.

Etting and Schrader did their attorney dances in and out of a labyrinth of tax law. There were the usual attempts by Etting to sever the progression of evidence presented by IRS agents on the more entangled charges and the customary patching job by Schrader. Arguments lumbered for two hours before merciful breaks were called. It was not an easy case to follow. Glenda was among those drowning in legalese.

At the start of the third day, when Schrader called Harry Jensen to the stand, the trial shook off some of its tedium. Jensen was an accountant at Riverside Pack, the man who handled Bremer's tax returns. It quickly became evident that Jensen, while holding a two-year accounting certificate from South Dakota Business School, was adrift in the complex swirls of corporate and international tax law.

After both attorneys waded through that maelstrom, Etting questioned Jensen about the $15,000 church donation. He was sure he already knew the answer, but it was one place where he could score a point for his client. Yes, Jensen admitted, it was an error on the tax return. The amount donated should have been listed as $150. Somehow Etting felt he had made a mere dent in the IRS case.

Etting then pounded away at the notion that Bremer was the victim of bad accounting, defective tax preparation, and general malfeasance by those who worked for him. But Shrader time and again returned to the old legal proverb that while people lie and make mistakes, documents "always tell the truth. And whose signature attests to these tax figures? The defendant's." His rebuttal catalog was suffocating.

The "victim" methodology continued when Etting called Bremer to the stand. Opening his client to cross examination was an indication of his grim assessment of Peter Bremer's chances. Glenda was relieved when she heard the judge ask if testimony had concluded, and the lawyers said yes. The final afternoon was devoted to summation.

Judge Mullin said he would review the evidence and testimony and "in due time" issue his judgment. He gave attorneys two days to submit summaries. The IRS agents, while privately confident Bremer would be found guilty, issued a friendly "no comment" when asked by a reporter about expectations. Schrader said he was confident the government had proven its case against Bremer. The always affable Etting could not hide a look that his house had just burned down.

"How do you assess the proceedings? Are you optimistic now that the trial is over?" the reporter asked Bremer as he and Glenda left the courtroom. Bremer, too, appeared defeated, not the suave executive who came out of poverty in Arkansas to dance among a six-figure income with an attractive woman on his arm. He glared at the newsman, shocked that his life was unfolding before the public's eye.

"You are writing about all this?" he asked, as if he just entered Earth from another planet.

"Yes. It's my job," Tom Wendling explained with a baffled look. "I've been in the courtroom every day."

"You realize your stories will ruin my life," Bremer said. "Our life." And he nodded toward Glenda.

"Perhaps you will be found innocent," Wendling replied lamely. He was surprised by Bremer's naïve response and searched for a more lucid comment, one that would draw the big picture. "Keep in mind, our business desk has been running stories of Riverside Pack's recent earnings troubles, including investor claims about poor management. And there have been several advance stories about your tax problems." It was also an attempt at diversion.

"I have nothing further to say," and Bremer walked away.

The next morning Bremer telephoned Wendling.

"Your story in last night's newspaper was incomplete," Bremer complained. "There are things you don't know."

He did not sound angry, but instead despaired and bewildered. Beyond tax and mob loan problems, Riverside Pack fortunes had dimmed. Third quarter was a disappointment, and fourth quarter financials looked even worse. What some had seen as a questionable venture at the onset now took on a lurching perspective.

Wendling said his news story was based on testimony given at the trial. He said if some of the complicated aspects of tax returns and foreign investments had been misconstrued, he would be happy to correct or amplify them. He invited Bremer to come to the newspaper offices, "or I can come to your office." Bremer took up the offer and said he would be at the newspaper by eleven o'clock.

The two-story Gazette building covers a half block on the eastern side of downtown, near Greene Square Park. The newsroom occupies the western portion of the second floor. As you reach the top of the stairs, the morgue and editorial offices are to the right, and sports, local, and national news desks to the left. It is a place of typewriters clacking, paper shuffling, chairs scraping, friendly bantering, and sometimes not-so-sociable yelling.

Word that Bremer, and perhaps his attractive wife, were coming to the newsroom spread like a three-alarm fire. Town blather had illuminated them both as Vogue Magazine models. Compounded by all the intrigue at Riverside Pack, interest spiked like a page-one bulletin, even among a supposed dispassionate crew of writers. As the appointed time approached, reporters and editors drifted toward the windows like carnival gawkers. If the room had been a boat, it would have tipped to one side.

Bremer's black Cadillac pulled curbside on Fifth Street. He got out, ignored the parking meter, and opened Glenda's door. An expensive-looking fur was wrapped about her neck, topping a camel-colored coat and protruding red dress. Matching stilettoes rounded out her ensemble. Bremer, too, was neatly attired, his suit covered by a black wool overcoat. The winter wind tossed his thinning hair. Her blond tresses danced about.

Wendling, not known as having the most orderly desk environs, scurried to find chairs for the forthcoming guests. He grabbed a heavy low-backed chair from the business editor for Bremer and pulled it adjacent to his Smith-Corona typewriter. Then, as the visitors approached, he hastily rounded up a wobbly castor-wheel chair for Glenda. It had a swivel seat, a narrow, torn back, and it looked like it came over on the Mayflower.

Bremer removed his coat and folded it on his lap. She unbuttoned her coat and sought stability on the junky chair. He looked around the noisy place but was not unnerved by the commotion. Glenda felt a collection of eyes as the pretense of normal business persisted. She jumped as a pneumatic tube clunked into a box, returned via a vacuum system after delivering news copy to the back shop.

Wendling removed the papers and scribbled notes that had been suffocating his typewriter and instinctively inserted a clean sheet of paper. He offered neither guest newsroom coffee, which was a thick, black swill that simmered in a forty-cup percolator last scrubbed before Christmas.

It was a peculiar scene, a contrast of seeming wealth and the hoi polloi, designer attire vs. Sears kakis, the kind of diversity unseen at the country club. Having a company president among ink-stained wordsmiths was a rare curiosity. There was an uneasy lack of conversation until Wendling spoke.

"Thanks for coming. You found a parking place?" he asked stupidly. He had a copy of the previous day's story in hand. "What part of the report did you think was lacking or in error?"

Bremer's eyes looked tired. Their sunken posture did not fit his dapper nature and spelled profound anxiety. He was drained of his normal buoyancy. His words seemed to be stuck at the bottom of his throat. They finally wiggled outward.

"The story could have put more emphasis on the hard work that went into the startup of Riverside Pack and our attempts to build a truly diversified company." He looked at Wendling's typewriter as if it held the secret to renewed life. "I really didn't notice any errors. My attorney didn't tell me he saw errors. It could have been more positive." He paused again, searching for words. "It's just that there is so much more to the story."

Wendling waited. Bremer's thoughts were engaged in a tug-of-war. He wanted to explain what he was facing, the peril he perceived from his mob connection. But that could complicate things even more, even escalate danger to Glenda and himself.

"Mr. Bremer?" A puzzled Wendling attempted to reconnect.

By now the usual newsroom hubbub had resumed with local, national, and world life stories unfolding on teletypes and typewriters. AP, UPI, and weather machines pounded out world conditions. Deadlines were approaching for the first edition, and the various newsroom egos searched for common ground, in this case agreement on what should go on page one and what should be prominently displayed inside.

Bremer's "full story" was on hold.

"Mr. Bremer? Are you OK?"

"Yes, yes. I'm sorry," Bremer responded, his hands shaking.

"Here's the thing," he continued softly. "I've made some bad decisions. I'm not talking about these tax issues. There are people trying to kill me."

Again, he hesitated, and Wendling wondered if Bremer was about to totter off his chair.

"When I drive to our plant at Chelsea, I no longer take Highway 30. I take back roads in hopes of living one more day."

With that he rose. He looked defeated. He steadied himself on the chair and looked at Glenda.

They were about to leave.

Chapter 32

1963, Western Kansas

"Welcome to God's country!" he bellowed.

Henry Bexler's wide body filled up the entrance door at the Welcome Inn at the edge of Cold Springs, Kans., like a west-driven squall occupies a weather front. He alternately chewed and puffed on a Roi Tan cigar that bobbed between his words like a pointer stick. His neatly trimmed brown mustache had flecks of white turned yellow.

"By damn! I'm a guessin' you're Bobby Bremer," Bexler said, remaining in place and exhaling another cloud of carcinogen-producing chemicals. "You look worse than a mound of month-old buffalo turds picked over by starvin' crows. It's my wild guess that you didn't get them duds from Rothchild's in Kansas City."

He was enveloped by a blue haze, his head in a smoky ethereal cloak that made him appear as if he was from outer space. It was a daunting site. It caused Bremer to pause, unsure if he was meeting the writer of columns about plains injustice or someone from the netherworld. He stepped up the broken concrete sidewalk and extended his hand to Bexler.

"That's me, Bobby Bremer, No. 174926, at your service," he said softly.

Bexler got the drift, chuckled, sending both the cigar and his girth on a jog.

"I gotta say, Mr. Bremer, you got the nerve of a one-armed rattlesnake tamer, bustin' out of Lansin', feelin' your way across Kansas. Or maybe it's the luck of a cross-eyed chicken that meandered across the road. Anyways, it's good to meet your face, to get a look at the letter writer."

"Nice to meet y'all too, Mr. Bexler."

"I mean to tell ya, I was surprised as a jackrabbit lookin' down the barrel of a shotgun when I got your phone call from down in Oakley this mornin'. And here ya are, the recent enrollee of Lansin' penitentiary. I 'magin' there's swirlin' red lights lookin' for ya all the way along I-70. But you'll be safe up here. Hell, no one knows the town of Cold Springs even exists. The only time we get noticed is when taxes are due."

Bexler touched the rim of his sweat-stained Stetson, then gave a hand of welcome to Bremer. A cigar was a fixture of his sun-burned, stubbled face. His nasty love affair with stogies, friends surmised, was probably another reason for his bachelorhood. Jake Spietz, an alleged friend, once suggested that Bexler and his pervasive cigars could transform a sterile hospital room into a smelly poolhall in minutes.

"Shut the damn door, Bex," someone yelled. "This old stove can't heat all of west Kansas."

"Come on in," Bexler motioned, pulling on the red suspenders that appeared to have a substantial task in keeping his pants up. "Come on in, young feller. Take a load off, and I 'spect you got a load to take off." Bexler ushered Bremer over to one of the three booths in the Welcome Inn. "This ain't exactly the Ritz. Won't see any escargot on the menu, but they got good vittles here."

It could be said that Henry Bexler had a sandpaper personality. However, life's experiences had ground away much of his gruffness, and like most of mankind, aging had mellowed him and imbued him with the inherent need of human contact that former years may have rebuffed. The hard work of ranching had labored to offset his bad eating and smoking habits, so he appeared healthy for a man in his sixties.

His blue-and-black checkered long-sleeved flannel shirt had no restrictions to stay tucked in his pants. His sheepskin coat with fur collar had seen many miles but few trips to the wash machine. Grime from several years of winter wear secured an indelible presence. He hung his coat on a nearby hook and invited Bremer to do the same.

The Welcome Inn had served up generous portions of high-cholesterol food to northwest Kansas for thirty years. Not once had the restaurant received grateful acknowledgement from area heart doctors.

"Hey, Rosie. Come over here and feed this stray doggie. He's been roped and tied for some time and is hungry as a bear just out of hibernation."

"Hi, Henry," Rosemary said, pulling an order pad out of her apron as she approached. "Who's your new friend?"

"Rosie, this here is Jeb, my nephew. He just blew in from Missouri and will be stayin' out at the ranch for a while. I don't presume to know what he wants to order from le menu, but I'm hungry enough to eat pickled pigs ears stickin' out of a bramble bush. She's a looker, ain't she, Jeb? Cuter than an albino grasshopper sittin' on the nose of an Angus steer. Hah, that's a good one."

Bremer's world continued to spin like an off-center top. In a matter of twenty-four hours he'd gone from Bobby, a ward of the Kansas prison system, to Jeb, the free man "nephew" of a Kansas schmoozer. He removed his gray prison jacket, then looked down at the stolen coveralls that hid his distinctive penitentiary wardrobe. He was tired. He guessed he smelled like a mixture of sweat, pine sap, and cattle droppings.

"Hello, Miss," he said feebly. She handed him a sheet of paper with coffee stains that listed four main choices. Bexler was right about one thing. She was cute. And a fellow who's been in prison has an especially keen eye for cute. His appetite overpowered any lingering. "Ah'll take, please ma'am, that special of meatloaf, mashed potatoes with gravy, and green beans. And could ah have a glass of milk, please?"

"Got it, big boy. Imagine someone actually sayin' *please*. And, how about you, Henry?"

"I'll take the 16-ounce steak, rare so's I can hear the moo when you serve it, half-burned potato fries, and a generous helping of cooked carrots. Good for the eyes, you know. Better to see you, Rosemary, honey." He snickered an attempt at humor. "Oh, and Rosemary, would you set aside two pieces of coconut cream pie for our palate la fin?" He laughed again, cigar ashes tumbling on the table.

Rosemary Hitchins gave Bexler a look that, when translated, spelled *idiot*, then wiped the cigar remnants off the table. She was used to the full range of coarse language, leers, and sophomoric behavior. Her body language also fended off conduct that stepped out of bounds, and when that failed, she told bores where to go in clear terms.

Life had not been easy for her and her family. Her younger brother was killed by a drunk driver who was the son of the biggest landowner in the region. He received a minimal sentence of a week in jail and $1,000 fine. It left a sour taste in her mouth. When her father's Uplands Seed Co. in nearby Richland was closed by the banks, she lost her job there and, as the oldest in a strict Methodist family, was sent out in search of a paycheck.

Now twenty-seven, she had worked at the Welcome Inn for four years. She rented a room at the edge of town. Every day the top item on her mind was to find a way out of the Welcome Inn and Cold Springs, Kans. She maintained a friendly smile that disguised a disgust for the likes of Bexler. He never threatened her in any way, but politeness was far off his radar.

Age and greasy restaurant fare had not yet made a claim on her figure. She was a pert five foot six and wore her hair in a frizzy style that looked like she just lost a skirmish with a windstorm. Her red-and-white checkered apron had more grease spots than a mechanic's shirt at the end of the week.

"Tell me, boy," Henry said as Rosemary rounded up their order, "how you flew the coop and got out here."

Bremer explained the peculiarities of happenchance. It was the serendipity of Christmas trees, the Kiwanis Club, mooing bovines, and kind-hearted truckers with obliging curiosity that brought him to Cold Springs. The entire odyssey was mysterious to him too. Crazy, also, was the brief time he had to wait for rides, subject to the hitchhiker-escapee role. He walked a mere half mile from the junction outside Cold Springs to the Welcome Inn.

"The trucker who let me out at Oakley gave me a dollar, or ah wouldn't have any money to telephone. And the feller at the feed store there looked up your number."

"Well, you're sure a lucky sumbitch." Bexler employed his philosophy. "We'll get your belly satisfied, then go over to Maud's Western Wear and get you some clothes to replace that fancy tuxedo your wearin'. When we get out to the ranch, we'll conduct formal rituals and bury the prison garb deep so starving coyotes won't dig it up to revel in the smell of cow dung."

"Mr. Bexler, do ya really think it's necessary to be callin' me Jeb? Ah mean, don't the people around here know who y'all are, and if'n you have siblin's and nephews? And b'sides, ah don't 'zactly talk like a Missourian."

"Oh, hell, son. Do you think we'll be going to dances and coming-out parties and rubbing elbows at church picnics? Only a few people will know you as Jeb. The rest won't give a damn. Hell, I live in nowheres.

"With a strong wind pushing us and the F-250 cranking on all cylinders, we'll be out to the ranch in twenty-five minutes. Half of that is on a winding dirt lane with bumps that will rearrange your molars if you don't keep your mouth closed. My lane is bounded by winter wheat that's a couple inches high, and when the wind is right, it's as pretty as a south sea lagoon.

"Further up, near the house, there's an assortment of foxtail, witchgrass, jimson, and other weeds that seek to squeeze out the wheat with the tenacity of a banker. And about a hundred yards beyond the house is a spring-fed stream. You can see this is action central. In other words, you'll damn near be at the end of the world."

Bremer got the message, and Rosemary brought the food.

Bexler looked around the room and leaned toward Bremer, a nod to precaution even at the end of the world.

"Your mom lives in Arkansas?" Bexler asked.

"Yes, sir. In Little Rock."

"She know you escaped?"

"Doubt it."

"Well, if she doesn't know now, she will in a short time. They will call your mom to find out what she knows about your disappearance. They might even think you went to her home."

"Do you think ah should call her?" Bobby asked meekly.

Bexler chewed on the question and his steak at the same time.

"Damn this is good," he said. "Done just right." And he waved his fork like he was symphony conductor. "Angus, corn fed, straight from the feedlots. Helluva a lot better than that tough range beef. That's like eating deer that pump iron." He finally sliced off another piece of beef, seared on the outside and hot, juicy, and tender red on the inside.

"There ain't no buffalo out here anymore, is there?" Bremer said quizzically and with the hesitance of a freshman in history class.

"What are you talking about? Buffalo?" Bexler was puzzled for a second. "Oh, I see. The buffalo turd thing. Son, did you ever hear of metaphors and hyperbole? I don't know about your callin' your mom or writin' her. Let me think on that."

Bremer told him of his family history, the fact that his dad took off when he was twelve. He lavished praise on his mother and told of her hard work during the war to provide for the family.

"Mom was the glue," Bobby said, surprised at his own candor. "Y'all don't mahnd havin' an escapee in your house?" Bremer asked straight out. "That's takin' a big chance, but ah sure do thank y'all".

"Look, I sure as hell would rather have one of those shapely cheerleaders from Kansas State, but none of them has called. So I'm stuck with you. You're no killer. From what you say, you're like a lot of folks in this world. A victim of injustice. We read your letters, at our meetings too. I think you were railroaded in Garden City and then again at the prison."

"This sure is good pah," Bremer said.

Bexler took time out from eating, placed his fork reluctantly on the table, and gave Bremer a repulsive look. It was almost as if Bremer had said something offensive about Henry's family.

"Look," Bexler said, shaking his head, "the first thing we have to do is teach you how to talk. You mutilate words like a tongue-twisted auctioneer. It's *pie, p-i-e, pie*, not *pah*. The *i* is long. It's *f-eye-ve* o'clock, not *fahv*. With that cornpone talk and okra slobber, you'll stand out in these parts like a feral pig. Not that you'll be rubbing elbows with anyone from the literary club.

"Let's get another thing straight. My hired hand quit two weeks ago. I need muscle, and you fit the bill. I'll pay you thirty dollars a week plus room and board. I'll even toss in the duds at Maud's. Can you ride a horse?"

"Never been on one."

"Well, son, your rear end is in for a shock. We finish about 200 head of steers and feed the same number of calves. Anyways, you'll have more blisters on your butt than a dog has fleas. By the time you get comfortable on your horse, your ass will be like saddle leather. You'll get the hang of it. And remember, there's no one around here to complain to."

Bremer finished his pie and looked around. He didn't see a single indication that Christmas was a short time away. No tree. No stars. No colorful decorations of any kind.

"Do you observe Christmas out here?"

"Yes, we do," Bexler said, wiping a speck of meringue off his lip. "It comes on December 25 every year, just like in New York City. Our calendar has all sorts of holidays. Thing is, we do chores every day." He nibbled on some stray coconut. "If you wanted to put up a Christmas tree, you should have brought one along. You were in the middle of a truckload of them. Won't find any cedars on my place, but you can go up to the bluffs where the spring comes out. Ask old Gus Nemmers if you can cut down one of his trees."

They left the Welcome Inn and walked over to Maud's. From there they headed out to Bexler's ranch.

"I didn't mean to sound like a soul without redemption back there," Bexler said contritely as they turned off on his private lane. "I'm a Christian. My parents belonged to the Episcopal Church, down in Goodland. But out here, there's not much opportunity for church. A person becomes adrift regarding religion and things like that. But I believe in Christmas and all that it stands for."

The old Ford pickup lumbered along like it rested on steel girders. Bexler had nursed it through two revolutions of the odometer, and while the body displayed chips, dents, and rust—all the stains of life on the plains—the engine still had some remnants of its showroom years. Like all farmers, Bexler could fix things, and he had not only performed regular maintenance but did major repairs.

After some time and Henry's run-away babbling, they turned off the main road. A mailbox that leaned in the direction of the postman signaled the Bexler lane. In less than a hundred yards, the right front tire dropped into a six-inch hole and nearly yanked the steering wheel from Bexler's grip. Parts for an electric generator jumped and clanked in the bed of the truck as if shocked into action. Bremer got an education on Bexler's short fuse.

"Goddamit!" he said, gaining control of the vehicle and readjusting his Stetson. "I've hit that same damn pothole three times now. It's like a bad dream, an old adversary. I have a notion when we get to the house to grab my shotgun, come back out here and shoot the son-of-a-bitch."

A few more miles soothed his temper like aloe on a burn.

"Got a better idea. I'm gonna send you out armed with a half load of sand and gravel, and if that hole ever shows up again, I'll shoot you."

He seemed satisfied with that.

"At home, when we was little," Bremer said, "Mom helped us make popcorn strings for the Christmas tree. And we assembled paper chains."

"Were you really a bad ass prison guy? You're going all mushy on me kid," Bexler said with a sour look. "We ain't goin' to make any damn paper chains or string popcorn. Holy Moses and Ezekiel too. Maybe you should call your mother."

Bexler slowed down as he guided the truck over the narrow bridge a quarter mile from the buildings.

"You got me to thinkin', son. Maybe there is some way we can celebrate Christmas. Maybe there is some way an old coot like me can observe the beliefs of past years. Maybe."

Bexler lit another cigar. Bobby gave thanks that they were in sight of the ranch house. He could hold his breath that long.

"Anyways, you've shaken the dust out of my belfry."

———————————

He didn't just disappear from the planet," said Warden David McNabb. "It's been twenty-four hours. You've talked to his mother, his previous places of employment. Early on you called the Kiwanis Club driver and people at the truck stop. Can't believe somebody didn't see something out of the ordinary."

"There was that one store clerk who said she saw a young man who seemed sort of lost. But as she rambled on, it was clear he faded into the crowd of her memory," one of the prison supervisors said. "The only thing, this guy didn't purchase anything. And she told a state trooper that the fella claimed his car broke down. Was looking for a ride west."

"How was he dressed?"

"She was fuzzy on that, but thought he was wearing a dull reddish uniform with some type of logo on it. Doesn't fit prison attire. Didn't have a hat."

"For God's sake, men. Read between the lines," McNabb said with disgust dripping through his words. "That's Bremer, sure as hell. He probably stole the uniform. Alert police in western Kansas, especially in the Garden City area. I realize we're talking Siberia out there, but we'll find him."

"Mr. McNabb," the supervisor asked timidly. "Are we going to let the media know about Bremer's disappearance?"

"Hell, no! Bremer is no threat to the general population. He's no Perry Smith. The guy is a dime store troublemaker who thinks he is always the victim. He's not worth a notation under Missing Pets on the classified page. His running off is about as newsworthy as roadkill."

"Keep in mind," the supervisor said, "Perry Smith served with the Marines in Korea and was an OK guy too, until he ran into Richard Hickock. Then the two murdered an entire farm family out in Holcomb."

"Point taken, but I'm not going to turn this into a media circus where we'll be the clowns. I can see the headlines: 'It's Christmas Time at Lansing Prison; Prisoner Escapes, Sings "Oh Tenenbaum."' Or, 'Prisoner Escapes in Pine Cone Capper.' Can you imagine the shit we'll take inside? Inmates whose hobby is creating jokes will be working overtime. 'How does a prisoner break out at Christmas? He puts up a Christmas tree and believes in Santa Claus.'"

"Well, boss," a determined assistant chimed in. "The prison jokes are bound to come. News travels faster around here than at the *New York Times*. We can either have the PR folks put out our version of the escape or have some pin-striped customer in here sneak the story to the newsies. In such an account, you'll likely be depicted as Father Christmas with reports you handed Bremer a fancy-wrapped gift just before he left."

"How far away are you from retirement?" McNabb scowled. "Fucking reporters!"

Chapter 33
1964, western Kansas

Heavier-than-normal spring rains turned the Bexler feedlot into a swamp. Cattle labored to walk through the muck, which at times sucked them down as if it were quicksand. One calf was so handicapped by mud that Bremer had to tie a rope around the bawling critter and pull it out with his horse.

Ordinarily, dry winters and springs induce the threat of fires on the range, but this year weather systems out of Texas and Colorado met with frequency over the high plains. The result was rain.

For Henry Bexler, the greatest concern was the impact of the wet weather on his winter wheat. The Kansas subsoil would inhale the moisture in the barn area within days after the sky spigot turned off. However, mold, stem rot, rust, and a host of other issues could reduce wheat yield by the time of July harvest.

"Not a damn thing we can do," Bexler said to his new hired hand, Bobby Bremer. "We've had wet years before, but this one is straight out of a Rudyard Kipling jungle book. "This keeps up, we'll have to outfit the bovines with life jackets."

As often is the case, when life seems ready to squeeze the last juices out of you, relief breaks out, and what seemed impossible yesterday is now back in play. And so the month of May entered with glorious sunshine. A northwest breeze caressed the prairie and sent the yearlings kicking like broncos and tickled Bobby's fancy. Even Bexler's mood was enhanced.

"A few more days of this weather, and normalcy may reappear," he said between gnaws on a cold beef sandwich. "Would you pass the mustard?" He held out his hand in expectance. "How you gettin' 'long with that horse? Is your hinder in full tune with the saddle by now?" Bexler laughed at images of healed saddle blisters.

"By this time, that sorrel should know your middle name."

"We're gettin' along fahn—I mean fine." Bremer emphasized the *i*'s. "Think the wheat will be OK?"

"Excellent!" Bexler said. "You remembered my *i* lecture. The wheat? Too early to know. That's like figurin' out what a woman is gonna do right after she tells ya. I expect there will be yield loss, but it's a rare year out here when you get 100 percent of what you hoped for. Anyways, if I had any kids, I'd tell 'em not to go farmin'. When you buy machinery, they tell you what the price is. When you take cattle and wheat to market, they tell you what the price is. And then, of course, there's the weather.

"You're young enough." He looked at Bobby. "Get an education."

"Right, like my name ain't skunk piss already in every college and public information file," Bremer said. "Not much hope down that path. Say, Mr. Bexler, when are we goin' back to town? I mean so's I could go along."

"I've been workin' this place all my life." Bexler ignored the question. "My Daddy farmed, as did his father. They call Montana the big sky country. Who ever thought that up hasn't been to west Kansas. We've got more sky than President Johnson has promises. Oh, it can be pretty out here, peaceful. But it also can be lonely as a doggie without its mama."

It was dinner time, and the two men were eating leftovers from last night's supper. Bexler was a fair cook, nothing fancy, but beef was nearly always the main dish, and of course potatoes. Potatoes were the only thing in his garden. He tried sweet corn one year, but the crows devoured most of it. He purchased pork in town, and they usually had vegetables and fruit from those trips.

"About takin' me along to town," Bremer prompted.

"By golly, you're about as big a nuisance as an army of ants at a pest control picnic. Tell ya what, son, I think you should continue to stay low as an earthworm's toenail. Law enforcement has a long nose, and it's only been a little over four months since you and the Christmas trees left prison. What I suggest, and mind you it's just ole Henry foggin', but I think you should meet Jake Spietz and others in the Less Government group. Whaddia think?"

"That'd be OK," Bremer said without a lot of enthusiasm, "but wouldn't mind goin' back to town, either."

"Maybe this summer. Anyways, it still seems a little too soon. I'll check with Jake about the next meeting and see if he has any objection if I invite an ex-con. Just kiddin', son. I know that's what you technically are, but I don't think of you that way. You seem like a pretty ordinary fellow to me. One who's maybe's gettin a little antsy. Right?"

Bremer didn't answer, but Bexler was pushing close to the truth. The subject lie fallow until a month later, when Bexler announced they would be going to the next meeting of Prairie People for Less Government in late June. The session was twenty miles away at the old Osage Creek school, which served as an occasional gathering space for farmers in the Kerwin County region.

Temperatures stayed mild. Bexler's grousing about wet weather and possible damage to the wheat crop was unfounded. Nature, in the face of self-inflicted trials or man-made distress, has amazing resilience. Kansas, typically brown, was splotched with green. Pastures were lush. The spring rains poured energy into the cottonwood trees. They responded by filling the air with a snowstorm of seeds, making June look like a January blizzard.

"Goddamn cottonwood trees." Bexler found a new topic for complaint. "I swear the stuff is flying in from Colorado and Nebraska. Anyways, I have this inkling that you'd like to get into town to see Rosemary. Can't say I blame you. She's not only an attractive young lady, but smart and a hard worker. How far is my ole thinker off target?"

"Okay, Mr. Bexler, maybe I wouldn't mind seein' Rosemary, but my main thinkin' was givin' a call to my mother. She ain't heard from me in nearly six months, and I know she suffers over it. She's the worrin' type. When my older brother disappeared in 1942, she almost lost her mind. Even though I'm an adult, she'll worry just the same."

"Great Horn Spoons! Bremer, you're more determined than a starved mosquito. Tell ya what, let's get them yearlings into the new pasture, and if all that goes well, maybe we can drive into Cold Springs tomorrow for dinner. Just the thought of one of them juicy, rare steaks make my taste buds tingle. Sorta like your loins when you think of Rosemary, don't you think?"

"Fine, that'll give me a chance to call Mom."

The trip into Cold Springs was routine, except for human anticipation. All the usual bumps in the road had endured the winter and wet weather and had reestablished their positions. The windows on the truck were rolled down, giving the plains breeze free reign. Both men matched the unbound atmosphere. It was as if they were destined for the state fair.

Bexler began to whistle "Zip-a-Dee-Doo-Dah" with the enthusiasm of a demented elf. Bremer viewed the endless miles of winter wheat, thinking what he'd tell his mother. He wouldn't say where he was, only that he was safe and doing fine. He would also ask her to keep their conversation private, not tell others that he had called.

"Like my whistling?" Bexler smiled as if he were a contestant on Sid Caesar's *Show of Shows*. "My Pop was a great whistler. If he wasn't whistling, he was humming. Drove my mother crazy. Tell me,

Bremer, what in the hell do you young people see in this 'Sha-boom, Sha-boom' crap? What kind of song is that? This rock and roll, I'm telling you, will knock the good Earth off its axis."

The truck rocked and rolled toward Cold Springs and the Welcome Inn without appreciation of Bexler's insight on music.

"Got your mind on Rosemary?" Bexler asked during an interlude of his tootling. "Better get your act together, what you're going to say to her. Maybe I should give you some pointers, Bremer. You don't want to stumble around with your words and spoil an opportunity. First impressions out here are harder to change than a hundred dollar bill. There aren't that many Rosemarys in these parts."

Bobby maintained silence and was grateful when the dot on the map marking Cold Springs showed up for real. He would like to see Rosemary again, but he wasn't going to waste breath in trying to convince Bexler that his mother was foremost in his thoughts. From the looks of things there was no big noontime rush at the Welcome Inn. A single truck was parked in front of the restaurant.

Bexler resumed his whistling, this time to something that resembled "If I Knew You Were Comin', I'd've Baked a Cake." He stepped through the front door, his musical medley warbling along. Relief came when he greeted Glendon Thomas, the eatery's owner.

"Bonne journee, Monsieur Thomas," Bexler said, mocking the ordinariness of the place. "A table for two, s'il vous plaite."

Thomas raised his eyebrows in forbearance and then showed the two to a booth.

"What? No Rosemary today?"

"She saw you coming, Henry, and decided she would rather scrub the toilets."

"Hah! That's good, Glen. Imagine that," he said to Bremer, "good food and entertainment. Glen, you could double as a comedian. Oh, Oh! Here's one for you. How do you break the finger of a west Kansas café owner?" He paused the obligatory interval. "Give up, Glen? Okay. You punch him in the nose. Hah. That's a good one. Heard it at a cattlemen's gathering down in Goodland.

"There she comes. Rosemary, Rosemary. It's good to see you again. Got the toilets all cleaned?"

She was puzzled initially by the question, but that dissolved when she considered the source.

"Mr. Bexler. Nice to see you again, I think," she responded. "Assuming one likes off-key whistling, bad jokes, smelly boots, and loud talk. Mr. Bexler, I have a favor to ask. Would you please go up to the bar and visit with Mr. Thomas for a few minutes? I want to talk in private here with your hired hand. Do you mind? I'll take your orders first."

Bexler hem-hawed but consented to her request. In the process, he puckered his lips and twirled his right index finger as he rose, leaving translation for others. After she relayed their orders to the kitchen, Rosemary sat down in the booth opposite Bremer. She rested her arms on the table, fingers clasped in modest but resolute manner. His face began to flush warm and rosy. He wiggled in discomfort. Suddenly, calling his mother became the second item on his agenda.

"I know who you are." Rosemary looked him in the eyes. "You are not Jeb. You are not Mr. Bexler's nephew. You are Bobby Bremer, an escapee from the state prison in Lansing." Bremer was stunned even though she had uttered his pedigree in a quiet, non-accusatory fashion.

"Don't worry," she continued. "I'm not calling the authorities. How do I know all this? Sometime after you arrived, two Kerwin County deputies stopped by to inquire if we had seen any drifters, anyone out of the ordinary. They showed me your picture and said you were serving time for being in fights, that you escaped shortly before Christmas. I asked them if you were armed and dangerous. They didn't know. I knew it was you, and I didn't remember that you looked dangerous."

Her large brown eyes absorbed his consciousness like a sponge inhales water. Her frizzy dark hair brushed her ears like a furtive whisper. She had an upturned nose that spoke spunkiness. Simple silver hoops dangled playfully from her ear lobes. She wore no makeup, yet her lips and face were aglow with natural radiance. The more he stared at her the more he became awash in her unpretentious spirit.

What did she say about deputies? he asked himself.

"Did you hear what I said, Mr. Bremer? I told the deputies that the picture didn't look like anyone who had been in the Welcome Inn. But I knew it was you. Mr. Thomas was gone, and I didn't tell him about their visit. I haven't told my parents either. If you want to tell Mr. Thomas and Mr. Bexler, that's your decision."

She waited. "Mr. Bremer?"

Rosemary Hitchins' slight but athletic stature complemented her authentic disposition. In a few brief minutes, Bremer, unaware of his innocent calculations, mutely observed a woman confident in who she was, both in her convictions and her forsaking of synthetic enhancements. She was plains tough and plains natural, a perfect fit for life in the middle of nowhere.

"Hey, you two gonna talk all day?" came a strident inquiry from Henry Bexler. "Must be some hot topics under discussion. Maybe we could declare a time out from all that coziness and get something to eat. Whaddia say, Rosemary?"

The gaze between Hitchens and Bremer contained nuances that surpassed mere revelations about prison escape and searches by lawmen. Such normally blockbuster disclosures inaudibly yielded to the mysterious elements that poets write about. Volumes were transmitted before Rosemary, her eyes frozen on Bremer, slowly exited the booth.

A minute later she delivered warm homemade bread and steaming baked potatoes. Next came green beans and butter. Finally she brought the 16-ounce steaks. She rounded up catsup and steak sauce in perfunctory style and asked Bexler if he wanted another Falstaff or if he was ready for coffee. She had already brought Bremer his glass of milk.

"If you need anything else," Rosemary said, "I know Mr. Bexler will beckon."

"Right, Rosemary. And happy Flag Day to you too! Just don't forget to save some coconut cream pie."

The business of consumption and appetite fulfillment lasted for less than two minutes before Bexler's hunger was overwhelmed by tittle-tattle curiosity. He washed down a slice of rare Angus hindquarter with a gulp of beer and fired off questions with the vigor of a Warren Commission investigator. He was surprised by Bremer's answers and disappointed in their lack of amorous content.

"Rosemary said a couple of sheriff's deputies showed up here in early January," Bremer began. "They said they were seeking information about an escapee from the Lansing State Prison. They even showed her my picture and asked if she'd seen such a person or heard of any vagrants in the area. They told her the escapee was a Bobby Bremer who was locked up for being in fights."

There was a halt in his synopsis, and then came his conclusion.

"She said she knew immediately that I was the escapee, that my name wasn't Jeb, and that I wasn't your nephew."

Bexler put his back molars at rest. The news that local authorities were on the hunt for Bremer and, more significantly, his recognition that he was harboring an escapee, temporarily clotted his taste buds. Like a passionate defense lawyer, Bexler immediately began to deliberate how he would frame his story to protect his own hide. Bremer's vulnerability took a distant second. He placed his knife and fork on the table in a shocking display of inward anxiety.

"She didn't tell them anything, that you are staying with me?" Bexler asked in an uncharacteristically subdued tone.

"No."

"She didn't give them any information that would suggest a prison escapee was livin' in these parts?"

"No."

"Did she say if they talked to anyone else?"

"There was no one else in the café at the time, she said. Mr. Thomas was not here, but y'all can assume that the deputies showed my picture all over the county. If they showed it at the Welcome Inn and asked questions around here, they hit every other spot."

"Shit," Bexler summarized.

"So, at this point, the only ones who know about you being out at the ranch is Rosemary and Jake Spietz. Is that right?"

"Ah don't know, Mr. Bexler."

They finished dinner as if they had just returned from a funeral. It is baffling how events headed north in anticipation and gaiety can so quickly plunge south in a cloud of fear and uncertainty. A sumptuous meal loses its appeal. An uplifting spring day transforms into a squall of apprehension.

"Are you ready for your coconut cream pie?" Rosemary asked upon return to their table.

"I'm full," a withdrawn Bexler replied. "I'll pass." He rose and groaned, a combination of a satisfying roast beef dinner and indigestion about the visit from sheriff's deputies. "I'm going for a walk."

She looked at Bremer, silently passing on the same apprehension.

"Rosemary," Bremer uttered shyly. "Ah want to telephone my mother and tell her ah'm OK. She worries a lot, and ah haven't talked to her since before Christmas. All she needs to know is ah'm doin' fine. She'll be relieved by that. Guess it's the nature of moms to worry, but she puts in overtime at it. Got any ideas about where ah can use a telephone in private?"

A man's expressed concern about his mother, while perhaps not intended to have any external effect, can convey a powerful message. That was how Rosemary read it. She saw kindness, devotion, and thoughtfulness. And she saw love.

"Bobby," she said softly, "I don't have a telephone where I live." There was a tinge of apology in her voice, and Bremer quickly sensed it.

"That's OK, Rosemary. There's a phone at the ranch, but I hate to ask Mr. Bexler to leave while I call Mom. It's long distance, and she likes to talk a while."

"Listen," she suggested with renewed hope. "Right after the lunch period, Mr. Thomas and the cook leave for a couple of hours. You could use the telephone here. If Mr. Bexler wants to return to the ranch before then, I could drive you out there later. I don't use my car much. Walk everywhere. That old Plymouth could use a little exercise."

"I don't think Mr. Bexler intended an early return. He has his usual stops, what he calls an exchange of lies. But how are you going to explain a long-distance call to your boss?"

"No problem. When the bill comes, I'll tell him I called my cousin in Little Rock and pay him for the charges. He won't care. Bobby"—Rosemary smiled—"do you want a that coconut cream pie now?"

————————

"Hello, Mom?"

Except for Rosemary, who was cleaning up the kitchen, the Welcome Inn was empty of patrons. For that matter, Cold Springs was mostly a ghost town. Like the meager morning dew, noon time customers had evaporated into the wide spaces of Kansas. She heard the dial clicks on the wall telephone near the entrance and retreated further into the kitchen to afford Bobby privacy.

"Mom. It's Bobby."

He could hear her breathe. But there was no response.

"Mom? Are you OK?"

"Bobby? Yes, I can hear you. I'm OK. The question is, Are you OK?"

"Ah'm fine, Mom."

"Where are you? What are you doing? Why did you take so long to call?"

"Ah'm working on a ranch. Ah'd rather not say where. I was afraid to call you sooner, knowing the police would be askin' if you'd heard from me. Ah'm sorry, Mom. Ah've been a real pain for you."

"Bobby, I'm just happy to talk to you, hear your voice, and know you are safe. You've had a tough time growing up. You've made some bad choices. You know that, but it's not entirely your fault."

"Mom, it's nice of you to say that it ain't entirely my fault, but nobody pushed me to get into trouble. That's my doin'. It ain't Dad's fault, and it sure ain't yours. You have always been there for me."

"It's so good that you called, just to hear you. I love you, Bobby. Don't ever forget that no matter where you are or what happens, I love you."

"Mom, I love you too. I enjoy working on the ranch, and I like the people out here. They are hard workers and take care of their families just like you did. Ah'll always be grateful to you. I know it was difficult for you after Dad took off, but you never complained.

You always put us kids first. Even when I was causing problems in school and afterwards, you were there beside me. And patient."

Silence broke into the conversation. He could hear her sob. He wished he hadn't called, added to her pain.

"I don't think I could have put up with me," Bobby said. "Thanks, Mom. And please don't cry. Ah'll be OK." More silence. "How's Grandpa Orval and Grandma Aliza?"

"Oh, they're fine."

"And Madeline? Does she still work with you at Timex?"

"Yes, she does. But she's planning to retire in a couple years. Ted—you remember her husband, Ted—is now a captain at the police department, and they have good insurance. Timex has a good health insurance plan, but benefits decline after retirement. Bobby, I still have eight years before I'm eligible to retire, and maybe I won't then. I'm hoping that new federal health care program for retired persons gets passed.

"I did hear from Peter, and Hattie calls almost every week." Her voice brightened. "Peter still works in St. Louis and says he's doing well."

"Mom. Ah don't know when ah'll be able to call you again. Ah just wanted you to know ah'm working and doing fine. Ah wish ah could tell you more."

"Bobby, please be careful. Promise you'll call if you need money or anything. Are you eating well? You never liked vegetables much, but they are good for you. Fruit too. Don't just eat meat and potatoes like your grandfather."

"Sure, Mom. Have to go. Long distance is expensive. I love you."

"Bobby!" She sounded upset. "You know you can reverse the charges, so don't use that as an excuse!"

"OK, Mom. I won't. Goodbye."

He hung up and saw Rosemary walking toward him. She smiled.

Chapter 34

1976, Cedar Rapids

Tom Wendling's mind was parked in the middle of a news story maze, surrounded by questions and groping for direction. Usually, during an interview and research into stories, he would check off—in his thoughts and with marks in his notebook—the potential emphasis of an article. Story leads and the general format would take shape before any typewriter was punched.

However, Peter Bremer's declaration that he feared for his life, that he avoided main highways to duck gangsters, held conflicting prospects as a news story. On the one hand, there was the page-one, blockbuster-story approach, complete with mob overtones. Opposite was the possibility that public exposure of Bremer's alarm could heighten the couple's vulnerability to harm. Or, he thought, a story may help protect them.

And it could be Bremer was playing his own con game or, at a minimum, escalating the potential of physical injury to generate sympathy and create a diversion from his tax case and deepening troubles with Riverside shareholders.

"Before you go, could I ask you one more thing, please? What evidence is there that someone wants to harm you?" Wendling asked.

Bremer and his wife had been in the newsroom for less than ten minutes, and already the complexion of a possible follow-up story had changed. Sure, this was a tax evasion case involving a somewhat prominent person. Yes, turmoil inundated Riverside Pack and put the company's future in jeopardy. But the fear of being murdered? That was a story changer.

"Last August I was severely beaten by goons from Chicago, people representing a company that gave me a personal loan. At the same time"—Bremer almost breathed his words—"our apartment at the Roosevelt Hotel was broken into. I feared for Glenda's safety, but thank God she was not home at the time. Mr. Wendling, do you see what I'm trying to say? We don't know what to do."

Wendling was not in the counseling business. His job was gathering and writing news, and like any reporter he relished exclusive stories that would have the town talking. Hell, this had all the marks of a running saga, maybe even a series, and one that would leave the TV competition sucking dust.

"You and Glenda have not been threatened or harmed since those events in August?" Wendling asked, not sure where he or the story was going.

"I paid them $20,000 in September, like they ordered, by leveraging some of my stock in Riverside," Bremer confessed, as if cleaning his soul would somehow bring relief. "For some reason, maybe because of all the commotion at Riverside Pack or the IRS case, they haven't contacted me and demanded more money. I know this. They haven't forgotten."

"How much more do you owe them?"

"I'm not sure, something in excess of $45,000."

"Mr. Bremer, your life and that of you wife are endangered, and you don't know precisely what you owe these people?" Wendling was dumbfounded.

"Look, I think Glenda and I need to be leaving. Thanks for your time. Thanks for meeting with us. I suppose we'll continue to see you in court."

They walked out of the newsroom. Three dozen heads of gritty journalists turned in choreographed-like, spellbound form. Wendling looked at the blank paper in his typewriter. It matched the blank in his mind. He walked over to the window, looked down as the Bremers got into their car. They drove off, leaving him still standing in a fog of uncertainty.

Five minutes went by before his gears finally slipped out of neutral. He tapped lightly on editor Jack Nelson's door, then walked in. Nelson was not a person of formality. No appointment was needed. He encouraged talk about stories—angles, organization, leads. Wendling asked if city editor Phyllis Flanders could sit in, and Nelson said to call her.

He explained the short meeting with Bremer and related what the Riverside official had said. Flanders, perhaps more than Nelson, was able to diagnose a news story's impact quicker than a doctor could identify a runny nose. She was respected for her news judgment and fairness. Her recommendation was to sit on the new information given by Bremer.

"This is one helluva story," she said, "but sometimes it's better to let incubation occur. It's not likely he'll talk to some other reporter. I suggest we continue to have the business desk cover the evolving Riverside saga. That in itself is a page-one story. Conflict between investors and management. Glamor meets the ordinary. Trust betrayed. Farmers once again teetering on disappointment. Hope dashed.

"It has more turns than a damn TV soap opera."

"I would agree," Nelson said. "Wendling, stay on top of all developments in the courts. If my guess is right, this will soon spill over into the state courts, and it will be a lawyer free-for-all. Anybody who has ever eaten a Riverside steak will be sued. Before it's over it will make the Ringling Brothers Circus look like a mere pony show.

"One more suggestion," Nelson said, looking at Wendling. "I think you ought to accompany the business desk people at Riverside meetings, just to cover our ass in case there is violence. It could be in the form of disgruntled shareholders or a professional hit man. Holy crapping Moses! This is a nutty story. And take a camera. You do know how to run one?"

"When is the annual meeting?" Flanders asked.

"I'm not sure," Wendling said. "There's this special meeting first. I understand many shareholders demand an immediate status report. Some are meeting in advance to plan strategy. I don't know if we can attend those sessions."

"Well, find out," Nelson said. "Or just go."

Days later Wendling received a telephone call from a man who identified himself as a minister and friend of Peter Bremer.

"I don't think you know me," the man said. "I have been following the court stories and those involving Riverside. I will tell you my name and what I know about Mr. Bremer if you will keep it in confidence."

Red flags fluttered in Wendling's mind. Did this have anything to do with Bremer's story about threats from mob goons? Was it pure coincidence for this person to call now, right after his meeting with Bremer? How deep does a reporter get into a story that he cannot write?

"Why would I be interested in what you have to say?" Wendling answered. "Why would I want to know things I can't write about?"

"I suppose that's a good question," the caller said. "I would simply say that it might help you evaluate Mr. Bremer's situation. Life, as you know, is complex, and we, the people who are part of life, can sometimes be complicated characters. My experience with Mr. Bremer certainly speaks to that. Or, as we sometimes say, God works in mysterious ways."

"I have a personal policy not to give much credence to information given on the phone, unless I know the person or the source," Wendling said. "We get news tips but always check them out for ourselves." There was a pause in the conversation. "I guess I don't understand the secretiveness of your call, why you don't want to say who you are. You say you are a minister."

"Actually, I'm retired. I met Peter some time ago when he was selling life insurance. Funny thing is I didn't buy from him. He recommended, instead, that I invest in income-producing securities, a diversified and conservative retirement plan. Recently, he told me his own difficulties. I guess I'm saying there is more to Peter Bremer than people know."

"You are right there," Wendling said. "There are a lot of things investors are learning about him, most of it not on the asset side of the ledger. Look, telling me your name and what church you were affiliated with gives me standing for meeting with you. Phone talk with a stranger does not work. Whether what you say has any bearing on how we cover Mr. Bremer in the future, I can't say."

"OK. I suppose you are right. My name is James Sandler, and I was pastor at Prairie Church on the west side of town. Perhaps we can meet over a piece of pie at the Butterfly Café. I hope you can keep our conversation private."

They met the next day. After introductions, Wendling was intent to clarify Sandler's reason for calling in the first place.

"I'm still not sure, Reverend Sandler, why you want to talk to me about Mr. Bremer," Wendling said. "I thought a minister's relationship with a church member was private."

"It is. And I appreciate your comment, but it's almost as if no one is speaking out on behalf of Peter. Maybe what I have to say is not newsworthy, but we all have weaknesses, and as you say, Peter seems to have overindulged on that count. But I can tell you that he helped others at our church. I'll bet you didn't know that he volunteered every month at Greene Square Meals, the program for feeding needy folks.

"He and Glenda helped a family find housing. They paid for another family's stay several nights at a motel. They helped serve at our Thanksgiving dinner."

Wendling didn't take notes but listened.

"Peter Bremer is his own worst enemy. He is addicted to the notion of success, and I would even say he venerates it. I have a psychiatrist friend who describes him to a T. Peter wants to get rich too fast, my friend says. Peter thinks he's wasting time when he's asleep. He tells me I'm his confessor. He realizes his unquenchable ambition. Mr. Wendling, I rode with him one time when he was looking at possible plant sites. He drove a hundred miles per hour at times."

Sandler went on for another five minutes, alternately relating a story about Bremer's compassion for people in need and his uncontrollable craving for success. Wendling was unsure what it all added up to, except, as Sandler had said once before, Bremer was an erratic and complicated man. He decided that none of Sandler's details about the president of Riverside Pack would fit into an immediate news story.

"Thanks for telling me another side of Peter Bremer," Wendling said as the two parted. "I'm afraid none of that will carry any weight with the unhappy Riverside shareholders, the federal district court judge, and especially the people in Chicago to whom he owes a substantial amount of money. He has difficult times ahead. Wouldn't a minister also say that you reap what you sow?"

"True enough, Mr. Wendling. But if what he told you is true?" He looked directly at the reporter. "He doesn't deserve death. Peter never mentioned details to me about his association with unsavory people and the terrible loan he made.

"But he does not deserve death."

Chapter 35
1964, Western Kansas

After a twenty-minute drive, they approached Jake Spietz's farmyard, with roiling dust as their calling card. Henry Bexler's disposition matched the hot July weather, except that the elements were moderated by a southwest wind. Henry was as wound up as a Kansas tornado. He exhaled cigar smoke as if he were an old Santa Fe railroad coal burner laboring up a grade.

"I wish these highly educated weather forecasters would tell me why the hell there can be so much rain in the spring and none in summer, why Mother Nature is so damn fickle. Seems we either drown in water or choke in dust."

When Bexler gets to pontificating about anything—the weather, markets, taxes, or judges—those around him may as well settle in for an ear bending. Bobby Bremer was glad they had arrived at their destination and a temporary lull to Henry's complaining. Maybe.

"You would think ole Jake would find time in his busy schedule to fix that broken barn door. See over there? Wouldn't take but a half hour to put a new hinge on, but I don't think he gives a damn. Don't understand why people don't fix things. Damn door could swing and hit him in the head but doubt if he'd notice. Been that way for years."

Bobby saw that there were nearly a dozen cars and trucks parked in the yard. Two men were leaning on a gate near the machine shed, one pointing to a grassy knoll where Hereford cattle were either grazing in the afternoon sun or chewing cud, reposed in the shade of sycamore and cottonwood trees. From a distance, Bremer thought the cud chewers looked like they were a bunch of Henry Bexler types arguing politics. "Don't you have an opinion about anything?" Bexler submitted his last complaint in the form of a question. "You didn't say five words the entire trip over here."

"When would I have slipped in a word edgewise?" Bremer shot back.

"By golly, you are alive. Let's go see what ole Jake has on ice."

The only thing that competed with Bexler's vocal reverberations was the rhythmic singing of the windmill on the far side of Spietz's barn as it responded to the breeze's steady persuasion. Spietz had released the windmill's gearbox and water from the well below flowed into a huge metal tank.

"It wouldn't take that long either to climb up to the top of that windmill with an oil can"—Bexler pointed upward—"and squirt a little quiet on that squeak. Banging doors. Squealing windmill." Bexler shook his head in disgust. "Maybe ole Jake is going deaf. Losing his eyesight too? He's in terrible shape."

"Why do you call him ole Jake?" Bobby inquired. "He looks younger than you."

"You don't say. Well, I'll call him damn well what I please. And you can keep your opinions to yourself."

"Hey! There's ole Henry Bexler," Vic Hayes hollered. Hayes walked up from behind and slapped Henry on the back. "Hell, I thought you died several years ago." Hayes slipped his Irish wit into high gear. His impish blue eyes were separated by a thin nose, all underpinned by a wide smile.

"Henry, are you still spreading cheer in Middle America as usual? Come in search of answers to some quibble, I suspect. And wearin' a clean shirt. My oh my. Look at you. Seem to be OK. Upright and all." He measured Bexler's face to determine if he had poked hard enough. "How's it hanging, Henry?"

Hayes ran a 1,500-acre spread out toward the Colorado line, a combination of farms that once were individual homesteads of three brothers. Vic was the survivor. In addition to farming, he had served terms on the local school board, county commission, and several township offices. At one time he considered running as an independent candidate for Kansas Secretary of Agriculture.

"How are you doing, Vic?" Bexler responded. "Bobby, this fellow here in the fancy overalls with patches on his billfold pocket is Vic Hayes. Claims he's a farmer west of here. Vic, I thought the state gerrymandered your place into Colorado. Would have made Kansas a friendlier place and improved our IQ."

"Good to meet you, Bobby," Hayes offered his hand. "You look smarter than to hang out with a crusty dispenser of hot air like Henry. Why, there are days when it gets so windy in west Kansas that one is not sure if it's nature or Henry talking somewhere."

"Yeah, yeah. It's nice to see you, Vic." Bexler extended the jostling. "I think."

"Well, it's downright nice to be seen," Hayes replied.

"I suppose that's true, at your age," Bexler responded. "And Vic, I know I'm slightly older than you, and twice as wise. I started workin' for justice issues out here while you were slobberin' Pablum on your bib."

"Say, Henry. I thought your hired hand's name is Jeb."

"It is. His middle name is Bobby, and he prefers that."

"Whatever you say, Lorraine. Ain't that your middle name?"

"It is. But the last guy who kept bringing that up had to have his jaw repaired."

Bobby was amused by the prairie needle exchange. He momentarily pondered Hayes' questioning about his name and whether Henry's quick alteration of the truth had gained any standing. However, his attention was quickly diverted to the wind-tousled, dark brown hair that was getting out of an older car near the Spietz house. It was Rosemary, a pleasant surprise.

Suddenly the heat and discomfort of Kansas's summer was displaced by a different kind of atmosphere. A shiver wiggled down

Bremer's spine as if he'd just gently touched an electric fence. It was a mysterious sensation, foreign to both his physical and emotional being. She was wearing blue jeans and a blue checkered top that was untucked. She slowly walked toward the house. A wind gust grabbed the end of her shirt and upturned it high enough to reveal her suntanned skin above the beltline.

"I see your eyeballs have refocused and doubled in size," Bexler said as they walked to the Spietz ranch house. "She is easy to look at."

Bobby ignored the comment, but his attention followed her as if he were being hypnotized. His walk veered to the left to sustain eye contact with her movement, but then she disappeared into the house. Spell broken, he glanced aimlessly at the parked cars. Immediately his mood shifted. He spotted a vehicle that caused his legs to freeze. He stopped as if confronted by a brick wall.

The vision of Rosemary, and all its illusory spinoffs, was replaced by that of a white star on the side of a black Ford and all its ramifications. The unknown became fear.

Bexler looked back at the immobile Bremer, saw the change in his face, and followed Bobby's alarmed eyes to the large black sedan. After a few seconds and some mental calculation, he began to snigger, and then full-blown, rib-rattling laughter erupted. He placed his hands on his belly and began to dance. He tossed his head back in a hilarious roar.

Bremer was a mixture of bafflement and uncertainty. His panic was partially offset by Henry's peculiar behavior. Yet he did not move. It was as if his boots suddenly were filled with cement. Henry pointed at him in uncontrollable hysterics.

"You, you," Bexler stammered. Frenzy disabled his ability to finish. A serious and threatening look on Bremer's reddening face tempered Bexler's joviality.

"What's so damn funny?" Bremer's latent rage stepped forward.

"Now, Bobby." Bexler held both hands outward in a calming gesture. "Don't get your neck hair uncurled. That car with the star on the side, the one that looks like it's from the sheriff's office, belongs to Ben Putman. Sorry about my chortling, but your face was something to behold. Ben bought that old lumber wagon at a county sale two years ago. I think he believes it gives him some distinctive authority. Ben runs a ranch to the north."

The explanation eased Bremer's anxiety, but it did little to sooth his sour feelings toward Bexler.

"Thanks for telling me," he said, his brow in a locked furrow, "but I still feel like punching you in the nose."

"Calm down, boy. Can't say I blame you for bein' upset. Guess I'd feel the same way. But you have to appreciate an old feller like me seein' your face go from sublime to alarm. Come on. We'll meet Rosemary and have a beer."

The small ranch house was filled with people and chatter. Bremer looked past and beneath the cowboy hats in search of Rosemary, but she had faded into the human milieu. His search was sidetracked when Jake Spietz thrust an icy Falstaff beer into his hand.

"Welcome, Bobby. I'm sure glad you were able to come along today. Delighted Henry didn't stick you with a list of chores. Knowing him it wouldn't strain the imagination that he'd create three days of work if he wanted to. He must be in an extraordinary good mood."

"Well, Mr. Spietz," Bremer replied, "I wouldn't really know how to describe Mr. Bexler's mood. He slips from hot to cold, sunny to cloudy like the climate out here. But he's a fair man, and he's been generous to me."

"Glad to hear it. Seems like you got him figured out about as well as the rest of us do. Bobby, or do you want me to call you Jeb? I'd like to introduce you to the group today. And if you have time, I'd like to personally visit with you later on."

"You can call me Bobby. That's my name. Jeb was Mr. Bexler's creation. Do you think, Mr. Spietz, that most of the people here know who I am? I mean, that I escaped from the Kansas State Prison six months ago? News travels fast, and gossip has wings, my mom says."

"I don't know Bobby. I can tell you that I never broadcast our correspondence while you were in prison. Didn't think it was anyone else's business. But some here may very well suspect that you are more than a drifter ranch hand. It's sort of odd, but there wasn't a lot of news at the time that anyone had escaped from Lansing. I have a brother in Kansas City, and he didn't mention it to me. If someone asks about it, it's up to you where to take it."

Bremer nodded.

"Thanks for writing to me. It's great to get mail when you are in prison. As for today, if I'm asked about my past, I'll just say that I'm a native of Arkansas, worked at a nursery there and at a feed lot in Kansas. I hope questions don't go too far beyond that. Excuse me, Mr. Spietz. I see someone in the kitchen I recognize. Oh, and I will look for you after the meeting."

He spotted Rosemary helping a woman place sandwiches on a tray. Another person retrieved a jar of what looked like bread and butter pickles from the refrigerator, and yet another stacked small dessert bowls on the table. Someone had brought freshly picked strawberries. Mustard, catsup, and barbeque containers were arranged next to the sandwiches and Frito Lay corn chips.

"Did you bring your appetite?" Rosemary greeted Bobby with a smile as he approached the luncheon crew. "I'm happy you came along." She walked closer to him and whispered in his ear. "I was afraid I'd be the only person here under fifty. The Prairie People for

Less Government tend to be older. In addition to less government, some may be concerned about having less hair." She chuckled. "I guess that wasn't nice."

Bobby tried to recall what she had just said. What stuck in his mind was a gentle voice coming from gorgeous lips, her breath on his neck, and the intoxicating lavender smell of her perfume. Or cologne. Or whatever. Her eyes sparkled like sunlight on a bubbling stream. He noticed a blue headband that graced the top of her head and was tucked beneath her brown hair in the back. It matched the blue of her shirt.

"I'm sorry," he said. "What was it you said about nice hair?"

"Never mind," she beamed, as she decoded Bobby's confusion. "Do you want to give me a hand with the pitchers of iced tea? With all that beer out in Jake's tank, we'll probably have enough tea left to last the summer."

People straggled in even as lunch was in progress. No one kept minutes for this informal gathering, but there were more than thirty men and women present. Neither was there a formal agenda. Jake Spietz opened the session with a second invitation for anyone who desired another beer. And, he noted, there were still sandwiches that needed to be eaten.

"First order of business is to introduce newcomers. Bobby Bremer—stand up Bobby—has been a ranch hand for Henry Bexler for some months now. Some of you may know him as Jeb. But he prefers Bobby. Comes from Arkansas. Must have a lot of patience to work for Henry." That drew laughter and a few amens.

"Any other newcomers or visitors?" There was none. "Okay, then. I want to bring to your attention"—he held a flier in his hand— "this article suggesting we are doing too little on soil conservation. Where there are hills, and I guess we don't have to pay too much attention to that, they are pushing more contouring and strip farming.

For those of us in the flatlands, less tilling and perhaps no tilling or plowing in the autumn is being recommended. Next thing you know, suggestions will become government regulations."

"Well, Jake, I expect that people are worried about drought and the possibility of a dust bowl like we had thirty years ago," said Chester Brown, a farmer from near St. Francis. "I can see where a field plowed in the fall exposes soil to wind erosion all winter long. It might be better to wait until spring to till. 'Course, this year, with all the rain, it would have taken longer to get crops in."

"I just don't like the idea of government telling me how to farm," Joe Kesler piped up. "We pay all these taxes, what, so some guy in a white shirt and fancy tie can tell us when and how to plant and how often we should grease our equipment. By dammit, won't be long and they'll tell us when to pass gas."

"Now, Joseph. Watch your language and keep your heart rate down," said a strong voice overlooking the sandwich tray. It wasn't the first time Julie Lynn Kesler had to moderate her husband's penchant for exaggeration and anti-government diatribes. "I can remember when you got on your high horse because the county nurse urged everyone to get measles shots for their children. You were happy our kids had the shots after that boy from Goodland almost died from the fever."

"Julie Lynn is right, Joe," said Norris Steines. "Just because someone in government recommends something doesn't make it wrong."

"Yeah. Yeah, Norris," Kesler answered. "Julie Lynn is never wrong."

Spietz recognized it was time to steer the conversation away from family dialog. He asked if anyone else in the group had been following the protests by "draft dodgers" in California. His view was that they were college students with deferments "while kids of working people and farmers are fighting the wars. If young people want to avoid the draft, they should be compelled to do two years of public service somewhere."

In a group where many were war veterans, no one disagreed. However, Jimmy Tegeler, who was among those who landed at Omaha Beach on D-Day, said President Johnson "made a big mistake in taking McNamara's advice and jumping full body into this Vietnam mess. Mark my words. It will be a disaster."

Helen Hargrave noted that Israel has mandatory service for young men and women, either in the armed forces or in volunteer work. She also held up an article from the *Progressive Farmer* about the migrant worker issue. While it was a problem in California, she said, it could become one in Kansas too.

"I think it's terribly unfair to turn these migrant workers out in the cold when we need their labor," she said. "I think President Johnson and Congress need to rethink what they're doing in California as well as Vietnam. This is a terrible injustice to the migrant workers and their families. We should pass a resolution in support of them."

Spietz picked up Helen's concern and explained the history of the Bracero program. He said the World War II agreement with the Mexican government brought Mexican men to the United States to pick grapes and other produce while US men were off to war.

"The program expired last year," Spietz continued, "and now Secretary of Labor Wirtz wants to replace thousands of migrant agricultural workers in California with high school students. Dumbest damn idea since Ford invented the Edsel. The migrants are experienced workers. Male high school students are unskilled testosterone factories."

"I move we send a letter to our senators and representatives asking the migrant program be extended," Rosemary offered. "The option is to have migrant families suffer and crops rot in the field. We should send copies of our letter to Hispanic groups in our area and in California. Maybe we should go down to Topeka and protest. We could build signs that say 'His Wirtz Idea Yet!'"

That injected much-needed laughter in an assembly accustomed to serious matters. Vic Hayes seconded the motion. All approved. Helen said she would write the letter on behalf of the group.

"Did everyone notice the ruling by a judge over in Colorado, not far over the border, where a farm family was evicted because they were six weeks late paying on a mortgage?" The question came from Myrna Thompson. She and her husband, Sean, rent a small ranch in western Kansas.

"Wasn't this the third time they were late in making payment?" asked Chester Clayberg.

"It was," Myrna replied. "But out here the judge ought to know that wheat don't ripen on the exact day payment is due. Cattle aren't ready for market according to some banker's calendar. By that way of thinking, the judge ought to pay for his steak at the restaurant before he eats it. This isn't exactly cutthroat Wall Street out here."

"I believe, Myrna, the couple in question moved back to their place when members of their church took up a collection and made the payment," Claude Jennings said.

"True enough," Myrna shot back. "And the family sold their first winter wheat to repay the church people, those who accepted repayment. But they had the humiliation of being escorted off by a deputy sheriff and forced to stay with relatives. That shouldn't happen in a civilized society. And Chester, they always made those other late payments."

Several other issues were raised as the afternoon sun headed downward. Did someone from the group want to run for soil commissioner? No one responded. A few comments were made about President Johnson's Great Society plans, mostly negative. Surprisingly, little was said about the president's push of new health care bills—controversial proposals known as Medicare and Medicaid.

And the subject of presidential primaries was shunned like sour milk. While Kansas was predictably Republican, most members of the Less Government group were fiercely independent, people who may go in any political direction and change their minds on the way. Some leaned toward Goldwater for president; others tended to favor reelection of Johnson.

A lull in the proceedings was interpreted by Henry Bexler as a time to rehash old matters involving taxes, and whether farmers and ranchers were paying in more than they were getting out. That soon led to yawns, people standing up to stretch, and a call by Jake Spietz for people to help themselves to beer, iced tea and, of course, the stack of sandwiches.

Rosemary and Bobby, as natural as the Kansas wind nudges wheat fields to sway, drifted out the back door. They sat on a porch swing that looked to the southwest, their eyes captured by each other and the prairie panorama. The gentle breeze busily fluffed her hair, sent sunflowers bowing this way and that, and maintained the pulsing squeak of the windmill.

The ever-so-slightly undulating landscape offered a blend of art. The reddish-brown cattle and their white faces complemented the deep green pasture. The horizon seemed to stretch forever, with golden wheat, masses of sunflowers, and emerald alfalfa competing for attention. With sporadic exception, cottonwoods and willows showed no intention of meddling with the plains portrait.

"Bobby. See that cloud? It looks like a buffalo running across the sky." She pointed upward, and he strained to filter the sun and discover the object of her imagination. He cupped his hands over his eyes, searching for the galloping beast. She feared the buffalo image would soon stumble and dissolve into ethereal nothingness.

"Right there! Are you blind?"

"I'm trying. The sun is bright." He pled pretext. "I can't make out the buffalo, but I do see something that looks like a scowling President Johnson. See that up there?"

She slugged him in the shoulder.

Perhaps that fell short of a sensual peck on the cheek, but Bobby read major shades of affection in her punch. His mind galloped in several directions, a mixed-up collection of discombobulated feelings that produced sensations that were peculiar to someone who never experienced real love. It is the kind of experience that can cause a U-turn shift in life.

"Bobby. Are you OK?"

"Yeah. Why?"

"You have a funny look on your face, like you just discovered something."

"Maybe I did."

"Hmmm. You're being mysterious."

"No. I think I did see that buffalo racing across the sky."

"Now you're being silly, or maybe poking fun at me."

"No. Not at all."

The "funny look" on his face suddenly took on a reddish glow.

"It's just that, Rosemary, it's nice being with you," Bobby stumbled.

"Oh, I see," she replied softly. "It's nice being with you too."

It surprised him when his left arm rose spontaneously, as if on some impromptu journey, and found its way around her shoulder. He almost withdrew it, but decided it felt comfortable and right. She did not object. They listened to the flute-like warble of a meadowlark. It mingled with the unvarying squeak of the windmill, the lowing of a cow and their own breathing.

Some kinds of chemistry are difficult to analyze.

"I think we should go in," Rosemary said after a minute or two. "People will wonder what we're doing. And I have to help Mrs. Spietz clean up."

"Okay," Bobby said with a reluctant tone. His arm surrendered.

"I would like to see you again," said Rosemary, "and soon. Perhaps at my house. And Bobby, I think you need to call your mother again. I know you talked to her in April, but you should really call her every month."

Nearly everyone, including Rosemary, had left when Jake Spietz motioned Bobby to step outside. Henry Bexler, in a customary role, was talking and chewing at the same time, still close to the sandwich and cookie trays. Leftovers were not part of his gastronomical glossary.

"Would you be interested," Spietz asked Bremer as the two walked toward the still-singing windmill, "in becoming more involved in justice issues? We have a citizen group that is more activist-minded than today's gathering." Spietz stopped near the large cattle water trough, grabbed a tin dipper, and collected a cup of cold water from the one-inch galvanized pipe. He offered the drink to Bremer.

Spietz was more serious, less gregarious than Bexler. He was in his mid-fifties, and the wind and sun had already carved the Kansas brand on his cheeks. His forehead carried a shade line created by his seed corn cap. His full head of hair, black already speckled with gray, was well groomed and swept straight back without a part.

He spoke gently, and his jaws flexed with visceral resolve. His face held no imprint of holiness, but justice and fairness were clearly part of his being.

"Many of the people here today don't like to stick their necks out too far when it comes to advocacy," Spietz continued. "It takes a little moxie to picket a judge, or to march in front of a bank with signs when an unfair foreclosure has come down. It takes time and money to raise hell in Topeka when it's necessary, or to print fliers pointing out bad legislation."

He waited for Bremer to react but was met with silence and an uncommitted face. Bobby endorsed the idea of citizens watching its government, even taking overt action to confront perceived unfairness. But he also was cognizant of his impulsive nature, and the trouble that created in the past. And, of course, his personal relationship with the law.

"It takes courage to link arms and attempt to block a fancy suit from delivering eviction papers to some poor farm family," Spietz went on. "Justice Now does that. We do it because these folks can't afford a lawyer, and while there are legal aid groups and public defenders to help a fellow accused of a crime, we are the only ones who stand alongside these farm families in financial trouble."

"Mighty fine water you got here," Bobby said, licking his lips. "I know one thing. You're lucky to have such a good well. You must be tappin' into a strong aquifer out here. We had good wells at the prison. Needed it to keep the nursery goin'. And that water tasted good too. Didn't have a iron or chemical taste like some city water."

"Henry is a member of Justice Now. Does most of the writing in our fliers. He spends too much time bitching about taxes, but he's on the right side of fairness when it comes to banker decisions and the bullish way their hand-picked cronies in law enforcement push some people around. I wouldn't be surprised if bankers sometimes slip them a Jackson or two."

"I like Henry," Bremer said. "He's a smart guy. Likes to act the country bumpkin, but like my grandad would say, he's wise as

Solomon's teacher. Heck, Henry, you, and Rosemary are really the only people I know out here.

"Yes. Rosemary," Spietz said. "She's a very active member of Justice Now."

"Rosemary?"

"Yep. You should talk to her. Maybe convince you to join in."

Bexler and a cloud of smoke approached the two men. The cigar wiggled from side to side like a divining rod. He patted his stomach as if it was his best friend.

"What the hell's goin' on out here?" Bexler barged in, determined to rub somebody wrong.

"This is a private conversation, and you are the subject," Spietz said evenly.

Chapter 36
November 1964, Kansas

"I'd better get back to workin' on that fence behind the tractor shed. Henry will be wonderin' why it's not fixed."

Their relationship thickened as summer moved into fall. She regularly visited the Bexler place.

Bobby Bremer's blood galloped in his veins. His entire being tingled, his manhood expanded, forcing him—out of embarrassment—to turn away from Rosemary Hitchens and her lovely lips.

Her embrace, the warmth and smell of her body, the freshness of her hair, the tenderness sent shock waves through his system. He staggered from her elixir, woozy with serenity and delight.

"Rosemary," he said, looking back, "we're gonna have to do something about this."

She flashed a receptive smile. He drank in her accepting glow and, as he backed away, stumbled over a badly placed two-by-four.

"I'm not sure you're ready for the harvest ball," she laughed, her frizzy hair flying like an untended wild fern. "What do you mean we have to do something about this?" Her eyes sparkled, and she wiggled her eyebrows in a tease.

He picked up his hammer and bucket of nails just as Henry Bexler rounded the corner of the main barn. Bremer expected his ears would soon burn with Henry's job assessment.

"Good grief, man," Bexler bellowed. Bobby braced for a tongue flogging. "I could have ordered a section of fence from Sears Roebuck, and it would have been shipped here while you're still gabbing with Rosemary." Bexler paid tribute to overstatement. "When you and that woman gonna do somethin' about it?"

"It" seemed to be on everyone's mind. Bobby had met Rosemary's parents, and "it" seemed to go well. "It" was well accepted by regulars at the Welcome Inn and at meetings of the Less Government and Justice Now groups. Mr. and Mrs. Spietz were excited about "it."

Bremer was careful not to hit his finger as he pounded a nail into the fence railing while contemplating what he was going to do about "it."

He was scared.

Both were aware that chemical processes had advanced beyond the test tube stage. In the ensuing weeks, their minds were so occupied with each other that Bexler once threatened to search for his family Bible, read an appropriate section about two becoming one, "and gettin' on with the business of operatin' a ranch."

His attempt at matchmaking fell short on the romantic barometer, but it nevertheless quickened the young couple's decision on the matter of "it." In early December, Bobby asked Mrs. Spietz to travel with him to a Goodland jewelry store, where she helped him pick out an engagement and wedding ring. Everybody knew "it" was going to happen, and at Christmas, it did.

Rosemary and Bobby became engaged and settled on a spring wedding date. There were a few problems that had to be worked out. She wanted to tell his mother. He did not. She was not worried about obtaining a Kansas marriage license listing his name as Bobby Bremer. He was. She wanted to be married at her family's church. He was nervous about that too.

As the new year moved into springtime, some answers developed. Proximity to Colorado helped. Bexler had recommended that they drive over to Holyoke, Colo., to obtain a marriage license. He said he knew the Phillips County, Colo., clerk, and offered to accompany the couple in case there were any questions. Rosemary desired to be married at a Methodist chapel in Amherst, Colo. Bexler's suggestions were accepted.

Matters proceeded with minimal bumps.

It was determined that Bremer's Social Security card, issued in Little Rock, Ark., would be sufficient identification for a Colorado marriage license. Parental consent was not needed. The minister at Rosemary's church agreed to perform the ceremony. That soothed Bremer's anxiety about marriage information finding a way back to the Kansas State Prison. Rosemary was happy about a church wedding, even if in Colorado.

She still wanted to invite Bobby's mother to the wedding. He said his mom could not possibly limit her excitement for her son's pending marriage to the immediate family. He argued that "the Little Rock gossip train" could somehow transport the news all the way to Lansing before the ceremony took place. Rosemary said he was being paranoid. It was their first disagreement.

"Look, Bobby," she persisted one day. "I think you can trust your mom to carry around a secret for several weeks. She carried you around for nine months without any major complications. Think of that." She elevated her appeal. "She loved you so much to give you life, and now you don't think that merits an invitation to our wedding?"

He never had any doubts about his mother's love, despite the many opportunities he had given her to do that. Molly Bremer stood by her children when they failed her. She shed insults and slights, patiently listened to problems and complaints, weathered infrequent communications, and still maintained her role and love as a mom.

She was a single mother with double duty. Bobby Bremer reviewed all this silently.

"You are right, Rosemary. Mom should be here for the wedding." He looked at her with gratitude and a different sense of love. "How did you know that my mother is such a wonderful person?"

Rosemary smiled like a woman who graduated from Harvard with honors and a degree in psychology. Bobby's grandparents, Molly's parents, would also be invited so she would have company on the trip from Little Rock. Otherwise the wedding celebration would be local and small. The following day they called Bobby's mom.

Bexler was so excited about the impending marriage that he offered Rosemary a job as cook and housecleaner at the ranch. He said the couple could reside, free of charge, at what was once a bungalow for ranch hands. In recent years, Henry had converted it to storage and used it as a wash house.

Rosemary frowned at both employment by Bexler and living near him, but agreed it offered the best situation for starting out married life with Bobby. It provided financial stability, and she and Bobby could work as though they were a farm couple on their own. Bexler would just be the ever-present pain next door.

The arrangement would also allow the two to remain active in Justice Now. Rosemary had personal motivation to be upset by what she believed was unfairness by both the banks and legal system. She told Bobby of her family's wearing experience, one that sent her father in a near state of depression. Her mother, who was forced to take in washing and clean homes for others, refused to talk about the matter at all.

It was a painful story for Rosemary, personally, but more so because of the trials undergone by her parents. City and county business leaders and bank officials had urged her father, Anderson Hitchins, to purchase the assets of the defunct Uplands Seed Co. They appealed to his sense of community and service to area farmers.

It meant he had to surrender his rural mail route job, borrow money from the bank, and mortgage the family's 130 acres. The run-down Uplands building and its rusted machinery and old bins had been taken over in foreclosure by the same bank.

That was in the mid-50s. Operators of the bank, a branch of a large financial institution in the Kansas City suburb of Olathe, Kans., wanted to impress superiors of their involvement in economic development and the important role the bank played in the community. However, beyond stimulating backslapping, the top item on their list was security of the bank's investment. Shared risk-taking and supportive management help for Uplands and Hitchins turned out to be nonexistent.

Hitchins was required to make a substantial initial investment to relaunch the business. He had to teach himself, with advice from farmers, what sort and quantity of seeds were needed in the region. At first he was able to pay his bills and interest on the bank loan with a meager amount left to support his family. For a short time, he was even able to pay down some of the loan principle. Then the rules of size and service hit him like a one-two punch in the stomach.

Regional agriculture companies not only offered a wider variety of seeds, but also expert advice from trained agronomists. And they had spraying services for both weeds and insects. While some farmers continued to buy from Uplands, Hitchens could not compete at a higher level. His business dried up like Kansas topsoil in a drought. After two more years of struggle, the bank called the loan.

He lost the business and part of his farmland. There were some ranchers who offered to help financially, but a humiliated Hitchens rejected any outside assistance. He worked as a farmhand before finding a full-time job at a lumber yard.

"It really ticks me off the way Dad was treated by both the bank and some town people," Rosemary bluntly told Bobby at one of the

Justice Now sessions. "If they hadn't sold him on the idea of coming to the rescue of ranchers, and if they had put investment money where their mouth was, I'd feel different. But they dumped all the risk on Dad. He may be guilty of bad judgment, but most of that bad judgment was in expecting more help from the bank and others.

"And once when he was ten days late with a payment on the loan, did they call him with a friendly reminder? No, they called the sheriff's office, and a deputy delivered the overdue notice. That is unadulterated bullshit."

Rosemary and Bobby set Saturday, May 22, for their wedding. That was her grandmother's birthday. While the wedding ceremony would be for family only, Bexler offered to host and pay for an elaborate reception party at his ranch. For that, he insisted on an open house. The wedding couple could hardly object.

There was one proviso. At the insistence of Rosemary's mother, there would be no dancing. Dancing, in accordance with her rigorous interpretation of Methodist standards, was one level above gambling and drinking, all instruments of the devil. Bexler's appeal to fill the stock tank with beer was also routinely dismissed.

It was a gorgeous spring day. Colorado was bursting with new blooms. Flowering crab trees, brilliant red peonies, and early roses competed to give the Kansas wedding party and guests a joyous welcome. Molly Bremer and her parents arrived the day before and visited the ranch. Bexler invited them to stay there, but they decided to rent a motel room in a nearby town.

The next day they were seated in the church in Amherst when the wedding party arrived. Like the outdoors, the church altar was arrayed with flowers. Hydrangeas and roses were sprinkled with anemones and, of course, bridal wreaths, packed in mason jars perched on short stands. The minister appeared from a side niche. A woman who cranked out "The Wedding March" on the church organ looked to be ninety years old, but she did it with pride, a happy smile, and mostly the right notes.

As Anderson Hitchins walked his daughter down the aisle, the pain and memory of Uplands Seed Co. faded like a scar subdued by time. There were no bridesmaids, no attendants, just Rosemary and Bobby. When he gave her hand to Bobby, the usually stoic Scotsman leaked moisture around the eyes.

The ceremony took ten minutes. When the minister asked for anyone "to speak now or forever hold your peace," silence followed. Not a soul from the Lansing prison was there to protest. The couple kissed, and "it" was done. The organ struck up the recessional, and the three-dozen gathered smiled their best wishes as the newlyweds left the church. Several sped out first to toss rice.

Before Rosemary or Bobby could speak, Henry Bexler took over like a carnival hawker, announcing that all were invited to his ranch for an afternoon of celebration. He recited a menu of various sandwiches, chips, cookies, and "other goodies" that would complement lemonade, coffee, and soda. But no beer. Otherwise, pretty much the same fare as for Justice Now meetings.

"Oh, and Mrs. Spietz is bringin' enough cake with sugary frosting to sweeten a sour banker. Anyways, it's what's on the agenda, and we have not set a closing time. All are welcome." After pictures were taken, most headed for Bexler's ranch.

The couple's friends and family had a good time. Several hours later, Bobby, seeing some were full of refreshments, cake, and Henry's malarkey—and about to leave—astutely stood and thanked everyone for coming. He acknowledged Henry for hosting. By early evening, all but Rosemary's parents and Bobby's family had left. Even Bexler made himself scarce.

"I remember when you were so little, Bobby." Molly looked at her son as if he were still a baby, that mom appraisal that absolves everything from dirty diapers to fights in the schoolyard or pool hall. "His fists were so tiny." She looked at Rosemary with loving delight. "He jabbed them around like a drunken boxer." She mimicked her verbal portrayal, and her small audience laughed. "Drool, though, seeped from his mouth, betraying his toughness."

More laughter.

Seven people, their hearts beating in sync and awash in tenderness, savored the contentment of family. Had Albert Einstein been alive, he would not have been able to unravel the mystery and depth of such newly formed fusion. For a moment, Molly silently recalled the joy of her own marriage and the pain that followed. But those thoughts quickly evaporated in the renewal of love expressed through Rosemary and Bobby.

The newlyweds dreamily sat at the top of the three steps that led to the porch outside their bungalow. The elders occupied chairs on the porch, with Molly's father claiming the worn wooden rocker. A soft northwesterly breeze flowed across growing shadows. A nearly full moon was gaining brightness on the eastern horizon.

The specter of prison was forgotten, barred by enchantment.

"Well." Orval Price broke the stillness. "I can remember a time when Bobby wasn't so cute." Molly's father was less inclined to pay tribute to romanticism. "You remember, Bobby. You had to be four or five. Sitting in the small backyard swimming pool? You had a fit over something, shucked your trunks and ran bare-assed down the block. Molly, you didn't think it was cute either. You chased after him and laid a not-so-gentle hand on his derriere."

"Honestly, Orval." His wife, Aliza, launched her chastisement. "Your timing is as graceful as a train wreck."

Her scolding was vetoed by the laughter from everyone else.

"Say, Grandpa." Bobby sought to add a little gasoline to the fire. "How are you and Adora Mae Marston getting along?"

"Heavens to Murgatroyd," Aliza quickly injected in a bid to cut off a blistering rant by her husband. "You could have gone all year without seeking your grandfather's opinion about Adora Mae. Those two have been feuding longer than the Hatfields and McCoys. So far, no one has been injured."

Bobby was then obliged to provide the necessary history of combativeness between his grandfather and Adora Mae.

"Aliza tends to embellish things," Orval responded with level proclamation. "Bobby, Adora Mae has turned into a domesticated pussycat, claws intact, mind you, a rose, wilting around the edges but with all her thorns in place." He paused for effect. "I've come to kinda like her, Bobby. Why, Adora has become short for Adorable."

Aliza's eyebrows raised again in hopeless editorial reaction.

"I also lie a lot," Orval confessed roguishly. "She is a circus specimen, really, a mouth without a body."

"That's enough!" Aliza pronounced.

Bobby was sufficiently entertained, satisfied that he had pulled Grandpa Orval's trigger.

"Does anyone want any more cake?" Rosemary offered, an attempt to substitute sugar for Orval's vinegar. All said no.

"Ma, we want to thank you, and Grandpa and Grandma too, for coming all this way," Bobby said. "Everyone here knows my situation. I was worried that too much news of our wedding might find its way back to prison officials. So maybe we can continue to keep everything between us."

"Oh, Bobby. We will," Molly said. She looked at her parents for a sign of support. "Twice you were given a bad deal. You come to the defense of a friend and what's the reward? Back to jail. You defend yourself from attack at Lansing, you jeopardize your parole. Somehow fairness never shows up."

She looked at the porch floor, then into Bobby's eyes.

"I love you, son. Nothing can change that."

"I love you too, Ma."

"We probably should get back to the motel. It's getting dark, and Dad doesn't like to drive in the dark. I should tell you that Hattie and her husband are doing fine. They both work at the Mayo Clinic in Rochester. I wish they'd come visit in Little Rock. And Peter. He's very successful," she said proudly. "He still works in St. Louis. Hardly ever calls. He hasn't been down home for several years."

Bobby could read his mother's face. Life without physical contact with her children was painful.

"Ma," Bobby said, first looking at her, then at Rosemary. "I promise we will come to Little Rock to see you, maybe this fall when ranch work slacks off. For sure we will call."

Molly smiled.

Chapter 37
1976, Cedar Rapids

The auditorium at Riverside Pack headquarters was filled with angry farmers and businesspeople, investors whose attitudes were poised with pitchfork tenacity. By 9:45 a.m., all the seats had been taken, and those standing had another reason to be unhappy. The temperature in the poorly ventilated room was rising as the mid-January winter temperature outside clung to below freezing. It was not a contrast for contentment.

Since the first annual meeting, in 1973, at which the toddling amalgamation of rural and urban shareholders showed some signs of survival, the company's financial health had been fragile. There had been indications of an upswing last summer, but those trends withered. It was claimed by many that bad management decisions aggravated by the vagaries of the market led to losses. Confidence evaporated among restless investors.

Farmers especially read Peter Bremer's fancy attire and Cadillac lifestyle as symptomatic of the company's problems.

"Too much speculative spending in an uncertain climate," was a theme that permeated those gathered. "Livin' too high off the hog" was the farmers' way of putting it. A significant number were ready to heap their frustration on the always dapper president. His ouster was high on their agenda.

A revolving door of directors and management personnel contributed to the growing skepticism. There was profound fear that Riverside's trouble may be fatal. It would be one more crushing experience to those who for years tried to patch together a farmer-investor operation in a time when the old packing house structure was gradually collapsing.

Some came to propose a fire sale. Others proffered a less drastic plan that sought purchase by an outside packer. It was a mixture of those devastated by what they saw as a sinking ship, others willing to seek an unknown lifeline, and then the ever-optimistic minority who preached patience for unknown ballast. A near-mutinous atmosphere prevailed, but a majority agreed it was the helmsman who was to blame.

Company officials had called the special assembly as an attempt to explain market problems since last year's annual meeting and the corresponding impact on Riverside. But the mood of investors went beyond meatpacking economics. Their agenda was aimed at company directors and, more specifically, Peter Bremer, the scheduled speaker.

While the Riverside Pack meeting was front page news, the headline this day—Jan. 20, 1976—went to a little-known former Georgia governor who was the talk of presidential politics. While Riverside investors were doused with bad news, Jimmy Carter was basking in victory. He had just won, in surprising fashion, the Iowa Democratic caucuses.

It was 10:05 a.m. The podium was empty, the microphone silent. Jimmy Carter could have donated a pickup load of Georgia peanuts to munch on, but the Riverside delegation was more inclined to chew on Peter Bremer.

Some shareholders pulled pocket watches from their bib overalls while others double-checked their wrist watches. Then they stared fretfully at a big clock on the back wall above the American flag. All timepieces agreed. The meeting start was delayed. Seed corn caps were taken off, then put back on in a ritual of nervous impatience and building wrath.

"Where's Bremer?" came a shout from somewhere in the middle. "Yes, where's Bremer?" another echoed. Soon it multiplied into a chant that engulfed the entire auditorium.

"Where's Bremer! Where's Bremer! Where's Bremer!"

The escalation swelled into a cascading roar that penetrated every corner of Riverside Pack headquarters. It demanded attention and action. The little man from Little Rock, who had fought his way from poverty to the presidency of a company, was on the verge of being tossed out into the street.

A slightly built man in a navy suit and red tie walked up on the podium, but it wasn't Bremer. He was a public relations flack, dispensed to bargain for more time and forbearance, but he was greeted like a slow squirrel on a busy highway. The shouts were for blood, and the poor PR fellow was unable to talk around it or even be heard.

"Have you ever seen anything like this?" reporter Tom Wendling asked the newspaper's business editor. The two, along with a photographer from the paper, were standing toward the front of the room, but on the side. They had a good view of several hundred jugular veins, all pumping blood as if doomsday had arrived.

"This is supposed to be a business meeting, full of boring financial information and good manners. Instead, it's more like the atmosphere at a professional wrestling meet. Are we going to see chairs bashed over people's heads and eye-gouging?"

Bruce George shook his head in a dumbfounded response. He had covered a lot of business meetings, including sessions where unhappy shareholders lined up to blister management, but this level of angst and anger was new. George loosened his bow tie and took a deep breath.

"Farmers are generally a peaceable lot," he responded in his quiet, pastor-like fashion. "They are neighborly sorts, ready to help, and when there are differences, they are prone to work things out. Life is hard, and days are long on the farm, and I guess they figure there's little use in added aggravation. But this is different.

"These folks believe they've been taken down the road once more, financially, and betrayed. That hurts. They not only have to go home and face themselves but listen to comments of farmers who decided not to invest."

George summoned years of knowledge gained in watching businesses succeed and businesses go bust.

"If Riverside fails," he said, "the ripples of destruction will run off in many directions."

It was 10:20 a.m. when a stocky, red-faced farmer climbed the podium and raised his hands like Moses. The unruly crowd quieted to a shuffling murmur. Moses rubbed the whiskers on his face and stepped to the microphone. He looked at them empathetically, sweat running down his neck. He, too, had bought into what many looked at as a Golden Calf.

"I know you are upset," he said, adjusting his Pioneer seed corn cap. "No, you are angry. I am too. Very angry. But this fella here with the red tie has information to put out, so why don't we be farmer-courteous and listen. OK?"

It was close to a miracle. No one knew this Moses chap, but his credentials were there for all to see. He looked like most every other farmer at the meeting. He was family. He was the guy you had coffee with at the town café on a rainy day. Belonged to the Farm Bureau. Once played softball, didn't he? I swear his boys, and the daughter too, displayed animals at 4-H.

"Thank you," Moses said, and he relinquished the microphone to the red tie.

"Ladies and gentlemen," the public relations man began with quivering voice. Clearly, this was new territory for him. He not only came with no manna, but his message was as sour. His shoulders shook. He grabbed onto the sides of the podium in search of steadiness and pluck.

"I'm sorry to inform you that Mr. Bremer has not arrived at Riverside headquarters."

The room took on the sound of a muffled explosion. Red Tie looked at Moses, who nodded as to say "go ahead."

"Mr. Bremer was scheduled to be here. We have tried to reach him at his residence. We have tried contacting him at several other places. No one at the plant has seen him. I don't know what else to tell you. I'm sorry. The board of directors has suggested we wait until 11:00 a.m., and if Mr. Bremer does not show up by then, we will have to reschedule the meeting. Again, we apologize for the delay."

"That's unadulterated bullshit!" shouted a strapping man in a green-and-black checkered wool shirt and jeans secured by gray suspenders. "Who ever heard that the top dog of a company fails to show for a meeting he scheduled? Maybe he's back in his office, hiding under a desk, tail between his legs."

The comments brought laughter and soothed the collective testiness.

"Unadulterated bullshit!" Moses repeated evenly as he glanced at Red Tie. "Be sure you get that in the minutes."

Eleven o'clock came, and Bremer didn't. It was announced that the meeting would be rescheduled in two weeks at the same time of day. Investors slowly filed out into the cold, defeated by the postponement and deepening fear that their investments were destined for losses. Some spoke of lawsuits. Opinions differed as to what should be done, what could be done.

The dream called Riverside Pack had painfully transformed into a wide-awake nightmare.

"I'm afraid my story is going to sound more like an obituary," George said, as the two newsmen headed back to the paper. "This one investor told me he was headed for his lawyer's office. Several others hinted the same but planned to first meet with some of the downtown heavy hitters who are investors. It's depressing. The meeting, though a waste of time, provided valuable insight about the future of Riverside Pack."

"Well," Wending cracked. "At least you could write that nobody was physically injured."

"Maybe so," said George. "But a lot of people suffered psychological pain, and some may be crippled financially. What did Leo Durocher say? 'Nice guys finish last.' I think you saw a ballpark full of investors assume that role today."

Judge Mullin, though sometimes less than punctual himself for court times, had little patience for tardy principals in litigation procedures. Most of the federal court cast—the bailiff, recorder, probation officer, clerk, and US Attorney—were present when Mullin entered from his private offices. Defense Attorney David Etting was seated at the big table opposite the prosecutor.

IRS representatives sat in the public section of the courtroom, ready to answer questions if needed. In the back of the courtroom were a deputy US marshal and news reporter Wendling. There were six other observers. Wendling was surprised that more investors were not there. All rose when Mullin entered.

Peter Bremer, the defendant in the tax case and the central figure of the proceedings, was absent. The empty chair next to Etting, where Bremer was supposed to be sitting, became the focal point for everyone. For Mullin it became a symbol of disrespect for the bench, the undermining of law and order. His glower, Wendling thought, could set the chair afire.

Bremer's trial had been held several weeks before. Now was the time for the judge's decision. Inside Mullin's case file was his determination that Bremer was guilty. Also the judge was prepared to pronounce a sentence of one year in prison and a fine of $25,000. The prison time would be deferred subject to probation conditions and arrangements to pay back the taxes and the fine.

"Mr. Etting!" Mullin bellowed with an accusatory look at the defense attorney. "Where is your client?"

"I wish I knew," Etting replied. "I tried to reach him this morning. I've tried contacting him for several days, but without success. I inquired at his office. The people there informed me he failed to show up for the company's special meeting of shareholders last week. I've called the company's plant in Chelsea, and I've tried reaching him at his apartment at the Roosevelt Hotel. No one has seen Mr. Bremer or his wife."

"This is highly unusual, Mr. Etting. I'm accustomed to having defense attorneys keep better track of their clients. I can tell you this much, and please relay this to Mr. Bremer. He faces contempt of court charges along with his other troubles. In the meantime, I'm directing the marshal's office to issue an arrest warrant for Mr. Bremer. One way or another, we will have this matter settled."

Mullin seemed to take the matter personally. He would show this pipsqueak president of a bloody meatpacking operation who was in charge.

"Yes, your honor. I understand," said Etting. "I will continue to search for him, and if I locate him, I will convey your message. I will also notify the court."

With that, a piqued Judge Mullin slammed the gavel and ended the proceeding that never was. He left a two-inch thick file of reports, background, and other data pertaining to Bremer's case on his bench, spurning the documents as if they were a useless accumulation of paper.

Reporter Wendling was unable to wrangle any more information from Etting, except that the lawyer was unaware until a day ago that Bremer had also missed the Riverside Pack meeting. Etting said he had been out of town and missed news coverage of the postponed meeting. Wendling rechecked sources at Riverside, but no one had seen Bremer for three days. He questioned the manager, desk clerks, and three cleaning personnel at the Roosevelt Hotel. Same results. Bremer and his wife had not been seen in three days.

The big black Cadillac was gone from the hotel garage. Hotel management refused to show Wendling the Bremer suite.

Before returning to the newspaper, Wendling drove down to Riverside offices. He again talked to office employees, secretaries, janitors, and maintenance workers. No one had seen Bremer for three days. That seemed to be the time frame most consistent. Three days. Bremer and his wife could be anywhere in that span.

Or, Wendling thought, they could be nowhere.

The reporter recalled Bremer's dark disclosure that he feared for his life because of ill-advised loans and delayed repayments to Chicago mobsters. He had said he a dreaded driving on US Route 30 to Chelsea, feared he may be intercepted and dispatched by mob hoodlums. As a result, he took backroads to access the Riverside plant at Chelsea.

Wendling returned to the newsroom, wrote the story of Bremer's no-show in Federal Court, and finished lesser articles from his beat. Then he put the finishing touches on a Sunday follow-up story on the Iowa Democratic presidential caucuses. Could former Georgia Gov. Jimmy Carter, the surprise winner of the caucuses, carry on in New Hampshire and other states to defeat Indiana Sen. Birch Bayh for the party's nomination?

The following day, Wendling worked sources at the Federal Courthouse and discovered, in a roundabout way, that the FBI was already involved in the hunt for the Bremers. However, Jim Ryan, agent in charge of the Cedar Rapids FBI office, refused to confirm or deny that the nation's top cops were involved in the search. For the moment, Wendling decided to sit on the information. The fear and mob angle and rumored FBI involvement would have to wait for another day's press run.

If the FBI is involved, Wendling pondered, the case of Peter Bremer is more than a warrant for failing to show up in court on income tax evasion. The Bureau reserves its long reach for major crime matters, such as murder with interstate complications, kidnapping, and racketeering.

Chapter 38
1965, Kansas

"Rosemary. I think we'd better head back to the house. It looks like a storm is brewing."

She was still cuddled to him, engulfed in his broad arms, her face caressed by the soft texture of his flannel shirt. His chin was nestled in her frizzy hair as he inhaled her sweet aroma.

Both were consumed in a rapture that can only occur when a couple become one in the full dimension of love. They had ridden their horses to the far end of Henry Bexler's ranch, picnic lunch in tote and love-making on their minds. They had discovered the perfect shade of a seventy-foot cottonwood tree, roots stubbornly lodged in Kansas's weather whimsey, a pastoral pillar to many generations.

The Lansing prison was locked out of their minds.

"That cherry pie was wonderful," Bobby said softly, rubbing his stomach. "Almost as good as my grandma makes."

She poked him with an editorial nudge.

"Really, you're a good cook, Rosemary. I knew there was a reason I married you."

She poked him again, this time with extra vigor.

The pure blue sky was gradually being overwhelmed by the churning black clouds of a northwest front. A cooler and building breeze carried the scent of approaching rain. A distant, deep-throated thunder, unhindered by hills or forests, muscled into the swelling overture. They quickly packed the picnic remnants, climbed onto their horses, and headed home with urgency. No sooner had they removed saddles in the barn and turned for the house when the skies opened.

These were delightful days for Rosemary and Bobby. The honeymoon chapter of their young life was filled with endless pages of bliss. They were in their thirties, submerged in each other's love in the obscurity of the Midwest, far from the pain of bashed black freedom marchers in Selma, Ala., and the buildup of US involvement in a war southeast Asia.

Kansans were still talking about the April execution of Richard Hickock and Perry Smith for the 1959 murders of four members of the Herbert Clutter family near Holcomb, a tiny town less than an hour's drive south of Cold Springs. The killers were hanged at the Kansas State Prison at Lansing, Bobby Bremer's alma mater. The dominating drama surrounding their arrest, conviction, and hanging smothered interest in a prison escapee who had been in a bar fight.

Summer folded into autumn, and winter flipped the calendar to a new year. Time bolted unrestricted, even for newlyweds, though the lackluster life of the open spaces sought to drag things down. Other than the weather, little changed on the plains. Like everyone else, the couple hunkered down in the cold, snow, and long nights of winter. It was a time when they began looking less at themselves and talked more about the happenings in the outside world. It was a natural maturation.

Beyond the Beatles mania, a near nonevent in western Kansas, the news from Vietnam became darker. Bremer was especially dismayed by a CBS radio report that outlined the dimensions of a Viet Cong attack near Da Nang, home to a major US base along the coast of Vietnam. Da Nang was thought to be a safe place, but a large force of guerillas attacked the Marines with mortars and small arms.

Among the defining aspects of the assault was the discovery that a thirteen-year old Viet Cong boy killed in the fight had Marine map positions on his body. The same boy had sold soft drinks to the Marines the day before. As if Bremer were among the Americans attacked, his mostly noncommittal stance regarding the war took a bellicose turn.

"This is what you get when you play with the enemy," he remarked to Rosemary after hearing the account. "Force, unrelenting force, is all the enemy understands, whether it's the Viet Cong or a goddamned banker treating customers like a piece of shit." He ranted another thirty seconds before Rosemary's waving hand cut him off.

"He was just a boy, Bobby," she said calmly, "doing what older people told him to do. Cuss his superiors if you want."

"Is that how you regard the pissant prairie bankers who talked your father into a mortgage to buy Upland Seeds, so they could impress their bosses back in Olathe? Were they doing what their bosses told them to do, at the expense of some innocent customer? If I had been your father, I might have taken a pot shot at one of them bankers."

It was Bobby Bremer's surly side, resurfacing after having been masked all through his courtship and first months of marriage. Rosemary knew the man she married was no escapee from the monastery. And the truth was she shared many of his viewpoints about government and people in power, especially those who controlled the purse strings of people's lives.

Time and the rebellious air of the 1960s regenerated some of his militant notions. While many in the country protested US involvement in Vietnam, Bremer's frustration grew in a different direction. While both continued to attend meetings of the Justice Now and Less Government groups, Bobby became irritated by the lack of any "real action" to achieve change. Lack of money was always cited as the barrier to increased encounter.

It was months after their first wedding anniversary, in the fall of 1966, that their love combined to create a new human being. It was the night they returned from a Less Government meeting at the Spietz ranch, Bobby speculated, that Rosemary conceived. They would later joke that it was the time when "less" became "more." They were excited, closer than ever.

"Perhaps," Rosemary giggled, "it was seeing all the other couples. Their love for one another seems to obscure all the problems we hash over. I'm not talking about a Hollywood kind of love that's showy on the outside and feeble on the inside, but plainly sincere and caring. I think our love is that way, Bobby."

"What about Henry? How does he fit into your analysis?"

"Henry," Rosemary suggested after deliberation, "while he hates to show it, loves everybody. I know. That doesn't exactly fit with some of things I've said about him. But if a psychiatrist got him to lay down on a couch, pried off his filthy hat, and pulled back his mustache so that his mouth could speak freely, he might admit that he is just a teddy bear. He would help anyone. Look how he has helped you, helped us."

"I love you, Rosemary." And he rubbed her belly, which was already showing signs of dimensional adjustment, making room for another human life. "I remember back to our wedding and how happy Mom was after meetin' you. Like me, she loved you on first sight. She will be ecstatic at news she's becomin' a grandma. Rosemary, she'll want to come to Cold Springs when the baby is born."

Molly Bremer, indeed, had loved Rosemary Hitchens the moment she met her. That was at the ranch, the day before the wedding, and Henry Bexler had spotted the accepting sparkle in Molly's eyes. He felt compelled to share his opinion with Bobby as the two savored cold beers out near the barn.

"Your mom has taken to Rosemary," Bexler said, "like taste buds cherish a mixture of grain, water, and hops." He took another swig and groaned ecstasy. "I don't know if you are aware of it"—the back of his hand wiped away his drool—"but moms ordinarily shield their sons like a new coat of paint protects wood. But your mom spotted Rosemary's sheen right off."

Molly had said as much in a private moment with her own mother. She noted Rosemary's confident yet supportive manner, her independence mixed with a willingness to pitch in. No primping and self-coddling the day before her wedding. Molly had plunged into sandwich making, up to her elbows in chicken salad and barbeque. Molly was happy for Bobby and Rosemary, and happy for herself.

It appeared, back on Bobby's wedding day, that Ma Bremer's boys had settled down. Peter was happy, making money in St. Louis, though she was concerned that he placed so much emphasis on what Pastor Clendon called a false god named Success.

Bobby Bremer was changing too. He had become more Kansan, casting off some of the Little Rock vernacular after Bexler's nagging tutoring. His character struggled to incorporate the softness and pride engendered by anticipated fatherhood with the growing militancy and hardness associated with his definition of injustice. Rosemary prayed the baby would be the antidote for his conflicts.

They faced other questions. When she visited the doctor, and she would soon have to, would it be as Rosemary Bremer? Perhaps more critically, would the baby's last name be Bremer? Should she see a doctor in Colorado, where they were married, in hopes it would keep Bobby Bremer's prison history concealed? Both wanted the baby's name to be Bremer, so Colorado again became the choice for camouflage.

There would always be the specter of Kansas authorities finding Bremer. It hung over their lives like permanent winter. The baby's coming both added and subtracted from that apprehension. Perhaps, they discussed one day, they should pull up stakes and move as far from Kansas as possible. However, it was amazing how much the child had to say in the matter.

Would he or she miss being close to his grandparents? Should the child be denied the same endless skies and open prairies that they had come to love? Would the people anywhere else be as supportive and neighborly? As the developing baby grew, their lives slowly converted into a threesome with all the attendant joys of parenthood.

With mysterious powers, the yet unborn child melted anxiety, allowing escape from the shadows of the Kansas State Prison once again.

Rosemary knew life could be cruel. She had seen it in the treatment and struggles of her parents. She had heard about it at Justice Now meetings. But she was not acquainted or prepared for painful devastation. Her first visit to the doctor indicated a normal pregnancy. He estimated the baby's stage to be at about the thirteenth week. When she started bleeding three weeks later, she was shocked and terrified.

A frantic and tearful trip to the doctor confirmed the worst. She had a miscarriage. The physician provided both medical and emotional attention to Rosemary, but clearly her mind had suffered the greatest wound. Every time she felt her stomach, the emptiness produced screams of lamentation. At the request of the doctor, she and Bobby stayed in the lone treatment room overnight. Neither slept.

"I want to leave now, right now," she told the doctor first thing the next morning.

The anguish, for both, was severe. However, Bobby was unable to grasp the piercing and prolonged impact the loss had on Rosemary. For days she sought solace by staring at the empty spaces of Kansas, as if its depths could absorb her anguish. But her pain only magnified. After three weeks of depression, he convinced her to ride out to the cottonwood tree, a totem whose broken limbs and tattered bark proclaimed the hazards of life and the prerequisites of survival.

They sat there, holding each other, drinking the cup of lost expectation and undefined future. Their silence filled volumes. The cool northwest wind hinted at the winter weather to come, Earth's endless cycle of dying and rebirth. He brushed the hair from Rosemary's eyes. Her shivering told him it was time to go home.

After they returned to the ranch house, he fixed her a peanut butter and jelly sandwich. He was in the process of pouring her a cold glass of Dad's Old Fashioned root beer when she smiled lightly and giggled faintly. To him they were hearty markers of healing.

"Did you know," she said softly, "that when you and Henry came into the Welcome Inn that first time, I was enjoying my favorite lunchtime snack? A peanut butter and jelly sandwich."

She looked at the lowly concoction as if it were a medical breakthrough, an ostensible cure being prescribed by none other than her loving husband, Dr. Bobby Bremer. Time, in Rosemary Bremer's case, had a stretch to go to claim healer status, but it certainly dispensed the salve of endurance.

The winter of 1966–67 was mild by history's averages. Bexler was in excellent spirits as the normal ravages of nature yielded to moderation, making ranch life far less demanding. Livestock thrived with minimal concern. Winter wheat signaled a bumper crop. Repairs to fences, buildings, and roads were minor. The only negative in Bexler's mind was that fewer expenses meant higher income taxes.

It was as if Mother Nature sensed the importance of extraordinary calm to counter Rosemary and Bobby's terrible storm. Slowly, they pulled themselves from the darkness of loss, but the shadows were never far away—especially for Rosemary. Bexler was not blind to their despondency. He suggested what he thought may help recovery.

"Why don't you take a week or so off and visit your mom and relatives in Little Rock," he suggested to Bobby in the spring of 1967. "We're caught up on work around here, and I'll pay for your gas and lodging, if necessary." Bremer's eyes brightened at the thought of pleasing his mother and moving Rosemary's healing another step forward.

"What do you think, sweetheart?" Rosemary was kneading bread dough when Bobby first repeated Bexler's proposal. "We could see Ma, and travel through the Ozarks. Mighty pretty there." His enthusiasm grew. "Think your '57 Plymouth can waddle down there?" Baking was therapy. She had punched down the leavened dough, kneaded it again, and now applied the rolling pin as if she were stamping out bad memories. She sprinkled in sugar and cinnamon and looked up at him.

"What do you think?" she replied in a meek voice that did not match her attack on the dough.

"I believe the old Plymouth can handle the trip," Bremer responded in male-like fashion.

"I'm not talking about the car, Bobby. I'm talking about us. Are we ready? Yes, it would be nice to visit your ma. It would be nice for a change of pace and scenery. And Henry is generous in giving us time off and money for expenses. But what do we tell your ma about the baby? Do we mention it all? Or is it better not to relive the pain with her?"

These were all questions—good questions—that the prospect of going back home to see his mother had overshadowed. Like an x-ray examination, they also revealed that the scar from the miscarriage was still just below the surface of Rosemary's life. She rolled the dough, cut it, and put sections in pans to raise.

Bobby followed her around the small kitchen like a detective in search of clues. The pacing eventually led him to another stumbling block. While it had been more than three years since his escape from the Kansas State Prison, was it safe to venture out? Just how long is the memory of Kansas state police and small-town cops?

"I just thought of another issue." Bobby sought her attention. She put the cinnamon rolls in the oven. "Me. I'm an issue. It's one thing being tucked away in the outskirts of nowhere, but what if we get stopped by police? What if we're in an accident? As Henry would say, I'd be back in the lockup faster than flies sit on manure."

"Don't you start on those Henryisms," she said behind a muffled chuckle. "Here's what I think. You are still on the prison books, and for sure the first chapter of some of those guards back at Lansing, but most everyone else has forgotten. But to be safe, if we went, I would do all the driving, and we'd take the Colorado detour." She was referring to the same pathway they took for marriage.

He agreed to such a plan, but the bigger questions, and the trip itself, remained in the air. It came as a surprise when the next day, without a word to him, she personally thanked Bexler and said the trip idea was great. Bexler gyrated through his customary harrumphs, then announced there was indeed a price attached to his offer.

"I suppose you thought you could sneak the smell of cinnamon rolls baking in the oven past my proboscis," he grunted. "In case you didn't know it, my sense of smell is sharper than a bloodhound's in pursuit of rabbits. My guess, and my deductive abilities are second only to my olfactory powers, is that there is an uneaten pan of those rolls on the top of your kitchen counter."

"The price is paid," Rosemary laughed, shaking her head at how she had come to accept a man she once despised. Life does unfold in perplexing ways. She reviewed her brief life as she went back to the ranch house and rounded up Henry's order, just like in the days at the Welcome Inn. Three days later they headed for Little Rock.

Chapter 39
Little Rock, 1967

"I didn't realize Oklahoma City was such a big place," Rosemary said as they headed east on Interstate 40. It was a trip with mixed outlooks—happiness for a change in life's scenery and a visit to Bobby's mother, but also anxiety that the long arm and eyes of the law that may be looming around the corner or in their rear-view mirror.

"Maybe we should have stopped at the Cowboy Hall of Fame, as Jake Spietz recommended," Rosemary said, "but I'm still nervous about accidentally spreading the Bremer name around. Never know who is watching registrations. That's why I use my maiden name at motels."

"I suppose," Bobby replied flatly, absent of endorsement.

He had been pondering the hide-and-peek lifestyle they had been forced to live in the last several years, and it was grating the sullen side of his temperament. His mind was slowly bending to a less restrained existence, maybe even one where the name Bremer found its way out of obscurity and back to routine. He yearned to have the fullness of his life back.

Anonymity is a different kind of prison.

Henry Bexler sensed his restiveness, and it was one of the reasons he had suggested they take some time off.

It was an unusually warm early April. Patches of wild violets began showing off in the shady spots of roadside ditches. Red-winged blackbirds warbled their return from southern nesting regions. The fresh spring breeze, like time itself, hurried past the open windows of their car. It rustled their hair and minds into a tangle of directions.

Bobby imagined freely mingling with other residents of northwest Kansas, having his own name on a driver's license and on the mailbox, openly participating in prairie governmental issues. He would like to share his views with the governor on several matters percolating under the capitol dome in Topeka. But that would be like flashing a red flag in front of Lansing prison officials.

Rosemary pondered the child who wasn't there and what to say about that to Bobby's mother. She imagined a youngster with bright eyes, crawling on the floor, exploring the pots and pans in the kitchen cupboard as if it were a safe full of jewels. Would he or she have had curly hair like hers? A short nose more like Bobby's? Oh, the wonder of a child who encompassed a couple's love.

A parade of their thoughts rode silently along. They had stayed in a small motel the night before in Geary, Okla., another of the hundreds of US towns established after the American Indians were chased out. The plan was to make it to Little Rock that evening.

"Your mom was really excited when we called and said we were coming for a visit."

"Rosemary," he said over the rush of wind. "Have you thought any more about a different life, moving on from this business in Kansas, starting over somewhere else where nobody knows us?"

"Aren't you excited to see your mom and grandparents?"

He shifted his eyes from an emerald-green pasture dotted with black Angus cattle to the woman who had become part of his life and accepted all his baggage. The thought that she loved him enough to risk her future toned down his response.

"Sure, Rosemary. You know that I'm delighted to see Ma again," he said with a slight color of testiness. "But you ignored my question. How much longer are we going to be holed up like outlaws in the wide-open spaces of nowhere?"

They zipped past the "Welcome to Arkansas" sign.

"I don't know." She looked back to his eyes and searched for words. "I don't plan much. I'm afraid to."

For him it sometimes seemed like a perpetual trip down a mud road. There were periods when the going seemed to get better only to bog down again in a rain of tedium and uncertainty.

"I know how much losing the baby pained you, but we have to leave that behind too. As hard as that is."

Like Ma Bremer, Rosemary was able to see his good side, the soft side of Bobby Bremer. Perhaps his vulnerable nature was part of what attracted her. And she usually was able to calm his churlish outbreaks. She sympathized, too, that justice fell short in some of his issues with the law. But she had no answers. She struggled to convey her feelings on lasting loss.

"See, Bobby," she said, fighting back a bleak and barren feeling in her stomach that sought release through tears. "You don't know about my pain. You can't know. Often I don't understand it myself."

The sign said "Alma, two miles." Another displayed the ubiquitous golden arches logo. She was sure further attempts at explanation about the baby would be futile. However, she had made up her mind about whether to tell Bobby's mother.

"I don't want to bring up the miscarriage to your ma," she said as the car sped past Alma and McDonald's.

"I agree with that," he said. "Ma would bawl her head off, and it would make matters worse for you."

It fell short of the definition of empathy, but Rosemary accepted his declaration as the best things could be. The Ozark Mountains galloped past their senses, an undulating tableau of shadows, emerald hills, and misty recesses.

"I worked in this part of Arkansas." He changed the subject. "I'd say it's one of the prettiest places in the country. Never been to the Smoky Mountains, but I read about them, and my guess is the Ozarks are every bit as handsome. I liked my job, too, working for a landscape outfit. Maybe we could move down here, and I could get my old job back."

"Bobby. Have you gone mad!" Rosemary gasped. "You skipped out on parole in these parts, said you were looking for new adventure. It's my guess the name Bremer is among those still on the minds of every parole officer in Arkansas. You may take your past lightly, but I'm positive the law doesn't. Makes no difference to them if injustice played a role in your troubles."

"Yeah, yeah, Rosemary. I was just dreamin' a little change for us, maybe a new adventure."

"I can see why you love the Ozarks. The trees just roll together in a massive canvass. Over there," she said, pointing, "the pines embrace a suspended haze. It looks as if the trees are letting off steam. It's beautiful. Sure different than Kansas."

"I think those are white pines. Some get ninety feet high," Bobby said. "When I had that landscape job, we went on roads that never saw sunshine. You have to get off this big highway to really appreciate the mystery of the Ozarks."

Rosemary's Plymouth purred along like a stroked kitten regally smirking at the family dog. The Ozarks and Clarksville quickly disappeared in the rear-view mirror as I-40 dipped southward toward Little Rock. She monitored her speed like a small-town cop eyeing out-of-state drivers. The speed limit was 70 mph, but she maintained a steady 65. It was one more example of restraint that caused Bobby Bremer to twitch as if he had sandburs in his britches.

"I'm looking forward to hearing the latest adventures between your grandfather and his friend Adora." Rosemary rekindled family talk. "Those two have a natural distaste for each other. How did that nasty relationship get started?"

"Maybe, when we get back home, we should consider how we can get more involved in Justice Now." Bobby ignored her question. "I know the group lacks money, but somehow we should get more involved in opposing injustice, wherever it shows up. I think there's some in law enforcement who are tired of looking the other way when the banker's son is involved in some shenanigan."

"You may have a point, Bobby, but now you've ignored my question."

"Grandpa and Adora Mae? I can't rightly say when they started fightin'. Maybe it was in first grade." He laughed. "Maybe he stuck her pigtail in the inkwell of his desk. Who knows? One sure thing. It's been as regular as the ocean tide." He glanced over at the shimmering waters of Dardanelle Lake. "Probably turned into intense dislike over war issues. Adora was a strong isolationist. Even Pearl Harbor didn't change her mind. No matter what one of them says, the other disagrees. They are like red flags in a bull ring."

"Speaking of red, what are those flashing lights ahead?" Rosemary asked nervously. "Looks like cars are stopped." She slowed.

She soon found herself in a queue of red taillights. The line advanced forward to where police had established four checkpoint lanes. Each lane had several officers quizzing drivers. The process seemed to move quickly. She knew her brake lights worked. Her driver's license was in her maiden name as was the registration. She glanced at Bobby who responded with a shrug. It irked her. He seemed to be amused by her discomfort.

"What if they ask to see your identification?" she said.

"I'll just say who I am and throw my hands in the air!"

"Bobby! I swear I will..."

She was interrupted by a tap on the driver's side window. She reached for the crank and rolled the window down.

"What's all the commotion?" she asked the young state trooper. He had peach-fuzz cheeks and looked as if he just exited high school.

"Ma'am," he said, his conduct nervous. "Could I see your driver's license, please?"

She handed it to him, matching his tentative manner. He studied it as if there would be a test later.

"You live in Kansas, then?" he asked.

"Yes, sir. Northwest Kansas."

"And this is your husband, Mr. Hitchins?"

"Yes. We are headed to Little Rock to see his family."

"I see." He looked in the back seat and saw two tan, worn suitcases. "Would you mind if I looked in the trunk?"

"No. Feel free," said Rosemary. All he would discover, she knew, was Bobby's mud-caked overshoes, an inflated spare tire, and wrenches. The inspection took less than a minute.

"Thanks, ma'am. There was a bank robbery in Fort Smith this morning. Banker was shot. Word is they were headed east. A man and woman. So we're checking all vehicles. They had a white Chevy but ditched it and stole a bluish-gray Pontiac. We don't know if they're still drivin' it. Thanks for your cooperation."

With that, Rosemary was flagged through the blockade. She took a deep breath and gave Bobby a look as if they had just escaped the beheading block.

"Isn't this lake beautiful?" he said, grinning from ear to ear.

"You weren't worried?"

"I thought it was exciting. Kinda made my day. Bank robbed. Banker shot. Seems like maybe justice was at work this morning."

"Bobby, that's terrible. You are lucky that cop was young. Probably never saw your picture on the post office wall." She thought over what the officer had said.

"I guess I'm not sorry the bank lost some money," Rosemary reflected. "But I don't like the shooting part." She thought about Bobby's restlessness, his itch for something different. She strained to read what really was bounding around in the back of his mind. Did he want a new life far from Kansas? Or did he merely feel handcuffed by his history?

"This whole delay made me hungry. What do you say, Mr. Hitchins? Want to stop for a hamburger?"

They arrived in Little Rock an hour and a half later.

Chapter 40

"I don't think I ever saw my grandmother so angry."

Bobby started to chuckle. Then he burst out in laugher that grew into an uncontrollable roar. Rosemary had never witnessed her husband with such wild, massive mirth.

"Don't hurt yourself," she cautioned. But then she fell victim to contagious hilarity. The more they reflected on that scene outside Good Neighbors Baptist Church in Little Rock, the more they roiled in laughter. They were heading back to Kansas, but their minds centered on images and words from Sunday's after-church spat between Bobby's grandfather and Adora Mae Marston.

All and all it had been a most enjoyable visit. For some time, Rosemary had wanted to visit Bobby's mother and see her husband's childhood home. The trip was a much-needed break from the solitude and routine of northwest Kansas.

It turned out that Molly's sixtieth birthday was the following week so her mother brought a cake for the small family gathering Saturday evening. Even Hattie had driven down from Rochester, but Peter said he could not make it. Rosemary was treated to albums of family pictures with verbal illumination provided by Molly's father. He reveled in storytelling and hyperbole. Discretely absent from any explanations of past events was reference to Jack Bremer, Bobby's father. No one had seen him or heard from him since he abandoned the family in 1942.

There was no mention of Rosemary's trauma in losing the baby or of Bobby's restive spasms. Neither was there any talk of Bobby's prison life. His escape was more than three years ago. If the matter came up at any time during the weekend, Bobby planned to simply say he was on parole. Attention was fixed on the family reunion and Rosemary in particular.

Molly was ecstatic. Two of her three children were home. Her parents Orval and Aliza Price were there. Though she felt hurt by Peter's absence, she invoked the magic of motherhood and concealed it in the joy of being surrounded by Hattie, Bobby, and Rosemary. Her father pronounced that Peter Bremer should have canceled his business plans and attended his mother's birthday party.

The bungalow on Cumberland Street had not experienced such joyfulness in years. Molly gladly gave Rosemary a tour of the house. The visiting couple would stay in Bobby's old room. They walked outside and Molly pointed to the spot where the children often played beneath the Southern Magnolia tree. It was fully grown now, and burgeoning buds indicated that showy white flowers were on its Spring calendar.

The two talked about the future. Molly was thinking of Bobby's past, his escape from prison, and where that would lead, but she avoided such direct questions. Rather, she asked if the couple planned to make west Kansas their permanent home, and if ranching was a satisfying life. Rosemary said Bobby enjoyed working with livestock and had made many friends in the area. Yet she acknowledged that he had expressed a yearning to do something different, maybe move further west.

"And how do you feel about that?" Molly had asked.

Rosemary said it would be difficult to leave her home region but was inclined to agree with Bobby that they should set out on their own. She elaborated no further, and the topic evaporated like morning dew in prickly heat. Molly had a feeling it would reappear with each new day of their lives.

After birthday cake was served, she was asked about her own plans. Molly said she intended to work another five years at Timex. She would then be eligible for the company's full pension. And, she said, it would allow her to build up her "rainy-day fund."

"I'm much relieved now that we have Medicare coverage for retirees," she added, "although my health has been good." While heart disease plagued the Price family, yearly checks showed that Molly had so far escaped any coronary complications.

However, the strength of her heart was surely tested after Sunday services when Adora Mae Marston and Orval Raymond Price met outside church. It coincidently followed a sermon on forgiveness and peace. The familiar Christian message was made more poignant by the recent assassination of Martin Luther King and the continued quagmire in Vietnam.

It was not long after a few of Molly's church friends had been introduced to Rosemary when the fireworks began. Adora Mae felt it was her duty, mostly to relieve pent up opinion, to comment on the sermon. She decided to link peace to the worsening conflict in Vietnam. Her antiwar views were gaining ground across the United States, especially among protesting college students.

"It doesn't seem President Johnson is doing anything that will bring peace to Southeast Asia," she said as bystanders were still casually rolling the church bulletin in their hands. "We should never have sent troops over there in the first place. Our boys are waddling around in rice paddies, ironically like ducks out of water, totally outside traditional warfare."

Sunday serenity dissolved. Everybody looked at Orval, knowing he disagreed with nearly everything Adora said, especially in matters involving armed forces. And they knew the vigor of her tongue grated on the ex-Marine. A slow burn was tempered by a "keep your mouth shut" look from Aliza, and it caused him to purse his lips as if he'd just chewed on a teaspoon of habanero peppers. The atmosphere was intensified by Adora's generous use of toiletries.

"I'm surprised, Orval," she continued, with full knowledge she was pulling the pin on his grenade, "that you, a staunch Kennedy

Democrat, would condone the idiot policies of Lyndon Baines Johnson and his half-baked secretary of defense, Robert McNamara."

She paused for designed effect.

"This domino theory about communism taking over all of Southeast Asia is malarkey. Should never have been in there in the first place," she repeated. "We learned nothing from the French. Why do we have to be the world's policeman? It's crazy. Take care of things at home first."

Her lungs had Olympic-like capacity.

Smoke drifted out of Orval's ears, a precursor to ignoring his wife's warning. Human tolerance, even after a sermon on peace and forgiveness, has its limits. For him, Adora Mae took on the persona of Jane Fonda at best and Ho Chi Minh at worse. He took a step toward Adora Mae and extended a wagging finger.

"I didn't realize," he began solemnly, "that you were an expert on foreign policy and military operations. Someone with your wisdom should be a consultant, I would think either for Mao Zedong or Leonid Brezhnev." Orval omitted a check with Aliza for editorial review. He knew her eyebrows would be raised in red-line objection.

"Our boys, as you falsely claim to respect, would size up your rantings as scum on week-old borsch." He avoided Aliza's contorted facial objections. "Would you like me to schedule you as guest speaker down at the American Legion? I am convinced they would suffer through your warped ideas about our place in the world, not to mention that you believe our troops are ill prepared to fight the Viet Cong.

"And then you may explain to the South Vietnamese people, who by the way, Adora, were invaded by the North, that they are less than human and not worthy of help from someone else. You were against Roosevelt's aid to Britain, and you argued against Truman dropping the bomb."

He, too, paused on purpose.

"I suppose you opposed French intervention in our War of Independence. I'm guessing you were there."

With that, Adora's offense quickly switched to a higher phase. With her big purse on one arm and her Bible tucked under the other, she wound up like Bob Feller and hurled her black-bound Holy Scripture directly at Orval Price's mostly bald head. Orval long ago had professed receiving Jesus, but now he was getting the Lord's full message by air mail.

Fortunately he was still agile enough to dodge the full impact of the holy book, which was caught by a startled Bobby Bremer. He held Adora's bible nearly a half minute, perhaps a record time for him. He was unsure who to hand it to until his mother came to the rescue. She nestled it reverently in her arms as Orval sputtered a sequel.

"Perhaps, Adora," he said with a devilish smile, "you should consult Paul's letter to the Ephesians. That's Ephesians 4–22, in case you forgot. It says you should lay aside thy old self, which is being corrupted in accordance with the lusts of deceit. Or in Hebrews he suggests not to throw away your confidence, or perhaps your Bible, lest you have need of endurance."

Orval doubted those were precise quotes from the Bible, but he figured it was close enough to counter Adora's surprise attack. He turned away just as she swung her purse. Molly was dumfounded. Aliza was blistering angry and headed after Oval. Everyone was stunned by this face-to-face confrontation that erupted outside Good Neighbors Baptist Church on an otherwise placid spring Sunday morning.

There was an upside to the clash. Adora Mae made no reference to Bobby Bremer's prison past. Perhaps she had forgotten. More likely, her venom was exclusively prescribed for Orval Price.

"Grandma Aliza was so ticked she could hardly speak," Bobby recalled as the couple drove west.

"Didn't your parents plan to come to your mom's for Sunday chicken dinner?" Rosemary asked.

"I think so, but when Adora opened up and Grandpa responded, then she tossed her Bible?" Bobby resumed his belly-bouncing laughter. "I guess that was enough to digest for one Sunday. I have never, ever seen Grandma so upset. Way more than that time he tried to light the cook stove only to have it blow up, leaving coal dust all over her face."

Henry Bexler was waiting on the front porch of his house when Rosemary and Bobby drove up. A timothy stem danced from side to side in his mouth as if it were conducting a silent concert. He waved, then walked up to their car. Rosemary read his mind, and it said he was itching to tell them something. A wrinkled brow and pressed lips confirmed it.

"What's the big news around here?" she asked.

"Oh, not much." He betrayed his thoughts. "Tell me all about Little Rock. Bobby, did your Grandpa behave himself?"

They gave him a report on the visit with Bobby's mother, and an abridged version of the Sunday scuffle, enough of the details to put a comic sparkle back in Henry's eyes.

"I like your Grandpa, Bobby. He is a courageous man. Come on in and have a lemonade, or something stronger if you want."

Inside, Rosemary made a peripheral housewife check of things but then zeroed in on the unknown, prompted by her intuition.

"Tell us what's bugging you, Henry," Rosemary prodded. "I can tell there is something on your mind that is aching to spill out. Something go haywire on the ranch? Bad storm? Problems with your health?"

"No, none of that," Henry answered with a wave of his hand. "You may recall, the same day you left, there was a meeting of Justice Now. Over at Spietz's place?" Bobby nodded. "Well, we come to find out from Jake that a sheriff's deputy arrested banker Smith's boy for drunk drivin', some two months ago, 'cept nothing was ever done about it. Seems County Attorney Langston dismissed the charges."

"Well, maybe he had good reason," Rosemary suggested.

"Not from what we heard," Bexler continued. "You may remember that Smith and his money helped get Langston elected. It was no secret young Langston had been starvin' for business as a lawyer. He couldn't find his way around the law code if Rand McNally was his guide. So, his daddy gets him to run for the county attorney office and lines up the cash to accomplish the task.

"The sheriff, who happens to be on the other side of the political fence, lets it out to Jake Spietz that young Smith, on his way home from Bud's Tavern, was speeding and almost hit a car with a woman and her two children. He had two other witnesses saying Smith was weaving all over the road. The deputy said there were empty beer bottles in Smith's car and that the kid himself smelled like a brewery.

"That got Jake's dander flying. He's none too fond of them bankers to begin with. So, he tells the sheriff to take his case to the newspaper down in Goodland. Well, the sheriff says he can't do that, but someone else could. The arrest and court proceedin's is public record, he says. So, off ole Jake goes to the newspaper."

"Did they run a story?"

"Yep, by golly. They did. That was last month. News doesn't travel very fast out here. Now Jake tells us he and the newspaper are being sued. Smith says his boy was found innocent of drunk drivin' and that the newspaper story tarnishes the lad. Well, most people know the kid had plenty of tarnishin' before."

"Wait. How does that concern Mr. Spietz?" Rosemary asked.

"Smith found out it was Jake who filled in the newspaper. So, he's suing Jake too. The newspaper claims they merely reported public record, but the problem is Jake doesn't have the kind of money required to hire a lawyer. Case will probably take months before trial unless, of course, the judge dismisses it."

"Now you know why I didn't collapse in sorrow about that bank robbery down in Ft. Smith." Bobby looked at Rosemary. They told Henry about the traffic stop north of Little Rock.

"This bank, the one suing Mr. Spietz, is that the same bank that foreclosed on my father?" Rosemary asked, knowing the answer beforehand.

"One and the same," said Henry. "A real community booster. But Justice Now has agreed to help raise money for Jake's defense. It ain't cheap to hire a lawyer, especially seeing no legal eagle in Goodland will take his case."

"I don't know what we can do, but we will help," Rosemary said. Bobby rose from his chair, pulled on his jacket, and went outside. He kicked at a five-gallon pail full of hardened concrete, Henry's idea for a door stop. It wasn't smart to accost an immovable object, but it wasn't the first time Bobby Bremer acted before thinking.

The pain in his right big toe intensified Bobby's sour mood. It also helped advance a bizarre notion in the back of his mind that only prudence and Rosemary's known level-headedness had kept concealed.

Chapter 41
1976, St. Louis

"Peter," she begged, "I know you are scared, but I don't see why I can't come with you. Please! Please!! Please!!!"

Glenda's eyes were red from hours of on-and-off weeping. Mascara streamed down her cheeks like rivers of lava winding down a pristine mountainside. She grabbed him by the shirt collar with both hands in a desperate plea to change his decision. Her mind was a haze of emotion—fear, confusion, and loss, all wrapped in a mist of uncertainty.

"Look at me and listen," she implored.

They sat on the edge of a bed in a motel room near the St. Louis airport, exhausted from endless discussion about the future. In mere hours, their lives had transformed from a settled routine, albeit filled with worry, to scrambling distress. They were like two penniless people who had just been evicted from their apartment, with doubt the only sure thing in their grasp.

"I'm so sorry, Glenda."

A single lamp struggled to illuminate the bleak scene. Blinking lights from the motel marquee filtered through the thin beige drapes, adding intermittent shadows to a room already colored with gloom. For Peter Bremer discomfort had run its course. His world, his life, was more a saturation of torment.

It was as if he had arrived at the wide-open gates of hell.

He stood. He stared at the floor, his hands locked behind his back as if shackled. Then, slowly, he walked to a big-armed faded-blue chair that had all the symptoms of original furniture in a motel overdue for remodeling. Finally he sat down, hesitantly, perhaps unsure if the chair, too, would come crashing down like everything else.

Bremer did not have the courage to look at her eyes, just as he had avoided confrontation with Riverside Pack shareholders. He shook his head in absolute defeat, still reluctant to confess the full dimension of his failures, including the portended collapse of their future as husband and wife. Worst of all, for him, was his overriding reluctance to part from the goddess of success, his primary love.

"Sorry," she said, trying to regenerate his Baptist upbringing, "means you should atone for any mistakes, and that begins, Peter, with being honest with me, completely honest, so we can try to work this out—whatever may be involved." She threw her hands in the air in exasperation. She struggled to push aside defeat and intuited alteration of their future.

Glenda walked over to his chair, grabbed his hands, and pulled him back to the bed beside her. She rejected his solution of submission to circumstances, just as she had done since they left Cedar Rapids some fourteen hours ago. She clasped his face with both hands and steered it toward hers, forcing his attention, holding on with the tenacity of a mortally wounded soldier.

Tears again bubbled from her eyes.

"Look at me, Peter," she pleaded. "I understand you have made bad investments, that you owe large sums of money to unsavory sorts in Chicago, but we can work that out. My father will loan us what is needed to pay off these debts. We can start over. We can—"

"No, Glenda," he interrupted brusquely. "I have been trying to tell you there is no way out, no wiggle room, no plan B or C, or anything else. I have used up all the answers. There are no more solutions." He did not expect she would understand. Acceptance was still beyond her reach. That is where they teetered, on the edge of a motel bed, outside any plausible resolution.

"I'm sorry that I brought this horrible situation on us," he said, "on you."

He shunned total honesty in deference to devotion to an unrelenting need to hang on to a last shred of self-reverence. His mind drifted to his boyhood days, when he cowered to his father's meanness, when he did what he had to do to survive. While his brother Bobby looked eye to eye at their raging father, defying his threats and suffering the consequences, Peter was not about to risk approval in exchange for a smack around the ears.

Bobby was reluctant to follow orders, whether from his father or teachers. And he had a strong sense for justice and an intense and sometimes aggressive attitude to achieve it. Peter, always conscious of his small stature, was driven by a need for approbation and recognition. Growing up, his mother was that unwavering reinforcement.

Mom was there to pull him from the shadows of fear cast by an insensible and insecure father. She was there to reshape family love during those unsettled months of 1942. She always bolstered his self-worth through high school and college, even during his early years as a struggling novice in business. She was always in his corner.

He wondered: Was this the root of his predicament?

SLAP!!!

The sound was magnified by the small room and lack of competing clamor. Almost immediately after she had swung her open hand forcefully against his cheek, Glenda began apologizing. Her action was involuntary, completely out of character for her. It was verification of the depths of the quandary that engulfed her.

"Oh, Peter. I don't know what came over me," she sobbed in heaves. "I'm sorry. I didn't mean to hurt you. Forgive me." She struggled to speak. "Let us... let's go... go to my father. I know... let's ask..." She could scarcely talk. "I just know he will lend you the money to pay off the Chicago debt, repay your back... back taxes and any other debts you may have."

She breathed deeply.

"It may take us a while, but together we can make it. Please, Peter."

Peter Bremer rubbed his reddening cheek, but the greater wound was inside.

———————————

They had left Cedar Rapids shortly after 5:00 a.m., long before the winter sun struggled to rise amid freezing temperatures, long before most of the city thought of waking up. The car was packed with most of their clothing and a few other possessions. The hotel parking garage was void of people. The streets were like barren paths. Highways waited quietly for the morning rush.

Bremer had an empty feeling in his stomach.

They drove to Hannibal, Mo., before pulling off for breakfast. On the day before, at his request, she had withdrawn all they had from savings, closed the checking account, and cashed in a small amount in federal savings bonds. It was, except for Bremer's Riverside stock shares, a complete abandonment of their connection to Cedar Rapids and Iowa. Like Huckleberry Finn, they had become drifters, floating down a turgid river of ambiguity.

It was Glenda who asked that they stop in the famous Missouri river town. She was not hungry, but eating was an opportunity for her to temporarily slow down this rush to uncertainty. The black coffee did little to ease the tension and bewilderment that permeated her being. She struggled to find new words, a different path to his intransigence.

"Do you remember, before we were married, when you left St. Louis to take that insurance job in Cedar Rapids?" Her eyes peeked over the coffee mug in search of reassurance. "We were in love, at least I thought so. I was devastated when you said you were leaving, taking what you said was a wonderful promotion. I had this awful feeling that I may never see you again. Do you remember all that, Peter?"

"I remember," he said softly, with less emotion than he would normally give a business prospect. He chewed on his eggs, then took a sip of coffee. "How does that change circumstances in the here and now?" It was an unbending response.

"All I'm saying, Peter, is that we were able to work it out. You took the job in Cedar Rapids, settled into a routine, and we were married. Sweetheart, we managed to find an answer, and we can do it again."

His failure to answer chilled the air like a January cold front.

Outside the restaurant, Bremer looked around, searching for anything out of the ordinary. Scattered tourists gawked at the weathered buildings near the Mark Twain Museum. Some pointed to the old white lighthouse, which clung to a hillside of barren trees north of Hannibal's Main Street, seemingly more concerned with its own precarious situation up on the bluffs than life along the Mississippi River.

Oblivious to history, Bremer drove aimlessly for nearly ten minutes, silently assessing his own perilous predicament. They ended up in Hannibal's Riverview Park, where he stopped the car, let the motor run, and got out with a blankness that cast Glenda as a nonentity. He walked to a bench and gazed at the never-ending flow of the river, unencumbered by any of man's troubles.

His behavior shocked her into action. She joined him at the overlook, unsure if Peter was contemplating suicide or otherwise refining his escape from reality. She tucked her gloved hand beneath his right arm, a spontaneous action of concern and affection. He nodded in her direction. Neither spoke. Below, a freight train clacked its way across the Wabash Railroad Bridge, headed for Illinois. Ice on sections of the river had halted barge traffic and most boat operations.

It was a place where the Mississippi River normally behaved itself, marking a nearly half-mile wide path past Hannibal on its perpetual drive to the Gulf of Mexico. Just to the north and south, during springtime binges, the river runs amok through lesser channels, backwaters, and vulnerable farmland. But in the depths of winter, it is placid.

Turbulent minds had invaded this peaceful refuge.

"Peter, I'm cold."

They turned back to the warmth of the car. The overcast day, just above the freezing mark, had a sniff of snow in the air. There were still small ridges of soiled snow along the park's roads where it had been pushed by plows. Otherwise, the ground was mostly bare, full of dancing oak leaves.

Bremer checked. No one else was in the park.

He was always on the lookout, believing the black Cadillac was marked, a blaring billboard with his name on it. Since the death threats in August, he had considered getting a different car, maybe, he chuckled to himself one day, one of those used, rusty Japanese models. But that would require him to disfigure his self-image. The Cadillac was him.

"I didn't tell you, Glenda, that last week I received another letter from the Chicago people." Now, he looked into her eyes—for understanding and emphasis. "They made it clear it was a final notice. There was no suggestion of a new repayment plan, no proposal for compromise, no appeasement, no wiggle room in any direction. Now do you see? Do you grasp what they mean by final notice?"

She screamed. Had it not been for the Fort Knox-like containment afforded by the bulky sedan, her agony may have echoed off the Illinois banks. The painful shriek was acknowledgement that the matter was closer to conclusion than she knew. She felt helpless, so she yelled and cried and pounded her fists on the leather dashboard.

Does a distressed body ever run out of anguish and heartbreak? Is there a point when the reservoir of tears becomes empty? Is there a junction when disappointment, fear, and anger collaborate to erode love? Nothing was said for five minutes before he encroached upon her profound suffering.

"I was afraid of telling you about the new letter," he said.

He backed out of the parking space, slowly exited the park among the drifting leaves, and headed south on US 61. His head swiveled in every direction like a submarine periscope looking for the enemy, his eyes constantly searching traffic for the peculiar. His paranoia was fully engaged. The only words uttered for two hours were instructions he muttered to himself.

"I think we turn here. Yes." Later, "I better watch out for that truck." Finally, "Where's that frontage road? There. That motel will do fine. I'll park in back. This will do."

They checked in. He paid cash, using a false name.

How could he make it any plainer that his life—possibly their lives—were truly in danger, that he likely faced time in prison, would lose everything he had built at Riverside Pack, and as a result be condemned in the business world as a scam artist. His only option was to run. Run from the mob. Run from the Internal Revenue Bureau. Run with his shame to wherever it might be that he could seek to regain the most precious commodity in his life—respect.

Sure. He could have turned himself in to the feds. To what gain? He was already dead in Riverside and Iowa business circles. Would prison keep him physically alive? For how long? The mob had its own prison connections. And when he completes his term?

He knew how the mob worked. He already had one loan extension. There would be no more. He was now more than four months in arrears. That is a grave embarrassment to the entire mob collection apparatus. When Mr. Koffmann and his bosses are unhappy, there is a whole wide underworld that is unhappy. It's bad for their business. It's like poking an enraged lion in the eye.

Failure to collect is no way to run a loan-sharking enterprise.

Every now and then steps had to be taken to show that business was business. Those steps were clear in Mr. Ragno's "final notice."

After an hour of silence Glenda rose from her chair, drained. Her sobbing edged toward acceptance. She showered. Peter rubbed his left cheek where the sting of her slap still lingered. *I understand*, he said to himself. He doubted if he could ever make her realize the full gravity of his situation. *The mob's next move*, he feared, *may be to kidnap Glenda, threaten harm to her to make me pay in full. Does that make sense? Pay with what?*

Would they really harm her? Only if it caused me to suffer. Torture was a favorite instrument for organized crime. They would make me watch her suffer. Perhaps for a while. But only my death will satisfy them. Still, I am a danger to her. My presence is a danger to her.

She put on her robe and again sat on the bed. They hadn't eaten since breakfast in Hannibal.

"Are you hungry? Would you like me to go out and bring back something to eat?" he asked.

It was her turn to be impassive. It was unlike her, but she was exhausted, simply empty of reaction.

"Did you hear me?"

"Do what you think best," she said.

He decided to order pizza. He checked the yellow pages, consulted the front desk, and called a nearby pizza place. It would be delivered in forty-five minutes. He pulled off his gray sweater vest, sat in the worn chair, then in a minute arose and walked to the window. He pulled apart the crease of the drapes. No one was near the big black Cadillac.

"The letter indicated they may harm you," he said, barely audible. She did not respond.

"I said," he repeated, "that Mr. Ragno suggested that they may harm you, Glenda. I can't have that. I am poison to you. I am sorry it has come to this. Not in my greatest fears did I think it would come to this. Call me immature. Call me stupid. But I swear I had no idea who these guys were connected to."

Glenda sat in a stupor, still trying to piece together the last few months of their lives. Was she naïve also? Did she miss signs along the road? Could she have interceded in some way? Peter was always private with his business dealings. Her life had really been confined to a small circle of friends, and none cared about the boring routine of business.

It all happened so fast. As they were packing, Peter asked her not to notify anyone. The evening before their departure had been weird, a surreal bustle in which she thought they looked like Laurel and Hardy characters racing around to nowhere. Clearly, now, nowhere seemed to be the destination. She stepped out of her meditation.

"Peter," she began, less guarded than usual, "do you believe in the intrinsic goodness of people?" Her question temporarily obscured the elephant in the room. Bremer's panic about the mob was interrupted. She extended her theme. "Do you think we are born benevolent, with trust and a loving nature? And then life happens?"

She paused and pulled the robe tight around her neck.

"Do you think God made us as with decency and civility, having respect for life, respect for each other and our humanness? Absent of self-centeredness? And then we bend to evil winds like a vulnerable fruit tree, and our good intentions go sour, and ultimately, as we grow older, we become destined to rot?"

He took refuge in the frazzled chair.

It was not the first time he half-listened to her ideas and comments, treating them as inconsequential. But these words of hers had a more cryptic edge, certainly uncommon, as if they were being uttered by a stranger.

"What are you talking about?" he said in an aggravated tone.

"About life, Peter. Why, if we are born in love, and if we begin so innocently, why do some people grow mean and selfish?"

"I'm not sure I understand what you are saying."

"How, for example, do people like your Mr. Ragno become so removed from the human race, so uncaring, so greedy, so violent?"

"How should I know. And he's not *my* Mr. Ragno."

The fissure in their union was something neither had foreseen several days ago. Nor wanted. But it was as real as their intense love once was. Perhaps, given the cauldron they had been tossed into, it was inescapable. He had come to believe it was the only way forward. She was unsure if he sincerely considered any other options.

"Glenda," he said, grabbing her by the shoulders like a parent preparing to lecture a child, an uncomfortable position for both, but that is what he did. The gesture steadied him as much and sent a signal to her. Reflecting the weakness that inhabited his being, he addressed her shoulders more than her eyes.

"Glenda," he repeated. "I would like you," he stuttered, "I... I would ask you to find an apartment where you can live for several weeks. Or stay at a motel. I don't believe you should live with your father just yet. They may try to look for us at your father's residence first. They may stake out his home for a time, I don't know."

New alarm spread on her face. She wiped her eyes with the sleeve of her robe. Her breathing skipped in between the sobs. Her emotions had been affronted from every angle. She had not considered that the threats to Peter may have dangerous tentacles.

"Do you think my father is in danger?" she asked with more than a tinge of fear.

"No. They won't harm him. They want me. I am their target. I am the death certificate they need for their collection brochure. It is my body they will use to convince other creditors to pay up."

Peter Bremer, for once in his life, faced reality straight on. It was a solemn declaration and recognition of how business is conducted in the underworld. Glenda exhaled a string of shrieks muffled as she buried her mouth into his chest and black corduroy shirt. He put his arms around her, holding her as if she might try to escape.

For a moment, the spreadsheet of his life and bond with Glenda came into focus for him like the stark figures of an annual business report. Oh, the sins of commission and the sins of omission. Wouldn't it be nice if we could rewind the clock and change our decisions? He clung to her as if it were their wedding night, but the honeymoon was long over. No reversable clock.

Minutes passed as they danced in what had been.

Peter relaxed, gently moved her back, and shared his thoughts.

"There is no turning back, Glenda. Time only flows in one direction."

"What will you do?" she sniffled.

"I will miss you, Glenda, My Magic. I do love you. Please know that." This time he subdued the frailties of his ego and fixed on her eyes. "But I must have you safe. My love cannot bear the thought of harm coming to you. Keep most of our money. You will need it to get settled in St. Louis. I won't need much."

"I meant"—her voice exhausted and bleary countenance void of hope—"where will you go?"

"I don't know," he said.

"Will you call me? Should I call your mother?"

"I will call if I can, and please don't call Mom."

There was a knock at their motel door. A flash of fear ripped through Bremer's body, and then he remembered the pizza order. The keyhole revealed the boy from Domino's. Peter retrieved two Cokes from the hallway dispenser. That was their farewell supper.

His plan was decided. Lay low until the morning, and then head south, immersed in traffic.

Shortly before 7:00 a.m., Peter Bremer grabbed his briefcase and left the motel and Glenda.

Chapter 42
West Kansas, fall 1968

"All rise." There was a scraping of chairs on the worn courtroom floor as lawyers and clients stood at the oak table in front of the elevated bench. "The Honorable Judge Finias Korbell of the Sherman County District Court presiding," the bailiff dutifully intoned in a tenor voice that sounded prerecorded.

The black-robed Korbell stepped up to the bench, grabbed the gavel, rapped it on the wooden block and ordered people to be seated, and business commenced. For all his twenty-six years as a magistrate and judge, he attempted to substitute implied gruffness for his slender, five-foot, six-inch physique. Not only was he short in stature, but he finished 83rd in a Kansas Law School class of 104.

He never attended class reunions.

Still, he could teach fellow judges a thing or two about jurisprudence, with emphasis on the prudence. He had a reputation for fairness and was considerably less pompous than many of his colleagues. While perhaps not the sharpest blade in the drawer, no one said he was dull, and he cut no favors based on country club membership or business standing. Off the bench, he was a storyteller, always a popular trait on the range.

Korbell was a proud citizen of Goodland, Kans., no stranger to community and high school events. He was a Republican, but some thought him to be a Democrat. He liked that. He was a Civil War buff and could recite every detail in the history of William Tecumseh Sherman, the county's namesake.

"Good morning, everyone," the judge said, rubbing his white mustache, a nice complement to his snowy hair. "I'm happy to see there are citizens here to observe the judicial branch of government at work and see how your tax dollars are being spent when two parties cannot settle a disagreement."

Details on this disagreement fattened the manilla folder before him. He opened it. The civil lawsuit before the court claimed libel and malicious intent against Goodland Newspapers Inc. and Cold Springs rancher Jacob Spietz. It had been continued for months, largely at the request of attorneys for the plaintiff, Junior Smith, son of banker F. W. Smith. Junior was busy in college, his attorneys argued, either with tests in business school, functions at his fraternity, or participation on the golf and fencing teams.

"This case has been on the docket longer than James Arness has been on Gunsmoke." Korbell tossed his hyperbole at the attorneys. "Let's get to it gentlemen. There will be no more continuances. Do you understand that, Mr. Junior Smith and Mr. Senior Smith?" he said, also addressing the father sitting in the courtroom gallery.

Smith's attorneys were from a law firm based in Wichita. It may have helped his son's case if Mr. Senior Smith had employed local counsel to represent his son rather than big city outsiders. At least that was the town scuttlebutt. Not that the newspaper was overwhelmed with community support. Being one step ahead of visiting lawyers in the public opinion race hardly qualified the newspaper for a standing ovation.

"As agreed, there will be no jury in this matter," Korbell said, addressing the parties. All attorneys nodded agreement. "As the pin said to the cushion, you are stuck with me." He searched for a smile. "That's a little levity, in case you people from Wichita don't know. Soon enough we'll get into the complexities of the here-ins and wherefores. Just so you'll know, I prefer the term *spit* to *expectorate*."

Hank Jackson of Goodland, who represented the defendants, translated the judge's admonition, but the attorneys from Wichita may have wished they had opted for a jury.

"Gentlemen. Proceed with your opening statements."

"Thank you, your honor," the lead attorney from Wichita pronounced with Harvard-like decorum. He stood as erect as a bowling pin and with matching charisma. "It is with great respect and sincere gratitude that we appear before the court in western Kansas," he droned. "We are flattered to play a role in the administration of justice and the inculcation of statutes in this great state," he said, continuing his sycophant stroll.

He and his partner appeared to have arrived straight from Hart Schaffner and Marx, fashion plates with white shirts full of starch and suits free of lint. Mr. Lead Attorney, whose navy ensemble disguised a bulging girth, fingered his red tie. Looking up at the judge, he then steadied his hands on the lapels of his suit coat and rocked on his heels as if ready to proclaim eternal deliverance.

"If it pleases the court..."

"What would please the court," Judge Korbell injected, "is if these matters moved along."

In addition to the Smiths, family and friends of Jake Spietz were also in the courtroom to observe the trial. Among them were members of Justice Now, including Rosemary and Bobby Bremer and Henry Bexler. Many had contributed money to Jake's defense. Rosemary, aware of Bobby's temperament and dislike of bankers, warned him not to voice any opinions during the proceedings.

"This entire case of Junior Smith's arrest, your honor, should have been settled when the county attorney determined there was insufficient evidence to prosecute," Mr. Lead Attorney said.

"Matter settled. End of story. While there were two empty beer cans in my client's car, there was no proof he had been drinking and driving," he quoted the county attorney's conclusive report. "In fact," he added, "the sheriff did not even observe Junior Smith driving.

"Moreover, while witnesses claimed he was driving in an erratic manner, the truth was our client was distracted by a bumble bee inside his vehicle," he continued. "No one refuted this. No one was injured. There was no accident. There were no sobriety tests conducted." He proceeded to elaborate on young Mr. Smith's achievements "in school, in church, and in the community."

"You are right, sir," Judge Korbell injected. "This is not a criminal matter. Please get on with the issues at hand."

"Yes, your honor. Junior Smith was maligned by the newspaper in dragging him through the mud with information dismissed by the county attorney. This was hurtful to him and his family and sullied his good name in the community. The fact that Junior Smith's father supported the county attorney's election campaign is immaterial. Dozens of other people also contributed to his campaign.

"As for Mr. Spietz, it was his defamatory remarks to the newspaper and others in the community that forms the basis for compensatory damages sought against him. Whether its libel or slander, young Mr. Smith is entitled to reparations to offset the harm done to his reputation."

After additional legal mumbo jumbo and claimed case precedent, which consumed another five minutes and caused the judge to shift in his seat, he sat down.

"Mr. Jackson," Judge Korbell prompted, "please offer your opening arguments."

It was not Jackson's first time at bat in Goodland County courtroom skirmishing. He was a native of Goodland, and locals had long forgotten or forgiven the fact he earned his law degree at the State University of Iowa. For two decades he represented the good, bad, and ugly in human life, nearly all in western Kansas. He was respected in legal circles and, as importantly, in the community.

His frequent rise to a point of law in the courtroom gained him the name of "Mr. Objection." Opponents were unsure if he was onto something, had a legitimate basis for objecting, or was bargaining for time while mulling his next move. The bottom line, he was more successful than not.

"Yes. Your honor, we believe this lawsuit flies in the face of the First Amendment. It is simple. The newspaper, acting on a tip from Mr. Spietz about the county attorney's handling of the drunk driving case, merely reported what was in public documents. It's public record. Anyone, all the good citizens of western Kansas, can demand and be shown these records.

"The same is true for all public bodies, not just the county attorney's office. The public, and that includes the news media, is entitled to peruse these records. The county attorney does not own these records. The sheriff does not own these records. At City Hall, the mayor does not own the records. These officials work for the public. These people are employees of the public."

Jackson paused here to let the elements of his sermon settle. He chose not to include Judge Korbell on the public's list of employees. Discretion.

"Your honor, that's how democracy works. It's what distinguishes our system from many others. Of, by, and for—"

"Mr. Jackson. Move on. I took government in both grade school and high school. Had some in college. You needn't list every branch of government and all the tenants of a democratic system."

"Yes, your honor."

Jackson concluded is opening remarks in less than three minutes, and the first witnesses were called by the plaintiff. Sheriff's deputies and other officials verified all the pertinent documents. A string of persons testified as to the accomplishments of Junior Smith, including his high standing in academics and sports. College grades read into the record confirmed his study habits.

The pertinent newspaper articles were then presented into evidence, and Mr. Lead Attorney noted that it was not the first time the newspaper was a defendant in court. "Twenty years ago—"

"Objection, your honor." Jackson popped up like a wounded jackrabbit. "Immaterial. No foundation. For all we know those involved at the newspaper twenty years ago may be dead."

"Sustained, unless plaintiff can fortify its implications," the judge said.

None was offered. Other witnesses were presented, and then the focus was turned to Jake Spietz. When Spietz was charged as being "a known troublemaker in west Kansas" and "having a unique dislike of bankers and the banking profession," Jackson objected again.

"Your honor. Plaintiff's attorney is testifying. He's pulling stuff out of the air, and it's hot air." He turned up his nose while saying it, corroborating claims he coated his arguments with body language. "Who, besides plaintiff's counsel, says Mr. Spietz is a troublemaker, and on what grounds? Perhaps counsel should take up fiction writing."

Jackson felt like he was running downhill.

"And I believe you could search Kansas statutes back to Adam and Eve and find nothing that says trouble making, to use the eloquence of the plaintiff's attorney, is against the law. Furthermore—"

"Enough, Mr. Jackson. This is a courtroom, not the handball court," Korbell smiled. "The gist of your objection has merit, and objection sustained, however, minus the colorful annotation."

It was all over in slightly more than an hour. A week later Judge Korbell dismissed the case against the newspaper and Jacob Spietz.

Two weeks after that, at the insistence of Junior Smith's father, the verdict was appealed. It meant more lawyer expenses, added court costs and an upsurge in aggravation for Spietz and his friends. It pushed Bobby Bremer over the top. His festering dislike for bankers and banks came to a boil. Rosemary was upset too.

In addition to the cost of court proceedings, delays had put Spietz, his family, and other ranchers behind in farm work. Now, in September, the appeal by the plaintiff. Incredibly, there were new postponements—first due to court docket complications and then because the appellate judge had surgery. It pushed the new date for rehearing the case to Monday, March 9, 1969.

While it allowed more time for Justice Now to seek contributions for Spietz' defense, it also gave longer fermentation to the sour mood inside Bremer.

By late December, he had cajoled Rosemary into a daring and criminal act to raise money on behalf of Spietz and Justice Now. The rogue juices of frontier action and citizen involvement had been brewing in Bremer's mind for some time. She was a reluctant participant and held off his plans until the new year. Now she had run out of delay maneuvers. She succumbed to his resolve.

They told Henry Bexler they had decided to attend a family reunion in St. Louis. The old rancher posed no resistance but questioned the notion of a midwinter reunion. "Bad weather and all," Bexler noted. Bremer lied, said it was his brother's birthday that prompted the gathering. Bexler was unconvinced, but he didn't question it further.

Bobby was comfortable with the plan, indifferent to its outrageous dimensions. Trouble was not new territory for him. He believed it was worth the gamble. Moreover, in his mind—forged by personal experience where he believed he was the victim of injustice—it was the honorable thing to do.

There was a time when Rosemary would have vetoed the idea forthwith. Even though her family had been treated shabbily by the bank, and suffered hardships, she would have said no. But the loss of her child reordered rationale and allowed the unthinkable to take root.

Her meeting Bobby Bremer some five years ago was awash in serendipity. Getting married to him certainly had its quirks of misgiving and disquiet, but love has a way of overpowering the factors of uncommon equations. Uneasiness had been her companion before. This time it had a front row seat.

They drove off immediately after breakfast on a cold February day. The prospect of snow drifted through the air. The leaden sky portended a candid appraisal of the entire picture.

Chapter 43
Suburban Kansas City, 1969

"What in the hell?!"

Police Chief Norm Effron talked out loud to himself and instinctively crouched near the black-and-white-tiled floor of his new office inside the sprawling Overland Park, Kans., City Hall. The boom outside sounded as if someone had lobbed a grenade. He looked out to the hallway.

"Hey, you out there!" he shouted to a passerby. "Get down," he motioned. "I think we've been hit with a bomb." The woman, head of Public Nutrition, flattened herself on the cold slate surface like a collapsed cake.

"It sounded like a bad car accident," she yelled back from her prone position.

"I don't think so," Effron replied. He was right.

The early morning explosion ripped through a brick wall and air conditioning enclosure at the northwest corner of the building, spewing dust and whitish-blue smoke in an otherwise clear sky. After a half minute, Effron slowly rose from his crouched position and looked out the window. He saw no one.

Effron, in his twenty-sixth year as a police officer, was stacking pictures on a shelf when the day took a terrible turn. He was in the process of moving into new quarters. Some welcome. This was no time to think about finishing his career in space that was plush compared to his cramped, old workplace.

"I suggest you return to your office" he told the prostrate woman. "Be prepared to evacuate."

He ran outside and saw the smoke. Crumbled bricks and red dirt coated the drab wintry lawn along the two-story building. Based on the sound it could have been worse, he measured. The lingering sweet odor suggested nitroglycerin-based dynamite. Experience caused him to suspect—almost immediately—that the detonation, external and the noise disproportionate to the damage, had an ulterior connection.

Could it be a diversion? he thought. He did not know.

"Everybody go to the east side of the building," he ordered those near the entrance. People who had heard the boom ran without asking questions. He raced inside to communications. "Sound a building evacuation. Immediately! I think the building has been hit with bomb of some kind. Tell occupants to exit east or south doors."

Eerie alarms filled the building. Effron doubted if there would be another explosion, but training taught him not to challenge doubt. Quickly the building was emptied. Some raced out without coats and shivered in the thirty-five-degree winter. Effron huddled with his command staff and several detectives on duty. Soon fire department crews were on the scene.

Keep all radio and telephone channels open," Chief Effron ordered, still operating on his best instincts. People began drifting back inside City Hall as police and fire personnel made their initial examination of the still smoldering explosion area. Damage was mostly confined to the air conditioning units and the nearby building wall. Effron was more tuned to expectations.

At almost the same time, a short distance to the south, a man casually walked into the Plains and Farmers Bank in Olathe, the next city beyond Overland Park in the string of Kansas City suburbs. He approached a young, female teller at the right side of a trio of windows. Above her window was the number three. The center window was vacant. The woman intently peered into a mirror held in her left hand and simultaneously straightened some loose strands of hair. She was oblivious to the advancing man.

He looked like any other customer, except he had a crumpled pillowcase concealed in his left coat pocket. The bulge in the other pocket was a Smith & Wesson .38 Special. He wore jeans and a greenish flannel shirt. "Jones Heating & Cooling" was printed in white letters on the back of his gray winter jacket. He had no hat, and his face was not concealed. There was no reason to believe he was anything other than a regular working stiff in this fast-growing suburban area.

"Did you and Harry have a good time at the movies last night?" Teller No. 1 asked No. 3. She examined her fingernails as if they were some sort of precious metal. No. 3 smiled. "And what did you do afterwards?" No. 1 pried. "I know"—she looked up at No. 3—"you are wild about Harry."

"Ma'am. Excuse me. Could I have some help here?" the man said.

"Oh, I'm terribly sorry," Teller No. 3 apologized. She put the mirror aside.

"Yes. Thank you," he said. "I would like for you to fill up this bag with cash, big bills only, please." He handed her the pillowcase. "And don't try to push any alarm buttons. I don't want to harm a pretty young woman like yourself. Harry wouldn't like that. Get going! Now! Feel free to take some of those Ben Franklin C-notes from the other drawer.

"You, over there at the other window. Push your chair back and stay sitting. There is no need for you to be involved."

The young teller's eyes popped out like high beams in the night sky. No bank training sessions can prepare you for a real holdup. She picked up the whitish bag and began filling it with bills. She had no idea that this bank had a branch in far west Kansas, that it was selected specifically for a heist.

Bobby Bremer watched the process, emotionless, as if she were sorting mail.

"Stay calm," he said softly. "Just act as if this is a normal transaction. And keep both hands where I can see them. Do you understand?"

She nodded as she continued the stuffing process. Twenties and bigger bills were slipped into the bag. She grabbed a stack of $100 bills from trays number one and two. She transferred the cash with a proficiency befitting orders from the bank president. After a little more than a minute, Bremer asked for the loot and ordered her to push her chair to the back of the teller's cage, just as the other woman had done. She obeyed.

"I'm going to step backward," he said, "and I don't want to see either of you move. Is that clear? Please don't force me to mess up your hairdo." He stuffed the bag beneath his jacket, zipped it up, and slowly backed away. After five steps, he waved to the tellers, turned, and briskly walked out the front door. Rosemary and her blue Plymouth were curbside.

Rosemary and Bobby Bremer, the night before, had stayed in an Overland Park apartment rented by an acquaintance. The friend was out of town on work. The lower-floor two-bedroom unit was part of Greystone Village, a complex of eight two-story buildings just a few blocks east of City Hall. They were alone in the apartment.

"This is a nice place, Bobby." She looked around, delighted with the large bedroom and walk-in closet, the double-sink bathroom with tub and shower, and the living room with modern furniture. "Look at the cupboard space in this kitchen. Maybe we should settle down here and forget about the bank." He said nothing. "Bobby? Did you hear what I said?"

"I heard," he replied with more than a tinge of annoyance. "We have a job to do, Rosemary. Don't go all homey on me. Keep your eye on the mission. Remember that asshole banker in Goodland. Remember justice."

"I know the lack of justice as well as you. No need for a lecture. I see nice things and wish we had them. Wish we had our own place."

Greystone was only a few years old. The fourplex buildings had front and back entrances that led to interior hallways. The apartments also featured outside patios and balconies. That and an outdoor swimming pool in the middle of the development boosted appeal. It was the fanciest place she had ever been in, but she didn't want to argue with Bobby.

Rosemary had taken their suitcase with clothes into the apartment. Bobby lugged a box containing a disassembled pump shotgun and ammunition for both it and his .38 pistol. His bearing was that of a person on a business trip. He memorized his strategy. The sequence, he believed, was as orderly as work planned at the ranch. Her sense of resolution was adrift in misgivings.

But then there was Bobby's determination.

It was his reckoning that they would not be able to outrun police and escape the Kansas City area after the bank robbery. He assumed someone at or near the bank would provide a description of the blue Plymouth, making it necessary to ditch it and find other transportation. Or walk. Either way they would find their way back to the apartment, stay low for several days, and then leave the area by bus.

"Are you sure we should go ahead with this?" she asked the night before. Her reservations bubbled into the open. "I know we want to help Jacob, but have we thought this through, considered all the options, all the things that could go wrong?"

"I thought we'd been over all this," Bobby said stiffly. "Hundred times. This goddamn bank is getting a big withdrawal, and when we're on our way home, I'm going to send an anonymous thank-you-note to the asshole banker in Goodland. Goddamn jerk should be in jail along with his son."

"Bobby! Must you take the Lord's name in vain?"

The next morning, Rosemary dropped him off at City Hall. He boldly deposited a paint can containing five half sticks of dynamite in bushes near the fenced-in air conditioning compressors. The fuse was set for ten minutes, the estimated time to reach the bank. Rosemary picked him up and then dropped him off at a street corner near the bank. She drove off slowly. Pick up would be in four minutes—tops.

He exited the bank, on the run. She was there. The plan was intact.

"Hit the alarm button!" bank teller No. 3 yelled to her coworker. She then ran to the bank president's office. The robber had barely cleared the front door. Others in the bank shifted their collective eyes to the entrance but saw no disturbance outside. Just out of their sight next door, near a raised flower bed and flagpole in front of Kentucky Fried Chicken, a blue sedan pulled away from the curb.

Two KFC employees on cigarette break witnessed a running Bremer jump into a blue car. It all looked suspicious.

"I'll be damn. I think we just saw a bank robbery," said one. "Guy with bulge in jacket runs from bank? Hell, yes! Bank robbery." He flicked his smoldering stub into the day lilies and ran inside the restaurant.

The telephone rang at the Olathe Police Department. The bank president relayed the robbery information and a description of the suspect. Less than a minute later another call to police from the KFC worker added information about the blue car. He had no license plate number.

Olathe police issued an APB. The report was radioed to every area law enforcement agency, including the Kansas and Missouri highway patrol. Four minutes later another call. Witnesses, the KFC duo, provided their information.

Effron's hunch was confirmed. He coordinated response with Olathe police. Three Overland Park squad cars sped off to comb the neighborhood. Olathe dispatched all available units.

Ten blocks away motorcycle cop Scott Zwinker was watching for heavy-footed drivers on I-35 and Route 69. He angled onto Antioch Road when the APB blared, "All cars. Be on the lookout for a blue sedan. Occupants may be those wanted in Olathe bank robbery."

Seemingly on cue, a light blue car, behaving normally, materialized out of the approaching traffic. As it drove past, Zwinker saw a woman at the wheel, and no one else in the vehicle. Not likely the suspects, but worth a check. He made a U-turn with his Harley and quickly came up behind the car. It was a Plymouth with Kansas plates. Just as quickly, a man leaned out the right front passenger window and fired a gun.

"Pop, pop, pop."

A round struck the cycle's metal frame just below the windshield and two others zipped past Zwinker's head. He backed off slightly and the car sped up. He removed his own weapon and fired twice at the rear window of the Plymouth. Glass shattered. Then another bullet from the car nicked him in his right ear. He pulled back, able to keep control of the cycle.

"Shit!" he muttered as he swung to the curb. His hand automatically sought out the sting on the side of his face. The wet substance was blood. "Shit! Shit! Shit! Nine years in the department and my first gun fight involves a rusting Plymouth driven by a woman," he grumbled. He clicked his radio.

"10–71! I repeat. 10–71! Struck by bullet, not serious. Antioch and 131st. May be robbery get-away car. 11–19."

"Rosemary," Bobby ordered. "Turn into this shopping area. Look for somebody getting out of their car. We will swap. The old Plymouth is hot. Goddamn cop was lucky. Out of a couple million people, he spots us. It's damn fluky. Maybe he wasn't so lucky, Rosemary. He backed off. I think I may have winged him." He scanned the lot without success.

"Why did you have to fire at him?" Rosemary yelled.

"Where the hell are all the damn old people when you need them."

"Bobby," Rosemary scolded. "There is no need for you to use foul language. Maybe I should wash your mouth out with soap, like your mother did."

"Over there, at the end of the parking row." He pointed. "See the old guy with the furry black hat. Looks like a goddamn Russian. Pull over there. His passenger is just getting out of that black car."

Rosemary drove down the one-way lane. She pulled into an empty parking space two cars away from the older couple. Bobby jumped out and raced to the startled couple.

"Give me your car keys! Now!" he yelled. "Look, I'm not shittin' you and have no goddamn time for games. I have a gun in my coat pocket. I don't want to use it, so give me the keys." The man handed them over, and Bobby shoved him aside. The shocked woman covered her mouth to muffle screams.

Bobby and Rosemary jumped into the 1966 black Chevrolet and sped off. Bobby drove.

"They will report their car stolen within minutes. We can't drive around for very long," Bobby assessed. "We are sitting ducks. Damn!" He glanced at her, but she stared straight ahead as if void of any suggestion. "This place will be crawling with cops." He drove east, then north, wending his way back to the Greystone Village apartments. He decided to park the hijacked car a block away. They walked quickly back to the apartment, entering a rear door.

Once inside, Bobby stuffed the bank loot deep into Rosemary's suitcase. He assembled his shotgun and removed shells from a cartridge case. He checked his .38, reloaded it, and placed more rounds on a table in the kitchenette. The arsenal, once insurance, now became policy.

Rosemary tossed her coat on a chair. She crossed and uncrossed her arms in a fidgety cloud of bleakness. Slowly she walked over to the front window and peered into the inevitable.

"Maybe we outfoxed them," he said with the enthusiasm of a felon parked in solitary confinement. "Maybe they won't find the stolen car. Maybe they will look to the south, thinking we are headin' out of town. Maybe it is our turn for a little luck."

"Maybe," Rosemary mocked, "it won't get cold in the winter."

"I want our motorcycle units to head south on I-35 and other major roads," Chief Effron barked to his dispatcher. "Olathe and Kansas troopers are taking the immediate bank area. Our squad cars are covering Overland Park and west. Olathe has asked Missouri departments to cover areas to the north and east." Off-duty officers were called in.

"We'll catch the sonofabitch."

As she did most weekdays, Helen Haysley, a retired nurse, was listening to Art Linkletter's *House Party* radio program when the local CBS affiliate broke in with a news bulletin. A bank in suburban Olathe had been robbed, the broadcast said, and a police officer shot by suspects. Authorities, the report said, were looking for a black Chevy with whitewall tires that was hijacked from an elderly couple.

Haysley lived on Robinson Street in Overland Park, just over a block away from Greystone Village apartments. She parted the lace curtains in her living room but saw only the mailman making his rounds. The curious type, she checked again about a half hour later. This time she spotted a parked car fitting the description outlined in the news bulletin earlier. She called police.

Kansas State Trooper Eldon Koob was among those who heard the possible ID on the stolen car. He was fifteen blocks away, scouring the Olathe area. He headed for Overland Park and Robinson Street. Overland Park police units were first on the scene. It took Chief Effron only minutes to conclude that the robbers were likely held up in one of the Greystone buildings.

"We are going to search these units one by one," he informed his officers at a quickly established command station. "A vehicle with safety vests is coming, and I want everyone to wear a vest. We believe a man and woman are involved. There may be others. These people are armed and dangerous. We have already had one officer shot. I don't want any more people hurt.

"Sullivan," he yelled at a captain from the bunco squad. "Take three other men and circulate in the neighborhood, in the unlikely chance the suspects decided to walk their way out. Police units continued to fill Robinson Street and the apartment building environs.

Like bees swarming to a hive, nearly thirty officers from various departments arrived at the scene over the next few minutes. The collection of black and whites parked helter-skelter looked like bumper cars at the county fair. Bobby Bremer saw the gathering taskforce. It was a response he had not anticipated, and he fell into his old mindset of being the victim and subject of authoritarian overreaction.

"Goddamn it!! Rosemary, we may be trapped. I'm not sure we can escape unless we shoot our way out." He rechecked his shotgun, Smith-Wesson, and ammunition supply. "And even if we could break out, where would we go? They're watching the car. The building is fenced in by cops. We're like two goddamn homesteaders surrounded by Apaches."

"I think, maybe, we should give up," Rosemary urged. "And, Bobby, blaspheming will not help matters."

"Give up?! Are you nuts? No damn way. I say we wait. They don't know we are here."

His warped persistence dominated remnants of good sense and overwhelmed his own calculations.

Quiet occupied the room. After several minutes, Bobby's tolerance for dithering expired. He paced. He could hear the stir and muffled talk outside. He again looked out the window at the cop brigade.

"If I wanted to, I could pick off several of them right now," he said impassively, as if he were talking about the opening of pheasant season.

"I don't see you doing that," she said.

His restlessness intensified. She could see despair and panic build in his face. Beads of sweat formed on his forehead. He ran his fingers through his hair. More pacing. Then, suddenly, his emotions seemed to relax, as if turned off like a faucet.

"Rosemary," he asked softly, fixed on her eyes. "Do you like poetry?"

She looked at him in disbelief. Was Bobby diving into the shallow end?

"What?!"

"Do you like poetry? In prison, we had this librarian who talked me into reading, even writing, poetry. It's real interesting. It's way more than words that just rhyme."

"You are talking goofy, Bobby."

"The hell I am. Poetry is wonderful. I can see you were never exposed properly to poetry. I wasn't either. Schools have no time for poetry. I guess teachers feel lucky if they can get their students to read regular books. Poetry gets lost in the shuffle. Like a lot of people."

"Whatever, Bobby. I have a strong feeling this is not the time to be discussing the merits of rhyme."

Truth can present drastically different choices. One trapped general will lucidly recognize reality and either negotiate or surrender. Another will spit certainty in the eye, ignore the living, breathing souls under his command, and charge ahead with blinding rage.

Rosemary and Bobby certainly shared attitudes about justice, or the lack of it, particularly as it played out in the unpretentious lives of plains people, where distance seemed to create closeness. Being a neighbor had nothing to do with proximity and everything to do with need. One rancher's problem was everyone's problem.

"Bobby, do you ever dream that you are flying?"

"What?!"

"You mentioned poetry. I'm thinking about flying, how sometimes in your dreams one is able to magically spread one's arms and fly away from trouble. Just like that. Escape from the inevitable. I'd like to do that now."

She looked at him but found no response.

"Is that poetic, Bobby?"

They were jolted by steps in the hallway. Bremer grabbed the shotgun.

"Go into the bathroom," he ordered her.

Chapter 44
Suburban Kansas City, 1969

"Brock," Effron instructed one of his police captains, "assemble eight two-man teams. Assign them to inspect all eight buildings, going door to door." He waved his arms and rattled on like a traffic cop trying to direct stubborn drivers bent on following their own course.

"I have talked to the building manager. Most units are similar in layout. There are one and two-bedroom apartments. Hallway door down the center. Check every mouse hole in every room."

He looked at the swelling sea of blue, enough manpower, he thought, to capture the gangs of Jesse James and Pretty Boy Floyd. It was Floyd's gang that in 1933 murdered four lawmen at Union Station in Kansas City in trying to free another gang member in custody. Floyd escaped, but he was killed in an Ohio shootout the following year.

"My God. We don't want anything like that," he mumbled.

"What did you say Chief?"

"Just talking to myself. I want officers to surround the entire apartment area. Get EMTs and an ambulance down here. We don't know what the hell may happen."

Effron, like Patton bound for the Rhine, took command without asking questions. Unlike the general, he worried about injuries or worse.

"Chief, what do you know about the robber?" Brock asked as he checked his .38 Colt Special.

"Not a damn thing, except he shot and wounded one of our motorcycle officers. What we do know is that he is willing to kill. A woman was driving the get-away car, which they ditched. Then they accosted an elderly couple and hijacked their car, the one found down the street."

"Are we sure they're holed up in one of these units?"

"No. We're not," Effron replied. His patience was thinning. "I'm going on gut instincts here. We still have other jurisdictions and the state patrol roaming the area. We'll get 'em. Go now! I think this will come down fast."

The officer read Effron's mood loud and clear.

"And Brock. Be careful. Repeat that to every officer team. Stay in radio contact. These people are dangerous. Get that out on the radio."

As Brock turned to leave, Effron yelled another instruction.

"One more thing. Have officers string crime tape around the area. TV news trucks and ink slingers will descend on the scene quicker than lawyers at an accident. Keep them back. I don't want anyone to be put in danger."

Teams fanned out to the eight buildings. Hunched-down, blue-cladded lawmen looked like giant ants creeping down dark, drab hallway tunnels. Guns were drawn. One person knocked on a door while the second, ready to respond, stood back on guard. Where no one answered, a notation was made, and another team would soon use a master key to enter and search.

It was a slow procedure, but one by one units were cleared.

Tim Busser, a reporter for the *Kansas City Star*, listened in the newsroom to bank robbery chatter on police radio. He knew the codes for police talk. Soon reports that a motorcycle cop was shot was broadcast. Busser, a twelve-year veteran on the cop beat, switched off his IBM Selectric, grabbed a camera and note pad from the equipment closet, and headed for the door.

"I'll be at the Overland Park PD," he informed the city editor. He was halfway out the door when the editor shouted. "Hey, Busser.

Hold up. Police radio just said a stolen car believed to have been used in the get-away was found near the Greystone Village apartments on Robinson Street. Get down there on the double."

Busser wasted no time. He jumped into his rusting red 1962 Rambler American and sped south on I-35. Morning traffic was light. *If I get a speeding ticket,* he mused, *I think the cops will forgive it. Who am I kidding.* What usually would be a twenty-two-minute drive took him seventeen minutes. He pulled into a triple driveway across the street from the apartments.

"...you can't hurry love, no, you just have to wait..." Carol Becker sang along with Diana Ross and the Supremes, oblivious to the gathering storm outside her apartment. It was one of her favorite tape recordings. Her husband and many of the occupants of Greystone were at work.

Becker, twenty-three, had eaten a late breakfast, fed their ten-month old son, changed his diaper, and vacuumed the living room. She had not looked out the window. She hadn't even changed out of her pajamas and robe.

"...she said love don't come easy," Becker warbled as she sipped her third cup of coffee. "It's a game of give and take..."

She smiled at the baby in her arms and made a silly face. With her straggly, bed-crumpled hair, and contorted countenance, she looked like Phyllis Diller on a good day. The baby popped a wide grin.

There was a knock at the apartment door. She wondered who would be calling at this time of day. She placed the baby in his crib and walked warily to the front door. Too much crime in a big city made the native of Kearney, Mo., nervous. Then there was a second rap. She peeked into the keyhole and was shocked.

The panoramic view revealed two police officers, their physical features grotesquely rounded by the peephole's aperture. She opened the door narrowly—all that the security chain would allow.

"Yes. May I help you?"

She combed her fingers involuntarily through her poofed-up blond hair, bringing frazzles in line.

"Police officers, ma'am. There's been a bank robbery," said one, addressing the keyhole. "We think the suspects may be in one of the apartment buildings. We're checking all units."

"There's no one here. I haven't seen anything or anyone."

"That's fine ma'am, but we have to check anyway. We need to look and clear every unit."

The Becker apartment was on the east side of one of the buildings near Robinson Street. The first-floor unit faced the swimming pool and center of the complex.

"Well, I guess it's OK. But there's no one here except me and the baby."

"Yes, ma'am. But we must check."

"Could you give me time to slip on a dress and shoes?"

"Yes, ma'am. Don't take long, please."

A minute later she unchained the door and admitted the officers. They inspected every room, including a storage area that housed the washer and dryer. Closets were examined. They checked under beds. Nothing.

"Cute baby, ma'am. Looks like he's getting enough to eat," an officer laughed as the process neared completion. "Could you unlock the veranda door?"

She retrieved the key. The area was empty except for stacked chairs and remnants of snow hiding in the corner out of the sun's notice. She looked through the open door and saw the collection of police vehicles. It looked like a cop convention. She knew the situation was serious.

"We're finished, ma'am. Thanks."

They exited and launched a similar process across the hall. A rap on the door triggered footsteps inside the west unit. But no one answered. There was a second knock, this one more forceful. The result was the same. Voices. The two officers exchanged glances and began working the math like Einstein. A third rap equally echoed ominously down the hallway. Still no response.

"Police!" the lead officer yelled. "There's been a bank robbery, and we're checking all—"

BANG!! BANG!!

This time the answer came loud and clear.

Bullets shattered the door, zipped by one officer's head, and slammed through the door of the Becker apartment. Both men leapt back.

"Suspect located! Shots fired!" one officer radioed.

"Copy," came a response.

The hunt was over. The standoff began.

"We need to get the woman and child out of their unit," half-whispered the officer in charge. On signal, both crashed through the woman's door. More shots pursued them like baying bloodhounds. Neither officer was struck.

"You and the baby must get out of here!" one shouted. She was stunned and overwhelmed by the turn of events. Fear froze her ability to respond. A serene winter morning in the comforting and blissful company of her baby had twisted into a hellish storm. This was no bad dream. Bullet holes in the front door were evidence of that.

With the prodding of officers, she numbly grabbed the baby. More firing erupted from the opposite apartment. A round zipped past the infant's crib. The four rushed to a bedroom with a window on the side of the building. Officers shouted for assistance. By now the shootout was evident on all sides of the complex.

"We need help here!"

Police rushed to the window. The ground dropped off sharply from the window, but there was no time to get a ladder. Officers yelled for the mother to drop the baby. Even though it was only five feet to outstretched arms, she could not release her son. The baby cried, and she squeezed him even tighter.

"Lady, you must drop the baby," a policeman pleaded. "They will catch him. You must do it now! We cannot stay here. It's too dangerous."

The terrified young mom could not part from her child. Finally one of the officers gently untangled her arms, took the baby, and dropped him to those outside. Then the woman climbed out and jumped to safety. When the two officers returned inside, they were greeted by a shotgun blast. The volleys ripped a larger hole in the door. Lead sprayed the Becker apartment. Pellets tore into the door jam. Others splintered a breakfast chair.

"Stop your firing!" an officer screamed.

Bremer answered with another shotgun blast.

"There is no sense to continue shooting! The place is surrounded!"

This time there was no shotgun response.

State Trooper Koob, forty-nine, a Marine Corps veteran, swung his motorcycle into the Greystone parking lot. Given the radio traffic, he was not surprised by the conglomerate of flashing red and blue lights. He parked behind a barren redbud bush, scuttled beneath the crime tape, and raced to the nearest squad car. He was not the sort to stand by in an emergency, waiting for time to unfold the consequences.

"Stay down!" someone yelled at Koob. "The shooter is unloading from that first-floor window on the left side, just behind those two bushes." The uniform pointed. "He has a shotgun and other weapons."

"I hear you," Koob answered. He crouched and moved laterally among the police cars, searching for a better view and clear aim at the suspect. He joined two other officers hunkered behind a Ford Galaxie cruiser. They filled him in on the off-and-on shooting pattern.

"Don't know if there are one or two suspects firing from the window," one of the officers hunched his shoulders in uncertainty. "I'm thinking one."

Koob assembled the pieces of information and assessed the situation.

"I assume he alternately shoots out front, reloads, fires out back, then repeats the process," Koob said. "He knows his future, but he must be insane. Sooner or later he will run out of ammunition. But I don't think we can let him shoot all day. The risk is too high."

Reporter Tim Busser arrived at the shootout scene minutes before Koob. He parked a half block away, grabbed his camera, and raced south to where cops and black and yellow crime tape halted his advance. He spotted a state trooper, later identified as Koob, running across the parking lot.

Busser had not seen such a display of firepower since the Korean War. Tubes of steel, long and short, were aimed at the apartment window. He calculated, just based on the manpower, that the suspect had little chance of survival.

The quiet interlude succumbed to an explosion of gunfire.

Shots sent police scrambling for cover.

The air in this normally peaceful urban neighborhood turned gun-smoke blue with eruptions of activated lead. There was a hailstorm of bullets in both directions. Some officers, like front-line infantry, had crawled toward the shooter's window. Now they hugged the ground to lessen exposure. A few rolled behind a dumpster enclosure and bushes for protection.

Two were caught in the open, unable to grasp cover. It seemed as if they were being attacked by a well-armed battalion. Shots whistled through the Kansas air. Koob pondered the law of averages that one would find flesh. The math made him nervous. Then, as if some heavenly force had brokered peace, the shooting ceased. However, none on the front lines moved.

"Stop! Stop!" a woman inside shrieked. "Bobby! We can't escape!" she pleaded. "Stop before someone is killed. This is nuts. I beg you!"

Bobby motioned her back as he reloaded his weapons.

Just as Busser steadied his camera against the trunk of a tree, Koob dashed toward an unattended police cruiser, its motor running. He jumped in, slammed the car in reverse, then weaved forward through the maze of vehicles. He pulled directly in front of the apartment window, less than fifty feet away, to shield the unprotected officers glued to the ground.

Just as he turned off the engine, the fusillade resumed. Bullets blistered Koob's vehicle, shattering the driver's side window. One round lodged in his chest. He slumped over the wheel.

Death was nearly instant. It was recorded on Busser's camera.

"Officer hit!" came a shout from up front.

The return salvo sounded like the siege of Bastogne.

Chapter 45
Suburban Kansas City

The woman screamed as police, guns at the ready, crashed into the shooter's apartment from the hallway.

She sat on the floor, legs crossed, like a frantic guru who needed guidance. She sobbed, the picture of desolate collapse.

Her shaking hands were bloody from the ripped flesh of the man's body. She held them outward, palms up, as if summoning an external order. Her face carried the psychological pain of someone who had staggered through hell without a map, looking for the exit door.

This time the pause in the bullet exchange had a mark of permanency. This time there was no reloading of weapons in the apartment bunker. This time the counterattack by police came with a rush from the rear.

It was over.

"Don't shoot anymore," she begged as the police stormed the apartment.

Two Glocks and a shotgun were aimed at Bobby Bremer's head. One false move would have converted his brains to grated head cheese.

"Please, please," Rosemary cried. "No more shooting!"

Bremer slumped on the floor, his back leaned into a beige cloth chair streaked with vivid red blotches that catalogued the combat. He looked down and examined the gaping hole in his stomach. Blood seeped from his wounds and trickled down his leg onto the floor. His mind slipped into a fog. Fading cognizance, nevertheless, informed him that he had lost the battle and maybe the war. Images once distinct, including Rosemary's face, became fuzzy like a distant memory.

Blood dribbled from his mouth. She grabbed a bath towel, dabbed his mouth, and then pressed it into his torn abdomen.

"Hold your fire!" one of the inside officers yelled, concluding that the firestorm was ended. "Hold your fire!" he repeated. "Suspect wounded and in custody."

Outside, Effron and a host of lawmen rushed to the front and to the squad car with Koob's collapsed body. The chief opened the car door and pressed his index and middle finger on Koob's neck in hope of finding life. There was none.

"Get that ambulance and EMT crew up here on the double," he ordered. But he knew.

"Anyone else hurt?" he shouted to the scattered upfront squadron.

"I don't think so, Chief," came an initial report. "Maybe some elbow burns from the asphalt. One guy hit his noggin on the dumpster."

"OK," Effron said. "Have another medical team go inside to check on the suspect."

"Let the sonofabitch bleed out," an officer bellowed from the still adrenaline-laced cop assembly.

Effron did not know the source of the comment, but it dented his notion of propriety and professionalism.

"Like I said, get an EMT crew inside to tend to the injured. They can go through the front door of the building over there." He pointed.

Slowly in the ensuing minutes, the blend of police, state troopers, and deputies began to untangle. A traffic cop would have helped dissolve the mishmash of vehicles. They made way for an ambulance to remove Koob's body. Another crew of medics tended to Bremer's serious wounds. By the time he was taken to a hospital, most of the police cars had left.

Crime scene experts combed the inside and outside of the shootout setting, amazed by the accumulation of spent shells and shotgun casings. They were shocked even more by the store of ammunition still in bags in the shooter's apartment. Effron walked into the room and examined the cache.

"Sufferin' Succotash!" He minced his words upon spotting the remaining arsenal. Years before, his wife urged him to moderate vulgar reaction in favor of more civil language.

"I'm glad we were able to stop him before he killed or wounded someone else." He shook his head in disbelief. "This place looks more like an ammo dump."

He inspected the blistered apartment walls and doors and shattered glass, imprints from the bombardment.

"How did he get out of here alive?"

"Maybe he didn't," one of the officers suggested.

"I'll leave all the picture-taking and measurements to you fellows," Effron said as he turned to leave. "I'm headed for the hospital to interview the suspects, if I can. We should have idents on both by now."

The collecting of evidence took most of the day. Residents came home from work to find ample signs of what hours before resembled the O.K. Corral. A few cop cars were still scattered around the complex. Mounds of crime tape and bullet casings were piled like confetti. Officers cleared all units for occupancy except the two apartments central to the battle.

At the nearby medical center, police were posted at the ER, where Rosemary was being examined, and outside the operating room, where doctors sought to reassemble the broken body of Bobby Bremer. Bullets had passed through his arm and shoulder. Some were still lodged in his body. At least two invaded his stomach and one nicked the esophagus.

He resembled a human sieve.

Rosemary's physical injuries were scrapes and bruises consistent with bounding about in search of safety from flying bullets. Far worse were the mental wounds from the traumatic standoff that had been heaped upon scars from life's previous dark days. She had been ushered to a waiting room.

After more than two hours, surgeons looked at one another in amazement—as if they had just put together a 5,000-piece jigsaw puzzle blindfolded. Bremmer's battered body had been stabilized. Foreign fragments removed. Torn organs repaired. Blood loss countered. They removed their surgical attire, satisfied that they had done the best they could.

"He is resting," one of the doctors informed Rosemary. "We believe he will recover, barring infection or other complications." The surgeon left. A floor nurse told Rosemary that she would have to wait fifteen minutes before she could see her husband, and then only briefly.

Police informed her she was under arrest.

Effron arrived at the hospital, and one of the officers filled him in on names and what little background information police had on the couple. It had been learned that Bremer had been living in western Kansas for the last five years, ever since his escape from the state prison. He and Rosemary were married in that time.

It had been one of the longest days in Effron's career as a police officer, certainly the most painful with the death of the state trooper. His mind turned to retirement, or perhaps something less stressful, like a greeter at Ace Hardware. He chuckled, remembering a recent news story about a fight among two shoppers over the last bag of bird seed.

He walked into the waiting room and saw a bedraggled woman smeared in blood.

"Hello." He extended his hand to Rosemary. "I'm Chief Norman Effron of the Overland Park Police Department. I understand you are Rosemary Bremer?" She nodded. At his suggestion they sat down. Rosemary talked freely, between sobs. She was, he thought, not much older than his own daughter.

He decided to accompany her to the recovery room, a fatherly gesture as much as a professional one. The visit was brief and without conversation.

"It's my understanding your husband will make it." Effron looked at Rosemary as they walked out of the room. "He is fortunate." He thought about Koob's death and the entire ordeal but said nothing to her about it. He gently took her arm, and they stopped in the hallway. "Go back in," he said softly. "Take a few minutes alone with him. I'll be outside the room."

Effron wondered if this husband and wife would have much, if any, opportunity to see each other in the coming days or years.

"Thank you," she faintly replied. "I want you to know how sorry I am, sorry that this all got out of hand." She placed a hand on the wall to gain stability. "This was not part of the plan, Chief Effron. All we wanted to do was get revenge on bankers who cheated my parents. My family will be devastated by this. I don't know how to tell Bobby's mother."

Rosemary's mind was half paralyzed by the day's trauma. She clung to the wall and handrail as if tottering on the edge of a cliff. Effron read the signs and held her arm.

"Are you going to be OK? Should I call a nurse?"

"Were any of the police officers hurt?" she struggled with a whisper. "Did anyone else get shot?"

"Mrs. Bremer. Now is not a good time to discuss all that."

"I want to know."

Her eyes stared at the gray tiles of the hallway floor. She was oblivious to the pattern of squares, blocks in which two-inch black borders hemmed in the grays like prison bars. Tears dripped off her cheeks and left no mark for posterity.

"I have to know."

"A state trooper was killed," Effron said.

The two, on opposite sides of the criminal justice system, stood side by side, more like grieving family members, each mourning mutual and diverse losses that crisscrossed in a funeral-like silence. More was said mutely in fifteen seconds than is sometimes conveyed in an hour-long speech.

The wordless conference ended when she glanced up at him.

Rosemary breathed deeply. Slowly, she reentered the recovery room and stood next to Bobby's bed, looking at the sleeping face. He was a tangle of tubes and bandages. Again, tears erupted as competing thoughts sped along the pathways of her mind like traffic on a busy highway. Their life as husband and wife was over. No children. No family. No one to care for. No one to love, to confide in, be close to. To share the ups and downs of living.

Clearly, she had been too obliging in this crazy and hopeless scheme? The hurt her parents suffered from bankers and the Spietz lawsuit had metastasized into revenge swollen by Bobby's notions of justice. Could she have stopped it?

What would she tell her family, Mr. Bexler, friends and acquaintances at Justice Now? Should she be the one to inform Bobby's mother? How do you tell people that your life is changed forever? Would things have turned out differently had the baby lived?

How do you manage yourself? Your own emotions? The reality of being alone? Confined. In prison.

Rosemary wept as she watched and wondered. She was a weaving basket of confusion as she left Bobby's room, uncertain when she would see him again. Effron steadied her as they left the hospital for a waiting squad car. She was taken to the Johnson County Jail in Olathe where he and another officer took her full statement. At a court hearing the next day, her bond was set at $50,000. Her request to call family was granted.

The jail chaplain offered to make the calls, but Rosemary decided she had to do it. She dreaded talking to Bobby's mother more than her own parents, shuddered at dumping another layer of grief on Molly Bremer's life—already scarred by heartbreak, physical abuse, disappointment, and enough unhappiness to sour a pessimist.

Molly had just returned from a routine physical at the doctor's office. Excellent health was the one consistent area of good news. She had no serious medical issues, but arthritis was creeping into her fingers. Her medium-length hair had become snowy, a harbinger of senior years as sure as autumn flurries ushered in winter.

It was sunny in Little Rock, temperature above average at sixty-two. The air had a teasing scent of spring, enough that she envisioned options for her summer flower garden. She made a mental note, as she walked in the house, to scan the new Burpee's seed catalog for lupine and other early bloomers.

The phone rang as she hung up her sweater.

"Mrs. Bremer? Is this Mrs. Bremer?" Rosemary inquired softly with a nervous inflection.

"Yes. This is Molly Bremer. Who is this?"

Rosemary began to shake with apprehension, imagining the impending scene on the other end of the line. More agony for Molly Bremer. Rosemary almost hung up, but there was no rainbow option on the horizon, only glum reality.

"Mrs. Bremer. This is Rosemary. Bobby's wife?"

"Oh, yes. Rosemary. What a nice surprise. How are you?" Molly asked, sensing tribulations like only a mother can.

"Mrs. Bremer, I... I," Rosemary stammered.

"Please call me Molly."

"Yes, of course. Molly, I have the worst news. Bobby and..."

"You haven't been in a car accident, have you?" Molly interrupted.

"No, Molly. It's worse than that."

"Worse? Are you injured? Has Bobby been hurt?"

"Bobby is in the hospital, but doctors say he will recover. It was not a car accident, Molly."

Rosemary worried that her faltering had created a false sense of hope, saving Molly from her worst fears only to have the truth plunge her into equal shock.

"Bobby and I have done a horrible thing, Molly. A crime." She paused, waiting as if this terrible nightmare would change. Finally truth regained traction. "We are both in police custody, Molly. It's probably my fault."

"But you are OK?" Molly asked as if she failed to hear the news of incarceration, failed to translate the despair in Rosemary's words.

"Molly. We are likely to be sentenced to long terms in prison. We robbed a bank, and then Bobby got into a shootout with police. It was terrible. A state trooper was killed."

Silence meant Molly had absorbed the information this time. Rosemary could only imagine the woman's renewed despair. She began to sob, deep weeping that flowed across the phone lines into the small house.

"I am so sorry, Molly." Rosemary cried. "I am so sorry. You don't deserve this, after all you have been through. I apologize for adding to your grief."

Molly Bremer suppressed the new sting to her swollen history of family struggles, girding her calloused life against one more puncture. Quickly she assumed the role of healer.

"Now, Rosemary, knowing well Bobby's short temper and distrustful nature I doubt if you are the root of any of this trouble."

Molly recalled the violent moods that consumed Bobby's father, his nearly chronic inability to overcome disappointment or slight, even presumed slight. More than once she considered if Bobby inherited any of that.

"Don't blame yourself. Try to calm down, dear, and tell me what happened."

Rosemary explained what she believed triggered the entire tragedy, the perceived injustice by bankers and government inaction that was interpreted as complicity. She closely guarded, like keys to buried treasure, any reference to the lost child and the subliminal role that may have played.

"The worst part, besides that Bobby suffered terrible gun wounds, is that, is that the policeman was killed," Rosemary recounted in a broken blabber of words. "The officer was only forty-eight."

It was this news that burned deeply into Molly's conscience, the vicarious absorbing of a tragic act. Where did she go wrong? What could she have done differently? Was Bobby really evil? She curled her lips inward and pressed them together in sorrow and relief that her feelings could not be seen. Again she gathered her resolve to be counselor and consoler.

She spoke slowly.

"I have a difficult time believing Bobby would have intentionally shot this police officer or anyone," Molly said for her own benefit as well as Rosemary's. "I can see him feeling hopeless, being targeted like he sometimes was at school, and flailing out like a trapped animal. For him to be a cold-blooded killer, a person who sets out to take someone's life? No, Rosemary." Her pause underlined her message. "That's not Bobby."

"He will likely have to spend the rest of his life in prison," Rosemary sobbed, with no respite from Molly's attempt at comforting. "Our life together is ended. Molly, I can't begin to explain my shame. For not being a better daughter-in-law. For not being a better person."

A hush reigned as both women gathered their thoughts, looking back and looking ahead, but mostly envisioning each other's pain.

"Rosemary. Listen to me," Molly implored. "We can't fix the bad things of the past. There's no turning back the clock. We can only treasure the good things, the good times. You are good for Bobby. I knew that when I first met you. You give him the depth of love he believed he never had growing up. I tried to tell him differently after his father left, that he was loved equally with Peter and Hattie, but he couldn't see it."

Again there was silence.

"I wish I could be with you and Bobby. Have you told all this to your parents?"

"Not yet," Rosemary cried.

"They will not love you less. Like me, they will be shocked at first. Saddened. But a parent's love of a child runs deeper than the sum of their mistakes. Please tell Bobby his mom loves him. And I love you too."

"Molly, you are so kind. I wish I were like you."

"You go call your parents now. And thanks for calling me and sharing these troubles. Goodbye, Rosemary. God be with you."

Bremer was released from the hospital after ten days. He was transported to the most secure section of the infirmary at the Kansas State Penitentiary at Lansing, where he had escaped more than five years before. Around-the-clock guards observed every movement of every stitch in his still-mending body. He quickly assumed the role of the prison's most famous inmate.

It was certain that he would no longer be lounging in the prison library, reading poetry and eating cinnamon rolls. The chances of crime boss Joseph Valachi becoming head of the Boy Scouts were better than Bobby Bremer ever again being allowed to join the prison Christmas tree farm operation.

Bremer's bond was set at $250,000. He and Rosemary were arraigned separately in early March. He was charged with first-degree murder, robbery, aggravated assault on a police officer, unlawful possession of firearms, aggravated robbery, and criminal damage. The criminal information said that some $13,000 was stolen from the bank and that damages to the Overland Park City Hall exceeded $3,000. She was accused of abetting murder and robbery.

The judge scheduled preliminary hearings and the time for entering pleas in two weeks. Court-appointed attorneys represented both defendants. Molly wanted to plead guilty, but attorneys recommended against it.

Rosemary and Bobby Bremer were found guilty in separate jury trials in Johnson County, Kans., District Court. Subsequently, Judge Harold Venter sentenced Rosemary Bremer to twenty years at the Kansas Women's Correctional Center. At the sentencing, she sketched her short life growing up in western Kansas. She told of working to help her parents after the financial disaster in which their seed business collapsed and part of their mortgaged farm was lost in the process.

The prosecution suggested a twenty-five-year prison sentence, but the court lowered that.

Two weeks later, in the same Olathe, Kans., courtroom, the state's attorney recommended death by hanging for Bobby Bremer.

Even in a state where capital punishment was much debated and on and off the books over the years, killing a state trooper stretched the limits of indulgence. Moreover, Bremer's indifference at various court hearings and during the trial seemed to chill any notions of clemency by the court.

The news crushed Rosemary. She had come to accept a life without Bobby. Death seemed intolerable.

Most murder cases in the United States take more than a year to process. It was just over seven months from that horrific shootout in Overland Park that Bobby Bremer appeared for sentencing. It was a blue-sky September day. The fresh late-summer air rendered a bizarre milieu for a man whose future was either death or life imprisonment.

Escorted by two deputies, Bremer shuffled his shackled legs past the granite marker leading up to the four-story, buff brick courthouse. The marker, engraved with oxen yoke, noted the path of the Santa Fe Trail. He awkwardly ascended the steps leading to the south entrance of the building and was ushered to a second-floor courtroom.

His head was drooped, fixed as if his neck vertebrae were locked. The deputies handed him off to his court-appointed attorney. Both sat down at a table, opposite the prosecutor, centered before the judge's bench. Bremer's body language gave no suggestion that his impassive, submissive demeanor had changed.

All rose when Judge Venter entered.

"Please be seated," the judge said. He then proceeded to recite all the geographic, time-stamp, statutory, case history and other perfunctory matters that judicial precedent and the Kansas Legislature mandated. Eventually he looked at the downcast Bremer.

Venter's hairless head sat on a sturdy six-foot frame, giving the misleading perspective of a judicial tyrant. To the contrary, he was regarded as judicious and fair. Proof came in the rare reversal of his decisions. A native of Emporia, Kans., he was a graduate of the Washburn University Law School.

Judgment about a human being's future is no comfortable task, especially in capital cases. Venter, like many, struggled throughout his adult life with the idea of killing a human being as punishment. He understood the reasoning about killing during war, as dreadful as that is. His Catholic faith was firmly set against the death penalty, but he had civil responsibilities.

At a presentence hearing, Bremer's attorney referred to conditions in the defendant's boyhood home. He focused on the dominance and violence of Jack Bremer and the difficulties of growing up in a single-parent family. He noted his steady employment in recent years and respect gained from his employer and friends. None of that gathered favor with Venter.

The only thing that caused him to pause in his deliberations was a touching letter written by Molly Bremer, a mother's cogent plea that would have impressed Oliver Wendell Holmes.

Venter had read Molly Bremer's letter three times, then took it home to share with his wife. They had five daughters, but no sons. He wanted her opinion, a mother's observation of another mother's petition. It probably violated some paragraph of ethics rules, but he needed her evaluation.

"Please read this," he requested after providing the case background.

Dear Judge,

My name is Molly Bremer. I am Bobby Bremer's mother.

I want you to know how sorry I am that my son wrongfully decided that violence was an answer to what he saw as injustice, violence that caused the death of Mr. Koob and threatened others. I want to extend my sincere sympathy and prayers to Mr. Koob's family. I cannot pretend to walk in their shoes, to experience their suffering. I am only grateful no one else was seriously hurt.

I would also like to express my personal distress for all others who were harmed physically or otherwise by my son's bad decisions. Violence, starting with Genesis when Cain killed Abel, is the terrible choice of too many.

Even so, as a mother knows her children better than anyone, I must say this on behalf of Bobby. He is not a cold-blooded killer. I want to say there is a difference between allowing violence to take over one's decisions and being violent by nature. Bobby is not someone who is indifferent to human life.

Please, Judge. Don't misunderstand. I am not trying to make excuses for what he did. He killed someone. But he did not set out on that terrible day with the idea of taking someone's life. He did not intend to kill a state trooper or anyone else. That's what happened in the course of violence.

My plea is that life imprisonment, rather than execution, would be a more just punishment for my son. Execution, in my belief, allows violence to have momentary revenge for the crime Bobby committed, an instant of satisfaction for some while his neck snaps. It won't restore Mr. Koob's life.

Life in prison will give my son time to think of his sin, time to ponder his losses. Being locked up, away from his wife, and knowing that won't change, is far greater punishment for him. He may prefer hanging, but let God judge if he is able to atone for his terrible actions.

Thank you for hearing me.

It was signed: *Molly Bremer, Little Rock, Ark.*

Mildred Venter read the letter twice. The judge reasoned that he really hadn't asked for her judgment. Or did he? As it happened, she provided him no escape from his life-and-death decision.

413

"Harold," she had said tenderly. "It's a beautiful letter." She looked into her husband's eyes. "You wouldn't expect less from a mother. She may be right, that her son did not intend to kill, that it was not a premeditated act in that he set out to kill someone. But neither was it an accident. He didn't stop shooting until they shot him."

Judge Venter nodded, folded the letter, and returned it to his briefcase.

Now, in the courtroom, in the stark moment of reality, the time for internal debate was over. He could argue with himself for another month, but no muse of justice would come forth with answers. It was his job to decide.

"Will the defendant and his attorney please rise," the judge requested.

Bremer had lost weight in the weeks while locked up, waiting for the court's machinery to grind its way to trial, presentencing, and now sentencing. He pushed back his chair, stood, and pulled up his orange jail jumpsuit with shackled hands. His dark hair, like his life, was in disarray.

"Mr. Bremer. Do you understand these proceedings?" Venter asked.

"Yes, sir."

"You understand this is the time for your sentencing?"

"Yes, sir."

Bobby Bremer studied the tiled courtroom ceiling as if it held some message for the future.

"You understand you have been found guilty of murder in the death of Trooper Eldon Koob?"

"Yes, sir."

"Please look at me when responding, Mr. Bremer."

"Yes, sir."

"Do you comprehend the gravity of taking someone's life?"

"Yes, sir."

"And you know the seriousness of putting other lives in jeopardy, robbing a bank?"

"Yes, sir."

Bremer's eyes took on a glassy appearance, an empty stare as if all the books in his library had been checked out. He looked out the courtroom window and fixed on construction workers across the street.

"You gaze out the window as if you have a lack of concern about these matters, Mr. Bremer. Is that the case?"

"No, sir."

Judge Venter's face reflected frustration and puzzlement. He saw surrender and hopelessness, not contempt.

"Are you sorry for your actions, the robbery, shootout, the death of the state trooper?"

"I guess so, sir."

"You guess?"

"Yes, sir."

"You guess? You don't know if you are sorry?"

The attorney whispered in Bremer's ear.

"I am sorry, your honor."

Venter shuffled some papers on his desk, still looking for a roadmap. It was times like these that the judge wished he'd gone to work on the railroad.

"Do have anything to say on your behalf before I proceed with sentencing?"

"No, sir."

"You have been in prison before, for fighting, then escaped?"

"Yes, sir."

"There is nothing more you want to say regarding your actions?"

"No, sir."

"Mr. Bremer, you are aware of the letter written by your mother on your behalf?"

"Yes, sir."

"And you have read it?"

"Yes, sir."

"OK, then."

The judge nodded to the court-appointed counsel for comment.

The attorney again cited conditions in Bremer's boyhood home, the father's violence and absence. He picked up on Mrs. Bremer's theme that the defendant did not set out to kill anyone, that his only premeditated purpose was to rob the bank that he believed treated his wife and friends unjustly. He advocated prison rather than the death sentence.

Venter shifted his body and rubbed his head. He had presided at murder trials before, but never one involving the killing of a law enforcement agent, never one where the state's attorney asked for death by hanging.

He looked at the defendant and saw Mrs. Bremer's son more than Eldon Koob's killer.

"Mr. Bremer," the judge continued, "I want you to know that none of the arguments made on your behalf by counsel, while important, are mitigating factors on the sentence I'm about to give. You could stack up explanations and excuses as high as the sky on a clear day in western Kansas, and they would produce no cause for what you did—armed robbery, eluding police, a gun fight, and eventually the slaying of Patrolman Eldon Koob.

"There is enough justification here to hang you twice."

For the first time words seemed to penetrate Bobby Bremer's anaesthetized mind. A wrinkled forehead, upcast eyes, and greater presence listened with new awareness. An image of Rosemary, happy times of riding their horses into a west wind on the open range, danced across his mind.

"I am going to make you several copies of your mother's letter. Read her letter every day. I want you to write her a letter of thanks, at least once a month, not a few paragraphs, but several pages. I want you to tell her how grateful you are for everything she has done for you, over the years, right down to this day in court. I want you to thank her for being your mother."

Courtroom ceiling lights reflected off Venter's bald head.

"Each time you write, thank her for saving your life."

The hushed courtroom waited.

"I sentence you to life in prison. This court is adjourned."

The following week, in the quiet of his new office, Chief Effron pondered events of the last months. He was unsettled that Bobby Bremer had escaped death row. He believed hanging would have been just in this case and additionally serve as a deterrent to violent acts against police. Yet he had conflicting thoughts. A small part of him accepted the sentence of life imprisonment.

Rumination about lost experiences and lost opportunity bounced around his mind like a dented ping pong ball. Officer Koob's grandchildren will never hear his stories, never see his faithful figure at softball games. Never feel his hugs. His wife will sit alone at evening supper.

Bremer's life as a husband, and perhaps that of a dad, gone forever.

Life is indeed strange, he mused.

In the tick of seconds, a man whose job is to save lives, dies. A man who tried to kill people lives.

How does that make sense in the cosmic code?

Chapter 46
St. Louis, 1976

"That's him, I tell you! I've got a fix on his license plate!"

Stefano Terdini, who at an early age was logically tabbed "The Turd" by inner-city classmates, fixed his binoculars on the black sedan ahead. It was already dark, but he was sure his eyes had found their target.

They were I-55 in West Memphis. Terdini was as excited as a jumping bean in a red-hot skillet.

Rusty Ragno glanced at his passenger with a face full of skepticism.

"I'm tellin' ya Rusty, that's the little prick. That's the car."

He pointed as if climaxing a successful hunt on safari. His uncontrolled, coal-black hair sprayed out the sides of a worn Chicago Cubs baseball cap.

"It's an Iowa plate and it has the number 57 on the left side. That's the county for Cedar Rapids. I know it! Plate number is— goddamit will you try to avoid the bumps in the highway—the plate number is... got it. EFQ921. *Voyler!* That's it! It's the same car."

"*Mi scusi*, Turd. It's *voila*, not *voyler*, you French cretin."

Ragno looked upon Terdini like a peacock appraises a sparrow. His disdain for the man was exceeded only by his lack of confidence. If Turd was the water carrier on the operation, Ragno feared his bucket was full of holes.

"I wanna be positive it's him," an aggravated and wary Ragno snarled. "No second guessing. What?" he again looked at Terdini. "This is your second rub-out, and you think you're a veteran?"

Chasing a pipsqueak piker demeaned Ragno's self-worth. However, loan collection, he knew, came in different sizes. And in gang governance, orders are orders.

The Outfit wanted Peter Bremer dead.

Terdini was a Chicago castoff as a teenager. He grew up poor and his life went downhill from there. Few people had less regard for him than he had for himself. He was a chameleon, an outside smile disguising inside suffering. A teacher said he seemed happy to be sad.

Always the downhearted clown.

His parents fine-tuned the art of fighting, so he ran away. They did not look for him. His mother's brother let him sleep in the garage for more than a year and fed him like he was a least favorite dog. He warned the kid to keep his fingerprints off the shiny 1950 turquoise Buick Super. Those accommodations ended when food scraps were found on the car's hood.

Tossed out by his uncle, he scrounged garbage cans near restaurants to stay alive. One day, outside a fancy chophouse, he found a billfold. He had never seen a fifty-dollar bill before. He looked at the picture of Ulysses S. Grant as if it were a Jayne Mansfield nude. And there was other folding money—a real cabbage patch.

He didn't know it, but the wallet belonged to a Mafia consigliere. He was about to run off like a juvenile hyena with a mouthful of antelope steak when a man with a bulge in his pocket appeared. The billfold, contents intact, was returned forthwith. Terdini's reward was a job. He was always a tough kid, an A+ student, street wise. Routine errands done faithfully earned him promotions.

At age twenty-six it became graduation time. After a secret loyalty ceremony that included the prerequisite finger prick, Terdini was given the biggest mob test: "taking care of business." Translated, he was required to kill another human being. That earned him money and respect, things he never had.

"What the hell! Do you have to see his passport?" an exasperated Terdini howled at Ragno.

"It's him! The asshole whose flashy suit is stuffed with stupid."

Terdini was afflicted with the disease of putting too much faith in a pair of jacks, pushing his luck and cheek.

"Gotta hand it to him," Terdini went on. "This guy we think has only an inch in his yardstick gave us the slip yesterday south of St. Louis." He glanced at Ragno, growing more irritated by his boss's arrogant mistrust. "Good thing you don't drive a race car. You'd get lost."

"Watch it, Turd. We can go to any horse stall and get a replacement for you. As I remember, you weren't entirely sure yesterday that we had the right guy. And you didn't tell me about the lane change. Some guide! You're not exactly Buffalo Bill with a saddlebag of maps."

"Rusty. Try something new. Pay attention. The car ahead is a Cadillac. It's huge. It's black. It has the right Iowa license number, the same number you yourself wrote down when you beat the shit out of him last August. I wasn't with you then, but you claim you hurt him bad. Your fingerprints are probably still on his jaw!"

The image of Peter Bremer's bruised and busted face relaxed Ragno like a double shot of forty-year-old Puni Malt. It settled his testy temperament and stirred his sinister juices. Getting this job done and returning to Chicago were tops on his agenda. Killing this small-town pseudo big shot who failed to pay his bills suddenly became a fulfilling mission.

Admittedly it was an amazing piece of luck, like betting on a 100 to 1 sway back nag at Arlington Park to show, and the horse comes in first. Like finding an honest politician in Chicago. Yes, they put on a full-court press to locate this scum bag, and sure enough he rises to the top like a dead fly in watery gruel.

Terdini was right.

They had spotted Bremer's car the previous day south of St. Louis. Bremer obviously sensed the tail, whipped the 190 horsepower V-8 into a frothing frenzy and created distance and relief. Ragno and his lumbering Ford Grenada snarled in rush-hour traffic and lane confusion and faded in Bremer's rear-view mirror like a misshaped idea.

Bremer had zipped off the interstate at Arnold, Mo., doubled back on urban streets, and left Ragno and his scout on embarrassment corner.

But this wasn't the mob's first hunting trip. Ragno was determined to placate his red face. He had stationed lookouts at the St. Louis airport, the bus terminal, and outside the home of Glenda's father. He even had a Little Rock hoodlum stake out Bremer's mother's house. Members of the St. Louis crime family were put on alert.

Every black Cadillac de Ville in the St. Louis area was inspected as if it carried a virus-infected rat. Bremer became the mob's plague cover-boy.

Wild with fear, Bremer knew traps tend to be tripped. He was familiar with St. Louis area streets. His hunters were not. Could he dance his way past them, tiptoe around danger, creating on-the-go moves that had become the hallmark of his problem solving—even at Riverside Pack? He had to do something.

But what?

"I know that sniveling piece of fraudulent capitalism will not stick around St. Louis," Ragno had surmised after Bremer had given them the dodge. "As soon as he finishes his attempt at being Houdini, he will head south. He knows we have major highways in the area covered, and that our noose will only get tighter."

Ragno circled the St. Louis suburb in vain before turning the watch there over to local henchmen.

"Notify our friends in Memphis."

The following day, Ragno's hypothesis appeared to be correct. Doubt transformed into confidence. Terdini's keen eyes confirmed it. The big black Cadillac moved through the west Memphis night like a hearse, five car lengths ahead of the mob squad. It crossed the Mississippi River on the Hernando de Soto Bridge into the lights of downtown Memphis.

This time Ragno kept a more discreet distance, allowing a semi to run in-between interference.

"We won't do anything in Memphis," he said. "We'll hang back and follow him outside the urban area. Do you have all the equipment ready?"

Terdini nodded, his sordid nature brimming with eagerness.

The tracking went past St. Jude Children's Hospital, then turned south. Late-night traffic was moderate in Memphis but quickly thinned by the time the tandem passed the airport exit and the Mississippi state line. Fortune then dealt Ragno an ideal hand. The black Cadillac slowed. Its right taillight began to blink.

"The dumb sonofabitch is pulling into the rest stop," Ragno fidgeted with macabre anticipation. He was like a starved lion savoring a blithe laggard from the gazelle herd. Except for a half dozen semis, the rest stop parking lot was empty. All the trucks, conveniently, were on the east side of the building. The west area designated for passenger cars was vacant.

"I don't know if his intention is to take a nap or take a piss," Ragno frothed. "Either way, I hope the fucker says a prayer first. It'll be his last chance at atonement."

He pulled parallel to the black sedan, several spaces away.

"Get going!"

Just that quick, the business of killing, uninhibited by any moral concern for human life, was launched.

Terdini popped out of the car, ran to the Cadillac, yanked open the door and in systematic fashion dispensed three bullets from the silenced pistol into the head of the diminutive figure sitting in the driver's seat. Blood and brains spewed throughout the cream-colored interior.

The man slumped. Death arrived quickly.

Insensible to his crime and the human form before him, he grabbed the dead man by the hair, yanked back his head, smiled with satisfaction, and walked back to the Ford unhurried.

"Is the main job done?" Ragno asked.

"He's dead. More than dead. At first, he looked surprised. Then he looked dead. You want to inspect for quality control?"

"I don't want to ever look at that little bastard again!"

Twisted by evil resolution, Terdini retrieved a Channellock pliers and returned to the death scene. First he double-checked the license plates. It was Bremer's car. He ripped the plates off the Cadillac. Next, in ghoulish indifference, he forced a two-inch piece of wood between the jaws of the lifeless form, prepping the mouth for his macabre exercise in dentistry.

Then he meticulously jerked and twisted off every tooth in the dead man's head and placed the remnants in his own pocket. It was no simple task and took several minutes.

He picked up the license plates and, as he tossed them into the back seat of the Ford, incurred the wrath of an impatient Ragno.

"What in hell are you doing? We aren't on a sightseeing tour here, you goofy numbskull."

"What I'm doing, oh learned one, is covering our asses. And now I'm going to permanently erase Mr. Bremer from the face of the earth."

Terdini grabbed two cans of gasoline. He doused the upholstery and interior of the Cadillac. He instructed Ragno to pull ahead a hundred feet.

"We need to wait a few minutes for the gas to soak into the seats," Terdini explained, "or we'll end up with one big poof and no fried Mr. Bremer."

Terdini had execution experience and, like a fire chief, knew the flammable properties of gasoline. Arson and murder were not electives for him but courses he had mastered.

"OK, Turd. But we ain't got all night. I want to be well down the road by the time Mr. Bremer enters hell."

Terdini grabbed his home-made ignitor, a four-foot stick with one end wrapped in kerosene-soaked rags. He waited.

"Get on with it, you fuckin' fire bug," Ragno ordered.

Terdini picked his own pace. He reveled in his role, the would-be protagonist prolonging his trip to the podium to pick up his gold medal as a hitman. He walked around the rear of the Cadillac like an assassin gloating over his defenseless target. He pleasurably exploited a calculated cadence as he performed his pre-arson ritual, fully aware it would cause a slow burn in Ragno too.

Eventually he pulled out a pack of Pall Malls and his Zippo lighter. He fired up his cigarette, inhaled a full dose of carcinogens, and torched the pseudo javelin. He took several more draws and released enough smoke to give him an authentic grim reaper appearance in the vaguely lit night sky. Then, slowly, he walked toward the Cadillac and its dead driver, tossed the burning spear into the car and departed like a winning Olympian.

"Holy crap! You sure took long enough," a seething Ragno spewed. "What were you conducting? Some sort of religious weenie roast?"

The two hoodlums slowly drove out of the rest area parking lot. Terdini looked back. The Cadillac began to glow brightly, smoke swelling as the flames grasped the gasoline-drenched interior. Minutes lapsed before the popping and exploding process of combustion provoked any attention.

A sleepy trucker lifted his head and peered out the dormer window to examine the source of the noise. He sat up, astounded by the flickering orange sky behind the rest area building. He rose and ran to the expanding inferno. He stopped to shield his eyes as he observed the flaming vehicle. Was anyone in the car? The intense heat voided any thought of rescue.

He returned to his truck, grabbed his CB radio mic, and called Mississippi state police.

"God Almighty!"

Jim Ryan shook his head in disbelief. Twenty years with the FBI and this was as gruesome as he had ever encountered. He read the yellow teletype three times as he walked over to his desk. The ghoulishness of the words seemed to magnify.

"Listen to this," he addressed agents Kellerman and Sedlacek of the Cedar Rapids FBI office. "This message was sent to the Linn County Sheriff's Office by the Mississippi Bureau of Criminal Investigation. The Sheriff's Office forwarded it to law enforcement agencies all over Iowa.

"*Murder Investigation: On 1-22-76 officers of Mississippi Highway Patrol discovered burned automobile and charred human remains at Mississippi I-55 rest stop south of Memphis. State criminologists recovered part of VIN. The serial number has been traced to registration in Linn County, Iowa. Victim not ID'd. Face burned beyond recognition. Teeth broken off. Please advise missing persons.*"

He looked up, the serious lines on his face signaling that his mind had already launched a search for answers.

"Anybody in particular come to mind?"

Ryan hoped one of the others would offer a guess that matched his own.

"Was there one body or two?" Kellerman asked.

"Good question," Ryan answered. "Not sure, but it suggests one. What are you thinking?"

"Well, Jim. There has been speculation about the Bremers. Peter Bremer doesn't appear at the Riverside Pack meeting. He fails to show up in court for a tax hearing. His lawyer says he can't reach him at Riverside offices or at the Bremer residence. We know he was in big-time hock with mobsters. Poof, they are both gone? I'm guessing they didn't run off to a family reunion."

There was a pause as the full impact of the message was digested.

"When was the car found?" Kellerman asked.

"January 22. More than a week ago."

"I imagine it took a while to run down that VIN number," Sedlacek offered.

Ryan gathered his thoughts, a plan of investigative attack taking shape.

"I'll call Mississippi to see what else they can tell us. Kellerman, would you please run down any information on Mrs. Bremer. Glenda Bremer. I don't see her as the deceased. Don't know her maiden name. If I remember correctly from IRS information, she is a native of St. Louis. Sedlacek, please check the Bremer suite at the Roosevelt. Get a court order if you need to."

Ryan, an Omaha native once bent on becoming a lawyer, switched professional gears after a Marine Corps stint. He finished second in his FBI class at Quantico and earned recognition for his keen analysis of case evidence. In his years with the agency, he gained a reputation for having an almost premonition-like aptitude for calculating the elements of crime.

His astute mind overshadowed an under-sized frame that more than one miscreant misjudged. He was high school state wrestling champ in the 145-pound division. Even at forty-six he led his YMCA basketball team in scoring. For fun, he exchanged mental hardball in duplicate bridge.

"And Sedlacek, pop upstairs to see if the US Marshal's office received the same teletype, and if so, what's their take on it."

The marshal's office was on the third floor of the downtown Federal Building. The FBI was located on the second floor.

"If there is any indication this burned car was a Cadillac," Ryan deliberated, "we'll have a key component of the equation. We know Bremer drove a de Ville, and we will know the plate number from local records. Any match, or partial, along that line will go a long way. Sedlacek, would you also please go down again to Riverside Pack. Talk to the front office, directors, anyone that may know anything about the Bremers."

Ryan first called the Linn County sheriff's office and Cedar Rapids police to review what they had in their Bremer files. Neither had much information on the couple. Police detectives shared their investigative report dealing with the break-in at the Bremer's suite last August.

Three hours produced scant new information. A secretary at Riverside told Sedlacek that Peter Bremer was unusually quiet and "even nervous" the last time she saw him.

"However, she attributed that to company business and the revolt by Riverside shareholders. She noted that Bremer stuffed an unusual amount of papers into his briefcase as he left that last day. And I found nothing of interest at their hotel suite."

Kellerman was unable to learn the whereabouts of Glenda Bremer but was still working on it. Ryan talked to Mississippi authorities.

"They said it appeared the front and rear license plates had been ripped off the burned car," Ryan related. "Shards of tin from the front plate were still in place. So no plates to help identify things. The interior of the car was destroyed, including the thirteen-digit VIN number on top of the dash on the driver's side.

"However, most of a second VIN tag—the same numbers— located on the rear upper portion of the cylinder block behind the intake manifold, was recovered," Ryan quoted Mississippi authorities. "And the scorched hood ornament—the Cadillac crest— was found. I think we can safely say it was the kind of car Peter Bremer drove."

"Did they have anything more to say about the body?" Kellerman asked.

"Only"—and Ryan's face took on a painful contortion—"that they speculated a pair of pliers was used to break off all the teeth. Can you believe that? The officer I talked to said it had the marks of a targeted killing done by a professional hit man. I agree. The killer knew if the teeth remained investigators would make molds in an attempt to ID the victim. Same reason they ripped off the plates."

"Only the killer forgot about the VIN on the motor," Sedlacek said.

"Yep."

Mississippi officials told Ryan that the victim's remains were sent to a laboratory in Jackson for forensic analysis. Those tests were not completed.

"They emphasized," Ryan said, "that there wasn't much left to work with. They doubt if any fingerprints can be retrieved. Arson experts made a preliminary conclusion that the fire was deliberately set—big news there—and gasoline used as an accelerant. The crime scene is still being examined. That's about it. Any questions?"

Shakes of their heads said no.

"Let's keep digging men."

Ryan decided to work the back door. He called FBI agents in Cleveland, one of the focal points for investigating organized crime's connection to the Teamsters Union and its pillaging of the union's Central States Pension Fund. Jackie Presser, a top boss in the Teamsters Ohio Conference and a Central States Pension Fund trustee, was also a paid FBI informant.

Could Presser, Ryan asked colleagues in Cleveland, inquire about Chicago mobsters "putting out the whack" for a particular person in Iowa? The Chicago underworld was especially active in loan-sharking, using the pension fund as a ready well for money. The next day, the Cleveland FBI forwarded a terse statement to Ryan: "He (Bremer) could have gone the way of Jimmy Hoffa."

That was it. Did it reflect authentic knowledge held by Presser or was it merely opinion? Did the name Bremer ever cross Presser's mind?

Ryan wanted more detail. Hoffa, everyone presumed, was killed by Mafia associates. The Cleveland FBI, unwilling to spend more of Presser's time over a paltry Iowa loan dodger, replied that no elaboration was provided.

The evidence, still piecemeal, was slowly building.

It was three weeks before FBI agents in St. Louis managed to locate Glenda Bremer. Howard Goodman, her father, said she had been living at a motel, talking to him only by telephone. He told agents of Bremer's flight, his daughter's secretive isolation, and that she finally had agreed it was time for her to move back home.

However, she made him promise not to reveal her presence. She insisted on living covertly, he told the FBI. Only recently, he said, was he able to convince her that she could not live the rest of her life like that. He urged her to talk with the FBI. At first she refused, but then reluctantly agreed to talk by telephone only after steps were taken to validate the identity of agents.

Subsequently, Glenda tearfully related her final days with Peter, their hurried departure from Iowa, and his consuming worry about being found by mobsters. Then his abrupt departure. She had not heard from him since.

Agents did not tell her about the investigation in Mississippi surrounding the charred body and Cadillac.

In response to questions, Glenda also revealed that Bremer had converted checking, savings, and other liquid assets into a significant amount of cash. He gave her $1,500. She said she urged her husband to send all of the money to the mobsters, "but Peter only laughed, saying they wanted the entire $45,000 immediately. And with added interest, maybe more."

Glenda agreed that if she heard from her husband, she would notify the FBI in Iowa. However, agents doubted she would do that. Even with remote contact, they knew Glenda Bremer still feared for her husband's life.

In the weeks and months that followed, Mississippi authorities learned little more from the crime scene and periphery investigation. The people at Riverside Pack had no new information. The Cleveland FBI was of no help. Glenda Bremer claimed she had not heard from her husband. And in truth, Ryan and his FBI team had no reason to doubt her.

"Where do we go from here, boss?" Sedlacek asked one late May day as the office was reviewing its open cases.

While Iowa was not a hotbed of murder and white-collar crime, interstate cases of prostitution, drug-dealing, and fraud kept officials busy. Much of their time was devoted to investigation of a ponzi scheme that covered several states, including Iowa.

"I don't know," Ryan said. "If you can think of some angle we have not covered, some alley we've not been down, please tell me."

The blank look on the agents' faces was telling. No one offered an untried path for probing the case of Peter Bremer. Neither did anyone want to say that the FBI and investigators elsewhere had run into a dead end. Yet the stark fact was that no evidence had been uncovered that tied the Mississippi murder to mobsters or anyone else.

"I think Peter Bremer is dead." Ryan finally broke the silence. "Everything points to that. As for finding the killers?"

He left the question hanging in the air.

"Just remember," Ryan said. "There is no statute of limitations in murder case."

Chapter 47
August 1979

"Yes, I'll accept and pay for the call."

Molly Bremer answered the operator while simultaneously untwisting the phone cord. After some clicks and electronic burps, the connection was completed.

"Hello, Ma."

"Bobby! It's good to hear your voice!"

"Yes, Mom. Nice to talk to you."

He was lucky, first in line to make a call. Sunday morning is a popular time for inmates to telephone loved ones. New rules at the Lansing prison allowed only collect calls limited to fifteen minutes. The person called must be pre-approved and the conversation is subject to monitoring.

"Have you had a nice Sunday breakfast? Did you go to church services this morning? Gee, it's good to hear your voice."

"Breakfast was fine, Ma."

"What did you have?"

"Ma. This is a prison. They don't hand out menus."

"I know that. You can still tell me what they served."

"Ma, I think the maître d' described it as SOS."

"Now you're being silly. Maitre d'. My word!" She chuckled. "What is SOS? Sounds like an emergency dish."

"It is. It means they don't have anything else to give us."

"No, Bobby. Really, what does it mean?"

"Ma, I don't know. I think it's an old military term for sumptuous omelet special."

"Sounds good. What did the prison chaplain talk about?"
"I'm sorry, Ma. I didn't make it to services. Have you heard from Rosemary?"

"Not since she called last spring. We had a nice visit then. She certainly is a wonderful young woman, Bobby. It wouldn't hurt you to attend church services."

"What did she say? Did she say anything about me? Did she sound OK, Mom?"

"I think I told you all that when we last talked. Are you all right, Bobby? Is there something wrong?"

"Yeah, Ma. Everything is wrong. Being in here is not the worst part."

Silence occupied the line.

"Are you still there, Bobby?"

"Yeah, Ma. I'm here. The worst part is being without Rosemary. If I could only see her for a half hour, see her face, touch her pretty hair, watch her walk. It's been almost ten years!"

"How often do you talk on the phone?"

"We are limited to one call per month to spouses. Still, that's more than at first. Ma, it is so wonderful to hear her voice. I can only imagine her perky nose. And her frizzy hair, always flying around without direction, free as leaves on a cottonwood tree. And those sparkling, devilish eyes."

"Bobby, thanks for writing. And such a nice, long letters. I am surprised. Your words make me happy. I wish I could have done more for you when you were growing up. I am so sorry about your situation."

"Ma! Please! I'm in prison for life because of what I did, not because of what you did or didn't do. These were my decisions, my mistakes. I deserve to be here. I am fortunate and grateful. Because of you, I escaped death row."

There was a momentary pause as both pondered his words. He gradually recovered his course and found the rest of his prepared remarks.

"Ma," Bobby said softly. "You saved my life."

Molly began to cry, partly out of happiness and gratitude that her son was not executed and partly in sorrow because he would spend the rest of his life in prison. Mostly because she thought Bobby had found rectitude.

There are times when the limits of physics are dissolved, and two people can feel the transmission of warm hugs zigzagging their way over 450 miles of telephone cables and lines, mere strands of copper silently carrying the love and emotions of a mother and son. These were occasions for such a phenomenon.

An embrace takes longer to transmit than the sound of voices. Finally he steered the conversation back to his mother and Little Rock.

"How's retirement, Ma?"

"What's that?" Molly answered, her thoughts still dangling in space.

"Your retirement, Ma. What are you doing?"

"Oh, yes. It's hard to believe I have been retired nearly five years. I meant what I said in that letter to the judge back when you were sentenced. I will believe to my dying day that you had no intention to kill that state trooper. One of your shots had to ricochet off a tree or something. I didn't tell the judge that, but that's what had to happen."

"Ma, whatever happened, I'm guilty. How is Gramma doing?"

"Bobby, I know that basically you are a good person. Rosemary knows too. The two of you just got caught up in a terrible predicament."

"Ma, please. I killed a person. I ended a human life. No one else is to blame. Can we leave it at that?"

"You asked about your grandmother. She doesn't like it at the care center, but they are nice people. Like you, she is lonely. When

Dad died, she lost some of her spirit. You remember Dora Mae died a couple months before your grandfather? I think he missed her challenge, though they both had mellowed. I visit Mom several times a week."

"Are you doing OK, Ma? Arthritis in check?"

"I remember when you and Peter tussled in the front yard. You were bigger and could have hurt him, but you didn't. You always let room for his self-esteem to survive. That was important to him, and you knew it. He was sensitive about his small stature."

"Ma, have you heard from Peter? What, it's been three years since he disappeared? Still no word about him?"

Molly Bremer sat down at the kitchen table. She ran her free hand through her hair, nearly all white now. She breathed deeply. Like so many times before she struggled to restore her resolve.

"I haven't told you, Bobby, but I think Peter is dead."

"What!? You think Peter is dead?"

"I'm sorry. I should have told you before, Bobby."

"But Mom. You said Peter is dead? He is dead?"

"I hesitated to tell you and Rosemary, and your sister too. You have enough problems of your own. I didn't —"

"Mom! He's my brother! How do you know he's dead? What happened?"

Her hands began to shake.

"Three years ago, I believe in late January, the FBI came by and asked a bunch of questions about Peter. I was shocked and nervous. They wanted to know if I had received any unusual phone calls, or if I had seen any suspicious cars or persons in the area. They said Peter had not turned up for some court meeting in Cedar Rapids, Iowa."

She hesitated. "I told them I had no such calls and had seen nothing unusual."

"Ma, what does not showing up in court have to do with suspicious persons? I don't understand."

"At first, the agents did not explain much. When they came back two weeks later, they said Peter not only had income tax problems but had borrowed money from some bad people. They said Peter had not repaid a loan and suggested these people, I guess mobsters, were looking for him and may harm him.

"I was worried out of my head. They kept saying the matter was under investigation and would let me know of any news. If only Peter had come to me, I would have helped him, loaned him what money he needed."

"But what makes you think Peter is dead?"

"Bobby, I was beside myself. The agents gave me their phone number, but I heard nothing more. I called them twice, but they said there was no new information, that Peter was still missing. After a month I tried to call Glenda, Peter's wife, in Cedar Rapids. But there was no answer. I didn't know what to do, where to turn.

"Then out of the blue, maybe in the spring of 1976, I get a call from Glenda. She was crying so much I could hardly understand her. But she tells me that Peter owed lots of money to these gangsters. Peter feared for his life. They fled Cedar Rapids, and in a St. Louis motel he told her they had to split up—for her safety as well as his. He drove off in the middle of the night."

"Ma, I still do not understand why you think Peter is dead. Did Glenda tell you that?"

"It's all so crazy. Bobby, why would they want to kill Peter?"

"I don't know, Ma. Mobsters usually don't leave explanations."

"Glenda said Peter's car was found in Mississippi. The FBI told her the car was burned and so was the driver. They believe Peter is dead, Bobby, burned beyond recognition."

Molly began to cry as she retold the FBI's conclusion.

"I'm sorry, Ma. That must have been horrible. Peter and I have caused you so much heartache. I'm terribly sorry. I wish I could turn the clock back. Please don't cry, Ma."

"I feel like I failed both of you," she sobbed. "I should have stayed in closer touch. I could have helped you over the tough times."

"That's nonsense, Ma. We've been over that ground. Both Peter and I made bad decisions. Ma, *we* made bad decisions, not you."

Again the overwhelming weight of unfolding life ground their conversation to a halt. Molly struggled to regain composure.

"Ma?"

"Yes, Bobby. I'm here."

"Ma, what did they do with Peter's remains?"

"Glenda said his body would be sent to St. Louis. She called again in a couple of weeks to say she had a small committal ceremony there. Glenda lives with her father. He paid for a stone to mark Peter's burial place, but I have not been there. I should visit his grave."

"My times up, Ma. There's a guy pounding on the door. I'll call again in a couple months. Love you."

"I love you, Bobby. Write a long letter."

Then she heard a click.

"Goodbye," she said.

Chapter 48
October 1979, St. Louis

"Glenda. Have you seen my measuring tape? I had it ten seconds ago. It's like a damn slithering snake trying to crawl into hiding."

Howard Goodman was a highly regarded businessman. Over the years, he had built his clothing store on Washington Avenue from scratch, or as he put it, with a few socks and underwear. He could teach the professors at St. Louis University Business School a few lessons on successful management.

Now in his later years, he could use a course on patience.

"Did you hear me, Glenda? Where is that measuring tape? I have little time to get these jacket sleeves to fit grumpy ole Ted Sims... oh for god sakes. Now the telephone rings. Next thing you know the St. Louis County tax assessor will drop by to brighten my day. Would you get that Glenda? I'll hunt for the snake."

In truth, Glenda Bremer kept Goodman Clothiers from turning into a pile of loose threads. Over the last three years, she assumed managing the books, billing, and paying the bills. She did the buying, double-checked her father's customer orders, and tracked inventory. She even swept the place.

Her father was taking on many of the maladies of old age— forgetfulness, bad back, shaky knees, and a remodeled urinary system that he diagnosed as a shrinking bladder. His forbearance was noticeably absent on days when he missed an afternoon nap. However, his vision was intact, and he still had a keen eye for tailor work.

Being immersed in her father's business gave her joy and satisfaction, a perfect tonic to heal the wounds of her husband's death. She had not forgotten their love. Memories of good times managed to subdue those of terrible times, especially the painful days

438

leading to their flight from Cedar Rapids and the agonizing separation at a forlorn motel room.

She still pictured his slight stature and dapper dress, how his lack of physique was more than made up by charm and confidence. He was that race car driver whose foot was always pressed to the floorboard, propelled by an impulsive nature that overwhelmed any consideration of sharp curves or what might be approaching in the rearview mirror.

"Glenda! Are you going to answer the phone?"

"Yes, Dad."

Sometimes she would envision the two of them exiting the elevator at the Roosevelt Hotel in Cedar Rapids, dressed to the hilt, walking arm in arm through the lobby and its Italian Renaissance Revival atmosphere, nodding to the doorman with a "good evening," and heading south on Second Street to the fine cuisine of the Flame Room. Peter always had steak, rare, and loved the sounds of the piano bar blended with the buzz of inaudible conversation.

Oh, he was good at pretense. The shatterproof builder of Riverside Pack could not wait to duke it out with the Big Four in the meat industry. He danced his way into a cut-throat business where no one curtsied, and blood was literally and figuratively spilled every day. He was a salesman long on passion and short on pragmatism.

She suffered when he suffered, when the bottom fell out of plans, dreams fizzled in embarrassment, and the fruits of bad decisions rotted his very soul. That's what she witnessed on that final day three years ago, when the demons of wrong turns coalesced to induce him into a final, fatal decision. They could have worked it out, she believed, found a solution.

But he was proud.

"Hey, Dad. I found your measuring tape," Glenda yelled to her father, who was back by the altering room still looking for that elusive "snake." It was serenely coiled around scissors under some newspapers.

"Wonderful, sweetheart. Could you bring it to me? But first answer that damn phone!"

Glenda placed the tape around her neck and picked up the receiver.

"Goodman Clothiers," she answered in her natural cheerful style. "Could you hold one minute, please?" She delivered the measuring tape and was back in thirty seconds.

"Sorry to put you on hold. What can I do for you?"

"Hi, my Magic," the voice on the other end said softly.

Glenda shifted the phone to her right hand and ran the fingers of her left hand through the end-of-the-day remnants of a morning hairdo. Her brow wrinkled in puzzlement.

"I'm sorry. I didn't hear what you said."

"I said hi, my Magic. What do you say we walk over town for a glass of wine and a nice dinner, and then, who knows what?"

Suddenly Glenda's head was thrust into what seemed like a swarm of bees, not threatening, but buzzing with the softness and harmony of a favorite melody. She blinked, but her eyes fixed on a mist that filled the store. Her entire being tingled, and a blurry sensation forced her to sit in a chair near the phone.

She feared she was hallucinating, being carried back to the past by a voice that sounded familiar, but a voice that could not be. A kaleidoscope of memories and history became unsettled confusion. It was intoxicating, simultaneously exciting and fearful. She stood, then sat down again, searching for bearings.

Her hands trembled.

"It's me, Peter," the caller continued.

"Cedar Rapids. Riverside Pack." He fed out clues as if it were a game. "The Roosevelt Hotel. A bottle of Louis Latour Chateau at the Flame Room."

Glenda felt like she was wedged between a miracle and a cruel joke.

"Really, Glenda. It's me, the guy from Little Rock. Insurance, investments, stock options. What do you want to buy?" He laughed.

Slowly, like fog in the early morning, the haze cleared. Her mouth gaped in wonderment. Glenda did not know if she should scream, cry, or do both. She muffled the phone with her hand.

It is common for life's history to be replayed in nighttime visions. Often the rocky pressures of the day wind up contorted on the spool of sleep's replay. You show up in the wrong class. You start the car, put it in reverse, but again forget to open the garage door. Dobermans chase you. You are always late. But there are those rare slumber fantasies where one can fly, soar free above the dark moments.

"Glenda? Are you there?"

"Tell me," she said with a skeptical whisper, her entire body shaking in a daze of doubt and dream. "Where were we married? What church?"

"We weren't married in a church. It was at your home in St. Louis," the voice said confidently, "by the pastor from Christ Episcopal Church."

Glenda's face began to warm. Her heart thumped like a Buddy Rich solo. Her toes began to wiggle freely, as if they had been locked in seizure.

Could it be true that Peter is alive? Can it be possible that he was not murdered? Is this real?

"Glenda!" her father yelled across the room. "Who's on the phone? Is it Ted? Tell him I'm working on his damn jacket!"

"No, Dad. It's a friend."

Who would do such a horrible thing as to represent her dead husband? Her mind raced in circles, suspicion chasing sureness. Ecstasy was disputed by circumspection.

"Glenda?"

"Yes," she replied, barely audible.

"Well?"

"Do you remember," she asked, pressing for proof, "that pottery piece you had to buy in New Mexico, the one that I believe you said was 'indigenous purity'?"

The voice on the phone laughed.

"You mean that Acoma jug that thugs busted in the break-in at our hotel suite?"

"Oh, Peter," she began sobbing with joy.

"What was the name of your grandfather's antagonist?" she probed. "The one at his church?"

"Do you mean Adora Mae?"

"That's it, Peter. Your mother told me all about your grandfather and Adora Mae, and the rest of your family, at our wedding."

Adora Mae's confirmation turned Glenda's sobbing into blissful bawling. She needed no more proof. Her father shuffled to her side.

"Glenda? What's the matter?"

"Just wonderful, unbelievable news, Dad, from my friend!" she blubbered, brushing away the tears.

"Wonderful, you say? What is it like with bad news?" Her father walked away, shaking his head.

"Peter, we thought you were dead," she whispered. "They said you were dead. Burned beyond recognition. It was so awful."

"I'm sorry, Glenda, for the pain. I thought I was dead."

"Where are you? What happened?"